And None Shall Remain
A Greta Steiner EUOPS Novel

Robert L. Fenton

"So shall it be with all the men that set their faces to go into Egypt to sojourn there; they shall die by the sword, by the famine, and by the pestilence: and none of them shall remain or escape from the evil that I will bring upon them."
Jeremiah 42:17

Cover Artist Elaine Pawski
Cover Design by Sunflower Creative Media LLC

ISBN-13: 9781072952862

And None Shall Remain
A Greta Steiner EUOPS Novel

Robert L. Fenton

ROBERT FENTON

Dedication: I am dedicating this book to Jennifer and Elaine who fought to win. Without their work this book would have never been published. They know what I mean.

ROBERT FENTON

Also by this Author

All the Gold in the World

ROBERT FENTON

Also by this Author

All the Gold in the World

TABLE OF CONTENTS:

CAST OF CHARACTERS:

American People:

Margret Perry

American Press senior correspondent, also CIA operative and messenger, she is very intelligent, mission oriented, vicious, and effective. She is very jealous of her position as a newsperson but she has been a CIA operative for years and that is partially why she is a very well-known newsperson. The Americans have quietly promoted her image and allowed her access to a lot of people and things.

English People:

General Sir Horace Meriwether Babington Smyth, VC, OBE, (Merry)

British Army active duty officer on General Staff, something important in MI5 or MI6 or possibly both, sometimes a director or minister of something hazy in the English government, also a member of the Royal Oversight Security Committee. Seems to have been in school with everyone important or is related to most of them. His wife Lady Pamela is Duchess of Cavingham and has royal connections.

EUOPS People:

Asim Halim-Toubon

Egyptian EUOPS operative, multilingual native of Cairo, specialist in disguise, infiltration, and observation. Asim is one of Dove Abraham's intelligence operatives. She is married to Maurice Toubon.

Colonel Benjamin Mac Glencoe, Ret. (Ben)

Former colonel in the English SAS and was in command of the SAS Counter Revolutionary Warfare Wing. One of the numerous people Merry, General Sir Horace Meriwether Babington Smyth, went to school with. After he retired from the army, General Babington Smyth had recruited him for EUOPS. As his current cover, he is Regional Manager in charge of the Southerland Oil office in Cairo. He is the Southern Armed Actions and Strike Force Commander for all EUOPS operations in the area and reports to Greta Steiner, EUOPS Southern Area Supervisor.

Dove Abraham

Ex-Mossad assassin and assassination squad leader. Now retired from Mossad and transferred to MI6, currently on loan to EUOPS. She is in charge of directing and coordinating direct action activities and is second in command to Greta Steiner in the EUOPS Southern Area. She is also the live-in companion of Greta and second mother of Elise.

Elise Julia Pamela Victoria Steiner - Francisci

Daughter of Greta Steiner and Mark Saint Martin, Goddaughter of Lady Pamela Duchess of Cavingham, Pam; Lady Victoria Dowager Duchess of Camenshite, Blossom; and Lady Julia Duchess of Montgreve, Julia. Elise is also the legally adopted daughter of Lucien Francisci the head of the Francisci Crime Family.

Francis Saint Martin née Schiller

Born Charlotte Angelina Fedorova in East German she is the oldest Daughter of Colonel Yuri Fedorova and his wife Angelina Tatiana Fedorova. She was born a "Blue Baby" and was smuggled out of East Germany for heart surgery by MI6 since her father was a double agent. She is the body double for Greta. Francis is brilliant and has several degrees. She was previously assigned to the EUOPS Department of Dirty Tricks lab where she was a specialist in exploding objects and disguised lethal arms. Francis is married to Mark Saint Martin. She is currently in an Agent-In-Place posting while recovering from being shot in the head.

Greta Steiner

Born Alexandra Maria Fedrovia, Youngest daughter of Colonel Yuri Fedorova and his wife Angelina Tatiana Fedorova, younger sister of Charlotte Fedorova Yegorov. Born in Germany and grew up in old Soviet Union. She escaped and became a EUOPS operative after the murder of her parents. Worked as an assassin and is also a qualified fixed and rotary wing pilot. She is the new EUOPS Southern Area Supervisor with an expanded area of operations to include all of Africa. Greta also has an identity as Brigadier General Juanita Anderson and has a daughter Elise.

Lady Julia Robertson, (Julia)

Duchess of Montgeave, Countess of Rhayader. Retired MI6 assassin, and operative, member of the Royal Security Oversight Committee, currently in charge of security for the EUOPS Welsh safe house village base, registered nurse with enhanced training in battlefield wound care and surgery. She is also the EUOPS expert in extracting information from people who would rather not talk. She is the designated successor for Lady Victoria Elaine Covington as the English Delegate to EUOPS. She is married to Sir Willard Robertson, a life peer and Director of Operations at the English mint. She has two daughters, Lady Julia Thomas, next in line for her title and Dr. Helen Robertson who is at the university doing research in biophysics and genetics.

Lady Victoria Elaine Covington, DCB, (Blossom)

Dowager Duchess of Camenshire, Permanent Assistant Minister for Economics and Policy on European Union Activities, English delegate to the EUOPS Control Committee, currently elected as chairman of the committee. She is the daughter of the Earl of Lindholm and her son is

Colonel Rupert Covington, 12th Duke of Camenshire, Baron of Insalady.

Mark Saint Martin

Former EUOPS Southern Area Supervisor, and also the Director of Middle Eastern Operations for Southerland Oil. He has been promoted to Vice President of Mediterranean Operations for Southerland Oil and the EUOPS Director of Southern Operations. Mark is the biological father of Greta's daughter Elise and married to Francis Saint Martin née Schiller.

Maurice Toubon

Algerian born EUOPS operative. Conducts infiltration, observation, courier, and sabotage operations and bombings, with an occasional assassination. Maurice is currently running the EUOPS Southern Area office for Greta Steiner as her executive assistant and Chief of Station Operations in addition to serving as head of intelligence and infiltration operations for the office.

Sergeant Major Charles Russell Whittingham, Ret. (Charley)

Retired SAS sergeant major. His last duty assignment was with the Counter Revolution Warfare Wing where the commander, Colonel Benjamin Mac Glencoe, loaned him to Greta Steiner as a bodyguard. He retired and has joined EUOPS. He is a driver and a bodyguard to Greta Steiner, Dove, and Elise.

Sergeant Major Joseph Omar Young, Ret. (Joey)

Apparently, his first name honors his paternal grandfather and is a traditional family name, his mother chose Omar as a middle name after going on a walking tour of Palestine with his father when they were both students and just before the wedding. ("A loaf of bread, a glass of wine and thou ... etc.") He is a retired SAS sergeant major and his last duty assignment was with the Counter Revolution Warfare Wing where the commander, Colonel Benjamin Mac Glencoe loaned him to Greta Steiner as a bodyguard.

11

He has joined EUOPS and is the primary bodyguard and assistant for Dove Abraham.

Sir Willard Robertson

Married to Julia, Duchess of Duchess of Montgeave. He is a life peer and Director of Reclamation Operations at the English mint. Former legendary MI-6 operations planner and policy analyst during the cold war, member of the Royal Security Oversight Committee, Head of Onsite Operations at the EUOPS Welsh safe house complex where his wife is in charge. Teaches the actual operations of International Finance and Economics to selected advanced students at Oxford.

Egyptian People:

Bryon McMillian

He goes by colonel but is actually a general in the Egyptian Army. He did not go to school with General Babington-Smyth but went to school in Egypt where he lived with his mother. He is a legitimate Egyptian and English dual citizen and his father is a friend of General Babington-Smyth's father, so he is one of the "Right People". He is in charge of Egyptian security operations in Northern Egypt and is also tasked with maintaining contact and providing cooperation and coordination with other western security agencies.

General Abdul El-Shazly

The Head of the Military Intelligence and Reconnaissance Department for Egypt.

Francisci Family People:

Alonzo Caparoni

Longtime bodyguard and valet for Lucien Francisci he is married to Clarissa Caparoni and is the father of Nicole and Celeste Caparoni.

Armand Gerard

Mr. Armand Gerard is one of the council of four senior members of the Francisci Family, an old Unione Course family dating to the fourteenth century. Mr. Gerard specialized in selling dubious to illegal weapons and military supplies to anyone with the required money. He is second in command to Lucien Francisci, the current head of the Francisci Family.

Carlo Conein

Mr. Carlo Conein is one of the council of four senior members of the Francisci Family governing council. He sells business and personal insurance for the Francisci Family. If you purchase the insurance the terms are easily understood, you pay up and nothing bad happens. Mr. Conein also supervises extortion, murder, theft, and collections.

Celeste Caparoni

Celeste is sixteen and attends Saint Teresa's Academy an all girl's school. This is her first year in Lycée where she is in the honors program as an advanced student. Her interests are history, language, and law. She has lived on the Corsica estate of Lucien Francisci since she was born. Her parents are Monsieur and Madame Caparoni who are on the staff of the estate.

Clarissa Caparoni

Housekeeper and bodyguard for Lucien Francisci she is married to Alonzo Caparoni Lucien Francisci's valet and bodyguard. She has been the housekeeper for Lucien

Francisci since she was nineteen and married Alonzo when she was twenty. They have two daughters, Celeste and Nicole.

John Carbone

Mr. John Carbone is one of the council of   four   senior members of the Francisci Family governing council. Mr. John Carbone is the only English born member of the council. He is in charge of drugs, sex, human trafficking and illegal immigration, smuggling, and normal and white slavery.

Lucien Francisci

Don Francisci is the head of the family. He is a well know international banker and financier, a past member of French Senate, and holder of the Croix de Guerre with silver gilt palm for service on Corsica with the resistance during World War II when he was a teenager.

Nicole Caparoni

As she said, "I am nine. I go to Saint Teresa's academy. I am in Cours moyen premiére annèe. I like to play too much according to the nuns and you already know who my parents are and the other stuff. I like sports."

Valentino Guérini

Mr. Valentino Guérini is one of the council of four senior members of the Francisci Family governing council. He is in charge of the casinos, betting and loan sharking, counterfeiting, property acquisition through various means, fencing stolen goods, securities manipulation and bank fraud and other white-collar crimes.

Other People:

Hamid Masoud

Freelance assassin and courier. Mr. Masoud works for whoever will pay him, although he has a number of steady repeat government clients in Asia. He has been extremely active in eliminating nuclear scientists for the past few years. It appears he is killing people who are experts in enriching uranium. Who is paying for these services is unknown.

Sara Kransky

Interior and exterior decorator and restoration and preservation contractor. Normally she works out of Paris, London and New York as a top of the market decorator. But she also has a Russian degree in electrical engineering and does freelance work in electronic building security.

Serena Watson

She is the producer and sometime cameraman for Margret Perry at American Press. She is also an operative for the ICCA, the International Currency Control Agency. They are the Switzerland based international money, bonds, and securities guards for the banking industry. She is a native of Australia and lives in Brussels.

ROBERT FENTON

CHAPTER 1: TAG

Hamid Masoud pulled the string that would move the awning a bit more to make the shadow fall into the ninth-floor apartment and keep the interior of the room dark. He looked at the green area of lawn and landscaping surrounding the buildings in the government administrative center two blocks away and at the conference building surrounded with its own green park. The conference building was enclosed in a tall masonry wall and had armed guards dressed in green berets, khaki shorts and short-sleeved shirts on the roof, on scaffolds behind the wall, and every ten feet along the perimeter of the building. The gate was blocked by two armored personnel carriers pulled up with their noses touching and local police cars were doing random patrols in the area and directing all motor traffic away from the closed streets in the two-block security area around the building.

He had been hiding in the apartment for the last two days. The young couple that lived here were away at a resort for a seaside vacation with their three children after winning a rigged drawing for the vacation that had been sponsored by a chain of local grocery stores with a sympathetic owner. After the family was gone, the building had been swept by the security teams and inspected again to make sure that there were no problems the week before the meetings and again the day before the conference started. The empty apartment had been duly noted as empty and no one cared about it anymore. Besides, the building was outside the exclusion zone and over a quarter of a mile from the conference building.

A pair of police cars on random sweeps had pulled up across the street from the apartment building and four officers got out and stood together talking. Hamid watched and tensed as one of the officers pointed at the building then another one shook his head and pointed down the street to a coffee shop in the adjacent building. The random search team made a checkmark on a paper on a clipboard and threw it in one of the cars and they all walked down the block and into the café. Hamid smiled and walked back to the kitchen table where he had set up his rifle and laser aided spotting scope. The scope was connected to a laptop computer with the latest targeting software. A USB cable that controlled the aim of the rifle ran from the computer to the motorized rifle carriage. The computer continuously updated the aiming point of the rifle by using an infrared laser sight that compensated for wind and also continuously measured the distance to the target to within a half a wavelength of the laser light. The screen of the computer showed a white circle about the size of a grape for the uncertainty at the point of impact, a zone of probability that made a head shot not only possible but also precise at almost five hundred yards.

It was mid-afternoon, and the meetings would be breaking up soon. The delegates usually held negotiations on the draft agreement until two or three local time and then adjourned so that they could contact their government before the end of the workday. If they quit at the normal time, the sun would be shining over the building he was in and illuminating the area under the portico of the conference building and highlighting the door so that when the delegates came out to drive away, he would have ample time to identify his target and shoot.

He walked back to the window and looked out. The chugging sounds of the helicopters and the chainsaw sounds of the drones circling over the meeting site blended to make a buzzing like the dragonflies and mosquitos in the reeds along the river where he had grown up. He wished he could have a smoke, but the young couple would notice the smell when they returned. He pulled the cord to move the shade again. As he did, he felt a hot spot on his throat and then looked down at the red dot of a laser gun sight on his chest.

He yanked the blinds shut and dropped to the floor. Then, when no shot came, he moved swiftly back to the kitchen table and closed the computer. He unplugged the cable to the gun carriage and curled it quickly around his hand and thrust it and the computer into a canvas tote bag. He released the two clips holding the stockless single shot rifle to the mounting carriage and unloaded it and put it in the foam carrier block. He slid the carriage's holding clamps off the edge of the table and hit the four detent release clips and folded it into a compact bundle of rods and tubes and put it in the bottom of the plastic tool box between the two one pound blocks of C-4 and then put the foam block containing the rifle on top. He closed the lid of the toolbox, swung

18

the tote bag over his shoulder and put on his ball cap. He picked up the toolbox then left the apartment after locking the door. He walked quickly to the end of the hall and glanced at the elevator indicator. It showed the up elevator passing the sixth floor. He unlocked the door to the service elevator and stepped in and slid the door shut, locking it. Then, he punched the button for the basement service area. When the elevator stopped, he opened the door and locked it open, so the elevator would not move.

Hamid wondered how in the world they had spotted him. He walked to the rear of the main heating furnace and opened the toolbox and pulled out the detonator for the explosives and then shoved the tote bag and toolbox into the furnace through the service port. He pulled the heavy iron door shut and then he set the controls for a test burn. The natural gas rushed into the furnace and ignited with a slight pop and the evacuation fans started pushing the smoke, and the smell of burning plastic and explosives, up the hundred and twenty-foot-tall chimney. He glanced at the furnace service sheet he had filled in yesterday and recorded the test burn then added the sheet to the furnace maintenance log notebook.

He stripped off the plumbing and heating company coveralls and hung them and the cap in a locker and took out his suit coat and put it on. He pulled a pocket protector with a badge identifying him as a power company engineer out of the side pocket of his dark suit and put it in the breast pocket. He put the detonator and the shell for the rifle in a small paper bag with the wrappers and fruit peel from his lunch and put the paper bag in his pants pocket then unlocked the door to the electrical, sewer and water utility tunnel and walked into it, closing and locking the door behind him.

****

Greta Steiner and her girlfriend, Dove Abraham, were sitting in the back room of the Cairo headquarters of Mediterranean Air Service, a new freight and charter service that served Africa and the Mediterranean area, looking at a computer screen that showed the picture from a Whirligig drone at the building where the assassin had been spotted. The picture also showed the four policemen that were standing by their cars and talking into microphones.

"Who was it?" asked Greta Steiner, new EUOPS Southern Area Supervisor to her second, Dove Abraham. "Anyone you know?"

"Not personally, I have absolutely no idea who he is, who he was here to kill, or who sent him. But, I do have good pictures and we will probably be able to identify him today. I want to do some blow-ups of the equipment in the back of the room, too, and that should tell us quite a bit."

"I don't think that he was after any of our people. As far as I know we don't really have a lot of interest in anything going on there and only have some lower level people to observe. Has anyone picked him up yet, Dove?"

"No, we do have a few people on the ground near the conference and they are going to be watching the ways out of town. No one local knows he was there. Should we let anyone know, Greta?"

"No, I don't think so. How would we explain that we knew he was there? How did we pick him up, by the way?"

"One of the monitors on the high-altitude drone noticed that there was a constant dark spot on the building. They called for a low altitude review and found out it was a shadow in a window on the ninth floor of the building that remained constant. Shadows do not remain constant, unless someone is adjusting them. I had them use a low altitude Whirligig drone with enhanced vision capability to take a peek and saw him and his rifle and we watched him for a while. Since the conference people were going to be busy for another couple hours we had enough time to set up a trap so I had some people dressed like local cops come and sneak into the building. There were a couple inside the building and a couple outside, but not too close since we thought we could follow him when he left without his noticing. When you said go ahead and spook him I used a visible laser pointer on the Whirligig that looked like a sighting beam from a rifle. We had a person outside in a car, one on a motorcycle, one in the elevator coming up, and one on the stairs but he apparently went down in the service elevator and got out. What do you want to do now?"

"Finally nurse Elise, before I blow up, and send the pictures out to get an identification on him. Have the people in the general area keep an eye out, if they spot him, put on a tail or plant a tracker and see what he does and where he goes. Then we are going to our apartment and see if there is anything left for cooking gear and make up a shopping list. Are there more diapers?"

"You want me to change her or take the pictures out? Why don't you just sit here and relax a minute and I will spread some orders and get the identity search going, then I'll change Elise and you can feed her."

"Right, you change her, and I'll feed her while you handle the search for the missing assassin. Then we can put the station on automatic for the rest of the day since we aren't even supposed to be active yet and everyone else needs to get settled too. Also, I am going to have to set up a meeting with Ben over at the Southerland Oil office sometime tomorrow. We are going to be handling all of Southerland's helicopter and light plane work in the area and they are just going to do the big jets."

"I don't get this," said Dove. "Doesn't Ben work for us?"

"No, Ben works for Merry and we work for Mark and Blossom," said Greta, "Ben retired from the Army into MI6 and took on African and mid-eastern business and service operations for Southerland Oil. We are the little eyes and ears in the woodwork and Ben is running a semi-legal division of Southerland Oil, Southerland Well Services chartered in Sudan, and providing equipment servicing and supplies to private oil production companies and individual owners in the area. He also has the troops and heavy stuff if we need them."

"I thought that they were giving the Southerland Oil operation to us, well you actually," said Dove. "What happened?"

"Dove, how much do you know about barite loaded drilling mud and fracking chemicals?" said Greta. "Yeah, well, me too, and Southerland is an actual oil well service company as well as providing cover for us. Ben doesn't know much more about oil than we do but he knows how to run things since he was, or maybe still is, a SAS colonel. Besides, he is a man. In the Middle East, private women oil company executives aren't. Southerland has to do a lot of legitimate and shady business, especially now with the Crete oil and gas development starting up. Ben can run an organization and he is being supplied with a lot of people that know the oil business and a lot of the other kind of people that we need for our work. I, on the other hand, know flying and so the charter business is something we can do convincingly and the charter contract with Southerland ties us together publicly, so we can get the work done."

"Here is Elise, with a fresh diaper," said Dove. "Feed her and I will go scatter orders and send out the pictures. Do you want anything else done or should everyone just arrange their desks and look busy until quitting time if they haven't left for the day?"

Greta waved her hand and slid the folder of pictures that they had selected and printed from the broadcast copy of the observation tape from the new low altitude drone across the desk. Greta took Elise and looked down at her. Elise looked up and smiled, or maybe it was just a gas bubble, but Greta hiked up her top and unsnapped the nursing bra. Elise took the offered nipple and started nursing and Greta leaned back in her office chair and put her feet up on the desk and relaxed.

"Send Mark the pictures and I'll call him later," said Greta.

Dove nodded and walked out with the folder. The low altitude Whirligig drone with the original tape had flown to a pickup area near the conference and been retrieved at altitude by one of the new supersonic Taranis drones in a low speed air capture maneuver. The supersonic radar evading Taranis was now on its way to the British airbase at Akrotiri on Crete where the Whirligig and tape would be recovered and processed. Greta would need to contact Mark and inform him about what was on the tape and request a selection of frames that would be best for maximum enhancement and printing so they could identify the man and his equipment.

This would be the first personal contact between her and Mark since Elise had been born. Mark Saint Martin was her nominal boss and former lover. Mark was also the father of Elise Steiner, Greta's four-month-old daughter. Elise had not been her idea and relations between Mark and Greta were still strained. She had taken over his old job as Southern Area EUOPS Supervisor. Mark had been promoted to EUOPS Director of Southern Operations, and also Vice President of Mediterranean Operations for Southerland Oil, one of the legitimate companies that provided cover for EUOPS. He had moved to Crete to supervise exploration drilling at the British airbase that apparently was sitting on a pool of oil and gas. Mark was recently married to a retired EUOPS operative named Francis Saint Martin née Schiller, who was Greta's body double and had recently taken a bullet through her head that had been meant for Greta and extracted a huge settlement from the Americans for doing it.

Well, thought Greta, now is as good a time as any to get in contact. At least they had something interesting to talk about besides Elise. She pushed the button that said Mark and the computer searched for the random number assigned to Mark's phone by Greta's phone that morning and dialed it. The computer turned on the scrambler program that would transmit a digital signal that was sixty five percent trash and thirty five percent scrambled message to a satellite that would pump up the power and broadcast a totally different re-scrambled digital string out into the waiting ether so that anyone listening on that particular frequency could receive it, and spend a significant part of eternity trying to decode it and only slightly less listening on that frequency for another message since the frequency might possibly be used by her phone again in maybe ten million years. The phone rang twice and then Mark picked up.

"Greta, what's up?" said Mark. "I assume this isn't just a test, since you are still a week or so out from active according to your last progress report. You got problems?"

"Well, kind of, Mark," said Greta and told him about the Taranis that was on the way and the tape of the assassin.

"You know anything about a hit that was planned at the conference?" said Greta. "Neither Dove nor I know the hit man. He looks to be local and not too old, but he was very professional in his reactions. Also, he managed to give four agents the slip. From the time Dove spooked him he took less than forty-five seconds to evaporate from the not crime scene and disappear."

"I don't know anything our side had laid on," said Mark. "It looks like whoever it is isn't an amateur though. He sounds good. As for who would try something like this, the meetings involve all the local parties affected by the Iranian nuclear program. The squeeze of the sanctions is starting to hurt Iran really bad and the loss of Syria as a go between is hurting them even worse. Prices in the area are going way up, even above black market abnormal, and they are astronomical for nuclear processing equipment and supplies. I don't even want to speculate on who sent a hired gun to do something since fifty percent of the participants at the conference would kill the other half if they thought they could get away with it. When will you actually be active?"

"I guess right now," said Greta. "The charter service is already going strong, but all my people are still getting sorted and we are in chaos here at the office, but we'll get on it since it looks like we have an interesting question or maybe even a problem in my area. I still need to get my apartment cleaned, re-done and furnished so I can move out of the hotel. I guess that the people that were leasing apartments, now own the building as a tenants' association, although the pilot that I sub-leased from is the actual owner, I guess."

"No, actually you were the one that held the lease, and the one the landlord was making films of, even if it was for the government," said Mark. "Neither he nor the government can actually admit that. The lawyers found out that the pilot was never a real tenant and you were the one with the lease. So, I put your name in the damage claim and when the judgment went against the landlord, you got your apartment free and clear and I got the films the landlord made."

"What," said Greta. "That is disgusting. You have all those pictures of us naked in the shower and you and me in bed and everything. Give them back. I want them right now!"

"Calm down. I am on Crete and you are in Cairo," said Mark. "If you run out in the street and turn north, you could get here by walking and swimming in a couple years. Now I can't give them to you since all of the original films are part of the evidence for the court case against your landlord, which will probably go on for at least two or three appeals and ten years, knowing the Egyptian legal system, but I have official custody of the films and they are locked in the vault here. If anyone gets a court order to see them, they have to come to Crete to watch the ones they can prove they need to see."

"How come you got the films?" said Greta. "It was my place that they were filming, and I was the injured party."

"Uh, well I was also in a large number of them," said Mark. "So the judge gave me custody of the films."

"Why didn't he give me custody," said Greta, "since I was in all of them, and was the named litigant and you weren't?"

"Well, you see you are a woman of demonstrated questionable character, which you proved by going to bed with me when we weren't married, and the judge thought that you shouldn't be, umm, trusted with the films since you might destroy them and so he gave them to me," said Mark. "Besides, he was worried about me just being married and you causing trouble with Francis."

"Tell me one more time about the prohibition on personal revenge killings as a corruption of agency policy," said Greta. "I am very disturbed, Mark. As a matter of fact, I am going to hang up now and go and see if I can figure out how to justify killing the judge and his whole damn family and his dog. How is Francis? Julia kept me informed from time to time while we were in Wales."

"She is doing a lot better," said Mark. "She has glasses now that seem to compensate for her double vision and she isn't having headaches very often. She has been hinting about going back to work or some other things."

"Like starting a family?" said Greta. "Julia said you two should get on with that since everyone's clocks keep ticking and it certainly appears that you at least are still fertile."

"Can we come see Elise?" said Mark. "Julia kept us informed about you and Elise, and well, she told me to stay out of the way until you decided things."

"I'll let you know," said Greta. "As soon as I figure out if I am hanging around in the job or not. Goodbye Mark."

"Greta, what do you want done with the tapes from the Whirligig?" said Mark. "Do you want a copy or an enhanced copy and when?"

"Oh hell," said Greta. "Do a low-level enhancement of everything and send it to the office tonight and I will come back in although I shouldn't. Honest Mark, I either need to go grocery shopping or give up eating."

Greta hung up and leaned forward in the chair and pushed down an intercom button and moved Elise to the other breast.

"Maurice, could you come in here for a minute," said Greta, "I need to leave and get supplies, and you are it. Dove and I need food and diapers and everything else. Mark is sending enhanced photographs tonight and I'll need to come back in later. "

Maurice Toubon was a senior operative from Algeria that had impressed Greta in the recent operations in Syria where her team had stolen several tons of gold. He was slightly older than the normal run of field people and had welcomed the job with the lighter physical and emotional demands that came with it. He was currently keeping company with Asim Halim, a young lady recognizance and observation agent that he had met during the Syrian assignment.

Greta had selected him to be her office manager at the Mediterranean Air Service operation and the chief of staff for the EUOPS operations. Mediterranean Air charter and freight service had originally been headquartered in Corsica but had announced it was moving to Cairo to be more centrally located in their service area of Africa and the Levantine, which was a logical excuse. Actually the office was the Southern Operations Area Headquarters of EUOPS, the direct-action arm of the European Union. EUOPS is an organization that does not exist, and if you don't believe it, just ask them. They will tell you EUOPS isn't and it is certainly not involved in directly influencing world events and shaping world affairs to the liking and benefit of the European Union and various other countries using bombs, bullets, assassinations, and bribery.

The head of the Corsican Francisci crime family, Lucien Francisci, had sold Mediterranean Air Service and its planes to Greta on the condition that a few of his people and things could still travel in the planes on an as needed basis while EUOPS used the business as a cover. The EUOPS Control Committee had approved the arrangement and Greta had bought the flying service with EUOPS money and moved the company headquarters to Cairo a few weeks ago when she came here from Wales to set up the EUOPS and Mediterranean Air headquarters.

Greta was still getting her life and her new organization organized and it had been a fluke that the staff testing some new unmanned equipment in an area that was temporarily overloaded with similar equipment so it wouldn't be noticed had seen something fishy and they had gotten involved in something totally unexpected that was probably not their business.

There was a knock on the door and she closed her bra and pulled down her top.

"Come in," said Greta.

Dove opened the door and stuck in her head and then pulled it back out and closed the door. Two or three minutes later she came back in.

"Here," said Dove, handing Greta a breast pump. "You're leaking. You should rotate the baby every two or three minutes. Maurice is out. What did Mark say?"

"Where is Maurice," said Greta, "I keep forgetting to change when I am busy, which is most of the time now, thanks for the pump and Mark said he was sending the primary enhancement pictures this evening, so I will be coming back to work. Here, take Elise while I finish up."

"Oh lovely," said Dove. "Chinese take away again and sleep on the couch in the office? I want a real bed, Greta. I want one with sheets and blankets and pillows and a mattress and all the other trimmings. Elise needs to sleep in her crib instead of in a paper box on a heap of coats. We want to go to a home, Greta."

"So do I, sweetheart," said Greta. "I was going to get Maurice to watch things and go and shop for food and appliances and furniture and that sort of thing before this all came up."

Greta finished pumping and handed Dove the pump and milk container and then straightened her clothing and took Elise, who whimpered and then dropped back to sleep, as Greta gently rocked her.

"You know we need an office sized refrigerator here," said Dove. "What am I supposed to do with the milk? I am not going to waste it. This represents two hours of sleep tonight."

There was another knock on the door and Asim stuck her head in and said, "I have Maurice on the phone, he is over in Heliopolis talking to his cousin who is a decorator and getting furniture for his place."

"I thought you two were together now," said Dove, "What's with his place and her place."

"It's like she can throw him out any damn time she wants him to," said Asim, "It keeps him in line. Do you want to talk to him?"

"Yes," said Greta, "put it on speaker. Maurice, your cousin is a decorator and has a source of furniture like beds and tables and chairs and stuff?"

"Oh hello, Greta," said Maurice. "Yes, she is fairly well known both locally and internationally, she is very busy but is taking a sanity break and she offered to come and arrange to have my place done by someone that comes and actually paints the day they say they will and charges what they quote. I doubt if I will have to have anyone killed to get their attention."

"We do not kill the locals, Maurice," said Greta. "Although I have to keep remembering that. Can your cousin be bought for gold, and I mean actual gold Sovereigns?"

"Probably," said Maurice. "What do you want?"

"I want someone to come to my place and look at it and make it habitable," said Greta. "I do not need my hand held, discussions of color mood, furniture styles or artistic drawings. I need furniture and an apartment that is plush enough to be convincing for the head of an air charter service. Now, get back here, we have a situation which I will explain when you get here."

"Hello," said a female voice. "Maurice had his phone on speaker. How about this, I will come back with him and we can visit your apartment and I will measure it tonight, arrange for a contractor to start tomorrow, buy furniture locally off the internet or from some of my contacts and put your place together as soon as the contractor gets what needs done, done. All transactions, including the contractor will be in gold and we can haggle about the prices after I see the place. Where is it?"

"In the Garden District," said Greta. "Maurice knows where it is. Currently, it is stripped to the bare walls and the place has been bugged, so I need it cleaned up and swept for bugs and made move-in ready. All gold Sovereigns okay?"

"Yes," said Maurice's cousin, "or actual British pounds or American dollars, gold preferred, and no checks or receipts."

"Done," said Greta. "Who are you, by the way?"

"Sara Kransky," said the woman. "I usually live in Paris, but I have been doing some work in the area for one of the locals.

28

I don't need to get back for a few days though while the cement dries and they cart off the rubble, and as they say a bit of extra off the books cash always comes in handy."

"Yes," shouted Dove, "saved by the decorator. Oh crap, I woke up Elise."

Elise started crying and Dove put her up on her shoulder and patted her back firmly. Elise screwed up her face and made a tremendous wet burp and then wet her diaper and started crying again.

"I now have a really nice Andree Saint Louis frock with pee on the front and urp on the back," said Dove, "and we are out of diapers. I am taking the milk to the breakroom fridge and I need to take a shower and dig a new dress out of a suitcase. We can meet Asim, Sara, and Maurice at our apartment and tomorrow I am going to see if we can get some kitchen supplies and put them away on the floor. If we get there before the decorator, fine, if not also fine. I am also buying a bunch of lab coats with waterproof lining."

"Who is here," said Greta, "anyone else?"

"No, everyone has long since gone home since it is past quitting time for the flight service," said Asim. "I am only here because I was waiting for Maurice."

"Okay, Maurice, bring Sara and come to the apartment. I am going to come back here later, and I will explain," said Greta. "I am ordering take out, no not Chinese, Dove, and we can eat on the floor out of boxes on whatever is flat at the apartment."

"I will order out on my phone," said Asim, "Maurice, stop by the Marrakesh Café and pick up dinner and get a couple of bottles of white wine. We are leaving now."

Dove spread a towel from the bathroom over the seat of the BMW 650 coup so that the leather wouldn't get dirty from her dress and pulled the seat forward so Greta could get in the back and put Elise in the rear facing baby seat. Greta strapped Elise in and sat down next to her while Asim got in the passenger seat. Elise was fretting, and Greta finally picked her up and took off the wet diaper and arranged a blanket from the baby bag over Elise and then pulled up her shirt again and started Elise nursing again.

"Swap every five minutes or don't come running to me," said Dove, "especially since we left the pump at the office. You will need to grab it and do a wash job on it when you go back. I think we need a dishwasher in the canteen and one at the apartment and we also need a laundry and decent closet space and a separate room for Elise when she gets a bit bigger and, oh hell, I don't know. What about Maurice's cousin, Asim, do you know her?

"No, not a lot, but she is definitely high end. The client she is working for right now is Princess Taja, the ruler of one of the United Emirate countries," answered Asim, "the word on the street is that she is also an expert in monitoring and security, which might be a really good thing for all of us, including the office. Do you need to get it authorized or can we ask her about the office?"

"I don't know about her," replied Greta. "I'll call around. Right now though, did Dove tell you about our assassin or pre-assassin?"

"Yeah," answered Asim, "you got a favorite? Half the countries and organizations there would like to kill the other half, but I guess you already know that. Without getting too deep into the Shi'a, Sunni, Sufis, Salafi question, there are already enough national and tribal problems to write a book. The stated purpose of the conference is to set up meetings to limit Iran's nuclear program. What is going on is that everyone is trying to either destroy Iran's nuclear program or to get a bomb themselves, at least that is what the briefings have been saying. Change the baby over, Greta."

"Umm I was thinking," replied Greta as she moved Elise to the other breast. "Who would actually benefit if someone was shot. I think we need to need to talk to an analyst about all of the combinations. I hear that MI6 has been working on a program to do an analysis on something like this for the English. Maybe I will check it out after we get the pictures back from Mark. I'll call Merry."

Merry, or a bit more formally, General Sir Horace Meriwether Babington Smyth, VC, OBE, and other things, was the usual primary English contact with EUOPS. The general is a serving British Army active duty officer who is on General Staff and is generally suspected of being something important in MI5 or MI6 or possibly both.

"I'll get hold of Merry tomorrow and ask him about the program," said Greta. "I wonder where I can get a nursing timer that rings a bell to tell you when to switch and some burp jackets made of toweling with rubber liners. We are going to need a washing machine at the office, or near it, and some crash quarters for people coming in from the field. And, I need to sit and think about physical facilities more and missions that really aren't ours less."

Greta looked out the window as Dove drove through the streets toward the Garden City District of Cairo. The area was a knock off of an eighteenth century European residential district that had been built in the 1900s. It was comfortable and tranquil and contained both the United States and United Kingdom embassies and top-rated hotels like the Four Seasons. The rent was ruinous, and parking was a mess. There had even been some violence here recently and armed thugs had set up roadblocks and demanded money if you didn't want your windshield smashed. It normally had more policemen than the usual areas because it was next to Tahrir Square and because of the embassies but it was one of the highest priced areas in town. It was south of the city center on the west bank of the Nile and a long way from the airport and the new office of Mediterranean Air Service. Greta sighed, and Dove drove into the street where the apartment was. As usual, there was no parking and Dove stopped to let Asim, Greta and Elise out.

"All right, I'll drive around and around until I find somewhere to park and get a cab back," said Dove. "You and Asim go on in and wait for Maurice and company."

"No, you go and get us a room at the Nile House and have them park the car and grab a cab from there," said Greta. "We are going to stay at the hotel tonight and both get a shower and sleep in a bed."

"Why don't you let me go," suggested Asim, "Dove can clean up a bit and I will go and book a room and get a bus and then come back here since I don't have baby all over me."

"Okay, I won't argue," agreed Dove, "I need clean clothes after my shower and my suitcase is here. We can talk about the place with the decorator and then go to the hotel after supper."

Greta and Dove got out of the car and walked to the entry while Asim walked around the car and got in the driver's side. Dove fumbled with her key while Greta stood with Elise against her shoulder and watched Asim drive away. When Asim paused at the cross street a block away, a truck pulled in front of her and three men with automatic rifles jumped out and ran toward the car. Asim slammed the BMW into reverse, spun the wheel and shot across the street backwards where the truck had caused a break in the oncoming traffic, then she jammed the accelerator to the floor and roared back up the street at the traffic that scattered left and right.

The men with the rifles looked at the scattering traffic that was ramming parked cars and jumping curbs and ran for the truck. A taxi driver stuck his left hand with one finger raised out of the window of his cab and rammed the truck in the front wheel with his cab, then he stuck an automatic rifle out the window and started shooting. The three men from the truck ran behind the truck and across the rush hour traffic and the truck driver slid out the passenger's side door and ran after them. The taxi driver screamed something foul and then got out and shook his rifle in the air and immediately everyone on the street, including the crashed vehicles, started blowing their horns and a few men got out and started shooting the truck or in the air. Asim drove back past the jammed uptown lane in the now empty downtown lane blocked by the truck. She waved at Dove and Greta and continued toward the Nile, then turned the corner. A minute later Greta's phone rang.

"Any ideas, boss?" asked Asim. "Obvious it was an attempt to snatch either you or Dove, since they didn't come out shooting. I don't think it was locals going for a few pounds ransom since they were wearing white tee shirts and uniform pants and combat boots not sandals like the local crooks do. What do you want to do?"

"Call Maurice and have him meet us at the hotel," directed Greta. "You ditch the car and we will report it stolen. Take a cab and book a suite and have them send up some food. We need to grab a suitcase with some clothes and diapers and sleepers. We'll go out the back of the building and walk to the next street over through the yards and flag a cab. We'll meet you at the hotel. Oh, get Elise's car seat and diaper bag out of the car before you ditch it though."

"You think that a cab will be safe?" asked Asim. "I could circle back."

"Yes, a cab will be safe. Cab drivers in Cairo only rob you, not kidnap you, and we need to sever all connections with the car as soon as possible," said Greta. "As a matter of fact, leave the keys in it and the doors unlocked. I think we need some new cars anyway."

"Okay boss," said Asim. "I just dumped it in a delivery zone with the keys in the ignition and the windows down. I'm walking off right now. See you at the hotel."

CHAPTER 2: LOCATION, LOCATION, LOCATION

Asim was holding Elise and rocking her while Greta drank tea with milk and Maurice, Sara, and Dove drank a white Algerian wine that Maurice had brought with the take-out dinner. Maurice had reported the car stolen from a parking space in old Cairo and had supplied a description, the plate number and VIN number. The police had given them an incident number to pass on to their insurance company and said they would keep them informed if by some miracle the car turned up.

"Do you think they will find it?" said Dove. "If they don't, I want a convertible. Red, red leather interior, white top and a full electronics package."

"Including machine guns and rotating number plates?" asked Maurice. "No, I don't think they will find it. By now it is a whole bunch of parts being loaded in a container to ship to Bulgaria. Handy tradition that way here in Egypt, no incriminating cars are left un-stolen."

"Umm, your cousin?" asked Greta nodding at Sara. "We need to discuss some things here."

Sara turned away from the window where she was watching the river and smiled at Greta. "Oh, go ahead and discuss whatever you want to, but I will tell it all to anyone that threatens me with a knife or even a sharpened sucker stick, although actually a sharpened sucker stick is dangerous in the right hands. No, I don't want to know what you people are doing, but I already know you are associated with Merry and he is associated with some of the people I do things for, but also a lot of people I do things for are not associated with him. Anyway, what did you have in mind?"

"I am really not sure now," said Greta. "I have a flat in the Garden District, combined living and dining room, kitchen, bath with a tub and shower, and a relatively small bedroom, a beautiful Juliet balcony big enough for two chairs, three flights of stairs and no parking. I was paying eighteen hundred pounds and utilities for it, but due to a lawsuit, I now kind of own it. I was awarded custody subject to twenty or thirty appeals and sessions of bribing the judge. I was thinking about having you fix it up so Dove, Elise and I could live there, but now I am not so sure."

"Yeah, having storm troopers try to kidnap you does make you nervous," commented Sara. "Not that I've ever been kidnapped, you understand, shot at yes, held hostage once or twice, arrested and tried, but as they say, sixteen arrests and no convictions. I was also a resident of Russia like you, Miss Steiner, but I left early."

"What do you mean by that remark?" asked Greta. "What makes you think I'm Russian?"

"No, what I mean is you were obviously a resident," responded Sara. "Unless you won the Russian civil helicopter wings in a poker game."

"True," answered Greta. "Been a while since I've been there although I fly in and out from time to time. Now, about the apartment, I am stumped on what to do."

"Rent it to Asim and me," volunteered Maurice. "We can live there."

"Wrong thought, bad idea, Maurice," said Asim. "His and hers is still the way it is now. However, why don't you swap with Greta? Swap your place in Heliopolis for her place in Garden City. Since the place in Heliopolis is in your mother's name, Greta and Dove can live there and get their mail at the office and drop out of sight for a while. If anyone asks, and they probably shouldn't, they can say they are renting from their family. Your family is large enough so that there should be some cousins lying around that haven't been used."

"What is the Heliopis place," asked Dove, "an apartment?"
"No," answered Sara. "It's one of the big old houses that was built right after the First World War. A dozen or so of them were built on land where there had been one of the public gardens that were redeveloped. It's a walled two-story brick English town house and has a gated entry and a large front garden with trees and turf. The place was split into two residences in the 1950s and rented out to some of the new government employees that moved there when the government set up all the offices in Heliopolis. The lower floor has a screened outdoor veranda, four large rooms and a large kitchen and four-piece bathroom. The second floor has a kitchen, a tub bath and a great room, two smaller bedrooms and a screened and

shuttered covered balcony or sleeping porch on the front. There is a carriage house that has been converted into a two-car garage at the rear of the property."

"That would sure be less cramped, Greta," said Dove, "and it is closer to the airport and the office."

"True, but then what about my more or less apartment downtown?" asked Greta, "

"Actually, the best option would be for me to buy the Garden City apartment," said Sara. "Well, actually take a lease option on it, since it still has to go through a number of shady deals in the courts. I need a place here for various professional reasons and can afford to buy it even at the ruinous prices. You can get rid of a place they, whoever they are, are watching and live in the Heliopolis place that is private and has a brick wall around it and a gate you can put a guard on. They will track you there eventually, of course, but if you work it right, you can find out who they are and what they want first. It will give you some time before they find you and at least you have off street parking and a bedroom for everyone upstairs. You can live downstairs, Maurice."

"If Asim moved in downstairs with me, we could carpool to work," said Maurice, "and save gas."

"Maurice, I may stop you from coming over if you don't quit this constant nagging," said Asim. "I said his and hers places."

"No, what I mean is there are four huge rooms," said Maurice, "and a big bath and kitchen and a screened in porch that we used to sleep on since there is no air conditioning. We could do the rooms up as three studios and a common sitting and dining room and even have a roommate if we want one or use it to stash people from work that are passing through. That way, we could split the rent three ways, actually four if Greta rents one of the downstairs rooms for the company. The rent that mother charges is a lot lower there than anywhere else around. But carpooling probably wouldn't be a good idea. Too many eggs in one basket, and apparently someone wants all or one of you girls."

"Good point," said Greta and nodded. "They went for the car even though someone must have seen Dove and me get out at the apartment. They wanted the driver and they didn't know who it was. All they had was an ID on the car, interesting. That means that it is probably someone who knows us but is using local help."

"Or at least someone that knows the car," said Maurice. "They apparently don't know who they would expect to find driving it and they could be acting on fairly sketchy information for someone that only knows the car from the apartment. Have you been there with the car?"

"Yeah a couple times to haul in some stuff to store," said Dove, "but this still looks like a fishing operation, or someone trying to pick up a few bucks from a kidnapping."

"All right, if you want to buy the flat, Sara, go look and figure out what you want to pay and then figure out what to do at Maurice's mother's house," said Greta. "I will probably want a separate exterior enclosed entrance added to the upstairs for a fire escape and we will need some more secure parking areas. Other than that, I guess I would like to see what you have in mind."

"How many bedrooms upstairs?" said Sara, "One or two?" "One, with a nursery," said Dove, "and a bed in the nursery. So, I guess two, but one is for Elise and someone to tend her. A girl should hold out for her own bedroom regardless of age."

"I agree," said Asim. "However, I am interested in the downstairs studio idea. They have jacked the rent up on my place and it is clear across the river from the office. Besides, I don't have a car, so it takes two bus changes and a long time to get to work if Maurice isn't there. Another thing is, I have been spending a lot of time out of town recently and people start to wonder where you are and get nosy. If I lived in a company compound no one would ask where I was, they would know."

"I was thinking today that we need a safe house, anyway," said Greta. "I think that the company should take the last studio for people that need a place to stay when they are here or need to disappear for a while. Asim and Maurice could set it up for a home office most of the time."

"All right," said Sara. "Now I need to go and take a look at the Garden City place and measure everything up and do a sweep of the places. You want internal house monitoring and grounds security at Heliopolis?"

"Yes," said Greta. "But to tell you the truth, I am going to need to get you cleared. We may have some other requirements."

"Call Merry and tell him you are working with me," said Sara. "I am off and so are you, Maurice. We can drop you off if you want, Asim."

"I would feel better if Asim stayed tonight," said Greta. "Since we have a suite, there is room and since someone tried to kidnap her, it might be best if she had company for a while. Also, I was going to go back to the office, but I think I will just go and meet with Mark and Merry tomorrow. I thought that I might take Asim and leave you to get things organized, Maurice. We can take my plane."

"I think that would be a good idea too," said Asim. "Maurice, we are without a car now, could you arrange a limo to take us to the Airport in the morning?"

"Yes," said Maurice. "I'll have one of the neighborhood boys pick you up in a taxi van. Less conspicuous if someone followed you here."

"Have him throw in some veils too," said Greta, "and we will check in through the front office before the local to Aswan flight. Load the flight up with people from the office so there is no room for anyone else and we can monitor who is there at that time. We need a babysitter for Elise, too. I don't want to take her."

"Why don't I stay," said Dove. "I can stay here at the hotel and watch her and then you can tell me whatever, uhhhh, no that isn't going to work, is it?"

"No, it isn't," said Greta, "since Merry needs to talk to both of us and you need to ask questions. This whole thing just isn't working is it? I don't know, maybe I should just quit. I don't know how to take care of Elise and run a spy agency. Crap, I don't know how to run a spy office. That is one problem with having a whole two-month career as a senior agent in control and also being the main operative for the field operation, Dove too. Both of us are playing with a big handicap. If Mark hadn't been such a shit, I probably wouldn't have taken the job."

"Look," said Asim, "there are a lot of us girls, well guys too, actually, I guess a lot of people, that have been wondering how you were going to do the job. The guy with no underwear, no condoms, and a freshly pressed tux riding around in a convertible sports car that had a flamethrower in the exhaust pipe, just isn't real. Everyone that doesn't actually know anything about our job thinks that none of us eat anything but caviar and never shit, but that just isn't so. I still have to go shopping and do the laundry, even when I am watching how the premier of Baloogaslovia goes to work so one of you girls can blow him up. Greta, if you can't do the job, all of us field people are going to get a black eye from the spin off and convince a lot of important people that marriages and babies are a no-no for operational people."

"Asim, I feel overloaded and totally at sea," said Greta. "I have no idea what to do first, or even second as far as that goes."

"I know it is hard to get around your feelings, Greta," said Asim, "but Blossom who is the head of the control committee was the only one questioning your appointment. Mark was in your corner all the way. He says you know things and figure them out and have a feel for situations. Julia and Willard both weighed in on your side, as well as a couple of the really, really, big you know who people, the ones that really do count. Everyone was impressed one way or another on the Syrian gold heist you pulled off. I think you can do this job, everybody else that works for you thinks that you can do the job and we will help all we can."

"Yeah, well Elise just did it too," said Dove, "Now with all the breast beating, probably a bad statement come to think about it, did anyone get any diapers, and jammies, how about a baby blanket and some wipes and all the other stuff?"

"Here," said Asim, "the baby bag was in the car and I grabbed it and the car seat when I ditched the car and I grabbed a package of diapers in the gift shop downstairs. Now, why don't I go and give Elise a bath and you can go and make her a bed in one of the dresser drawers in your room, Dove. Use a pillow that will totally fill the drawer or fold up an extra blanket that will totally fill it so she can't get tangled. Look Greta, you got problems with what we think was an attempted assassination, or an attempted kidnapping, getting a house set up, and organizing the office. You also have a problem with Elise, right?"

"Right," said Greta, "and?"

"Maurice has been an independent agent for ten years and is good at doing things. He is supposed to be your office manager and chief of staff, right?" said Asim. "Just tell him to get the office organized and living quarters organized. That's his job, after all. Sara will apparently be on the approved list to do the observation and security systems at your apartment and the house. Have Maurice check things out and take care of it all. I think that you should appoint me chief babysitter, please call it something glamorous like personal assistant for operations, or special live-in bodyguard so my record doesn't end up crappy and I will travel around with you since you don't want Elise to be too far from you, just in case she needs to eat."

"She could be hurt when I go in the field," said Greta. "But you're right, I shouldn't be going in the field now, should I?"

"No, and also it will keep me safe and sound in the office too," said Asim. "I guess you are elected to go run around in the field, Dove."

"Not I, unless I really have to," said Dove. "I'm Greta's second and that is the operation's director. That means traditionally I count bullets and arrange for taxis and bandages to be used in the field but not at the action. Besides I do have experience running field operations since I was a hit squad leader for the Mossad and had to move my people around and get them in and out and do the tissues, elastic bandages, machine gun bullets and bus tokens. I think that I can do what is needed without much sweat, especially since we got some good experienced people from Blossom and Merry. I think that you are going to have to let go and trust other people to do things, Greta."

"Yeah, well there is only one little problem with that," said Greta, "Rule one."

"Rule one?" said Asim, "Which is that one?"

"Never trust anyone," said Dove, "That's rule one."

"Oh, that rule one," said Asim, "Well, let's all go and give Elise a bath and get ready for bed, that way we can all watch each other to see if anyone is doing anything suspicious."

Greta was sleeping in a recliner the next morning when the sunlight came through the window and hit her in the face. She had come out of the bedroom to nurse Elise after her bath and Asim had used the extra milk from the office at two so Elise hadn't been hungry again until almost five. When she started whimpering, Greta had picked her up and gone out to the sitting room in the suite and fed her again and then just pulled a throw over them and gone to sleep cuddling Elise on her stomach. The sunlight on her face was warm and pleasant and Greta shifted a bit then opened one eye to check Elise. The baby was lying on Greta's stomach wrapped in her blanket and sleeping. She was making little whispery sounds with each breath and Greta smiled and pulled the throw over them again and turned away from the light.

She heard a noise of someone fiddling with the door and quickly stood up. She took two steps to the bedroom door and was passed by Dove who came out holding her Glock in both hands and centered on the door to the room. Asim came out of her room in a hastily tied bathrobe and holding an Uzi Pro with a thirty-round clip. The door opened, and Maurice backed into the room pulling a cart with several covered dishes on it.

"Ah ladies," said Maurice. "If you would care to put down the various things you have pointed at me, we have some breakfast and then I have some information to share."

Maurice parked the cart and walked back and closed the door.

"Is everyone decent?" asked Maurice. "Can I turn around without offending any sensibilities?"

"Maurice, you almost got shot several hundred times," said Asim. "Well, at least forty times. What in the hell are you doing sneaking in here. You should have phoned ahead."

"Oh, I doubt that," said Maurice. "There are still a few things you really don't want to discuss over wires or the air either, as far as that goes. We have an identity on the shooter at the conference. It is Hamid Masoud, he is a freelance operative that is loosely allied with Al-Qaida in the Arabian Peninsula, but he has been doing some work for other people lately. At least that is what the smart money is betting. Apparently, he is the one that blew up the Iranian nuclear scientist last year, but we don't know who signed the check."

"So, who was at the conference that he would be after?" asked Greta. "I need to change Elise and feed her and then me. Why was this so important that you needed to come by at whatever ungodly hour it is?"

"Merry is coming today and will be at the office in a couple of hours, so you won't have to go to him and can keep getting the office in shape," said Maurice. "He is bringing the pictures from the Whirligig and a list of who is at the conference. We can't tell them we saw a shooter, of course, but he can tip them off that we have reason to believe that someone or several people are in danger and to stay away from windows. I think that it would be a good thing for Asim to take Elise and come to the house with me and just lay low while you all talk and then hopefully you can come out to the house tonight. Sara looked around the house and decided that except for the kitchen and bathrooms, it was mostly furniture, painting, rugs and decorating upstairs and down. She has crews doing the painting and demolition now and is going to check a couple of companies that do staging and that also sell stuff and having a couple of trucks of furniture and knick-knacks sent over about noon. She has torn the kitchens and bathrooms out of both upstairs and downstairs but says that they will be functional later this week and has put some porta johns out back. Oh, she also said to bring your checkbook. Well no, actually a lot of cash."

"Why shouldn't I take Elise to the office?" said Greta. "That way it would be easier to feed her."

"Yeah, but we still don't have any place for a baby there and two bits says Mark will be there. It might be better if today was all business," said Asim, "besides, if we go to the house we can find a quiet corner and just relax behind the big thick fence and Elise can have a quiet day."

"Maurice," said Greta. "I want you to get the office up and running and take care of the living arrangements and get some cars and trucks and coordinate the security and surveillance systems with Sara. I assume she passed Merry?"

"Actually, I haven't called him yet," said Maurice. "I thought that you might want to ask Merry today since you are in charge."

"Um, plumping out my position, eh?" said Greta. "Okay-food, showers, Asim is on child custody duty and guard duty today and we will go and meet Merry and find out what he thinks."

"What do you think, boss?" asked Maurice. "Just curious."

"I want to see how many nuclear scientists and key men in their nuclear program the Iranians brought to the meeting," answered Greta. "If our boy did one, he might just be setting up to do two. Although, I don't know why for sure, I have ideas. One of them could be bent and playing for the opposition."

"Any word on my car and who tried to grab it and the driver?" asked Dove. "It is registered in Wales to a fictitious person. It was bought for cash in Italy and never registered there. I suppose someone could remember us, but we didn't give names."

"It hasn't turned up yet," said Maurice. "I reported it stolen and left a name and the number of one of the card phones. The police gave me a number for a case and urged me to call it in to my insurance. I doubt if it turns up. I have the phone I used in my pocket with a piece of tape with the name of the person reporting the car missing written on it. The truck that the kidnappers were driving was registered to the Department of Antiquities and apparently no one had missed it until we asked if it was theirs. I had one of the girls pretend to be a representative of the towing service that removed it and gave them the actual number of the service at the Department of Antiquities. I have a couple of people watching to see if anyone claims it."

"Who do you think it was?" asked Greta, "and who were they after?"

"I think it was the army, or one of the militias," said Maurice. "And why is still a work in progress. What do you want us to do about this, boss?"

"See if there is any surveillance camera video footage we can look at and see if there are any pictures of anyone we can identify," said Greta. "I doubt if there are and I really don't know what else to do but discretely ask some questions around on the street. We need to set up our own sources, Maurice. See who knows who and whom we can enlist."

"Greta, why don't we see if Lucien Francisci has a few people we can recruit or borrow or something?" asked Dove. "He said he would help. The other thing is, we need to take Elise to Corsica for a visit."

"You know, we should probably see if he knows anything about our would-be assassin, too," said Greta. "Maybe we should go this weekend. Ah, what day is it, Maurice?"

"Thursday," said Maurice, "It would probably be a good idea to get hold of him on both subjects. Now, we need to eat while there is still some heat in the food and then we need to get moving. Merry will be here in an hour or so."

Greta finished feeding Elise and handed her to Asim and said. "Go on with Maurice and take Elise to the house and see what we need for a nursery. Choose some space where she will be away from any gun battles and as safe as possible. Maurice, have Sara come to the office and figure out what she needs to harden the area of the building where the public isn't going to be, and see what she says about planning some security for the office when she gets done at the house. I will get her vetted today when I talk to Merry, and we had better leave now. What have you got laid on for transportation, Maurice?"

"I rented a microbus from one of the local guys I know," said Maurice. "He runs a private service between the hotels and the airport. He is parked up the street in an underground garage. When I give him a call he will come and pick us up down at the corner. The bus is full of our people and he will be stopping around the corner where there is no bus stop. Four of our men will get off and we will get on. The timing is a bit tricky and we will start him out when we get to the lobby. Have you paid?"

"Yes," said Asim. "I rented the room and paid cash out of the contingency fund, and I got a receipt, Maurice, so don't start sniping at me. I will need to check out. Why don't we take the baby and the suitcases and go down and you check out. If anyone asks, we had four people here last night, but your mother and cousin left early."

"All right, we will come down ten minutes after you leave," said Greta. "We will do full European tourist dress and just walk out and look around in the lobby a bit. We will follow you out and down the block."

Twenty minutes later they were all on the bus. Asim was sitting in the back of the bus next to Maurice holding Elise. Maurice had slung the suitcase and baby carrier up in the overhead rack and was sitting with one arm around Asim who was playing with Elise. They looked like a nice young married couple with their first baby. Every so often, Elise would chortle and wave her hands in the air and Asim would beam. Asim was wearing a plain brown western suit outfit and a niqab. The veil had never been totally displaced in Egypt and with the election of Mohammed Morsi, there had been more and more pressure from the Islamists for women to go veiled in public. Some young women and girls had been beaten and assaulted for dressing in western clothing and going without veils. There were also more and more burkas appearing in the street as women became fearful of reprisals.

The prevailing mood to wear a burka made things a lot easier for Greta and all her operatives to go anywhere undetected. As a matter of fact, she needed to get Maurice to lay in a supply of Muslim cover-ups for the various countries they operated in. Cultural traditions were not logical and if they persisted, you used them to your advantage. Somehow, people never thought that a small woman or a girl in a burka would be carrying an icepick and half a dozen concussion grenades under her blanket, which had made Dove so effective when she was a Mossad agent, or that when you couldn't see someone, it made determining the sex of the individual really hard. Greta smiled as she looked out the window. Well, there was one sure fire way to check someone's sex, but that was hardly an option in a public place and a lot more frowned on than looking at someone's face.

"What are you giggling about?" said Dove. "You are finally smiling, too."

"Oh, I was just thinking about verifying someone's sex in a burka," said Greta. "It could be interesting."

"Yeah, especially if they had to leave it on," said Dove. "Although a triple X large could be really interesting for a couple. Why were you thinking about that?"

"I was just thinking that we need to lay in a supply of them and some other stuff, too," said Greta. "Why did you have the make-up things this morning?"

"I grabbed a do-over bag when you were packing sleepers and burp cloths," said Dove. "Seems like it was a good idea."

Greta was wearing a frosted blond wig and a white linen dress with tennis shoes and large amber sunglasses. She had on a white visor that said EGYPT and carried a canvas handbag with pyramids on it and with a copy of a guidebook sticking out of the top. Dove had on white slacks, a white short-sleeve top and a brown wig. She had on running shoes, a panama hat, large silvered aviator sunglasses, and carried a small backpack and a folding hiking stick. Dove had gone down and purchased most of the clothing and tourist items at the hotel gift shop that morning for cash. They looked like two American schoolteachers on a summer holiday and not like Greta and Dove, which was the idea.

"We need more of these make-up kits for the office and I need to learn how to use them," said Greta. "Also, we need to get everyone to learn how to alter their appearance. Some specialized things things like the old lady Russian fat suit disguise were put together by the dirty tricks section. But we should get hold of them and have a talk about some simpler disguise kits. Okay, we are here, let's go in and ask about air tours and stand around and see if there is anyone we recognize."

Greta got out of the bus and walked into the flight service office and up to the desk. Dove looked around at the people in the waiting room. No one looked familiar. Dove pulled a point and shoot camera out of her backpack and took a few pictures, making sure that she included everyone in the lounge. Then she picked up a brochure advertising the flights to Aswan and Siwa.

The decision to fly regular flights to some fixed destinations had been discussed and the problems of actually hauling people around had finally come in second to having a reason to fly places on a schedule. This would allow people in the field to have a regular dependable way out that they could run for if a problem developed with any of their activities. Dove looked up when Greta called her and waved.

She walked over, and Greta said, "Okay, for two hundred bucks each, they will take us out and fly around the pyramids and the city, so we can take pictures. They guarantee a one-hour flight."

"Okay, why not?" said Dove, "We spend that much for a hotel and food every day and who knows if we'll ever get back. Where do we go?"

"Give them a credit card and they will take us out to the hanger," said Greta. "I'm going to the restroom now first."

"So am I," said Dove and handed the counter clerk a credit card.

They went down the hall and into the women's restroom. Asim was standing at the changing table finishing up with Elise.

"Okay, we will be meeting with Merry and Mark and Ben in the conference room behind my office," said Greta. "We'll cut through the hanger. Where is Maurice?"

46

"He should be in the conference room already," answered Asim, "He went to his office to take a call and I had to tend Elise."

"You two go on out and I will cover," said Dove. "I've got my Uzi in my backpack."

Greta nodded and held the door open. She glanced out and Asim and Elise went down the hall to the offices. Asim walked up to the door and it buzzed and clicked open. When she walked through, Dove and Greta turned and walked out to the passenger terminal and a young man in a light blue pilot's uniform escorted them down a hall and out through a door. While the passengers for the Aswan flight filed out to the sky-blue Shorts 300 and got on board Greta and Dove walked across the hanger and into the office area and then down the hall and into the conference room next to Greta's office.

When they entered, the four men in the room stopped talking and looked slightly confused, then stood up. Merry, General Sir Horace Meriwether Babington-Smyth, VC, OBE, MI5 and MI6, was in full tropical uniform and looking very well pressed and at ease, Mark Saint Martin, EUOPS Director of Southern Operations, newly minted Vice President for Mediterranean Operations for Southerland Oil and father of Elise Steiner, was looking very nervous, Colonel Ben Mac Glencoe, retired, now MI6, and ex-head of the SAS Counter Revolutionary Warfare Wing looked wary, and Maurice looked smug.

"Um Greta?" said Mark. "You are looking very well, actually quite different though."

"Just for this morning, Mark. We needed to get out of somewhere without being recognized. Now gentlemen," said Greta, "Why are we all here? Did someone come up with something?"

"Hello Greta," said Merry. "I'm not sure. As you know, we looked at the tapes from the Whirligig and did an enhancement and identified the shooter as Hamid Masoud, a freelance gun loosely attached to Al-Qaida. We started asking around and he has been identified as the one who blew up the Iranian nuclear scientist last year and a possible in the shooting of the Pakistani nuclear physicist that was the head of their gas centrifuge program. Apparently, he has been doing some work of thinning the ranks of nuclear scientists in various countries that are engaged in the development of nuclear weapons, especially those that have technology or pieces of technology for sale. This did give us pause, since as you know, everyone does not notify everyone else what they are doing, even if we have agreed to do so."

"What are you beating around the bush about, Merry," said Greta. "I assume you know something?"

"Well, mostly just speculation," said Merry. "As you are aware, EUOPS is a cooperative group that does things agreed to by a committee. Everything is normally chewed to such small shreds that there is very little substance. With nation states, such as I am employed by, there is somewhat more decisiveness and a government leader can make decisions and implement them. They normally do not advertise what they are going to have done since they can claim they didn't know what was going on if it goes in the toilet and people find out or claim full credit in their books later if it works out."

"What Merry is trying to not say is that we could have a situation here like the Syrian gold problem where one of the nations on our side, or kind of on our side, or around our side, has hired a freelance hit man to keep a lid on various nuclear weapon development programs, but forgot to mention it to everyone else," said Mark. "Israel bombed the Iranian reactor in 1981 and the United States and Israel and maybe a few others screwed up the Iranian centrifuge software and one of the chief Pakistani physicists disappeared without a trace, but ended up in the UK a few years later. No one cleared these various activities with their friends and neighbors and we could have something similar, if a bit more direct, going on now."

"True," said Greta. "Why are you grinning like a Cheshire Cat, Maurice?"

"Well, you asked me to see if we could borrow some people from Lucien Francisci to listen around locally until we get a network in place," said Maurice. "I, of course, didn't talk to Mr. Francisci directly, but got hold of Armand Gerard, the arms dealer for the family, and he said he would send me a few names of people we could use, but he also casually mentioned that he has been getting what appeared to be a few serious inquiries about whether he could supply some atomic weapons to a couple groups here in Egypt and did we know anything. I said we would look into it, but we were still getting the rugs laid and the paint dry. I asked him what he was going to do, and he said he was stalling. He also said that he thought Mr. Francisci would very much like you and Dove to visit him, so you could talk, and he said to bring Elise. He said it was important."

"Oh me oh my," said Dove. "Someone in Egypt is bomb shopping? I guess their army didn't explain some of the ground rules on atomic weapons to the new president."

"What are the ground rules?" said Maurice. "Whose ground rules?"

"You know I used to carry a gun for the Mossad, Maurice? Well the Middle East rules on nuclear bombs say if you get one, you get the other," said Dove.

"What do you mean?" asked Ben, "If you get one what other one do you get? I don't understand."

"If you get a bomb," replied Dove, "you get the Mossad. Like it has already been pointed out, Israel bombed the Iranian reactor and screwed up the Iranian centrifuges. I also heard, but can't swear, that a nonexistent reactor project in a country, that will not be named, ended up under a pile of rocks and a couple of missiles that some people bought blew instead of flew when they pushed the button. When you have an atomic bomb on a missile in an underground base, you do not want them to blow up even when the bombs are not armed since they are still full of really nasty stuff and explosions scatter it all over. This is not a good thing to happen in your secret underground base. The bottom line is that Israel will not tolerate a nuclear armed Arab nation and they already have the really big stick to enforce it if they have to."

"What about the major nations?" said Maurice. "Do you think that they would allow Israel to use the nuclear option?"

"I really don't think that Israel would ask around if they decided to go with the big one," said Merry, "and it is always better to beg for forgiveness than to ask permission. Well, this does cast a different light on it. It appears that someone is trying to upset the apple cart on the balance of power. I don't know if the Egyptian military is in on the secret and I really need to have a bit more information before I have a drink at the Officers' Club at the Military Academy. I think you need to nose around a bit, Greta."

"I would like you to do something, Merry," asked Greta. "I heard that you have a computer analysis program that does an evaluation of who benefits how much for various things. I would like to run an analysis of who would benefit if someone shot each of the participants at the meeting. Well, one at a time or all at once and, oh, you know what I mean."

"There are some of your people in the dirty tricks section that are working on something like that," said Merry. "I will ask if they can take a shot at it. It might tell us something, but I still think that you should ask around. Are you going to Corsica to see Lucien Francisci?"

"I hadn't planned on it right now, but maybe I should," answered Greta. "You said you talked to Armand but not Lucien?"

"Yes," said Maurice, "when do you think that you will go?"

"Actually, I thought I would call Lucien up and then fly up today," said Greta. "I don't have a place to sleep tonight and… Oh, Merry, Sara Kransky the decorator. I need to know if she is all right to do security and surveillance systems. She said she knows you."

"Well, it depends on how much money you want to spend," said Merry. "She is top drawer. Normally she works out of Paris, London and New York as a decorator, but she also has a Russian degree in electrical engineering and does freelance work in security. She's been involved in a few shady deals and does work for people that are less than sterling but she doesn't sell out clients. Why?"

"Oh, long story, but she is related to Maurice somehow and is doing some work locally," said Greta, "She wants to buy the Garden City flat, well, take an option on it since she knows about the legal situation and I was thinking about getting her to do up living quarters and security at the office and my new place. Can I trust her?"

"Rule one, Greta," said Merry, "but she knows better than to sell out a client. How is she related to you, Maurice?"

"I don't know for sure," said Maurice. "I think that she is the daughter of a second cousin by marriage of my Aunt Hermione. Not really a blood relation, of course, but still connected to the family. The old women know everyone's pedigree. I can ask my mother if it is important. Sara was around in

50

the winter at my Aunt's place when we were both kids. I think her family was in the Ukraine, but she came for the sun since she was delicate and went to school in Oran. Anyway, we consider that we are cousins."

"You got any objections, Mark?" said Greta. "I need someplace safe and quiet."

"Merry?" said Mark. "Any objections?"

"No," said Merry, "I think that she is suitable. If we have a problem we know where she is, and she knows that, too."

"Can we offer you a lift to see Lucien?" asked Mark. "We have a little jet here and there is plenty of room."

"No thanks, Mark," said Greta, "if I left now, I would need to swim back and live in one set of underwear while I was there. I'll meet with Sara, pack a few things and fly up myself this afternoon. I have a whole bunch of little jets here that I can use. Ben, you have been very quiet, what's up or did you just think that you would rather go to a meeting than work?"

"I thought that meetings counted as work,'" said Ben, "No, I am going to send Sergeant Major Charles Russell Whittingham and Sergeant Major Joseph Omar Young, both retired, over to you to act as your drivers and bodyguards."

"Omar?" said Dove, "Joey's middle name is Omar?"

"Ummm yes, his mother was a Classics major," said Ben. "Apparently his first name is traditional family, but his mother chose Omar after a walking tour with his father when they were students just before the wedding."

"That is rather curious," said Merry. "I wonder what that has to do with an Arab middle name?"

"Merry," said Dove, "Did you ever hear about this guy that wrote a lot about wine and paradise and various jugs?"

"Oh yes, him," replied Merry, "A country walking tour as students before the wedding and as perfect as a Hori and a jug of wine and so on. Yes, I see now."

"Well it will be nice to have them around, Ben," said Greta. "Any particular reason for this?"

"Yeah," said Ben. "I hear you need a new car and I really think you need a driver for it."

CHAPTER 3: MY LITTLE GIRL

"All right now, reduce power and set up a descent of six hundred feet per minute," said Greta. "You need to call the field now and check in and request landing instructions."

"Lord, how do you keep track of everything, Greta?" said Dove. "All right I know, the same way you get to Crown Hall in Jerusalem-practice, practice, practice."

Dove keyed the microphone and called the airfield at Calvi on the north coast of Corsica. During the time they had spent in Wales while waiting for Elise to arrive, Greta had been teaching Dove to fly and Dove had been teaching Greta how to use make-up and disguises. Now Dove was getting ready to solo and needed to make some long flights to build her confidence. Greta had handed the controls of her Turbo Commander to Dove about an hour after take-off from Egypt and told her to fly while she nursed Elise. Now, she was letting Dove set up for landing and Greta would follow through while Dove landed.

Elise had been asleep for the last half an hour and now she stirred as the plane descended and pressure in her ears equalized. She whimpered and shook her head and Greta picked her up and held her. Elise came awake and looked out the front of the cockpit at the array of flashing and blinking and rotating lights and howled. Greta passed the baby to Dove and took the controls. Dove dug around in the baby bag and got out a pacifier and stuck it in Elise's mouth. Elise started sucking and then spit it out, so Dove got out a bottle and shoved it in Elise's mouth. Elise sucked a few times and looked surprised and then started nursing in earnest.

"What's that?" said Greta.

"Water with pomegranate juice and a bit of Chambord," said Dove, "A stewardess friend of mine gave me the recipe. It keeps their ears from stopping up when they suck. They like the juice and a bit of a hit from the Chambord keeps them calm."

"You are feeding our baby booze?" said Greta. "Is that a good thing to do to a four-month-old?"

"She isn't fussing is she," said Dove, "and I think she is going back to sleep. Why don't you land the plane now since I can see the runway and the autopilot is good but not that good. Who is picking us up?"

"I don't know," said Greta. "I didn't get through to Lucien. Armand said he was a bit under the weather. Armand said it would be someone we know."

Armand watched as the Turbo Commander in the colors of Mediterranean Air Service dropped gently to the runway and slowed. The plane turned and taxied back to the Mediterranean Air Service hanger in the charter area and stopped. The ground crew set the chocks and started servicing the plane as the cabin door swung open. Armand watched as two women, no girls, in white outfits with loose hair and sunglasses climbed down the stairs and stood in the late afternoon sun. One of them held a baby wrapped in a pink blanket and the other carried a suitcase and had a baby bag over her shoulder. They waved, and he walked toward them. Lucien hadn't wanted him to call them. He said that they would know and come if they wanted to. Lucien's several nieces and nephews had arrived and so had two of his natural children. His legitimate grandson was here and so were three of his ex-wives and two of his mistresses, now these girls had come. The others were looking for what they could get but these two were different, at least he hoped so.

Armand knew Lucien had a deep respect for Greta and Dove on a professional level. They both knew who they were and, more importantly, what they were. He had known Dove ever since she was eighteen and a beautiful killer. He had met Greta when she had made the crossing from soldier to captain and then to Capo. Now, she oversaw a whole sector of EUOPS operations, and was a mother. More importantly, when Elise was born, Lucien had sent her a gift of flowers and jewelry. Lucien had received a picture of Elise, Greta, and Dove in return. Greta had been prominently wearing the necklace on a black sweater and holding Elise in her arms and there was a vase with the flowers in the background. Lucien had laughed and had framed the picture and had it on his desk. Armand wondered if Greta knew exactly what the exchange had meant. Well, now hopefully she and Dove would be in time to find out.

"Armand," said Greta. "I didn't expect to see you here, but I am very glad you are. I really need to speak to you, privately or with Lucien, and I must talk with Lucien, too. You said that Lucien was under the weather. What is it, a cold or something? I hope he didn't fall. Even with a strong spirit, falling and being confined to bed at his age is very bad."

"He had a stroke, Greta," said Armand, "He wouldn't let me call you or Dove but he has been expecting you. His family has gathered to see him off as fast as possible and divide the spoils. They aren't going to like you being here. Especially with the baby."

"How bad is he?" said Dove. "I really want to see him. I really do like him, very much actually now that I think about it, and he has always had a soft spot for me. Is he going to die?"

"We all die, Dove," said Armand. "But I think that he has a bit more left if the wolves don't take him down."

"What do you mean, Armand," said Greta. "What wolves?"

"Lucien has been the head of the family since the great war," said Armand. "When the Germans took over in France they hunted down our people and shot them in the street or tied their hands with wire and threw them off buildings or hung them over balconies by their arms to die and dangle and rot. We are criminals, but not barbarians and the Germans were barbarians. They killed and tortured and got names from people and then killed and tortured and got more names. They burned whole sections of towns to destroy our factories without bothering to locate them. Finally, they just killed people for standing around. If you were caught with drugs, they made you eat them and then tied you up to frames outside the Gestapo headquarters where people could see you die. If anyone tried to help, they shot them and let them lay in the street, including women, children and mothers."

"That is horrible," said Dove. "I mean it is even bad compared to what I do, well did. How did Lucien get to be the head of the family?"

"Lucien took over when the Germans killed our leader who was in France," said Armand. "Lucien was only sixteen, but he was brilliant, and no one would challenge him. All the young men, boys actually, including my father, were with him and the old men were either afraid or bewildered or dead. He decided that the Germans would kill anyone that stood against them, but on the other hand, they were killing anyone that made any waves.

Mussolini sent his Black Shirts to occupy the island and Lucien contacted the free French and they sent people and supplies from Algeria and we took over the countryside. It was death for any German or Italian to walk at night or go out to the country. When France was liberated, we had lists and went around collecting people. The French government didn't interfere, and we followed the war back to Germany and cut throats for years and gutted people in the street until Lucien said the score was even. During that time he reorganized things and assigned new responsibilities, set up the working groups and we prospered. He saved us and now he is old, but still we honor him. On the other hand, there must be a new leader and many people contend for the job."

"The contenders are who you are calling the wolves?" said Greta. "How about if he just retires or something."

"I doubt if anyone could convince him of that," said Armand, "and anyway you do not retire from his job."

"Where do you stand in the competition?" said Greta. "We need to maintain friendly relations with you and the rest of the family, as do the French."

"I have a large following and if I can sort things out with some other people, whom you have met, I could probably take on Lucien's duties," said Armand. "But, I will not take the job from him while he lives and there is the problem, so things are stalemated."

"Well, we need to get to the estate or wherever we are going," said Greta. "I have a little girl here that needs a bath and a bed, and I want to see Lucien."

"And she needs a guard or two," said Armand, "but I will explain everything later. I have Lucien's car here and the gentleman who you were with last time. He and his wife will be assisting you while you are here. Are you armed?"

"Yes, I have a micro Uzi machine pistol and a Glock and a lipstick single shot," said Dove. "Do you want them?"

"What about you, Greta?" said Armand. "Anything?"

"Well, there is an Uzi submachine gun in the diaper bag and I have a PPK automatic in a thigh holster," said Greta. "Other than that, no firearms or explosives."

"But you may have a knife or two? Well, I suggest you keep them all this time," said Armand. "You will not be searched, and I will go with you to your rooms. You will be on the third floor overlooking the garden and there is a knotted rope attached to the balcony and curled up on the floor and a door into the adjacent room that locks from your side."

"Umm, Armand," said Dove. "Is this a bad time for a visit?"

"Oh, get in the car, Dove," said Armand. "You are irrepressible, and we need to be careful. Especially with Elise here."

"You keep mentioning Elise," said Greta. "Why?"

"Lucien sent you a gift of flowers and jewelry," said Armand, "didn't he?"

"Yes, and that was very sweet," said Greta. "We sent him back a picture of Elise and Dove and me."

"Yes, and you were wearing the necklace he sent you in the picture," said Armand. "Why did you include it?"

"Because it is pretty, and he was thoughtful, and I wanted him to see I valued it," said Greta. "It is just polite when someone sends you a gift."

"I thought that was it, but here it means something else," said Armand. "When a man sends an unmarried woman who has had a baby flowers and jewelry and she takes them, he is acknowledging the baby is his and so is she. The picture is proof that Elise is Lucien's daughter."

"But she isn't," said Greta. "Lucien and I never…Well, you know."

"Greta," said Armand. "You can always tell who someone's mother is, but fatherhood is more an act of faith and as far as everyone here that counts is concerned, Elise is Lucien's daughter because he said so."

"Oh Lord," said Greta. "I need to feed Elise and I need a drink too, maybe a couple of them. Where is the car?"

Armand picked up the suitcase and walked toward a group of men with guns standing in front of a hanger. The doors of the hanger opened and a 1983 Cadillac Fleetwood armored limousine that had once been used by President Reagan rolled toward them. It stopped, and Armand walked to the rear and opened the door. Greta and Elise and Dove got in. Armand shut the door and signaled. Four black SUV's pulled into position in front and behind the Cadillac and the procession moved out to the road.

"Well that is a real surprise," said Greta. "I wonder what Lucien had in mind with sending me the flowers and jewelry. We are really going to have to talk. I did not mention Mark on Elise's birth certificate, but I didn't know we were in search of a father. Lucien knows we never had sex."

"Speak for yourself, Greta," said Dove. "Well, I guess we never had sex either, if you go by the Clinton Doctrine. I doubt if Lucien is slipping even with a stroke and he was definitely with it when Elise was born. I wonder if we can get in to see him. It appears that the family has gathered and will probably try to keep us apart. However, we have business that needs to be done and I believe that the other old men will see it our way."

"You and Lucien?" said Greta. "What was that all about?"

"Oh, strictly business on my part," said Dove. "Well, not totally. I have screwed a lot of people and things for various organizations, but I really do like Lucien. He got the hots for me when I first signed on with Blossom and one thing led to another and it was decided that it would be a good move on our part for me to get really friendly if you know what I mean. Anyway, he was grateful in more ways than one and I felt sorry for him when I got to know him, and we became, well, very good friends for a while."

"What do you mean in more ways than one?" said Greta. "I thought you were with Blossom in more ways than one."

"Well true, but we got a lot of information on people working for Russia from Lucien while we were involved, which is what Blossom wanted, and I got some really nice jewelry," said Dove. "I know from experience that the new wonder drugs don't help Lucien, so I doubt if anyone really thinks that he is Elise's actual father but being the recognized daughter of the head of the Francisci Family has a whole bunch of things going for it. I just wonder why he set it up?"

Greta handed Elise to Dove and tapped on the dividing window between the chauffer and the passenger compartment. The window rolled down and Greta saw the man who had served as their bodyguard the last time they had visited Lucien.

"Good to see you," said Greta. "Did you get over your disappointment for not preventing the little problems from the last visit? I told Lucien you had done an exemplary job and deserved a commendation or something."

"Yes, thank you miss," said the man. "I am most appreciative of your recommendation. First, I wasn't a suspect in the discussions of how the assassins knew where you were, which was a real relief, and I also received a very nice cash bonus after things were sorted. Did you want something?"

"Yes, are we going to see Lucien this afternoon?" said Greta. "We have some rather urgent business to discuss."

"I don't know miss," said the man. "Mr. Gerard, Mr. Guérini, Mr. Conein, and Mr. Carbone, are all here and are making the decisions as a council. I know that they want to see you, the baby and Miss Dove when we get to the house. We will be driving to the rear wing where the business offices and Mr. Francisci's apartment are. My wife and I will be assisting you while you are here and you will be staying in Don Francisci's apartments."

"Thank you. You know I don't even know your name although we fought off a bunch of gunmen together," said Greta. "We have never been introduced."

"I am Alonzo Caparoni," said the man, "My wife is Clarissa. We will be providing additional security and any help we can while you are here."

"Thank you, Mr. Caparoni," said Greta, "We appreciate the help. What can you tell us about what is going on? Armand said the vultures were gathering? Who are they?"

"They are Mr. Francisci's nieces and nephews, two of his natural children, three of his ex-wives and two of his acknowledged mistresses," said Alonzo," There is also his grandson, who is a student, but he at least was sent for. His mother, Mr. Francisci's daughter, is dead, killed in an auto accident some ten years ago. His two nieces are the daughters of his sister who died, oh twenty years ago. They have an allowance from Mr. Francisci and are worried about it continuing. They are in their forties and have never done a thing except get married and divorced a couple times. His nephews are members of the family but have never really shown much drive or talent. There are three of them and two of them work in narcotics distribution and one is in unions. I doubt if they are expecting much but hope for some kind of bequest. Mostly they sit on the terrace and stay drunk. Mr.

Francisci's two natural children are both made men and work as mid-level muscle in drugs and prostitution. They are the sons of the two acknowledged mistresses that are here to push claims for something. The ex-wives know that there will be something for them and they are very willing to get it."

"What about the grandson?" asked Dove. "You said he is a student and his mother is dead?"

"Yes, she was killed in a motor accident with his father. Mikael was raised by his grandfather and Lucien truly loves him," said Alonzo. "He is a student of architecture at the Sorbonne in his third year and is not involved in the family. He is a nice young man and a good student and also very talented. He is not dealing with his grandfather's illness very well."

"And then there are us and Mikael's, what great aunts?" said Dove. "I don't think there is anything like a half aunt is there?"

"Not that I know of," said Greta, "well, we are here, so let's see if we can get in to see Lucien. It would probably be a good idea to talk to the committee that is in charge now. They need to know what is going on, too, if Lucien is in trouble."

The four escort vehicles pulled into a parking area that had been built to the left of the driveway and the men who had been riding in them got out. The limousine pulled up to the newly reinforced gate of the estate. A guard came out of a new outside gatehouse that had been added next to the first gate since Dove and Greta had been there and walked to the car. He looked in the window at the driver and Alonzo and then walked to the back window and bent down and put his hand over his eyes as he gazed through the six-inch armor glass. He motioned up with his palm. Greta looked puzzled and the guard repeated the motion.
"He wants you to hold up the baby," said Alonzo through the car's interior communication system.

Greta smiled and held up Elise who looked out the window and obligingly smiled and waved her hands. The guard smiled and stepped back and saluted and then waved them through. The exterior gate opened, and they drove into the courtyard and the gate closed. Armand walked through the small main gate from the parking lot and came over to the car and rapped on the back window. Dove released the door and slid over.

"That was very nice of you, Greta," said Armand. "A lot of the people are glad that there is another child of Lucien. He is well respected, and his family is an old one. Well, if Mikael marries and has lots of children, it will be better. If not, there is Elise to carry on the family name."

"But she isn't his child, Armand," said Greta. "Mark is her father."

"Totally immaterial, as far as the family is concerned," said Armand. "Do you think an adoption makes a child any less to a family? No, you love them too."

"I don't think that you have a good argument for that one, Greta," said Dove. "Just go with it for the time being. Armand, we do need to talk to Lucien real soon to find out what he was trying to accomplish with this."

"I know," said Armand. "Everyone is here waiting. Take a few minutes and freshen up and then we can all meet and maybe you can see Lucien then. Why did you come?"

"That is a good question," said Greta, "but I think that together we may find an elephant. But we need to talk to Lucien."

"We have a tree and you have a snake?" asked Armand. "Yes, that has happened before, and you are one of the few people that can fill in the blanks this soon and see what may connect them. Come, let's go to your suite. Alonzo will get the suitcase but bring the bag with the Uzi. I don't think we'll need it, but we may."

Greta fed Elise while Dove showered and then Greta showered and changed. They both were wearing black dresses and low heels and Dove had redone their hair and make-up. Greta was putting on lipstick when there was a tap on the door and Armand announced himself. Greta took Elise and the Uzi into the next room and looked through the crack behind the door while Dove opened the door. Armand looked around and then motioned and a dark haired pretty woman walked in and smiled.

"This is Alonzo's wife Clarissa," said Armand, "she will be staying with Elise while we go to the meeting. Two of my other young men will be in here and one will be on the balcony. We will be moving Elise and Clarissa next door to a small interior room with reinforcements and an elevator and stairway to the basement. Alonzo will be outside that room's door. The room was built during the last war and used as a command post for our activities then. Lucien had it redone to provide a high measure of security and privacy for various special visitors."

"Oh, so now we're special?" said Dove. "I think that's nice."

"Actually, Elise is special," said Armand. "That is why we are putting her in the high security room and not you. Shall we go?"

Armand escorted them to an elevator and it went down until it was well under ground in the granite bedrock. The elevator opened into a small room with a blast door in one side. The blast door opened into a hall. The hall led to a hallway. Armand led them to another door that opened into to a small conference room in the basement bunker. Greta and Dove went in and the four men sitting at the table stood up, three of them bowed and one of them, the Englishman, nodded. They were the senior members of Lucien's management group for family activities.

Mr. Armand Gerard was the senior member and specialized in selling dubious to illegal weapons and military supplies to anyone with the required money, Mr. Valentino Guérini was in charge of the casinos and loans. Mr. Carlo Conein, supervised extortion, collections and murder operations. Mr. John Carbone, the only English member of the team, was in charge of drugs, sex, human trafficking and slavery. The fact that the organization was so quietly successful was because it was tightly knit, based on family relationships and well and quietly run by these men.

The organization had forged ties with the French government during the Second World War and the immediate aftermath and was still useful to various organizations like EUOPS, MI6 and the CIA. This was not a coincidence but a carefully thought out policy of all the organizations involved. The working arrangement provided for a degree of immunity for the Unione and a method of information collection and fielding deniable operations on the part of the cooperating agencies and governments. The gentlemen's agreement for countries not to assassinate heads of state did not stretch to cover using hired assassins, for example. Greta wondered if it might also stretch to hiring assassins to shoot another nation's nuclear scientists.

"Gentlemen," said Greta. "I am sorry about Lucien and the difficult position it appears you are in, but I need to talk to you regarding information that I believe is important. The last time that we were all together Lucien said that I represented the greatest evil imaginable. He told me that I represent governments, and said governments were a necessary evil, but one he didn't know if they were more necessary or more evil."

"What do you think he meant?" said one of the men. "More necessary or more evil?"

"He said that the Family could have me killed, or my family killed or burn my house and business but when it comes to destroying whole cities or countries and their populations he was powerless," said Greta. "He said that even a tiny country like North Korea could destroy a million people with their atom bombs. He also pointed out that they would then cease to exist forever in the time it takes to draw two breaths, but countries and governments are vicious mindless brutes and as he said are stupid and prideful and rampage through the world treading down the crops and killing the children with no regard as to what the outcome is."

"I have heard him say that and that we, on the other hand, are like fleas, we suck a bit of blood from everyone and get fat," said Valentino Guérini, "And he is right, but what is your point?"

"Armand?" said Dove. "Have you told them?"

"No," said Armand. "Gentlemen, I have been offered half a billion dollars for an atomic bomb by an unidentified group in Egypt."

"What?" said Valentino Guérini. "I trust you said we were fresh out. My God, if anyone suspected we would get involved in something like this we would end up like the Estonians. Did you call Miss Steiner about this?"

"Yes," said Armand. "She represents the European Union in the area and I, for one, did not want to end up like the Estonians. So I thought about it and decided to enlist her assistance. She and her compatriots have been involved in various things with us and if the people that want the bomb get one, I want everyone to know we did not participate in the sale or facilitate the transfer."

"Good thinking," said John Carbone. "I assume you have sent word up the chain to Merry, Miss Steiner?"

"Yes, I have, Mr. Carbone," said Greta, "and he has communicated laterally to certain trustworthy Europeans. I am here at his behest with his blessing and with additional information and questions."

"We were up at school together, you know," said John Carbone, "he was sixth form when I was third, so we knew of each other but were never close."

"My God, is there anyone that Merry wasn't in school with?" said Dove. "Well, I guess with the exception of women."

"Well, everyone really important," said John Carbone, "and his wife Pam was in school with them if they are women. She is related to the ladies she wasn't in school with if they are important. Anyway, it is a relief to know he is on board. He is, isn't he?"

"I'm not sure we have anything to get on board with yet," said Greta. "We had discovered an assassin targeting the meetings on limiting the Iranian atomic programs and that he has been going around thinning the international nuclear scientist crop for the last few years. Then Armand mentioned an Egyptian group that wants a nuclear weapon and I got this feeling that something is developing. It's like Dove said, if you get a bomb in the Middle East, you get the Mossad and if anyone actually uses a bomb on one of the developed countries, the response would be swift and overwhelming. Why would anyone in Egypt want a bomb? It would take two years for the Nile to fill the resulting crater where Egypt used to be if they got one and used it on anyone, including Israel."

"An interesting and probably reasonable scenario," said Armand, "but you are thinking of nation states. Groups like Al-Qaida are like the Loyal Order of the Kangaroo Rat or some other group that gets together and plays pool and drinks beer on Tuesday night. They are not a country and usually don't care about what happens in any particular country. They are more criminal than we are, actually both you and us. Neither of our organizations go around killing people at random or setting off truck bombs in markets. If any of the assorted radical groups got a bomb to blackmail people with it would be chaos and the scary thing is the people that are actually in charge of these groups are normally not part of the legitimate government, well not officially. So, if a group in Egypt were to make a lot of noise and set off a bomb in Tel Aviv, then Egypt would be flattened and two problems would be solved for them."

"What do you mean by that?" asked Dove. "What two problems?"

"Israel and the Egyptian Army," said Armand. "The hardliners that backed Morsi in the elections in Egypt are finding out that things are not all rosy among the Egyptian population and military. There is dissatisfaction with the new constitution and the move toward strict religious tendencies by the Morsi government is unpopular. Things have been shaky since Mubarak was ousted and Morsi's election and they are getting worse now. The military is not going to put up with any civilian government that doesn't play ball. There have been riots and there will be more from what we hear. This is not really what the international brothers want."

"So, you don't think that the Egyptian government is in on the bomb purchase?" said Greta. "Where do you think that the money is coming from? Half a billion is an awful lot for your average terrorist organization to come up with."

"Obviously a country," said Armand. "It's pretty obvious that some country is funding this and probably egging the group of malcontents that want to buy it on. That way they can avoid any repercussions against their country when and if it gets used. Actually, if you are a country, there is no really good reason to have a nuclear bomb unless you have dozens. One will just get you taken care of if you are an identifiable government."

"Well, since we have discussed all of the reasons that anyone in their right mind wouldn't want an atomic bomb, we are still faced with the problem of some group of nuts wanting one," said Dove, "and also we have the problem of Mr. Hamid Masoud. With your gentlemen's permission, I will dim the lights."

Dove stood up and walked to the light switch and turned off the lights. The soft glow of the baseboard safety lights didn't interfere with the picture quality when she turned her cell phone toward the wall and turned on the projector function. The enhanced digital picture showed the outside of a building in bright sunlight. The picture zoomed in on a window in deep shade and then stabilized and an enhanced picture of the room came up. It showed a young man sitting in a kitchen chair behind a kitchen table looking through a monocular spotting scope trained on the window. To his left was a long metal tube that on closer examination turned out to be a sightless stockless rifle mounted in a frame. A USB cable from a computer was plugged into the rear of the frame holding the rifle and the muzzle of the rifle appeared to move minutely and constantly.

The young man pulled his head back from the scope and stretched his shoulders and then felt his throat and looked down at the quarter inch round red spot on his chest. He dove to the floor and pulled a rope to close the blinds on the window. The picture switched to infrared. It was slightly blurry, but it showed the young man as he rolled over and stood up. When he stood up, a small digital timer started running in the lower left portion of the picture. The young man disassembled the rifle frame and stowed it in a toolbox along with the rifle and picked up a suit coat and put it on. As the timer reached forty-eight seconds, the young man had stepped into the hall and closed the door from the outside. There was a pause and then a still picture of the young man appeared and then slowly rotated to show him from all sides. This picture was replaced with a picture of the frame and rifle that again rotated to show the sides, top and bottom. Then the picture came back to the apartment and a circle formed around a small black object. It was a computer charger that had been left behind in the scramble to depart.

"We found the remains of the rifle, tracking device frame, and scope in the furnace in the basement," said Dove, "There was also some charred plastic and melted metal that had been the computer. The charger was for a model 5011, 504, or 5220 Ace Computer and also had three fingerprints on it. We did not have fingerprints for Hamid Masoud but now it appears we do. He was identified using facial recognition software and pictures supplemented by a visual identification by some of our associates and sources. We need to know if you were involved in providing his services or know who did and if you are aware who he was there to shoot."

"This would be handled by my associates and me," said Carlo Conein. "I will check and let you know. I am not personally familiar with the young man and I do not think we supplied him. Should we ask around, Armand?"

"Yes, yes, that would be good, Carlo," said Armand. "Greta, it is getting late and I gather you would like to take Elise and visit her father. Why don't you go and do that, and we will continue in the morning after Carlo has had time to ask around."

"Yes," said Greta, "I would really like to see Lucien. I have a number of questions to ask him."

CHAPTER 4: FAMILY TIES

Armand walked back to their suite with Dove and Greta and motioned to the young man standing at the door to open it. The young man was wearing body armor, a helmet, and a shoulder microphone. He was carrying a short-barreled pump action shotgun.

"Shotguns, Armand?" said Dove. "Not machine guns?"

"Dove, you do not shoot machine guns in your own house," said Armand. "For one thing the bullets will penetrate walls and kill people you do not want to kill, and for the second thing the damage a shotgun does is normally confined to just one wall and makes it easy to do repairs. These guns were manufactured in Holland for military and police use and have fourteen-inch barrels. We have them loaded with shells that contain thirty caliber lead balls and lead BB shot. With the short barrel the pattern is about six feet on a side at ten feet, you don't have to be very accurate with them to stop a man, even one in normal body armor since the pattern will overlap arms and legs and other places where the armor doesn't cover. You should really look into getting some for your security people."

"We may need to look at one tomorrow," said Dove. "I have so much to do now that I am really snowed, Armand. If Greta wasn't here I would go back to my old job of security for Blossom."

The young man looked at Armand and Armand nodded and the young man spoke into his microphone and opened the door. Greta and Dove followed Armand into the room and nodded to the two young men pointing shotguns at them. The young men relaxed when the outer door closed, and Greta, Dove and Armand walked to the interior room where Elise was staying. Alonzo was sitting on a chair in front of the door of the room with a sawed-off pistol grip Double Barreled shotgun on his lap.

"A Lupara, Alonzo?" said Armand. "Why that?"

"It was my father's," said Alonzo. "I am used to it and do not like the stocks on the new ones, sir. Besides, the ten gauge shells hold more shot and you can fire both barrels at once. Do you want in?"

"Yes please," said Greta. "I should probably top off Elise and then we need to change her and take her and go see Lucien. How is he, Armand, really?"

"You must judge for yourself," said Armand. "His mind is alert, but he can't talk clearly. His left side is useless, but he can still write, slowly. That is how we have been conducting business."

"When did the stroke happen?" said Greta, "You should have called."

"A couple days ago and he wouldn't have it," said Armand. "He said you would come in time and he was right, wasn't he?"

"Yes, I guess so," said Greta. "We need to go in, Alonzo. Do your secret knock or whatever and open the door."

Alonzo looked slightly taken aback and then stood and knocked three times on the door and then waited a few seconds and then knocked four times. The door opened a crack and Clarissa opened it. She was holding an automatic pistol with obvious confidence and dropped it in her apron pocket when she saw who was there. The door closed and there was a rattle as a heavy chain was disengaged and then Clarissa opened the door.

"If you are going to feed the baby, Greta, I should probably go," said Armand. "I need to see what else has transpired on the request for the atomic weapon. The group that is trying to buy one and I have been exchanging email on the subject and I hope to discover who they are. Have one of the young men escort you to Lucien's room when you are done but don't be too late, he is very tired and he isn't eating."

"Can I go up alone, Armand?" said Dove. "I would just like to talk to him about happier times a while."

"Yes," said Armand. "He would enjoy that."

Greta nodded and walked into the secure room while Dove and Armand walked away. She looked around the room. It was painted a pleasant but non-descript beige with a hardwood floor, bookcases and a desk, a settee with a coffee table and two wing chairs on an Oriental carpet, a television on one wall and a door leading into another room. She heard Elise giggling and walked toward the door with Clarissa following her.

The next room was a bedroom with a recliner, a double bed and a crib in it. There was also a changing table with an assortment of diapers and powder and lotions. A young girl of maybe fourteen or fifteen was sitting on the rug in the middle of the floor and holding Elise on her lap while she wiggled a sock puppet of some sort of creature at Elise and talked to her in various voices. Another girl a few years younger sat alongside the older girl. She had another sock puppet on her hand and was also wiggling her puppet and answering the other girl. Greta looked at the three children and smiled. The two girls were oblivious to her presence and so was Elise, who was enthralled.

"What is the story you are telling her?" asked Greta. "I don't speak French."

The girls looked up startled and Elise started screaming. The older girl picked up Elise and put her against her shoulder and rubbed her back and Elise quieted.

"We were speaking Corsican, Madam," said the older girl in English. "We learn English in school, and French, too and I have started Italian, but we speak our native language at home. We were telling her the story of the pigs and wolf. Nicole is doing all the pigs."

"You always make me be the pigs, Celeste," said Nicole. "I want to be the wolf sometime."

"You don't growl right," said Celeste. "I keep telling you that, but you have a very good squeal when the wolf eats you."

"Girls, this is Madame Steiner, she is Elise's mother," said Clarissa. "Say hello to her."

Nicole jumped up and Celeste looked around and finally gave Elise to Clarissa and then stood beside her sister. The two girls held out the sides of their skirts and curtsied.

"Enchanté, Madame Steiner," said the two girls.

"And who are you two young ladies?" said Greta.

"They are mine," said Clarissa. "The men keep forgetting that we have families that need food and help studying and someone to answer questions. Besides, they need to be around babies. How else will they learn how to take care of them? Celeste, please?"

"Hello Madame Steiner," said Celeste. "I am Celeste Caparoni, I am sixteen and I go to Saint Teresa's academy. This is my first year in Lycée. I am in the honors program as an advanced student. My interests are history and law and I have lived here on the estate since I was born. My parents are Monsieur and Madame Caparoni who are on the staff of the estate."

"Very good Celeste," said Clarissa.

Nicole stood up and licked her lips and then said, "I am Nicole Caparoni and I am nine. I go to Saint Teresa's academy. I am in Cours moyen premiére annèe and I like to play too much according to the nuns and you already know who my parents are and the other stuff. Elise is a very nice baby. Is she really Monsieur Francisci's little girl?"

"Lucien seems to have adopted her," said Greta. "I need to talk to him about that, but I need to feed and change her. Then we will need to go see Lucien."

Celeste looked at her mother and then took Elise and walked over to the changing table and expertly changed Elise's diaper. Nicole got out a new pink blanket and handed it to Celeste and Celeste put Elise on it and wrapped her up and walked over and curtsied to Greta and held out the baby.

"Thank you, Celeste," said Greta. "But you don't need to curtsy to me. You are very efficient and so are you, Nicole. I appreciate your help."

Greta walked to one of the wing back chairs and sat down then she tried to hold Elise with one hand while she reached behind her to unzip her dress. Celeste walked quickly over and took Elise while Greta finally found the zipper and undid her dress and pulled it down. Then she held out her hands and took Elise, slipped off one shoulder strap of her bra and started nursing Elise.

"There is one thing you girls should learn right now," said Greta, "don't get all dressed up in clothes that are hard to put on and take off while you are nursing."

"You should also change sides too," remarked Clarissa, "you are leaking, here."

Clarissa handed Greta a folded diaper and Greta smiled and stuffed it in the other cup of her bra to stop the leak while Elise continued nursing. Celeste stood to one side and Nicole sat down on the couch and watched.

"Mama says that you live in Egypt," said Nicole. "Where they have the pyramids and camels and the Sphinx and mummies. She said we may have to move there and take care of the baby."

"No, I don't think so," said Greta, "I already have a lady that helps me take care of Elise that lives there."

"Oh well, I guess I will get to see a camel someday," said Nicole. "Is the lady that takes care of Elise nice?"

"Yes, she is very nice, Nicole," said Greta, "but I think I had better get myself back together and go and see Lucien now. We will be back in a while Clarissa."

"I will take the girls down and they can get ready for bed," said Clarissa, "Will you be wanting me to come back?"

"No, not tonight," said Greta, "Will Alonzo be spending the night outside the outer door?"

"Yes, he will be staying out there," said Clarissa, "Would you want someone in the other room?"

"No, I think that Dove will be there and Elise and I will stay in here," said Greta. "Good night girls and thank you, Clarissa. Perhaps you can visit me in Egypt and see a camel, Nicole. We will see."

Greta finished getting her clothing adjusted and Celeste shyly offered to zip her up. Greta smiled and held up her hair and Celeste zipped her dress. Then Celeste picked up Elise and went to the changing table and got another blanket and another diaper and some tissues. Then they all went to the door of the room and Clarissa pulled the automatic out of her apron pocket and then fastened a long stout chain behind the door and over a stout hook. Clarissa knocked on the door and when it opened a crack she looked out and saw Alonzo he winked, and Clarissa nodded and pulled the chain off the hook. They all stepped to the side as the door swung open and Clarissa led the way into the rest of the suite. Three very serious young men with earphones and little microphones in front of their lips were walking around in the rooms.

"I need someone to take me to Lucien's room," said Greta, "Armand said someone would escort me."

One of the young men inclined his head and spoke into his microphone. There was a rap on the outer door and the young man motioned Greta back. He walked over and opened the door while the other two young men covered the door with their shotguns from adjacent doorways. When the door opened two young men with shotguns hung over their back and their hands in the air stood in the door.

"These young men will guide you, Madam," said the guard who was apparently in charge. "Mr. Francisci's room is just down the hall in this wing."

"Thank you," said Greta, "Coming Alonzo? You can stand outside the door of Mr. Francisci's room while I visit. The two guards can go first and then I will carry Elise and you can bring up the rear."

Alonzo nodded, and the guards put down their hands and turned around. Greta walked out followed by Alonzo and they all walked down the hall.

"Alonzo why all the guards?" said Greta. "I am starting to get nervous."

"Well, Elise is the heir of Signor Francisci. As his daughter, she is his nearest relative and will inherit everything if he dies," said Alonzo. "There are small bequests for others and his grandson gets a trust fund but Elise is his daughter and he is just a grandson. The rest have no claim beyond the will. Some of his other relatives or others might see things would be better for them if she were not here. Once she gets in to see her father and he acknowledges her, then it is a bit late for them since to kill her then would be punishable by death and the whole family would be sworn to uphold the vendetta against the killer and their whole family."

"Oh," said Greta. "How much farther is it?"

"We are there," said Alonzo. "Do you want me to come in with you?"

"Why don't you go in first," said Greta, "and I will just stay here. Just a second."

Greta put a hand up her skirt and pulled out her PPK automatic and clipped off the safety and then nodded to the guards and they knocked on the door. The door opened a crack and a young man looked out and then exchanged a few words with the guards. The door closed and then opened, and Alonzo walked in and looked around, then he nodded at Greta. Greta shoved Elise at one of the guards in the hall who took her and she then dove in and rolled on her shoulder with both hands holding her pistol. She stopped behind a sofa and looked around. Then she raised her hands and let the pistol drop on the floor and walked back and took Elise.

"Grazie", said Greta and walked back into the room and smiled at the two amazed guards.

Alonzo picked up her pistol and returned it to her and then one of the guards went and tapped on a door at the side of the room. Dove opened the door and looked out. She looked tired and a bit grim. She stepped out and closed the door behind her.

"Greta," said Dove. "He is paralyzed on his left side and has trouble breathing and is only sipping a bit of juice and water I got out of Elise's bag. I don't know when he ate last. He needs to go to see a doctor and get some better medical treatment or he isn't going to last long."

"Can he use his right hand?" said Greta. "Armand said they have been communicating by writing."

"I don't know," said Dove. "I have just been helping him drink and get a few sips of juice and talking to him. Sometimes he will try to say something, but it is hard for him to talk and mostly he just nods his head."

"Alonzo," said Greta, "Do your girls have a little portable computer or a pad of some kind that that they use for school and that you can type on by touching the screen?"

"Yes, they do, Madam Steiner," said Alonzo. "Celeste has a pad that the school uses for things. She gets assignments and turns in work that she does at home on it."

"Alonzo, go and get Celeste and her pad and bring them up here," said Greta. "She already knows how it works and I don't want to waste time. Now, Dove and I are going in and sit with Lucien and when you get back send in Celeste and her pad please."

Alonzo nodded and walked out and talked to the two guards that had escorted Greta to Lucien's room and they walked hurriedly down the hall. One of the interior guards closed the door and then barred it with a thick steel bar. Dove went to the door of Lucien's room and opened it and Greta walked in, holding Elise. Lucien was leaning back against a stack of pillows. He was breathing in short gasps and had a waxy look. He opened his eyes and saw Greta and motioned for her to come to the bed. He looked up and raised his right hand and put it on Elise's head and tried to say something. Greta gently took his hand and put it back down.

"Lucien, save your strength," said Greta. "It won't count until we have a witness like Armand. What are you trying to do, commit suicide? You need better care and you need to eat. Here Dove, hold Elise."

Greta took Lucien's left hand and said, "Now squeeze it. Fine, fine there is response. All you need to do is train your brain and get some strength back. I already know that your right side is better. What kind of horse doctors have you been seeing?'

"Nownn," said Lucien painfully.

"None?" said Greta. "You need medical attention right now. How long have you been like this?"
Lucien shrugged his right shoulder and then pursed his lips. Dove picked up a glass of pink juice with an ice cube in it and held the straw to Lucien's lips. Lucien drank greedily from the straw and then leaned back.

"What are you giving him?" said Greta.

"The last of the ear clearing drink I made for Elise," said Dove, "apparently he hasn't been eating or drinking for the last two days."

"Posn," said Lucien.

"Possible but I don't think so," said Greta. "Armand seems to be looking out for your welfare but still poison is a possibility. We need to get you the hell out of here and to somewhere you can be treated that we can keep you safe."

There was a tap on the door and Dove raised her Uzi machine pistol and pointed it at the door and Greta got out her PPK, picked up Elise from where she had been lying on Lucien's bed and moved to the corner of the room nearest the door.

"Who is it?" said Dove.
"It is me Celeste, madam," said Celeste. "My father told me to bring my pad and come up here."

"Open the door slowly and come in Celeste," said Dove. "Is Alonzo there?"

"Yes miss," said Alonzo. "I am here."

"Okay, you guard the door and just open it a crack for Celeste to come through," said Dove. "Now be careful. If the door comes open all the way you are going to get about a hundred rounds of soft lead nine-millimeter through the wall before I change clips. And I am behind something solid."

"Yes miss," said Alonzo. "Celeste is coming in now. All right?"

The door opened a little crack and an arm holding a pad was thrust slowly into the room. The rest of Celeste followed the arm. Celeste was wearing a white nightgown with a flannel robe over it and was bare footed. He hair was tied up in a ponytail and she looked slightly bewildered and excited. She looked at Lucien lying on the bed and curtsied and then looked at Dove who was still holding a sub machine gun pointed at the wall. She glanced at Greta and then came over and handed her the pad and picked up Elise and held her.

"Thank you, Celeste," said Greta. "If you would turn the pad on and hold Elise it would be very helpful. We need to communicate with Lucien and he has had a stroke and can't talk very well right now. Do you know what a stroke is?"

"Yes mam," said Celeste. "Here, it is on and I loaded the keypad and the note program. If you hold it, he can type on it."

Greta nodded and walked over and braced the pad against a pillow but where Lucien could type on it and held it with her hand. Lucien put out one finger and typed.

"Get me out of here!!" typed Lucien.

"Agreed," said Greta. "Do we have to smuggle you or what?"

"Get Armand in here," typed Lucien. "This thing print?"
"Does your pad print, Celeste?" said Greta, "Or do you have any way to send messages to a printer?"

"Yes, but I can only print at school," said Celeste, "I don't have a printer, but you can save things to a memory stick or chip."

"It'll do," typed Lucien, "Any more drnk?"
Dove went to the door and opened it a crack and spoke to Alonzo and Greta went to the diaper bag that Dove had been carrying around to disguise the Uzi and pulled out another small nursing bottle. It had breast milk in it.

"No, but we have a bit of milk," said Greta. "Which will probably be better for you than the whisky in the juice. Then we are down to water, but we have almost a liter of that."

Greta took the bottle of milk and poured it into the empty glass and then took another ice cube from the cold pack in the diaper bag and put it in the glass. She walked over to the bed and put the straw in Lucien's mouth and he drank. Then he put down the pad and patted her hand and drank the last of the milk. He leaned back on the pillow and then he pointed to Elise. Celeste brought the baby over and held her where Lucien could see her. Elise looked solemnly at him and then closed her eyes and burped. Lucien smiled a twisted smile and made a noise in his throat. Greta looked at him worriedly and then realized he was laughing. She patted his hand and he took her hand in his with a surprisingly strong grip and raised it to his mouth and pressed it to his lips then he released her and fumbled for the pad. Greta found it and put it back against the pillow. There was a rap at the door and Armand announced himself.

The door eased open a crack and Armand slid into the room. He saw the empty glass with the ice cube in it and smiled.

"Are you stopping being an ornery old goat, Lucien?" said Armand, "Or should I have brought some pretty nurses before. I would have called them if you would have let me."

Lucien typed with one finger, "And let everyone know they coming? Not to brite."

"Lucien," said Armand. "We are not trying to kill you, or them."

"Blsht," typed Lucien. "Someone will be."

"Too true," said Armand. "Now what should we do?"

"I am going with daughter and mother to somewhere. You in charge," typed Lucien, "Go get everyone and memory sticks. Greta type."

"Yes, that would probably be best," said Armand. "We can get back on the other issue in a few days. Can I ask where you will be taking Lucien?"

"Cyprus, the airbase hospital at Akrotiri," said Greta. "I want a medical helicopter from the airport and then I will take one of the little jets which I will choose at random. You square it with whomever, please. Now what should I type?"

"Here, let me," said Armand, "it will be quicker if you don't take dictation."

"Probably," said Greta, "Celeste, call your father and have him go with you and have your mother put some clothes and things in a bag for you and Nicole and your mother and father, a week worth. Stay there and have your father come back and wait outside the door. I want you all to come with me for a few days while we look after Lucien. We will square it with the school so don't worry. We will also arrange for Nicole to see a camel. Have your mother keep everything at your place and wait there until your father comes to get you all. Give Dove the baby now."

Celeste nodded and curtsied to Lucien and then handed Elise to Dove. She went to the door and opened it a crack. Armand passed the pad to Greta. He had typed a short statement that Lucien acknowledged Elise as his daughter and heir, that he was going with Elise and her mother Greta for a while to recuperate and that Armand was in charge in his absence. Greta read the statement to Lucien. He nodded and leaned back again. Greta saved the statement and then went and got water out of the diaper bag and filled the glass again and put in one of the last ice cubes and held the straw while Lucien drank. He patted her hand again and leaned back and closed his eyes.

His skin was decidedly less waxy, and he seemed stronger. His breathing was more regular, but he still rattled when he breathed. Greta put out a hand and smoothed his hair and felt his forehead. Yes, he had a fever. She went to the baby bag and got the bottle of liquid baby aspirin that Lady Julia Robertson, Duchess of Montgeave, Viscountess Rhayadr, retired MI6 assassin, one of Elise's godmothers and a nurse, told her to always carry to fight a sudden fever. She looked at the dosage and then poured half a bottle into the remaining water and held the straw out to Lucien.

"Here Lucien," said Greta. "Some aspirin. You have a fever and probably a headache too."

"Won't that make him bleed more?" said Dove. "I don't think aspirin is good for strokes."

"He had his long enough ago so that it is probably clotted up pretty good and he sounds like he is getting pneumonia," said Greta. "Anyway, he has a heck of a fever."

Lucien typed, "Mama nos bst. Giv me baby."

Then he held up the pad for Dove to see and pointed at Elise. Dove came over holding Elise who was sleeping and held her down for Lucien to see. He put up his hand and touched her cheek with one finger and Elise turned to the finger and took it in her mouth and started sucking. Lucien smiled his twisted smile and gently disengaged his finger. Then he patted the bed beside him.

Dove slid the baby down between Lucien's body and his arm and then stood beside the bed as Lucien leaned back against the pillows again. Greta walked over and stood looking down at Lucien and Elise.

"Why Lucien?" said Greta, "I know that you knew that I didn't know what the flowers and necklace meant and that I would accept them from a friend, but you are far too subtle to have sent them for no reason. Why did you need to stake a claim to Elise?"

Lucien opened his eyes and then slowly said, "Omm yuuuu."

"On me Lucien?" said Greta, "Why? You know I would always help you if you ask, well on most things, but you needed more than that?"

"Yess," said Lucien, "lis get all when die, save Mik."

"Your grandson?" said Greta, "You want us to protect your grandson?"

"Yes," said Lucien clearly, "Save Mik."

There was a tap on the door and Dove walked over and asked who it was and Armand responded and said he had brought the others. Dove crouched down in the corner that would be hidden by the door swing with the machine gun and nodded at Greta.

"I think we should save his grandfather first," said Greta, "I think they are here. Let me take Elise, Lucien."

Greta picked up the baby and walked to the far side of the bed with the Uzi 1 and crouched below mattress level at the end of the bed. The door opened a crack and a hand and arm in a blue school sweater came through the crack holding what looked like a silver pen in two fingers.

"Celeste?" said Greta. "Is that you?"

"Yes, Madam Steiner," said Celeste. "I brought the stylus so Don Francisci can sign the papers and some little memory chips to make copies."

"Well come in," said Dove. "Just you to start with, then the others in a minute."

The door slid open a crack and Celeste slid in. Greta motioned to her and Celeste came over to the bed. Greta handed her the baby and motioned her to get down. Celeste nodded and then reached in her sweater pocket and took out her mother's pistol. Greta saw the safety was on and nodded.

Then she stood up and said, "Come in, Armand."

The door opened and Armand stuck his head in. He saw Greta with the small Uzi and nodded. He opened the door slowly and John Carbone, and Valentino Guérini walked in with Armand.

"We have come to witness Lucien's statement," said Armand. "You are looking better already, Lucien. Well, we are ready."

"Where is Mr. Conein?" said Dove, "I thought you would all be here."

"He left to go back to France," said Armand. "Apparently there is some information about Hamid Masoud. He said he would phone back tomorrow if he had anything."

Lucien waved his hand in the air and made a growling sound, and then he coughed. Greta moved to the bed and wiped his mouth with a tissue. He nodded his thanks and made a drinking motion. Greta picked up the glass with the last of the aspirin and melted ice cube and put the straw in Lucien's mouth. He drank the last of the water and then cleared his throat. Then he pointed at Celeste and motioned to her to bring Elise. Celeste held out the baby to Greta and she took her, considered a moment and then laid Elise down next to Lucien.

"My girllll," said Lucien.

Then he held the pad out to Armand. Armand took it but looked puzzled and Celeste curtsied and then made a few finger swipes and curtsied and handed it back to Armand.

"Ah thank you, young lady. Here is his statement," said Armand, "You can all read Lucien's statement. He says the baby is his daughter and that he is going to go with her and her mother to rest and recover and that I am in charge while he is gone, subject to general agreement of you gentlemen, of course, and also to his veto."

"He said he would sign it if I brought the stylus," said Celeste, "and that you could all have a copy."

"We are going to go on by committee?" said John Carbone. "Like we are doing now?"

"No," said Lucien.

"I think that Lucien wants me to be in charge, but to listen to you gentlemen and discuss things," said Armand. "I will make a decision and convey my decision and any suggestions that you have to Lucien, if it is important."

"If it is God damn important," said Dove. "He needs time to heal. You all run your part of the organization now and you need to do that first. If you get bogged down going over everything you each do with each other, you will spend all of your time worrying about too many things that aren't your business and the whole operation goes to hell in a hand basket."

"Yes," said Lucien and motioned for the pad.

Greta took it and Celeste curtsied and gave him the stylus when Lucien put out his hand. Lucien scrawled a signature on the document and Celeste put a flash memory card in the pad and thumbed the surface. She curtsied and handed the chip to Armand who nodded and put it in his inside suit coat pocket. Celeste repeated the process three more times and Armand distributed the cards.

"John do you want to take Carlo's copy to him?" said Armand. "Assuming we don't meet tomorrow and you go home. I will stay here a while longer and clean things up with Lucien's family. I think I hear your helicopter, Greta. We should get Lucien on a stretcher. I will carry one end and John will carry the other. It will be landing on the heliport on the roof. Now, I am going to open the door for the guards to bring in a stretcher, please don't shoot anyone."

"Celeste, run get your family," said Greta. "No, is your father outside?"

"Yes madam," said Celeste. "Should I send him for mother?"

"Please," said Greta, "then change Elise, grab some diapers and put another blanket on her so she won't get cold outside and you can carry her. Stay behind me and to the left side. That way I will avoid you if I have to shoot anyone. If I yell drop, just do it and land on the bottom with Elise on top."

"Yes madam," said Celeste.

When everyone was finally assembled, the helicopter had been waiting on the roof for half an hour. Clarissa had found half a dozen juice boxes in Nicole and Celeste's room that would be safe for Lucien and packed more diapers and two loaves of bread and some cheese and a bottle of Mosel in a basket. Lucien was wrapped in a down blanket and then loaded into the helicopter and strapped in on a gurney and then Greta, Celeste, Elise and her family got in and crowded to the back. The medic looked at them and shrugged and started handing out hearing protectors. Dove took a pair and then stood on one skid, holding the open-door strap and her machine gun, and Greta walked to the front and motioned the copilot out and slid into the right seat with her PPK pointed loosely at the pilot. The copilot got out of the helicopter and stood on the pad by the guards.

"All right, lift off gently and remember I probably have more hours in this class of bird than you do," said Greta to the pilot, "don't act dumb. I know you speak English and if you do anything strange I will blow your head off."

The pilot looked aggrieved and the helicopter lifted into the air gently and swung toward the airport at Calvi. Alonzo helped Dove in and slid the door closed when the helicopter cleared the grounds of the estate and was out of range of anything but heavy weapons or a missile. Dove went and stood by Lucien and took his hand. The medic had put in an IV and attached a bag of saline to it and it looked like Lucien was finally sleeping normally.

"What's the fuel load," said Greta to the pilot over the intercom. "You full?"

"Yes, we are always at full fuel load," said the pilot. "You never know what you will need, so we always fuel and restock medical supplies when we land. Why?"

"We are going to Italy," said Greta. "Low and fast and if you don't want to do it, I can drop you off. I might even land."

"Is that actually Lucien Francisci back there?" said the pilot.

"Yes," said Greta. "He had a stroke and needs a doctor."

The pilot reached in his shirt and pulled out a Maure pennant on a gold chain that showed a black profile of a human head on a sliver background, the symbol of the Unione.

"Whatever you want, miss," said the pilot. "Whatever you want."

Greta nodded, and the pilot called Calvi and reported an emergency transport to Italy while Greta called Merry and told him to scramble a medevac transport jet with a medical team and full support for a stroke victim and meet them at the NATO base at

Avano. Then she nodded as the helicopter swung to the east and dropped down to a few hundred feet above the ocean and the pilot called and reported an emergency medical transport and increased the speed.

******

The medevac plane with a doctor and nursing staff had met them at the airbase in northern Italy and had immediately transferred Lucien to a treatment table in a fully equipped surgical and diagnostic area in the plane. The doctor had come back to talk to Greta and Dove and told them that Lucien was stable, dehydrated, awake and ornery. He also said the stroke appeared to be a stroke where a clot had closed an artery and killed part of the brain. He said that since it was several days since the stroke, it appeared to be minor since Lucien was alive, conscious, and responding fairly well but that they could tell more when they got to Cyprus and did some brain scans. He also said that Lucien was making strange wiggling motions with his fingers and were they a result of the stroke?

Greta had laughed and then asked Celeste if she could borrow her pad until they could buy one for Lucien. Then she had gone back and sat while Lucien typed a number of Email messages and finally went to sleep holding Dove's hand. When they landed, Dove went to the hospital to check Lucien in and sit with him and Greta went with Lucien and Dove then on to the VIP guesthouse in the officers' quarters area of the base to meet Mark and Merry.

When she opened the library door at the guesthouse Francis was holding Elise, and Celeste, Clarissa, Alonzo, and Sergeant Major Joseph Omar Young, SAS Counter Revolutionary Warfare Wing, retired, were standing around looking nervous. Merry was relaxing in a chair drinking a cup of tea.

"Honest to Christ, Greta," said Francis. "This kid has better security than the President of the United States. I talked to Mark and we were going to offer to take her on when you and Dove got your damn fool selves killed, but since she has three Duchesses, one of them royal, a general, and a senior member of the English government for Godparents and is now officially the daughter of the head of the Francisci Family, I feel kind of out-ranked. Mark told me about her, well after we were married, but before she was born."

"I hope he mentioned she was not my idea," said Greta. "But now that she is here, I am strangely attached to her, you might even say I feel motherly. What are you going to do now? Mark said you were getting restless staying home and dusting the good china. How are you feeling, Francis?"

"Well, not one hundred percent, Greta," said Francis. "But I really don't want to try to go back full-time because I still get headaches although the glasses help, but I still see better if I use one eye. One thing, though, is that the cousins came through with a huge settlement since we had them by the nose ring or somewhere two or three feet farther down. I hear you have a couple things that are guaranteed to keep them in line."

"Actually, more things than that, Francis," said Greta.

"Anyway the American number and letter people all got together and figured out that they couldn't clean their boots on each other and get away with it, so they fell right into line with a stunning pay-off," said Francis, "Actually, you owe Blossom more than me. I guess she has a little list that has everyone terrified of her and she has opened her umbrella over you."

"That's fairly normal," said Dove. "Her little list is not that little but adding people to her do not touch list is very rare."

"But what about you and Dove, Greta?" asked Francis. "I know that Julia and Willard are Blossom safe since they are part of the oversight committee that watches what she does, but Blossom is the Assistant Minister for Economics and Policy on European Union Activities, the English delegate to the EUOPS control committee, and Lady Victoria Elaine Covington, DCBE, Dowager Duchess of Camenshire, as well as your big boss and has more money that some small countries. I hear from Mark that she considers you to be a bit headstrong and need to be house broken."

"Well, a while back I was a bit nervous, even though some of the VIP people approved of me, but now I am not sure," said Greta. "As the mother of the daughter of the head of the Francisci Family, I think there are a few options open to me that are Blossom proof. Besides, we are on her like list now. "

"Yeah, now let me see," said Francis. "Lucien Francisci claims to be the father of Elise, but we know Mark, my husband, is?"

"Not that simple," said Greta. "I don't understand everything but, you see, Lucien sent me some flowers and a necklace when Elise was born, and I accepted them."

"Please Madam Steiner," said Clarissa. "Maybe I can help."

"Hey," said Greta. "Don't let me take the lead in something that I haven't had much exposure to. Go ahead, please, Clarissa."$

"My country Corsica has always been someone else's," said Clarissa. "There were the Italians, the Greeks, the Saracens, the French, and the Moors. They forced us into the mountains, used us as slaves and whores, and slaughtered us. Only once, for a few years, was Corsica ever a nation and the people that lived there were free to walk the streets and farm their lands in their own country without a foreign master standing on their neck. Then, the French crushed our nation and took us as part of France. Napoleon was born in Corsica and was an ardent Corsican nationalist and fought in the Corsican militia until he broke with the Paoli faction. Then he supported the French and when he came to the throne he was as bad as any other Frenchman. When he was emperor we were again under the heel of a dictator. So we had nothing left to do but to band together as outlaws. We formed a union."

"How does this explain what is going on now?" said Francis. "I am still at sea on this."

"We were not part of the rulers and had no power and in some cases were outlaws," said Clarissa. "The families in the Unione Course banded together for protection and survival against foreign invaders and we made our own rules. We lived how we could and sometimes, it was torturous and rough. We could not venture into the cities or go to church and so we developed our own ways of coping and our own codes. One of these was the gift of flowers and jewelry. When a child was born-the father, married or not, sent the mother a gift of flowers for his love and jewelry as a pledge of his financial support. This also was something for everyone to see and recognize. The thing was, when a baby turned up, the man who claimed it might not be the father since while it is fairly easy to tell who someone's mother is, fatherhood is more a thing of faith as they say. Sometimes a young woman would receive an embarrassment of gifts and too many are worse than none. We finally sorted this but there could still be more than one gift and the young woman would need to choose."

"But what about Lucien sending me flowers?" said Greta. "He knew he wasn't Elise's father."

"As I said, fatherhood is more a thing of faith and an offer of support, Madam Steiner," said Clarissa. "If a young woman was expecting and her man was killed, his brother or father might offer the gift of flowers and jewelry and it became not a marriage but an adoption. Our families recognize that Signor Francisci is past his prime, but he offered the gifts and you accepted, Madam Steiner. You agreed that Elise is the daughter of Lucien Francisci. Who Elise's biological father is, is totally unimportant. She is Signor Francisci's daughter and his heir, and that is very important."

"You mean she is going to be the head of the Francisci family?" said Francis. "That is ridiculous. She isn't even a year old."

"No," said Alonzo. "Women cannot join the Family, except under exceptional circumstances. It is for men only and membership is through the men in your family. Your cousins and father and uncles are the people who belong, and your family belongs through them. The little girl is the daughter of Signor Francisci and his heir but not a member of the family. Her sons would be eligible though, if they had a sponsor and wanted to join."

"So, what is Elise heir to?" said Greta. "Nothing that relates to the family, I gather."

"I don't know what all she would have if Signor Francisci dies," said Alonzo. "His villa in Italy and the estate in Corsica and some farms and vineyards in Sicily, Italy, and France. He has a ski lodge in Switzerland and another one in the United States and a few apartments there too. I'm not sure where they all are, and his yacht and his private jets and the car collection and art collection and I don't know what else. Then, there is his personal fortune. Signor Gerard would know about that."

"Jesus, why would he give all that to Elise," said Greta. "What about his grandson?"

"I believe that Signor Francisci gave it to Elise, so it wouldn't go to his grandson," said Alonzo. "His grandson is not a member of the family and is not protected. But Elise is protected now that everyone knows she is his daughter and his grandson's aunt."

"Okay," said Greta. "In short sentences and small words explain this to me because Lucien told me to save Mikael and I need to know what I need to do."

"Well, Elise is Mikael's aunt and Signor Francisci's daughter and heir, so killing Mikael wouldn't benefit any of the other people that have a claim on his estate," said Alonzo. "Also since he has acknowledged that Elise is his daughter, harming her would bind the whole Unione to finding her killer and killing anyone that harms her."

"Why?" asked Francis. "Sorry to interrupt but we need to know the local customs."

"Oh," said Alonzo, "yes, excuse me. One of the reasons the Unione was formed was to protect wives and daughters from the outsiders. This may not work exactly well if someone really important in the Unione becomes attracted to a woman of low rank and she is not willing, but nothing is perfect. Some girls and women go and visit family in France or Italy and things blow over but sometimes things get out of hand and people are killed on both sides of the argument, and arguments of this sort can go on for generations. But the thing is that as long as Signor Francisci is alive and the council respects his wishes anyone, and I do mean anyone, who would harm his daughter Elise, who is after all about as high a rank as a woman in the family can get, brings down the curse of everyone else in the Unione on his head not just the family. He is a dead man from the time he steps across my dead body to harm her."

"Okay, explain that to me," said Greta. "Why did Nicole say that you would need to move to Egypt to take care of Elise. I have a lot of people to take care of Elise or people would like to. Like her Godparents, and Asim, and Dove, and Francis, and remember me? I'm her mother but I would probably need to schedule time to see her if she didn't need to be fed. Is she fretting yet, Francis? She should be getting hungry."

"No, she is still asleep," said Francis, "You flying around all night and dragging her around on field operations is not a good idea, Greta. You should leave her with me."

"See what I mean, Alonzo?" said Greta. "Why are you guarding Elise? I grabbed you to come along to help me with Lucien until we get him to Egypt where I can protect him."

"Monsieur Francisci told us that we were to help you with the baby," said Celeste. "Monsieur Gerard said that Monsieur Francisci told him that since daddy had been with you the last time you were here, you knew him, and we should help you. Momma is Monsieur Francisci's housekeeper for his office and apartment and his personal cook and Daddy is his butler and personal bodyguard. We live right next to him on Corsica. Sometimes he helps me with my French and English and mathematics when he is at the estate. Sometimes we go to France or Italy with him on bank business for a few days."

"Well, looks like I grabbed the right people for Lucien," said Greta. "But what about Elise?"

"Since Daddy is Lucien's bodyguard, well, Momma is too, and Nicole and I are kind of, so we are your bodyguards too as long as Elise and you are with her father," said Celeste. "Besides, I like taking care of Elise. Can I feed her sometime?"

"Yes, I suppose so, Celeste," said Greta. "I have always kind of resented that girls play with dolls and boys play with guns but until men grow tits I guess there are some things that are inevitable, and you should learn about babies early. I'll pump you a bottle for later and you can feed her before bedtime and your mother can watch while you and Nicole give her a bath and get her ready for bed."

CHAPTER 5: SICK OLD MEN, DIRTY OLD BOMBS, AND NO ROOM AT THE INN

"Well?" said Greta.

"Okay, I have been talking to the doctor," replied Dove. "Lucien had what they call a Cerebellar Hemorrhagic Stroke, bleeding in his brain, because his blood pressure was off the charts. It stopped on its own this time, but this is probably why he has been in a wheel chair recently and having trouble with using his hands and standing up. The doctor is working to get his blood pressure down, which will help. Some of the problems may be temporary and the damage was mostly in the cerebellum where muscle and motor control are located. The damage was not too extensive but isn't something to shrug off and there is a good chance he may be partially paralyzed and have to use a wheel chair or walker and will talk with a slur. The good part is that his reasoning and memory will probably not be screwed up."

"Lucien isn't going to like any of that," said Greta. "But he doesn't get a vote, does he? How long do they want him to stay here?"

"They want to get his blood pressure down to where it is approaching normal and they want to do a few more tests," answered Dove. "They also want to try and get him to stand up and move around as much as he can. Therapy is going to be long term and I think that we should take him back to Egypt for that, but we need to talk to Armand. We also need to see what Merry and Mark want to do about the atomic bomb sale situation and the attempted kidnapping or whatever it was."

"Yeah, there is that little problem, too, and I haven't got that sorted," said Greta. "But the discussion we had about the pros and cons of having your own little nuclear bomb gave rise to some curious musings and theoretical situations."

"All right, teach me, great guru," answered Dove. "I am stumped about why anyone is dumb enough to want one. If they shoot it off they just as well sit on top of it since they have committed suicide."

"Okay, as you just pointed out having a bomb is dangerous to your health," agreed Greta. "A bomb is enough to attract everyone's attention and a lot of people are going to line up to take it away from you or destroy it, and you too. For example, there were the two old Soviet Tochka mobile systems with low yield nuclear warheads at that secret underground base in Chechnya where they shouldn't have been that just happened to blow up, and then there is the reactor complex that no one admits ever existed out in the middle of the desert under a pile of loose rubble rocks. It doesn't matter who you are, if you buy or barter for a bomb or two you get noticed and normally squashed. Second, anyone who sells anyone an atomic bomb also gets noticed and normally squashed, like the Estonians. Third, a nuclear bomb costs soooo much money that your normal dissident group can't afford one. The point, Dove, is that no one should want one atomic bomb, unless they are contemplating suicide or unless someone else is pushing them to get it, and only a country with lots of taxpayers can put up the money for even one."

"Okay, so this is all true but it's just a rehash of what we talked about with everyone in Corsica," said Dove. "What is your point?"

"I have been trying to figure out why a bunch of nutty Egyptians who apparently must have found Aladdin's treasure cave to finance the purchase want an atomic bomb, size unspecified, to do something unknown and probably dangerous with it," answered Greta. "So try this instead, they really don't want it. They are fronting for some country who wants to remain unidentified and that has absolutely no desire to use the bomb, they just want it for show and tell."

"Who in the world would want an atomic bomb for show and tell?" asked Dove. "That makes no sense at all."

"How about a country that wants everyone to think they have a functioning nuclear program and an arsenal," replied Greta, "but really don't?"

"Oh, now how about that? It is a possibility, isn't it?" responded Dove. "A new kid that wants to join the nuclear club and is not against doing it under false pretenses too. But who?"

"Well, the Islamic Republic of Iran immediately leaps to mind," said Greta. "But then so does Taiwan, and believe it or not the only country that ever got a couple atomic bombs for free, Japan. Both of them are having trouble with China and a nuclear arsenal would really give them some leverage. I don't think that North or South Korea would turn one down either. Then, there are also a bunch of the locals around here that would like to be taken a lot more seriously and could possibly make up a convincing story about their secret nuclear programs or all the leftovers they bought from the old Soviet Union with their oil money, but anyway someone who is desperate for some reason and is willing to gamble."

"So, what about our shooter?" asked Dove. "Why would he be gunning for someone at the nuclear limitation talks?"

"I haven't figured that out yet and I have done all the heavy thinking I can today," said Greta. "After I get a bath and some food, I am going to look in on Elise and her two or three baby sitters and guards and then grab her and go to bed. Are you coming?"

"Yes," said Dove. "There is food in the dining room. Can we just take the baby and go home when we are done here?"

"Yeah, fat chance," said Greta. "We don't even have a home that I know of, and then we need to make provisions for Lucien and Alonzo and his family and finish up the base and a whole lot of things I am not going to think about right now. We can call Sara in the morning after we sort things here a bit more and discuss housing with her. Now, I am taking a bath and then eating a bite."

****

The next afternoon the post store had delivered a new some assembly required baby crib to the guesthouse and Sergeant Major Charles Russell Whittingham, Charley, and Sergeant Major Joseph Omar Young, Joey, had inexpertly assembled it. After a couple hours of tinkering, it had finally been pronounced habitable by Clarissa who had thanked them and then shooed Charley and Joey out and quickly attached the mattress supports and slider rails the correct way, put in the mattress and made the bed. Celeste had spread out the extra diapers, tissues, lotions, and soap that had been purchased, on a long low chest of drawers that was doubling as a changing table, along with three or four sleeper outfits and half a dozen blankets that Francis had shown up with. Nicole entertained Elise with her pig hand puppet while the impromptu nursery was finished and then cooperated with Celeste in giving the baby a bath and dressing her in a diaper and new gown.

Elise was getting used to Nicole and Celeste and that evening when they took turns feeding her the bottle of milk that Greta had pumped during the day, she was content to be held and finally had gone to sleep holding Celeste's finger in one hand. When Celeste slipped her into the crib, she had come awake and started fussing until Celeste picked her up.

"You are spoiling that child, Celeste," said her mother. "Put her down in her crib and let her fuss a bit."

"Why don't I just lay her down on the big bed with me for a minute, momma?" said Celeste. "She has had a long day and not a really normal one for a baby. We dragged her here from Corsica in the middle of the night and she was awake and hungry and cold and scared until I put her inside my coat and zipped it up. Then, she got quiet, but she didn't sleep much. Mama, what is Dove?"

"Um well, Greta is Elise's mother and I guess you could say that Dove is her other mother," said Clarissa. "Dove and Greta are a couple, you know about things like that?"

"Yes," said Celeste. "There are some girls at school like that, but we don't talk about it in public because the sisters would mess their... ah, have a fit. But if Dove and Greta are a couple, then why is Monsieur Francisci her father?"

"He really isn't Elise's father, sweetheart," said Clarissa. "He is her official father and Greta is her real mother, but I don't know who her biological father is. Signor Francisci adopted Elise as his daughter for reasons that are his. His only real daughter was killed in a car accident years ago, although there was talk about the accident being too convenient. Enough, go on lie down and settle the baby, and take your shoes off so you don't dirty the spread."

Clarissa went out into the front room of the suite and sat with Alonzo and had a cup of coffee and took off her shoes. They discussed Lucien Francisci's condition and what they could do to help and what to do with the girls.

"I think we should wait a few days to see what is going to happen with Signor Francisci and then we can contact Signor

Gerard if we need to," said Alonzo. "Until then, the boss still needs an inside guard and a housekeeper. Well, I am off to sit with him tonight. Take care of his daughter and our daughters. How much ammunition do you have for your pistol?"

"Two clips," said Clarissa, "Why?"

"Well, I thought I would take it and leave you the lupara," said Alonzo, "it is rather hard to be inconspicuous with a sawed off shotgun. The two military men, Charles and Joey will be taking turns standing watch outside the door here and there are soldiers in the yard and at the entry to the house. I will try to be back for breakfast."

****

That night it was late when Greta had finally come to the guesthouse. She and Dove had talked to Blossom over the phone about the atomic bomb and their theory that someone in Egypt was fronting for someone else in the attempted purchase since even buying a little one was well beyond the means of anyone except a country. Blossom had thought about it and then said she would get ahold of Merry and have him look around and see what he could turn up since he had a lot of Egyptian military friends. Blossom had enquired about Lucien Francisci's condition and what the plan was there.

Greta had said they should see he got somewhere safe since EUOPS needed to stay on the good side of the Francisci Family and Lucien or his successor, whom ever that turned out to be. She told Blossom that Lucien would only eat things that Dove or Greta fed him and only drink water and juice from sealed cans that they provided.

Blossom had thought about it and then said, "That shows that his mind is not damaged very much. One of the last changes in leadership there was probably hastened by chemical means. What are his chances of surviving?"

"Fair to good according to the doctors," Greta told her. "The stroke was probably the result of astronomically high blood pressure and bad habits but high blood pressure had a number of effective treatments and bad habits can be changed, especially when there is a real inducement, like not dying. I thought I would see what happened but his condition is still uncertain."

"When he can be discharged from the hospital take him to Egypt and take care of him," said Blossom "After all, he is Elise's official father and we do need to stay on his good side, especially with this bomb thing happening."

Greta had agreed and then had gone in to sit with Lucien while Dove went to the guesthouse for a shower, clean clothes and a nap. When Dove left she had kissed Lucien on the forehead and he had struggled to pat her hand and smiled lopsidedly. Greta had sat down in the chair and read the morning papers to Lucien and fixed him tea using bottled water that she had brought in a locked carry-on bag and some canned soup with bread that Clarissa brought from Corsica and that they had all eaten. After dinner Lucien had held out his hand and she had scooted the chair up to his bed and he had taken her hand and kissed it and then napped while she read.

Dove had had come back for the evening and she and Greta and Lucien had watched a western movie and Lucien had dozed off and on until Alonzo came to relieve them. The armed guards on the door had been replaced with new ones and Dove and Greta decided to walk from the hospital to the guesthouse for a bit of exercise. Greta called Clarissa and then went outside. It was chilly but not cold and the stars were out. Charley and another soldier drove up and Charley got out and smiled. He was wearing a uniform with an SAS beret and a lieutenant's collar insignia.

"Dinner ladies?" said Charley, "We can walk to the club and get a bite and then either ride back or walk if you prefer?"

Dove had decided to take the car home and Greta had smiled and taken Charley's arm and they had strolled to the Officers Club and had a good dinner and a bottle of excellent wine that Charley had selected. Then they had sat and talked in the bar while Greta relaxed. Finally, Charley had called a car and they had gone to the guesthouse.

When she got there she had looked at the clock and then taken off her shoes and tiptoed into the suite. There were two SAS troopers standing guard at the door. She tried the door and it was locked so she knocked and announced herself and then used her key to open the door. She walked quietly into the sitting room and saw Clarissa very much awake holding a sawed-off shotgun and lying in a recliner and holding Elise.

"She is hungry," said Clarissa. "She didn't settle right after her bottle and bath and so Celeste lay down with her for a moment and they both went to sleep. Nicole climbed in with them a bit later since she is tired from the trip and all the excitement too. I just went ahead and put a blanket over them all before I sat down since I didn't know where else to put my girls."

"Thank you, Clarissa," said Greta, and held out her hands for Elise. "We need to discuss living arrangements tomorrow. I'll just slip in with the girls and feed Elise and then probably sneak back next door with Dove. Go on back to sleep."

Clarissa nodded and relocked the door. She checked the safety on the shotgun, pointed it toward the door and then adjusted her pillow and went back to sleep. Greta walked into the room that had been fitted out as a nursery and looked at the king-sized bed. Nicole and Celeste were lying under a spare blanket. Greta sat in the chair and nursed Elise and watched the sleeping girls. When Elise finished, Greta changed her and then put her down by Celeste, who instinctively put one arm over the baby to protect it. Elise whimpered and Celeste curled protectively around her without waking. Greta looked at the girl and the baby and then slid down under the blanket and put an arm over Nicole who woke up and then slid over next to her and they all went to sleep.

The next morning, Alonzo brought a tray with some rolls and a pot of black coffee from the dining room when he returned to the guesthouse from the hospital about sun up. Charley was watching the outside door to the rooms where Dove, Elise and Greta were sleeping with Alonzo's family.

"How is the old gentleman," said Charley in halting Italian. "Is he feeling better?"

"He is sleeping naturally and has some color back," said Alonzo in English. "Would you like some of the rolls and a cup of coffee? Or I could watch the door for a moment if you would like to take them in and get something."

"No, thanks," said Charley. "Joey will be along shortly and I will go down and get a proper breakfast. Of course, then I will need to run five miles to keep my weight down. Anyway, they are all still asleep, I think. I haven't heard anyone moving around. Clarissa checked with me a minute ago."

"Well, I have been up all night watching Signor Francisci and I intend to have some coffee and a roll and see where I can catch a nap. I expect everyone will be along in a minute. What time are the meetings this morning?"

"No set time that I know of, but the general went running with Colonel Ben a while ago," said Charley, "and they should be back and get cleaned up and have breakfast and finish the papers by nine."

"I'll check the ladies and let you know what's going on," said Alonzo. "If they are all still asleep, I will sit here until Signoras Steiner gets up and see if there are any instructions."

"Yeah, it would be nice to get roles and duties all straightened out," said Charley. "Well, go on in and see what's up."

Charley stepped aside, and Alonzo went to the door and knocked three times and then waited a minute and knocked four times. Then he opened the door and looked in. He looked behind the door and smiled. Clarissa was crouched behind a tipped over table holding the shotgun across the top.

"I brought some coffee and rolls," said Alonzo. "Let me set the table up and we can have some. Are you the only one up?"

"No, Signora Steiner is showering," said Clarissa. "The general called and asked if they could be at the dining room in an hour so I woke her. I will go and take her a robe and you can set up the table and put down the rolls and coffee and give me my pistol. If you are going to need one, I suggest we ask someone for one. That damn shotgun weighs a ton and I slept with it across one leg last night. I think it gave me a bruise on the thigh."

"Should I look?" said Alonzo, "I can tell you if it did."

"Set up the table, pig," said Clarissa, "and I will go and protect Signora Steiner's modesty from you."

Greta stuck her head out of the bedroom and nodded at Alonzo, "Clarissa, where is the girls' suitcase? I finished feeding Elise and Celeste is changing her, but Nicole and Celeste would like a shower and some clean clothes. Alonzo, I have some stuff here somewhere and so does Dove. Could you go and talk to Charley and have him scare up our kit? It would be appreciated. Is that coffee?"

"Yes, Alonzo brought it and some rolls when he came back, and we were just getting ready to have some," said Clarissa. "I will send him back wherever he found it and have him get more. The girls' suitcase is in the closet in the nursery, tell them to take out some clothing and put the dirty laundry in the laundry bag, please. They will need a shower before they dress. "

"All right, hand me the robe you have, and I will give it to the girls to share when they get their shower and then we can have a cup of coffee and everyone can get dressed," said Greta. "We can all go down to the library and get breakfast then. I assume Merry and or Mark have called?"

"Yes Madam," said Clarissa. "Dove will be up in a few more minutes."

"You want a shower and to change too?" said Greta.

"I would appreciate it, Madam," said Clarissa. "When you are finished, I will go in with the girls and keep them from wasting the hot water so Madam Abraham has some left for her."

By nine, everyone was dressed and sitting in the dining room. Clarissa was holding Elise and Nicole and Celeste were sitting on either side of her. Alonzo was standing stiffly behind his family and looking at the unfamiliar sight of a woman general.
Charley had handed in two uniforms on hangers and a duffle bag a few minutes after Alonzo had asked for their clothes. Greta and Dove had come out of the bathroom in terry robes and with their hair in towels and taken the hangers and bag into their room that was next to the nursery after telling Clarissa the bathroom was hers and the girls. Half an hour later, Greta and Dove had come out of the bedroom wearing stone colored uniforms with general staff collar tabs but with no insignia of rank. Greta was wearing a sky-blue Army Air Corp beret and had flight wings as well as a DFC and two or three other ribbons pinned on the chest. Dove was looking suspiciously at a Beige SAS beret with a flaming sword badge on it and at several metals and badges on her chest,

"What is the problem, Dove," said Greta. "You don't like the SAS?"

"I wasn't in the SAS that I know of when I was your sergeant," said Dove, "and I don't remember joining; and this is an officer's uniform. The little ribbons and bells and whistles and what not are unfamiliar, and I don't know what they imply."

96

"Well, I think the little one with a parachute on it means you do something stupidly dangerous and the other one with the rifles means you are more dangerous to them than to us," said Greta. "I was wondering about the things I have scattered around on my shirt too but I'm sure Merry will explain."

Greta had motioned to Alonzo and his family who had looked curiously at the two women in uniform. Celeste picked up Elise and a diaper bag and they had all gone down to breakfast. When they walked into the dining room, Merry, Mark and Francis were sitting at a table finishing coffee and the newspapers. Merry was dressed in a stone colored warm weather dress uniform like Greta and Dove but with all his metals and ribbons and the stars on the shoulder boards. He put down his empty coffee cup and smiled at them.

"Ah, I see that you are wearing your uniforms, good," said Merry. "Why don't we get this over and then we can have breakfast and discuss some things."

"What are we getting over?" said Dove. "I haven't had any coffee."

"Well, it has been determined that your rank in the Army should be adjusted to reflect your new level of responsibility in EUOPS," said Merry. "Also there have been a few other changes in your status that I need to tell you about. But first, Francis, will you do the honors?"

"Sure," said Francis.

"Normally, the wife or girlfriend of the officer will pin on their badges of rank when there is a promotion ceremony but since I doubt if either of you know where things go and there are a handful of little pins, I asked Francis to do the honors," said Merry, "first Dove. Dove you have been promoted to acting lieutenant colonel, Special Air Service, twenty second regiment, in the Air Troop and assigned to general staff duties. Both Charley and Joey, who are on detached duties while assigned to Greta have volunteered to assist you in completing your parachute training, Francis?"

Merry handed Francis an envelope and she took out the shoulder pips and pinned them in place. She stepped back and looked at Dove and then stepped forward and gathered Dove into her arms and kissed her long and hard.

"There," said Francis, "congratulations."

Merry handed another envelope to Francis and then turned to Greta.

"Your status and background make it a bit harder, Greta," said Merry, "After considerable consideration at a relative high level, and a direct suggestion from about as high as it is possible to reach in this world, it was decided to grant you English citizenship as a political refugee if you want it. The offer was discussed by everyone including your uncle, who retired from the Saint Petersburg police a number of years ago and also with your current employer. There is ample reason to make the offer, since there is still an open warrant for your arrest in Russia under your birth name, and your uncle thinks that the GRU is also troubled about some things regarding the ambassador. Anyway, I accepted for you and the paperwork has been done with your citizenship back dated to when you were sixteen and left Russia."

"Thank you, Merry," said Greta. "After a very brief consideration I accept the offer of English citizenship since it will make it a lot easier for Elise to get papers and things. Do you think there is a chance I could see Uncle Rolf? Is he still alive? What about the rest of my cousins and my Aunt? We have a lot to talk over."

"Um well, I will see what we can arrange," said Merry, "But first, you have been promoted to brigadier and seconded to the General Staff. You will be acting as liaison between EUOPS and MI5 and MI6 for your theater of operations. Mark will be coordinating area operations with me. Do your worst, Francis."

Francis opened the envelope and dumped out a handful of badges and then put them back in the envelope and held it out to Greta.

"Here, have Charley or Joey put them on," said Francis. "I would take an hour and they would still take them off and start over. Congratulations! Are you going to have the brains to fly a desk now and give your daughter a home?"

Then Francis leaned forward and put her arms around Greta and leaned against her in a hug then she kissed her on the cheek. Greta hesitated a moment and then returned the hug and kiss.

"I can't promise that, Francis," said Greta. "But I am not going to do anything totally foolhardy either. Which brings us to the next order of business, which is somewhere for everyone to hang their hat. Coffee, breakfast, and then discussions, all right?"

"Perhaps we should leave, signora, uh, general," said Alonzo, "congratulations on your promotion."

"No Alonzo," said Greta. "You two are the personal attendants for Lucien and the only representative of the Francisci Family we have here. Get you and your family some food and grab a table. Dove, get us something, if you would, and we can get this going."

Merry looked at Mark and then filled his coffee cup and sat back at the table with him. Francis filled a pot with more coffee and put a sweet roll on a plate and brought them back and sat down with Mark and Merry and started eating the roll. Dove came back with two plates of eggs and sausages with hot toast, marmalade and butter, a large glass of milk, and a pot of coffee all on a tray and put it down on a vacant table.

"Okay, come eat, Greta, or you will starve our daughter," said Dove. "Then you have the floor, I assume. Also, you can talk while you eat you know, it's called multitasking."

Greta sat down and poured a cup of coffee and leaned back in her chair.

"Okay," said Greta. "First Elise. She is my daughter and Dove is her other mother, Merry and Pamela are one set of godparents and Julia and Willard are the other. Blossom is also a Godmother. She is Mark's biological child and I just found out she has been legally adopted by Lucien Francisci the head of the Francisci Family. Now it appears that everyone feels compelled to have some say in her safety and we need to sort this out or she may get killed in the crossfire from her various guards. Let's start out with Alonzo. What exactly does Lucien expect?"

"Well, signora general," said Alonzo. "Don Francisci told me to guard her since you accepted the adoption and he filed the papers that were needed to make the adoption legal in Corsica and therefore France. I am also his sworn man and personal bodyguard and my wife has been told to help you with the baby. As long as you two are together, I will stay with you and him."

"Clarissa, what about you and the girls?" said Greta. "You have been a great help, by the way."

"Alonzo said that Signor Francisci told me to help you with the mite while you were at the estate," said Clarissa, "and I thought that Nicole and Celeste should learn a bit about babies since there is very little chance to practice with them on the estate. I hope you are not angry."

"No, not at all," said Greta. "It looks like Celeste and Nicole are better at tending her than I am. Asim, one of my operatives in Egypt, has been helping me with Elise while we get organized there and find somewhere to live. Anyone else want to chime in on Elise?"

"Well, Mark is her father," said Francis, "and we need to settle that right now."

"No, Signor Francisci is her legal father," said Alonzo, "and, well Signor Mark may be her birth father, but she has been legally adopted since she had no legal father and Signor Francisci discussed this with the lawyers and filed the necessary papers. Legally she is Signor Francisci's daughter and his heir and the French legal system and everyone in the Unione will support that."

"I don't think that it is a good idea to go up against the whole Unione Course and French law, Francis," said Dove, "so why don't you have a few of your own? It's not like everyone doesn't know who is who. Greta, what now?"

"The problem is, I am trying to sort is who is where, Dove," said Greta. "Remember when you said you wanted a bed and your own bathroom and Elise needed a crib? I need to know what the minimum square footage is we can get by with. We need to take care of Elise's adopted father, Lucien until he is well. I can explain this later, but Armand was very specific that Lucien didn't adopt Elise on a whim. He wants her and him and his grandson protected, and he thinks I, or we, can do it. Now, it is apparent that EUOPS and associated spooks need to maintain good relations with the family, because among other things there is the matter of the people looking to buy a bomb from them. Me being part of the family, granted with a dirty hem on a non-existent white wedding dress, is a pretty good way to start staying on their good side, I think. What did Ben mean when he said Charley and Joey were mine for a while, Merry?"

"Well, two things," said Merry. "First, they are his contacts with your office, second, they are your and Dove's army batmen and bodyguards, as such they look after you and carry guns and drive you around and make sure you have clean clothes and at least occasional meals. My batman has been with me for over twenty years and he is also my butler and runs my house along with the housekeeper, well my house and Pam's. When he chooses to leave military service, he will work full time for us at Worthold Grange and Highgate House. Anyway, Ben thought that someone whose only job was to take care of you and watch your back and keep watch on Elise would be a damn good idea, both Mark and I agree. Even more important, Sergeant Major Whittingham and Sergeant Major Young agreed."

"I've never had a batman," said Greta. "I've never had a bodyguard before either. I guess I will give it a try because it does make sense and Charley and Joey are good people. Okay, they are two, then there is me and Dove and Elise for five, I really want Lucien close and that means that we need Alonzo and Clarissa around to take care of him and to provide inside security, like they have been doing. Their girls need somewhere to stay and then we need to arrange for a school, unless Alonzo and Clarissa want to send them back to the estate on Corsica. We were going to have Asim and Maurice as downstairs boarders at our place, in separate bedrooms. By my count, we are well over the limit for the available space we had lined up and that doesn't even count any special stuff that Lucien might need."

"Didn't you hire Sara Kransky to do up quarters and security systems?" said Merry.

"Yes," said Greta, "But we have different requirements now."

"Then I suggest you call her and tell her," said Merry, "it would only be considerate."

"Merry, she only works for gold or British or American currency," said Greta, "I don't have a lot of any of them and I need furniture and appliances and stuff."

"Well, I can see that you need to be briefed on station operations and expenses," said Mark. "When you are a station chief you don't pay for your own apartment or car or your security system or guns and ammunition or almost anything job related. You pay for your groceries and clothes and vacations but everything else is picked up by EUOPS. I was going to have a little chat with you when you got up and running and give you the charge number manuals for Maurice to use, but we hadn't gotten that far. I believe you have analyzed the situation with Lucien Francisci and reached the right conclusion. Neither Merry or EUOPS can afford to lose contact there and we need to take care of him."

"So, my house, cars and living expenses are covered?" said Greta. "What about Dove?"

"Good question, but she lives with you, right?" said Francis. "She already gets a company car and bodyguard since she is the head of field operations and I don't think that even the pencil pushers in Brussels would try to make her pay room and board, although you may have to buy Elise's nappies and blankets and milk. I'm not sure the people at headquarters have ever had a station chief with a baby before, so they probably don't have a charge code for strained peas."

"I want a red convertible with a red leather interior and a full electronics package with a killer sound system," said Dove, "and I am going to have Joey bleach his hair and wear jeans and muscle shirts and silver sunglasses while he drives me around."
Merry looked at Celeste and Elise and sniffed and Celeste whispered to Greta.

"Okay," said Greta. "Celeste has just informed me that Elise has just commented on the discussion. We'll be back in a minute."

CHAPTER 6: HOME SWEET HOME, WITH LOCKING DOORS

Sara was leaning into the face of a furniture dealer who was holding a clipboard and screaming in French. The dealer was screaming right back at her and standing behind a van loaded with furniture. He was blocking the van door with his outstretched arms, so she couldn't reach the furniture when her phone rang. She stopped and shrugged and smiled at the contractor who smiled back. He walked away and leaned on the truck, lit a cigarette, and started chatting with the driver.

"What?" said Sara into her phone. "You want what and you want it when and why do you think I would get involved in such a stupid hair brained scheme anyhow? I have to leave Egypt in less than a week. I am rebuilding a royal palace and only took off for a while, so I wouldn't start drinking."

"Merry said we would pay you in gold sovereigns or euros and add a ten percent bonus in American money if you can get done in a week," said Greta. "Five percent if you can get done in two weeks and no budget limits on what you spend."

"Tell him that concrete doesn't dry that fast," said Sara, "I will get everything going and come back to check it as needed and I will charge a fifteen percent finder's fee on all materials and goods I find and buy. All of it is to be paid in gold. No, half in gold direct to me and half in euros to my bank account in Dubai. I will see what I can do about getting you somewhere safe to hang your hats in two weeks but no guarantees. Can I buy property?"

"No, but Maurice can," said Greta. "He will have the charge code book when we get back. I would apologize, Sara, but things beyond my control required the change. I can't tell you over the phone."

"One other thing," said Sara, "I went ahead and totally gutted everything down to the stone walls and sub floors in the Garden City place," said Sara, "Then I went out and swept the hall. There was a micro camera watching the door and another one bored into the apartment from the hall. I traced the wires and they went to a satellite uplink on the roof. I shut it down by throwing it off the roof and then swept everything. The building was bugged with the latest and best Chinese snooping gear but it was sending the info to a rebroadcast satellite link, so it is basically untraceable. I set a couple recorders and cameras myself and lo and behold a couple of guys claiming to be in the satellite TV business showed up and looked around on the roof and checked a couple of junction boxes and left. I have their pictures and pictures of their truck."

"What do you want to do?" said Greta. "I won't hold you to our deal."

"Nah, I will take it," said Sara, "I am going to finish the place up as a love nest for some general's mistress and lease it out for a bundle."

"Hi Sara," said Dove. "It's me, the general's mistress. But I think I will just stay with the general in her quarters."

"What?" said Sara, "You want to explain, Dove?"

"Look, we will be coming home this afternoon," said Greta. "Have Maurice meet us at the office and have him rent us two adjoining suites at the Hilton with two bedrooms each and would you please sweep them and stay for supper? We need to talk. We will leave Lucien and Alonzo's family at the airport in the secure overnight area with a nurse and some guards. Talk to you later, bye."

Sara looked at the phone and then shut it off and dropped it in her purse. She walked toward the van and looked at the man with the clipboard who was talking to the driver. He walked over and extended the clipboard and she looked at the list of furniture and furnishings.

"Mark it up fifty percent and I will sign it," said Sara. "Then start unloading."

"You said mark it up fifty percent and you will sign it?" said the man. "What happened? You were fighting me for a lousy three hundred Egyptian pounds a few minutes ago."

"New contract, I'm working on a percentage now," said Sara. "When you get done carting it all inside the house go back and get the set of antique marble top tables, the fireplace surround from the old Majestic Hotel, and the red room-size antique Turkish silk carpet. Come back with your crew tomorrow and I'll tell you where everything goes. Now, I have to leave."

Sara walked to her car and got in and started it and drove out the gate of the Heliopolis English Colonial house. Across the street, a man sitting in a bookstore reading a paper looked at a picture of a woman staring up from the floor at a camera somewhere above her and then nodded. Then he dialed a number on his cell phone.

"Yes, it's her," he said. "What do you want me to do?"

"Get ready to bring her in," said the phone, "figure out how to get her as soon as you can."

The man hung up and went and got on a motorcycle and shot off into the traffic looking for Sara's car. He spotted it ahead of him weaving through traffic with the abandon that only a resident of Cairo, or Rome, can truly master. He hung back tracking her to see if he could establish a routine or follow her home. It was obvious she was not living at the Garden City apartment or at the Heliopolis house. It looked like she worked for someone and was buying furniture for the project. Well, she would need to go home eventually then he could figure out how to get her and find out what was going on.

Sara turned in at the gate of Moussa and Sons Construction yard and beeped the horn. The guard smiled and opened the gate and she drove through. As the gate closed, she saw a motorcycle pull up and stop. The rider said something to the guard who gave him a flyer with the business office address. Sara drove to the shop area, where the enclosed steel fire escape for the second floor of Maurice's mother's house was being fabricated and stopped. She walked to the shop door and stuck her head in and yelled.

"Amir, where are you?" yelled Sara, "Changes."

A man over six feet tall with a bald head and bulging muscles walked around the corner of a pile of steel sheets and toward Sara. He was huge and had an expressionless face. He was brown from the sun and had pale blue eyes with no expression. As he walked, he kneaded a tennis ball in his left hand alternately crushing it flat and then letting it expand. He stopped in front of Sara and looked down at her like a lion looking down at a rabbit to see if it was worth eating.

"Sara, I just finished the damn thing," said Amir Moussa, the son part in Moussa and Sons, "let it cool before you have me cut it up for scrap and build one six inches wider or narrower or something. Did you bring money?"

"No, I did not bring money," said Sara. "Your mother handles the money. What do you need money for anyhow?"

"Girls, forbidden drink, wild living, new bicycle tires?" said Amir. "Actually, it was strictly metaphorical since I am going to make you pay for that monster even if you want to cut it up. However, I do need to get a couple hundred pounds to enter the contest at the athletic club, though. I think I can lift at least two hundred kilos without wrist wraps."

"The changes are not to the armored fire escape," said Sara. "Go ahead and have it installed and put in the fire brick lining and fireproof doors. No, we are changing the whole damn project. I want you to come with me and look at some properties that we are going to first find and then go see with my realtor as soon as I call him. Bring your clipboard and a calculator since we are going to do some fast retrofitting and construction. We need high security housing for twelve in six distinct private living spaces including an invalid apartment that is wheelchair friendly. It needs to be inconspicuous, plush, and high security. We got two weeks, max, to do it."

"Oh, me, oh my," said Amir, "a special client?"

"Yeah," said Sara. "Probably the specialist I have ever worked for and I have worked for some doozies. This one is so special that he can make you an offer you can't refuse, if you get my drift."

"Great," said Amir. "I was wondering if they are going to bother to pay us or just let us live?"

"Oh, they are not paying," said Sara. "The government is picking up the tab. I plan to charge well, extravagantly, and often."

"Lord, I love it when you talk dirty," said Amir. "Let's take my car since I would have to ride on top of yours. I think that we need to buy either a high security oil sheik's summer house, a small hotel-or how would you feel about a jail?"

"A jail," said Sara, "bars and one-hole floor level crappers with easy wash concrete floors, walls, and ceilings that don't show blood stains? Nah, I don't think so. The people that we are working for, most assuredly don't like jails."

"Well, this is not exactly a jail," said Amir, "It is the old transient detention building at the airport. Not exactly at the airport, it's about a block away in the low rent motel and business row on about half a city block. I've never been inside but it has a bit of a shady reputation. There is a nice mature garden you can see from the street, outside parking, and a tall exterior brick wall. There is a guardhouse already and we could put in a gate."

"Why is this available?" said Sara. "How big is it?"

"They built a new detention center in the international terminal that is located before immigration," said Amir. "That way no one that is shaky gets into Egypt officially and can't ask for asylum. With the old one, the detainees were officially in Egypt and had legal status because they had been admitted and could ask for asylum or protection and things. The old detention center is a poured concrete building with a basement. The top two floors are detention space but mostly like a hotel, there is a basement, too, but it is cells for people you don't want to climb the wall before you send them home. There is a separate one-story office building and administrative center on the front of the property by the gate."

"How do you know about this?" asked Sara. "I haven't heard about it."

"One of the guys at the lifting club is the cousin of one of the generals in the security service," answered Amir, "and he told me. Thought my dad might be interested in trying to convert the place to a hotel or something. I drove past but it is too small as it is and you would have to tear everything down and clear the site for a major development."

"How much are they asking or is it a bid situation," said Sara. "We need something now."

"Well the asking price is high but not that much," said Amir. "The price they are asking makes any project marginal at best for a full tear down, especially when you throw in a bit for the general's cousin as a finder's fee and enough to cover the necessary expenses for the general and the rest of the people with their hands out."

"Including you?" said Sara, "let's go look. Can you get in?"

"Let me call the general's cousin," said Amir. "I think someone may have a key. Why do we want to buy it? They are going to ask."

"Say we are trimming a bunch of foreigners who are looking for office space and overnight accommodations for workers going to and from oil jobs," said Sara, "We want to do minimum work and give the oil company a long-term lease."

"What oil company is that?" said Amir. "Anyone I know?"

"Sure," said Sara, "and I wouldn't tell you on a bet. I will see about a three percent commission on what I make on the purchase deal for you without mama knowing, okay?"

"Ohhhh, new bicycle tires for sure," said Amir. "Maybe some strong drink, pretty girls and wild living, after the lifting competition, of course. I'll call for keys and we can go look."

****

"Switch," said Dove. "You need me to remind you?"

"No," said Greta and moved Elise to her other breast.

Elise snorted and then started nursing again.

"Okay, I was distracted and she was gulping air and will need to be burped. Tell me why I would want to pay, what, forty million Egyptian pounds for a low-grade prison, Sara," asked Greta. "Especially one I haven't seen."

"You have got to relax and let someone else do the leg work, Greta," said Sara. "The place is a concrete building with all partition walls. I can tear them all out and make it into anything. It has a ten-foot-tall brick wall and has a guardhouse with a big steel gate. You can do whatever with the administration building and we can turn the cells in the basement into storage."

"It has cells in the basement?" said Greta. "Cells with lockable doors and everything?"

"They took out the lockable doors when they decommissioned the building," said Sara, "unfortunately, they left the plumbing. There is a functional holding cell and an interrogation area in the administration building basement, but we can do the basements and the administration building after we get somewhere for you all to live."

"I think this is somewhere we need but for various other reasons," said Greta. "I'm going to call Ben. He might want this a lot more than we do. Besides, it sounds like a major project."

"Okay, unless you haven't noticed, Elise is done," said Dove. "Let's change her and see if Clarissa and her brood are up for a bit of babysitting and run and do a quick tour of the building. You got keys Sara?"

"Yeah, I got a bootleg set," said Sara. "Let's go quick. Bring a couple flashlights."

"I'll take Elise down to Clarissa and pop in on Lucien," said Dove. "Put on some jeans and a sweatshirt, Greta. You don't need a business suit to go house hunting."

"Yeah, well I think I will get a robe and hijab to go over my jeans and sweat shirt," said Greta, "Things are getting dicey on the street again. They had more hair cuttings on the metro today. A couple of burka bunnies cut a Christian girl's hair with a straight razor and then jumped off. Besides, I don't want anyone to know who may be fronting the deal. I think we should put Maurice in a business suit and take him, too."

"If you want to pass him off as important, put him in sandals, khaki's and a white shirt and six gold chains and sunglasses. We can take my rental Audi," said Sara. "Actually, that might be a good idea anyhow. I need to get it back. We can pick it up at Moussa's construction yard. If anyone is watching they will have already seen me so I'll go as is."

Maurice, with sunglasses but only two gold chains, was driving, and Sara was in the passenger seat. Dove and Greta, dressed in abayas and hijab, sat in the back seat and looked out the window at the area. There were several large hotels visible out the window and a number of older large residences and a few churches and mosques. A scattering of multi-story international business offices crowded closer to the airport with what looked like government buildings and several cafés and restaurants. Maurice turned toward the airport and drove down a wide commercial street crowded with modern multi-story buildings and then turned into a driveway at a hotel. Maurice handed the attendant a bill and said they needed to make a cell phone call and would leave in a minute.

"What?" said Greta, "are we there?"

"No," said Maurice. "Sara, ever since we got your car there has been a guy on a motorcycle following us. I just forced him to pass us. Any ideas?"

"A guy on a motorcycle was right behind me when I went to Moussa and Sons today," said Sara, "he asked directions from the gate guard and then went on. I didn't think about it."

"Well, he had your car staked out," said Maurice. "He came out of an alley with a good view of the parking lot where the car was. You rode with someone else when you went to the building the first time?"

"Yes," said Sara, "I rode with Amir Moussa, the son in Moussa and Sons, in his truck. He is big and wouldn't fit in the car."

"He must be big," said Maurice. "Wide or tall?"

"Both and he lifts weights," said Sara. "He is in a contest this weekend and figures he can lift two hundred or so kilos without wrapping his wrists."

"Big, wide, and tall." said Maurice. "I think we should arrange for some backup before we go on to the detention center now. I bet we see our friend again when we get there. I know it is stupid to ask, but do you all have guns?"

Sara looked at Greta who nodded and at Dove who suddenly had a Glock in one hand. Sara smiled and reached in the glove compartment and pulled out a Micro Uzi with a thirty round clip then she shrugged and pulled a Walther out of her shoulder bag and then reached in again and pulled out a Taser. Greta lifted one eyebrow at the Taser and put her hand out to examine it. It was pink and small and had a snarling kitten on it with one paw raised and claws extended.

"Sometimes the clients get too handy or think they should get a bonus if you know what I mean but you don't want to kill them since they owe you money," said Sara. "It looks cute, but it is law enforcement quality."

"I have never seen a pearl handled kitty zapper before," commented Dove. "Where in the world did you get that?"

"At the cheerleader's supply store," said Sara. "It's just off the university campus in Austin, Texas. Apparently, the girls use them to keep the football team at bay. I guess the coach has cut a deal with the girls so that they are only used after the game though."

"Interesting" said Greta, "but I wonder what happens before the games. Shall we go and see if our motorcycle rider is around?" "That way we'll know if he's been following Sara all day."

Charley started the car and pulled out and turned around to go another way. He turned and drove to the airport and up to the private owner's entrance and stopped as the guard approached. Greta took down her veil and showed her owners identification to the guard and was waved through.

"Egypt is still one of the only places around here where the guards don't go bug eyed when they see me, as a woman who owns a private airplane," remarked Greta, "but why are we here, Charley?'

"I thought we would call Ben and then sneak across the field and get another car," replied Charley. "Actually, an additional car and driver and a couple of scooters and have them follow whoever is following us."

"Also, as long as we're here, I want to brief Ben and get him and Asim to come and look at the building," said Greta. "Asim can wear a burka and Ben can wear a beard so they will be hard to identify if we are being photographed. I'll phone them to get dressed up and bring another car with dark windows and have Ben and Asim drive over and meet us at the exit. They can follow us and if the motorcycle snoop is watching, it will look like we picked them up here from a plane. The other cars and motorcycles can leave at the same time as we do and take other routes to the property."

Half an hour later, the blue Audi, followed by a black Mercedes limousine with darkened windows, left the private operations area and drove to the detention building. Sara got out and spoke to the gate guard and passed him a few hundred Egyptian pounds and he saluted and raised the barrier. The Audi led the way to the administration building and stopped and the Mercedes followed.

When the limousine parked, a man in a black suit jumped out of the passenger's side front door and looked around. Then he opened the back door and a tall, dignified man with a full grey beard and dark sunglasses got out. He was wearing a white thobe and a black cloak with wide gold trim on the lapels and a red and white checked Saudi headscarf with a black cord with gold wrappings. A woman wearing a black abayah cloak and a blue headscarf and veil got out of the car and stood behind him. Maurice, Dove and Greta bowed, and Sara curtsied, and the man waved them up and then walked toward the administration building with Maurice. They stopped, and Sara unlocked the door and then nodded and stepped back as the party entered the building.

"This is going to raise the price a million pounds when the guard reports back," said Sara, "who is Ben supposed to be?"

"Tell everyone the banker needed convincing before he would put up enough money," said Ben, "then offer them twenty percent less but cash in Saudi riyals. Now, show me the cells."

****

Sara was sprawled on the settee in one of the suites in the hotel looking completely relaxed. She was dressed in a pair of sweats that she had borrowed from Greta and was barefoot. Her hair was wrapped up in one of the hotel towels after her shower and she had a glass of white wine on the coffee table.

"Oh wheeee, so now we need quarters for a high-ranking French criminal who is in the country without bothering with immigration, his housekeeper and butler and their two kids, also here sans permission. Then add two large, impressive, and cute military types that belong to you, Greta, and what should we do about Maurice and Asim?" said Sara. "Also what about Maurice's mom's place. I will have it finished in a couple of days."

"Finish it up, if you can," said Greta. "We may have to go back to the original plan now for at least a while, or maybe later. Ben wants the property we looked at today. He wants to use the Administration building for a branch office for Southerland Oil. The other building would be perfect to ship people in and out through. We can also smuggle anyone we don't want people to see over from the private airfield in my air service van. We can convert the first floor of the detention building to living spaces and a hospital with a surgery unit, a couple ICU hospital rooms, and a recovery area. A private hospital will be a nice thing for all of us to have. Upstairs, we can put in living areas for transients as well as quarters for staff that we need to pull in from the field or are just passing through. The basement goes to lock up storage with solid, no view, watertight, fireproof doors and we leave half of the cells as cells with concealed cameras and listening equipment in them."

"What needs done in the administration building?" asked Sara.

"Ben can keep the debriefing and interrogation room in the basement at the building as is and we can put in a reasonable kitchen and a dining area and lounge down there, too," answered Greta. "He can put offices for his people upstairs and call it the Southerland personnel office and transient assignment center or something. A single wall will allow him to separate his shop into a legit to marginally illegal oil field service company headquarters and an illegal to totally black intelligence gathering and direct-action operations group area."

"Oh, that is impressive," said Dove. "I can see the advantages, but shouldn't we keep it for ourselves?"

"I don't think so," said Maurice. "We really don't need that kind of space that often and if we do need to lock up someone we can borrow space from Ben. He is the one with the large number of troops and we are the snoops. Besides, we have a lot of space at the airfield that we keep clean for inspection by the locals if they suspect anything. We'll have to keep Ben's new area to where it can pass inspection too. I would fit all of the basement cells out as waterproof high security record storage with steel shelves for file boxes and put expansion plugs in the floor level toilet openings. If anyone needs to lock someone up we move the shelving out and take it apart and store it. We can hang bunks on the shelf attachment bolts or clip wrist and ankle restraint chains on them. We can pull toilet plugs when we need to, and I think we should take out the water lines and sinks and make anyone in the cells totally dependent on us for everything, including a drink."

"Greta, Maurice and I are getting married," said Asim. "if you want me to stay around and watch Elise days I will, but we will be moving in together, ah hell, we have already moved in together and are staying at my place. We will need to move eventually but you don't need to outfit living space for us right now."

"Well congratulations," responded Greta. "I suspected you two might want to do that. I know of no prohibition with you two getting married since you are a field operative and work for Dove, not Maurice. I might need you as backup for Elise when we finally get Nicole and Celeste in school, depending on how involved Clarissa gets with Lucien."

"I thought that spies didn't get married," said Sara. "You know, just naked passionate embraces at night on the beach in Tahiti, featuring your good profile and a camera angle on the tits so the lift scars won't show? Then a weeping maiden standing in the dawn watching an explosion in the distance as the burned out super spy and his hot car are forcibly retired with a missile."

"Nah, that was spying in the fifties when they couldn't afford computers and didn't have good high-altitude cameras and universal communication taps," said Maurice. "Things are a lot different and more organized now. For example, if Greta wanted to buy the property I will need to prepare a justification and cost estimate and do a title search and zoning evaluation. Then get the proposal documents to the property acquisition committee and budget section for review. Then do life cycle costing and get an environmental clearance from real property management, or we could just run it through Southerland Oil."

"Why do you think that I wanted to give it to Ben?" said Greta. "He can get a verbal authorization tomorrow and we can pay for it later in the day as a reimbursable operation expense."

"Excellent suggestion, Greta," said Maurice. "That way we can charge it to Operation Union, which is what taking care of Lucien is being called. We won't be officially involved, and Southerland will own the building. They can always sell it and probably make a good bit on it when we get done with it."

"Oh, that is rich," said Sara laughing. "I told Amir that I was going to buy it and redo it and then lease it to an oil company for an operations center and temporary housing for people going to and from oil jobs."

"Why is that so funny?" asked Dove. "That's exactly what is going to happen."

"Because I made the story up on the spot," said Sara, "and I lied my way into the truth."

Sara giggled again and drank her wine then she got up and filled her glass again. Maurice's phone rang, and he looked at the caller ID and thumbed it on. He listened for a minute and then drank his wine and walked over and took the bottle from Sara and filled his glass. Then he looked at Sara with a frown on his face.

"Sara," said Maurice, "Have you done anything to make anyone in the army mad at you recently?"

"Not that I'm aware of," answered Sara, "although I did rip out some wires and stuff at the Garden City apartment that someone had put in. I also threw their satellite uplink off the roof and busted their transmitter. I'm not sure if that was army equipment but it could have been. Why?"

"Well, our motorcycle rider showed up at the gate of the detention center about half an hour after we left," said Maurice, "He had a long conversation with the gate guard and then he rode off to the Headquarters of the Egyptian Military Intelligence and Reconnaissance Command. A minute ago the lone rider just came out with half a dozen armed men in police uniforms and they got in a van. I think that you should go back to your day job now, Sara, and the rest of us should go to mom's place."

"How do we do that?' said Greta. "Do we still have the limo downstairs?"

"Yes," said Maurice. "I had it wait downstairs to take Asim home."

"Okay, Asim and Sara, get on robes and veils and Dove help Maurice put on the beard and banker outfit," said Greta, "Have the driver pull the limo up to the side entrance. Asim, you take Elise and play nursemaid and walk behind Sara. Stuff all the guns and things we shouldn't have in the diaper bag. Asim, put any baby stuff you can't fit in with the guns in a shopping bag and everybody, go to Maurice's mother's house. Dove, Charley, Joey, and I will stay here to see if anyone shows up and what they want. Go!"

Greta walked to the door between the suites and opened her side and banged on the door to the next suite. Charley opened the door and looked at the controlled disorder. Dove was looking at Maurice and brushing and fluffing his beard. She handed him a pair of gold framed round eyeglasses and he settled his headscarf and then looked in the mirror and nodded. Asim had pulled the plainest thobe on over her western clothing and selected the plainest of the black abayah cloaks and put it on. Sara had managed the thobe but was looking at a white veil and headscarf. Asim grabbed a blue silk one and put it on Sara then put on the plain white veil and scarf and checked in the mirror.

115

Dove handed Sara a shopping bag full of baby things and gave Asim a baby bag with all the guns, tasers, ammunition and extra clips wrapped in diapers, so they wouldn't clank. Asim hung the baby bag on her shoulder and then everyone stood and looked at Greta and she nodded and then handed Elise to Asim. Maurice's phone rang again.

"Yep they are headed this direction," said Maurice, "They must have had another tail on Sara's car. We are gone. The limo is at the side entrance running and the driver is meeting us at the elevator. We'll meet you at the house later. Good luck."

A EUOPS operative in a dark suit that was acting as a chauffeur stepped out of the elevator and held the door. Maurice, Sara, and Asim, carrying Elise wrapped in a gold embroidered blanket, walked across the hall and got in the elevator and it started down.

CHAPTER 7: INVITATION TO THE DANCE

"Okay, Charley," said Greta. "We got some of the locals headed this way looking for Sara. Grab Dove's bag and take it in the other suite and throw it on the bed. You and Joey get on your Number five bush jacket uniforms, but you can skip the boots if you need to. As soon as you are dressed, you and Joey get in here. What do you two have to drink?"

"We have a fifth of thirty-year Glenmore and a fifth of hundred and fifty proof Shipshape Gin Ma'am," said Charley, "also tonic and some limes and a bottle of Algerian white wine."

"That'll do," said Greta, "Go and get it. I want to find out who they are, what they are doing following Sara, and why they are interested in us, so we are going to be putting on a little show. We are going to be a group of friends having a little fun and drinks before dinner on our way to you having a chat with the upper echelon. I'll call and have someone impressive come fetch us in twenty minutes or so. Here put these on your bush jacket and get Dove's stuff out of her suitcase for Joey, you both just got promoted."

Greta handed Charley an envelope with her brigadier's pips and other ribbons and flashes. He looked in the envelope and nodded. Greta pulled off her jeans and top and grabbed a thobe. It was royal blue with gold embroidery and crystal beads around the neck and on the cuffs. She took her suitcase into the bedroom where Elise had been kept and looked around. The bed was disturbed, and it definitely looked used. She pulled down the covers on the bed and then spread them back up and put her suitcase on the luggage stand and opened it. She pulled off her jeans and shirt along with her underwear and threw them on the floor. Then she grabbed a new set of underwear out of the suitcase and put it on and added a pair of white tights. She slipped the thobe over her head and took a brush and started brushing out her hair. There was a knock on the door and Charley stuck his head in. He was wearing his jump boots with bloused trousers and a white tee shirt that showed all of his muscles. He looked around and then walked out. In a couple of minutes, he came back carrying his bag and slid it into the closet. He pulled another uniform bush jacket with no insignia out of the bag and hung it in the closet. He dumped some uniform trousers and another shirt on the floor by the bed and rumpled them. Then he hung his SAS beret on the bedpost.

"Kind of like a claim marker, Ma'am," said Charley. "I assume you are sending a message?"

Greta nodded and walked out into the sitting room and looked around. Joey and Dove's suitcases had been moved into the other suite and some bottles and glasses had been arranged on a small table by the balcony door. Charley's bush jacket was draped over the back of one of the chairs. There wasn't anything to indicate that there had been anyone but Charley and Greta in the room. Greta opened the balcony doors and stood in the opening and watched as the last of the sun glowed behind the towers of a mosque to the west. She was standing looking down as a white van with no markings and a couple long whip antennas pulled in the hotel driveway.

"Would you care for a drink, bgeneral?" said Charley. "I have the liquor over here and some ice and the tonic and gin or you could have Scotch. I also noticed a bottle of white Algerian wine."

"I'll have a small gin for the smell and then switch to wine," said Greta. "They're here, I think. Get me the drink and come here. I just put on fresh lipstick and I want to smear a bit on your collar and face."

"Yes ma'am," said Charley.

Greta sat down on the couch and Charley handed her the small gin and tonic. Greta took a sip and then chugged it and put the glass on the side table and patted the couch beside her. Charley sat down, and she took his glass out of his hand and put it on the table and then sat on his lap and kissed him. Then she kissed him again and put her face to his ear and bit the lobe.

"Put your arms around me, sergeant," whispered Greta, "We are sitting in front of the open balcony doors and there are half a dozen places they could be watching from. I think I saw their van come in the driveway, but they probably have observers with glasses and cameras."

Charley put his arms around Greta and then tilted her chin up with one hand and kissed her thoroughly as her arm went around his neck. She leaned back and blinked and caught her breath after the kiss and there was a knock on the door immediately followed by the door opening with a bang as it hit the wall. Greta jumped up and stood with her back to the area of wall between the terrace door and the windows. She put one hand on her throat as Charley stood and turned and looked at the half dozen armed men in blue uniforms that rushed into the room and then into the bedrooms and the next suite. A man in a tuxedo stood with the key in his hand and looked nervously at Charley.

Joey walked out of the next room followed by two of the men. He had one arm around Dove, who was wet, barefooted, and wearing a hotel bathrobe and crying. She rushed over to Greta and Greta put her arms around her and comforted her. Joey had on his bush jacket with Dove's colonel pips, staff flashes and a chest full of medals. He looked at Charley and no one spoke for a moment. Charley nodded and picked up his bush jacket and slipped it on and then pulled it shut and started buttoning it. There were a dozen service ribbons and metals on his chest along with a DFC and a British Empire Metal, military division. The brigadier insignia and General Staff flashes were very plain to everyone in the room. Charley finished buttoning his bush jacket and looked at the only unarmed man among the invaders and smiled.

Then he said, "I bet you five pounds English, you are going to have to spend all night coming up with a really great reason for this before tomorrow when I get to where I am going, so you don't have to spend the rest of your miserable life standing in the sun without a hat shoveling camel shit into a pile and then shoveling it back into another pile and so on."

Charley walked to the table of liquor and poured two fingers of scotch in a glass and dropped in an ice cube then turned around, and said, "Now in a spirit of international understanding and peaceful cooperation, which I was told was the reason for me being here, I would like to ask something."

Then Charley tossed down his drink and shifted to his best parade ground voice and roared, "WHAT IN THE HELL IS GOING ON? AND PUT UP THOSE GOD DAMN GUNS BEFORE YOU BUNCH OF IDIOTS SHOOT EACH OTHER."

Then he slapped the pistol out of the hand of the nearest policeman, shook his head at their ineptitude and turned and poured another drink. Greta looked at Charley and blinked.

Joey walked over to the leader of the police and said in perfect Egyptian Arabic, "Can the brigadier and I be of any assistance? We were just getting ready to go meet some of your military people for dinner and talk over what we might do to assist them in what they are thinking about doing. Now, it would probably be best to have your men finish whatever they are doing and then go out and guard the hall against terrorists or something while we have a little chat. And your name is?"

The man barked an order and his men filed into the hall and took up positions facing the elevator. The man in the tuxedo bowed and walked out and shut the door.

"My name is unimportant," said the man in English, "We are looking for this woman and we have reason to believe she is here. Do you know her?"

The man held out a picture of Sara standing in a hallway and looking up at a camera.

Joey passed the picture of Sara to Charley who barely glanced at it and said, "Of course. It's Sara Kransky; she is an interior decorator and international home security consultant. I believe she has offices in London and Paris. She has done work for several prominent people like the President of France, members of the English royal family, famous film stars, and extremely wealthy and famous people in the United States. I believe she is currently employed by the ruler of Abassa in the United Arab Emirates to supervise work on restoring the nation's royal palace and other public buildings and monuments. There was a program on BBC two about it a few months ago. She is often on the front pages of various magazines and papers. I believe she has an international television program, too. I've never met her, but we do have a file on her since she seems to turn up in interesting places at odd times. This is interesting. Why would she be in Egypt? Any good ideas?"

"No, but we think she is involved with a terrorist group," said the man. "She hasn't been in your room today?"

"Not that I know of," said Charley. "We just got in and have only been in Cairo for a couple hours unwinding."

"Did you rent the room yourself? There is no record of you at the desk," said the man. "Who did rent the room?"

"A charter airline that arranges rooms for its passengers so that they don't need to," said Joey. "It's best if our presence here is not widely known. The airline gave us a key when we arrived."

"Was there anyone else here that this woman could have been seeing?" said the man. "Did you notice anyone else?"

"There was a couple from Saudi Arabia who were here in the room next door when we arrived, but they left and said we could take over the room," said Charley. "They needed a place for their nurse and baby while they did something. They pulled out, oh, half an hour ago. The man was older, and the women were in robes and veils but the baby was pretty young, so the wife was probably quite a bit younger than her husband. They had bodyguards that bowed to them and the man had a Saudi headscarf and a black silk robe with a couple of inches of real gold embroidery on the edge. I would bet prince someone, but I didn't know him. Kransky could have seen them about a job. They looked like they could afford her."

"We will need to search the rooms to confirm that there is no one else here," said the man. "If one of you would care to accompany me?"

"Colonel, go around with the gentleman and let him look under the beds," said Charley. "Why don't you ladies go ahead and go next door and finish getting ready. We should have someone picking us up in a few minutes. I'll stall them with a drink. Now sir, if you would like to go with the colonel? Check the next-door bathroom first, the ladies need to finish getting ready."

Greta and Dove walked out of the room and went into the bathroom of the suite next door when the policeman finished his search. Dove pulled lacey white underwear and skin colored tights out of her suitcase on the bed and then selected a white soft sheath dress with a long leg slit and grabbed a make-up kit. She threw the bathrobe on the floor and then dressed and started her make-up.

"My God, did you have to kiss Charley so good?" said Dove. "He had enough lipstick on him to qualify for after the senior prom and you two were sure looking cozy from what I could see, peeking through the crack behind the door."

121

"Yeah, well I doubt if you made Joey turn around for the striptease when you got in the shower and bathrobe," said Greta. "Would you believe it? I don't believe how they handled the cops. I thought I would have to do the talking."

"Okay, so they did good, which is not to say Charley wasn't handling you really well, too," said Dove. "You should be ashamed."

"Yeah, well it is really unfortunate they are part of the help," said Greta. "As someone important said, never start screwing the help, they get to expecting more than their paycheck. But he is definitely very accomplished at lots of things. Now, finish up and then get a fresh coat of paint on me and we will probably need to wipe down Charley, too."

Dove washed Greta's face and then did her make-up. She was just finishing Greta's eye make-up when there was a rap on the door. Dove and Greta checked themselves in the mirror and then opened the door. Charley, who had cleaned his own face, was there and behind him stood two armed men in the uniform of the Egyptian Republican Guard.

"Our ride is here," said Charley. "They have tidied up and taken our luggage down stairs. Are you girls ready?"

"Well, I was thinking about a scarf for my hair and a veil," said Dove, "but I guess I will have to do without."

"We can get one when we get there," said Charley. "Let's not keep everyone waiting."

Greta looked around and then took a bed sheet and bit the edge and tore a wide strip off of it for her and another one for Dove and they covered their hair and veiled then they went out. There were six Republican Guards, and a Guard Major who was holding a glass with a lone ice cube, standing in the sitting room with the policeman. The Major put down the empty glass reluctantly and bowed to Dove and Greta and scowled at the leader of the police and then walked to the door and opened it. Greta, Dove, Charley, and Joey walked out passed the police who were still standing around with bored looks on their faces guarding the elevator and hall. Dove, Greta, Charley, and Joey took the elevator down and got in a stretch limousine that had come with the Republican Guards. The Republican Guards got in two armored scout vehicles with mounted machine guns. The scout cars and the limousine drove to the airport and went in through the private operations gate and then onto the private hanger access road and disappeared into the hanger area.

About twenty minutes later, a Beech 1900 jet with Egyptian civil markings taxied out of the hanger area and took off. A young man loitering outside the fence sitting on a small motorcycle watched as it lifted off and turned to the south. He remained watching until the armored scout vehicles appeared and drove across the field to the guard base and the limo moved along the access road toward the car rental area. Then he started his motorcycle and rode off, followed by a young couple on a motor scooter that had been sitting at the coffee shop across the street using the free Wi-Fi and waiting to see if anyone showed up.

****

An hour or so later everyone was finishing Maurice's mother's house. Sara had dragooned Maurice, Charley, and Joey into moving furniture around and spreading rugs on the freshly polished floors and hanging pictures. Charley and Joey had hooked up the appliances, Greta and Dove made beds, and Asim had arranged a nursery corner in the larger upstairs bedroom. Sara had finally gone through and plumped pillows, scattered knick-knacks and flowers and put the final layer of chic on things. The place was beautiful. Finally, everyone had cleaned up and showered and was sitting in the downstairs sitting room eating takeout kosher vegetarian pizza that Asim had ordered in and drinking beer or sodas.

"I was truly impressed with how you handled things at the hotel, Charley," said Greta. "You got the answers we needed and did a very commendable job. Are you sure you haven't been involved in this sort of thing before?"

"I don't remember saying that, ma'am," said Charley. "I was wondering how you lined up the Republican Guard and armored cars, Ma'am? Were they real?"

"Yes," answered Greta. "I called Merry and had him request an escort for two members of the British General Staff here on confidential business that were having some problems with the local police because of some girls. He got hold of the airport detachment commander who also works for us as an informant. When I recently got my local station chief briefing I found out there are a lot of people who are available locally that will help, but I thought a request for assistance in this case would be better coming from the military. The decoy plane was one of Ben's of course."

"I'm glad you are pleased, ma'am," said Charley and smiled broadly, "I'm always willing to help out any way I can."

"I just bet you are," muttered Dove.

Greta laughed and winked at Dove who blushed.

Sara started picking up and was offering around the last pieces of pizza when Maurice's phone rang, and he looked and then brought up a text message. He read it and then shook his head.

"Greta, they had a man who followed the convoy to the airport and stayed around to see the plane take off," said Maurice, "A couple of people that we borrowed from Armand followed him to the Military Intelligence and Reconnaissance Headquarters. I don't think it was the local cops at all. What in the world did you do to make the intelligence service mad at you, Sara? They said they think you're associated with a terrorist group."

"I think I ripped out their wiring and chucked their transmitter off the roof at the Garden City apartment," said Sara, "I don't know how this would get me in league with the terrorists, whoever they are around here this week, but this interest in the Garden City place has me curious."

"I told you that the Egyptian military, probably Military Intelligence and Reconnaissance had spy cameras in the place when I lived there," said Greta, "they had the place wired and they rented apartments to people they wanted to watch. The military hung the landlord and owner of record out to dry as a pervert when we exposed the cameras and got the recordings. That is why I got the apartment in the lawsuit so easily. They never caught me doing any spy things there, although they got some very private moments. The judge gave the films to Mark, the creep."

"You think Mark, our boss, is a creep? I'm pretty sure there is some confusion about who is involved there now," said Dove. "Just before we left for Corsica, they tried to grab Asim at the apartment when she was driving our car before we dumped it. It was definitely a bunch of boys with short hair and combat boots.

What this suggests is they had a make on the car but not the driver. This means they had to have a description of the car from France or Wales from when we were involved in stealing the Syrian gold. We had only been in and out of the apartment once after we started setting up the office here, so I bet they didn't know who was involved. Either they didn't have camera equipment installed at that time or they hadn't connected Greta back to the apartment. Then Greta swapped it off to Sara and she started showing up fairly regular, but they didn't try to snatch her then."

"No, the judge is a creep, Dove, although come to think about it Mark is too for not giving the observation films to me. The Egyptians got a whole bunch of amateur smoker films of me and my assorted friends in bed for a couple of years but no hard evidence I was anything but a pilot," said Greta, "so why the attempt to collect Sara now, also why the attempt on Asim or the driver of the car? Also, who tipped them off to the car?"

Maurice's phone rang, and he put it to his ear and listened while he finished his wine.

"We may get a chance to ask them," said Maurice, "The gentleman who came to your hotel room today left the Military Intelligence and Reconnaissance Headquarters in a car. He is alone and dressed in an army uniform. Some of our teenage snoops started following him and it looks like he may be headed this way. What do you want to do, Greta?"

"Sara, you and Asim grab Elise and get out of here," said Greta, "Joey, you and Charley go with them for cover. Go to the airport and have the standby crew warm up a plane if you need to run. Get Lucien and Alonzo's family ready to go too and head back to Crete if necessary. I have some serious doubts about this whole situation. How could they have found this place, unless someone told them we were here? If it comes to a shooting match, we will go out the back door and try and head for the airport. Maurice, what have we got for transportation?"

"Well, Sara's car is still at the hotel, but we have an emergency backup service," said Maurice, "We can try that."

Maurice hit a speed dial on his phone and said, "All right, they will to be here in two minutes. Let me text the kids following the Egyptian man's car and get an arrival time. You sure you want to stay, Greta?"

"Yes," said Greta, "It appears they have us made and I may have to hand everything to Ben and quit, which actually has some real attractions right now. Okay everyone, grab the empties and pizza boxes and take them with you to eliminate fingerprints. Charley you and Joey do a quick wipe for prints on the furniture. Sara put things back together and Asim grab Elise, the baby bag and some formula."

The gate of the house opened and a delivery van from a large local grocery store entered the gate and drove to the covered and screened kitchen entry at the rear of the house. Maurice was watching the television camera for the rear entry and smiled as a young man dressed in a white apron climbed out of the van and slid open a sliding door in the side of the delivery van. He pulled out a box of groceries and walked to the kitchen door and knocked, then entered the kitchen and put the groceries on the counter with a bill and nodded.

Maurice nodded back, and Charley walked out and looked in the van and then motioned everyone else out. They got in the van and it drove to the gate and out into traffic. Two large sedans joined it, one behind and one in front, and it drove out of sight.

"That was slick," said Dove. "How did you get this arranged Maurice?"

"Actually, it is part of the services Armand is providing because of Lucien and Elise," said Maurice. "Normally, they transport cash from lottery ticket sales and other gambling enterprises, as well as the occasional person in various states of repair, but the police don't bother them since they are paid off. They also deliver groceries so if anyone gets overly curious they just might get a load of rice and broccoli. The one we just got is kept across the street in a condominium parking garage in a private enclosure with its cover cars."

"Greta, I'm not sure about all this involvement with criminals," said Dove. "I know that everyone agrees we should take care of Lucien because the Francisis are useful, but I thought we were some kind of international good guys. You know protect the people, punish the bad guys, arrest the guilty."

"Well right now we are cooperating with the Francisis on the atomic bomb thing and we need to work together. After all they came to us with the problem and everyone in EUOPS is curious about who wants an atomic bomb so I guess you can think of them as our criminal contacts or informants. Can we arrest someone, Maurice?" said Greta. "I really don't know. You know, Maurice, there are a lot of things I need to find out about the actual nuts and bolts of EUOPS. What if I actually want to arrest someone and charge them with a crime or something? Can we do that?"

"I don't know," said Maurice, "I'll find out. Someone must know. Normally, we just kill them."

"True," said Greta, "but I think that killing everyone every time is a bit extreme especially in some cases. Why don't you find out? What's the problem, Dove?"

"Oh, I don't know," said Dove, "It didn't use to bother me to kill people and steal things and blow up places but since Elise came I get worried sometimes. What about her future? I mean what is the difference between us and the crooks?"

"We normally don't have anyone trying to arrest us and lock us up for the rest of our lives," said Maurice, "and we get a monthly paycheck and a good retirement if we survive. However, right now it looks like we have what may be a policeman or army officer talking to the gate guard. He wants in. What do you want to do, Greta?"

"I'm curious," said Greta, "let him in."

"Want to throw on a veil?" said Dove; "He is going to recognize you as the little cutie that was playing footsy with our fake brigadier."

"Probably be a good idea to start with," said Greta, "You better cover up, too, so that he doesn't recognize the naked teen age hooker in the bathrobe from the hotel. That way we can see what he has to say to Maurice and take it from there. We'll go and slip into something less comfortable and then when we get back, let him in."

Dove glared at Greta and then got up and stomped out of the room. She came back with two heavily embroidered house robes and scarves and veils and threw one at Greta. Greta fielded it and slipped it over her tee shirt and jeans. Greta slipped on the scarf and veil and then went and pulled her chair back behind Maurice and sat down with her hands folded in her lap. Dove finished adjusting her cover up and pulled her chair back the same distance and then sat down folded her hands and looked at her feet.

"Everybody ready?" said Maurice. "Wow, don't you two look servile."

"Shut up Maurice," said Dove. "I'm still armed."

Greta nodded, and Maurice spoke into his phone. The street gate open and the car drove to the parking area in the front of the house. It stopped, and the door opened and a man in the khaki uniform of the Egyptian army got out. He was wearing a standard army beret but nothing to denote a branch of service although he had a major's rank insignia. He was not wearing a sidearm. He walked to the porch and looked up at the camera. Then he unbuttoned his jacket and took it off to show he was not concealing a weapon in a shoulder holster or tucked into his pants top. The Major put on his jacket and reached out and touched the doorbell.

"Let me," said Dove.

Dove slipped out of her chair and went to the door and opened it and then bowed and stepped behind the door. The major looked in and then stepped in and looked at Maurice where he was sitting at the table and nodded. Maurice stood and indicated the other end of the living room where there were several chairs and sofas and a cabinet with bottles and glasses. The major walked into the room and glanced at the bottles and then picked up a bottle of Glenmore and looked at Maurice. Maurice nodded, and the major poured an inch of the thirty-year-old scotch in a glass and swirled it around and then sniffed it and took a drink. He smiled and then put it down on a side table and bowed.

"Ladies, gentlemen, I said my name was not important this afternoon when it wasn't but now it actually is," said the man, "My name is Bryon McMillian, I am a colonel in the Egyptian security services not a major in the army. My father is General Sir Wallace McMillian, retired and one of Merry's father's friends. Merry and I never attended any schools together since I lived here with my mother and finished my education in Egypt, but we have been involved in several operations together since then. He and a certain lady that is involved with what I believe is your organization told me there would be several people here that I should introduce myself to. Who am I addressing?"

"I am Maurice Toubon," said Maurice as he the bowed and then extended his hand.

The colonel shook it and Maurice indicated a sofa and sat down. The colonel picked up his drink and sipped it and then looked at Greta and Dove.

"I believe you two ladies are some of the other very important people I should know," said Colonel McMillian, "especially in the current situation."

"What situation is that?" said Maurice, "and you mentioned a lady?"

"Yes, she is known by the operational name of Blossom," said Major McMillian, "and is a friend of my father who is also on a committee with the lady. I was told to identify her as Elise's godmother, who sent the message that she would be willing to pitch in if you needed to send her home."

"It would appear that you know a number of people," said Greta, "but what situation are you talking about and why would all of the people you referred to be interested in getting us together?"

"It appears that we have all discovered more or less independently, that there is an attempt by someone in Egypt to purchase a nuclear device," said the colonel. "This has resulted in a great deal of international unease and a demand for action by all the people who are aware of the problem. Since I am a member of an Egyptian agency charged with investigating and blocking such activities, we are taking the lead in the investigation here by common agreement. Your various superiors have consulted with mine and you are invited to assist us in discovering the facts and taking whatever actions are necessary to prevent such a sale."

"And if we decline the offer?" said Maurice, "Then what?"
"I believe it is as they say, an offer you cannot refuse," said the colonel, "now, if we could all introduce ourselves, please? We have a lot to talk about."

CHAPTER 8: LOCAL CONSIDERATIONS AND CONDITIONS

Greta reached in her robe and the colonel put his hands up. "My people, and more importantly, your people know I'm here," said the colonel. "I assure you that I am unarmed and am here to solicit your cooperation and aid."

Greta pulled out her phone and held it up. The colonel put down his hands, leaned back in his chair, and let out a long breath.

"Get another drink and relax," said Greta. "I'm going to call someone and check on you. Dove will shoot you if you don't check out."

"Can I take off the muffler, mama," said Dove, "it's too warm in here for two layers of clothes."

Greta nodded and walked out of the room. Dove pulled off the headscarf and veil and then took off the house robe. She smiled and stretched and then sat down again with her hands in her lap but this time she had a small blue pistol in her hand.

"Miss Dove?" said the colonel. "I believe I saw you earlier today. I would like to complement you on your acting ability. You were most convincing."

"Thank you, colonel," said Dove, "but what makes you think it was acting? You could have just walked in at an inconvenient moment."

"Oh, a number of things," said the colonel. "For one thing, all of the clothing was in neat little piles and not flung all over and nothing was ripped. Also, even though you were discovered in the shower, your lipstick was perfect. You do not climb out of bed with presumably ruined hair and lipstick to take a shower and stop to renew your lipstick and redo your hair on the way. Also, after examining the films from the other room we took from the outside, I was somewhat unsure about the fact that it appeared that the brigadier appeared to be coached to put his arms around the other young lady. I am well acquainted with the actions of military men and I found the activities to be a little too restrained."

"An interesting analysis," said Dove. "Are you married, colonel?"

"Yes, I am," said the colonel. "Why?"

"I was just thinking that your wife must have an interesting time of it when you come back from out of town," said Dove. "Now, since we are either cooperating or I am going to shoot you before we leave, let me introduce myself. I am Dove Abraham."

Greta walked out of the other room. She had removed the veil, scarf and house robe and was wearing a plain grey business suit with a white shirt and black string tie. She had brushed her hair back into a ponytail and removed her make-up. She looked like a very young high school business teacher.

"Well, you check out, colonel," said Greta. "But, there are still a few questions. First, why were you searching for Sara Kransky and pretending you didn't know who she was? She is about as well-known as beer."

"We were confused about what was going on with you and her," answered the colonel. "The only tie we had discovered was the apartment. We had been watching you previously because your actions did not quite square with what was normal since you had far too much money for a self-employed charter pilot and you were often found in company with a suspected foreign agent, Mark Saint Martin. Also, you maintained a relationship with him for a number of years, a first for him. This indicated either a professional relationship or an uncharacteristic commitment on his part. When we heard about the enquiries regarding the bomb we checked on all of the known organizations and also on what appeared to be relevant new sources. This is when we discovered Saint Martin had relocated and the renewed activities at the apartment, and that Miss Kransky was involved. Since she is an interior decorator, and one of the most exclusive and expensive in the world, we were immediately alerted since she doesn't do small apartments in Egypt so we started following her and located you."

"What about the attempt to hijack our car?" asked Dove. "I don't get to shoot him?"

"No," said Greta. "Julia and Blossom both gave him a clean bill of health. As a matter of fact, his father told Julia he thought the young rogue would be a jolly good choice for the assignment and could probably learn a few things from the professionals. Julia may be coming out with Willard just for a visit and to get some sun, but I think it's to check on Elise for her godmothers. Now, what do you know about the attempt on the car, colonel?"

"As you know, things are unsettled in Egypt at the present moment," said the colonel. "The Muslim Brotherhood has been outlawed in this country for over fifty years since one of their stated objectives is the establishment of Sharia law. With the revolution in 2011, the party was no longer outlawed and has widespread support. It won almost half the seats in the first election after the revolution with its political arm the Freedom and Justice Party. Then Morsi was elected in 2012 and it soon became apparent that the pledge of honoring the beliefs of all and the constitution was about as believable as anything else a politician says. There is a great deal of tension right now between the military, who were primarily trained in the British traditions of chain of command, obedience to your superiors, and fair play, and the civilian government who were raised on the values of the brotherhood which stresses obedience to religious leaders and the unchanging rules written in an ancient book."

"And how does that have anything to do with the attempt to grab our car and the driver?" said Greta.

"I guess what I am trying to explain is that everyone in power is not in agreement on actions and policy," said the colonel. "We think the attempt on the car was made by a faction in the brotherhood called the Secret Apparatus that is a paramilitary organization. They were the ones that tried to assassinate Nasser in 1954 and probably participated in the death of Sadat in 1981. We had someone watching the apartment that saw the car incident and your reactions there were one of the things that convinced me that none of you were exactly what you seemed. We have no idea about why they made the attempt or how they identified the car. Afterwards, I increased the attempts to find you and started following Sara Kransky myself because I didn't trust anyone else."

"So, what about Sara?" said Greta. "She is just hired help and a friend. She really isn't involved in anything else. I've had her doing some decorating for me. Actually, she did this place. I swapped her an option on the Garden City place for the work here. That's why she keeps showing up there. She's getting ready to fix up the apartment and rent it to someone important for a love nest."

"Ah, so you are Miss Greta Steiner," said the colonel, "I am very pleased to meet you. Also, I admire Miss Kransky's abilities and talent. This place is very nice. I am also glad that we were right about you. It gives me a great deal of satisfaction that we are actually doing our job in identifying foreign agents and tracking them."

"If you tell me you watched the films from my apartment, I am going to have Dove shoot you anyhow," said Greta. "I suppose I shouldn't feel any resentment, but I do. Especially with that damn judge that gave the films to someone else. I suppose that there are tons of copies, though, so I had better get over it. Actually, though, I am still madder than hell."

"What did Blossom and Julia actually say," asked Maurice, "and I suppose we should introduce ourselves. As I said, I am Maurice Toubon, I am currently Chief Administrative Officer of the EUOPS office here."

"I'm Dove Abraham," said Dove, "Chief of Operations, EUOPS Southern Area Office.

"I'm Greta Steiner," said Greta, "and I am the new EUOPS Southern Area Supervisor. Blossom said that the Colonel's father gave him a good report and said he was clever and adaptable. She also said his father said he was a damn fool for staying in Egypt which is going to collapse around his ears and would consider it a favor if we gave him a hand and tried to get him and his wife and the general's grandkids out if everything goes in the toilet, assuming the government is the one trying to buy a bomb."

"What about our secret operation here?" said Dove. "Blossom normally doesn't give out the address of the EUOPS area chief to the locals since we are supposed to be a secret organization. I think that the lady still wants to stick it to you, Greta. Is Julia on board with this?"

"Yes, we may have to move anyway. The general feeling among our experts on the area is that if the Morsi government or the Muslim Brotherhood does manage to buy a bomb and it is confirmed, the Israelis will give them another two or three for nothing the same day," said Greta. "The Israelis have already indicated they will not ask anyone for permission."

"That is what we in the military are afraid of," said the colonel, "as for EUOPS being a secret organization that is just the official position. We are aware you are here and generally ignore your operations and even provide assistance in some cases. You can go back to being a secret organization after we finish the bomb problem. Now, I was told that you discovered Hamid Masoud getting ready to take a shot at someone at the Iranian nuclear program talks. We have been keeping an eye on him and this is very interesting. You are aware that he was a prime suspect in the bomb death of an Iranian nuclear scientist a year ago and may be implicated in the death of a Pakistani nuclear centrifuge expert?"

"Yes, we caught him trying to take a shot at someone, but determining who was inconclusive," replied Greta. "There are just far too many equally probable possibilities. It is apparent he is thinning the herd on nuclear experts but there doesn't seem to be any other pattern that we have been able to discover."

"After analyzing the people that we know he assisted out of the world and the ones he may have helped that way we have come to a rather interesting conclusion," said the colonel. "It appears he is killing people who are experts in enriching uranium. It is highly likely that someone, I wouldn't say Israel of course, but someone is trying to prevent the spread of nuclear technology in the Middle East."

"I wouldn't say Israel any more than the United States or Norway or the French, Russians, Germans and Chinese," said Dove. "No one wants a bunch of nuclear armed people that are preaching terrorism. I just don't think that the wide-eyed nuts realize that if you stick your hand in the fire, you get burned regardless of how holy you think you are. Two will get you ten that if it is confirmed that the existing Egyptian government got hold of a nuclear device by buying it, stealing it, or saving enough trading stamps for one, you would suffer a whole series of little things that would finally have it blow up in your face. You know about the Estonians and the two rockets?"

"We are very aware of them and that is why we are nervous," said the colonel, "I will bring some files and we can go over them tomorrow. I will call off the detain order on Miss Kransky but leave a couple men on her as security just in case since she is involved with you and the apartment in Garden City and we are unsure about the attempted carjacking. We will also keep watching the apartment building to see if anyone is unduly interested. Now, I need to get home or I will be in serious trouble with my wife. I will need to pick up a gift anyhow since we had an engagement tonight that I had to miss."

"Just a second," said Dove.

Dove walked out of the room and returned a moment later with a slim white leather covered box that said Lady Le Gamilon in a thin gold script on the front. She handed the box to the colonel and he opened it. Inside was a small elliptical gold watch with a black face and a half-carat diamond at twelve o'clock. It had an expansion band made of alternating gold, white gold, and rose gold scales, each stamped with a small script g, the trademark of the House of Le Gamilon.

"This is beautiful," said the colonel, "but I can't take this. It would be a bribe."

"Don't be silly," said Dove. "It is also a tracking device and we are bugging your wife. This will be handy if we need to locate you or her or the kids sometime. Here, let me set it."

The Colonel handed the watch back to Dove who slipped a small pin from the case into a hole on the back and then looked at the face. Numbers started flashing on the face of the watch and the hands rotated. Dove manipulated the pin until the small numbers only appeared on the face with one under the hour hand and one under the minute hand and then selected the local time. As the minute hand advanced the numbers also advanced always showing the correct time.

"There, just stick this pin in the right-hand hole on the back to set it," said Dove, "the pin is magnetic, and the watch is waterproof to a lot deeper than you could survive. The hole on the top activates a signal. If you put a paper clip or toothpick or splinter or anything in it and leave it there for more than thirty seconds, the watch screams for help. We will track it and will come running. I would tell your wife about that feature and the fact your father is worried about your family but say that it is connected to a private security firm. And it is a genuine Le Gamilon, too, just several thousand pounds more than the normal ones, which are several thousand pounds."

"I am aware of the cost of Le Gamilon watches," said the colonel. "Wouldn't it be better if you had a man's watch for me if you want to track me?"

"Probably," said Dove. "But you crapped up her evening and not the other way around, so she gets the watch. Just be grateful we bailed you out for being a crumb."

The colonel smiled and shrugged and then put the watch in the box and put the box in his pocket. He nodded and walked to the door. Dove followed him with a pistol held loosely in her hand and opened the door. Greta walked to the front window and watched as the car drove out the gate.

"So?" said Maurice. "And what?"

"And he is a committed nationalist, speaks half a dozen languages, was active in the revolution on the Mubarak side, and is a Coptic Christian," said Greta. "His wife is a lawyer and a member of a local women's movement that was active in the overthrow of the previous government. Julia was not all that happy with Blossom blowing our cover but said that we did need to keep Egypt out of the radical Islamist camp and the bomb thing was real but a bit fishy. Merry said that the people that attempted the snatch were probably an extremist right wing group who could also be our best choice for the people trying to buy a bomb"

"And what are we supposed to do about him?" said Maurice, "Lead, follow, or ignore?"

"Cooperate," said Greta. "On the attack on the car I think that it looks like the only reason that they made a try for the car is that someone told them that anyone who was driving it could be squeezed for information. The thing is the car is only connected to us in France and Wales so someone from there had to be the source of the information. Julia said Blossom has several people looking into it since the most reasonable source of information would be someone in EUOPS. Blossom reserves the right to blow agents cover and when you are cooperating with someone there isn't any anyhow. Julia also said that she and Blossom and Pamela would appreciate a few baby pictures and how is Elise getting on. I suppose we should call everyone at the airport and tell them to come home."

"There is one more source that could tie you to the car," said Maurice, "the Francisci Family. I really don't trust them. If Lucien was dead and the fight over leadership over or if Lucien was back on his feet I would feel a lot surer of them."

"True," said Greta, "well, call everyone up, Maurice. If you and Asim are sleeping together, we have enough beds for everyone if Sara bunks in Elise's room and we scoot the crib into Dove's and my room, which would be handy anyhow. We need to check in with Lucien tomorrow first thing and tell him about the Egyptians and get him settled somewhere permanent."

****

Greta woke up to a rap on the door and opened her eyes and looked at the clock. It was five in the morning and she sat up and slipped out of bed. She pulled a robe over her pajamas and went to the door and opened it.

"You need a stronger door and some way to see who is outside or a way to block it, brigadier," said Charley. "Joey and I are ready to run, and Dove said you would want to run in the morning. Did you get enough sleep?"

"It would appear so," said Greta. "Let me grab my shorts and a top and put on my shoes and we can go. Where are we going to run to?"

"We thought we could run to the airport and have breakfast and then run back," said Charley. "It's only about two and a half miles each way but we thought we would take it easy today. We were wondering about the colonel finishing her parachute training. She has already done the five-mile accompanied HALO training jump, so she only needs a couple of solos for low opening and to complete the high opening jumps to a target sequence and, of course, the night jump into water with the five-mile swim, which is a piece of cake here. I had to do mine off the cost of Wales with the rest of E squadron and let me tell you, it was damn cold. Are you awake yet? You look like you were thinking about something."

"Actually, I was thinking about Dove getting you to have me run this morning," said Greta, "and her finishing qualifying for her SAS training. I think she should start almost immediately and get it out of the way. Be back in a sec."

Greta slipped back into the bedroom and pulled a pair of running shorts out of a suitcase, she slipped them on and pulled on a sport's bra then thought about it and changed into a bright red track suit and added a scarf and veil. She picked up her running shoes and socks and then went out and sat on the chair in the hall and put them on.

"Are you going to run in the track suit, ma'am?" said Charley. "Maybe we should run earlier when it is cooler."

"No, this is fine," said Greta, "but I may catch a ride back. One thing I don't want to do is offend local sensitivities. Besides it covers my face, and my shoulder holster."

"Good idea ma'am," said Charley. "We'll meet you at the gate."

Charley turned and went back into his room and Greta went down to the yard and started warming up exercises. She stopped and looked at the front yard for the first time in daylight. Sara had done a bit of gardening too. The house was now shielded with a perimeter planting of palm trees and blooming bushes. There were a series of offset precast concrete planters filled with soil and planted with flowers that were the right height for kneeling behind with an automatic rifle or submachine gun. The planters flanked a long stone path that lead to a paved seating area with chaise lounges and a table with an umbrella and the whole house was surrounded by a lawn that left an open field of fire to the front gate from any point.

A seven-foot deep and twenty-foot wide swimming pool, filled with water to within a few inches of the top, stretched totally across the front of the property from wall to wall and provided a blocking obstacle across the entire front lawn and the driveway. A decorative car bridge with a lacy open metal rail that provided no cover at all crossed the pool and led to the garage. To the left of the front gate, there was a water slide coming down from a blocky structure in a grove of newly planted palm trees. The building had a cement block privacy wall and a sun deck on top and was painted various shades of pastel pink and beige.

"You can see," Sara had said when she showed them a bit of what was there last night. "A frontal assault through the gate is in trouble unless they have a bunch of broad jumping basketball players over seven feet tall who can stand in the pool and shoot over the edge or broad jump six feet farther than the world record. The bridge is mined but it is also under crossfire from the water slide bunker on the left side of the drive and the planter barricades in front of the house."

"How in the world did you build a pool in a week?" said Dove, "It takes concrete considerably longer to harden."

"It's a kit," said Sara, "any shape any size plastic liners and a plumbing package. Just dig a hole and smooth it up and throw the liner in and fill with water. The pH, chlorine, temperature and water level are programed into a computer in the plumbing package and you only need a pool boy to look sexy and skim the trash. It took one day for the pool contractor to put it in. The bridge is a prefab and rated for a small van, then it breaks, and I also had Charley wire it. The water slide is fiberglass prefab sections and the supports are the building which is a bunch of reinforced poured concrete slabs with weld points. The pool controls, changing rooms and an armory for heavy weapons are inside the pool house. It is a bunker that has a firing platform on top for mortars and heavy and light machine guns and acts as an observation point up and down the approach streets. It also tends to attract attention away from the main house."

"My God, Sara," said Dove. "Do you think we need a fort in Egypt?"

"Yes," said Sara. "This whole place is a tinderbox. I lived here a long time and I know. It could explode any minute."

That, thought Greta, was true. The discussions with Colonel McMillian had underlined the seriousness of the current situation. Egypt had always been the large secular country that imposed peace and relative stability on the whole area and it could not be allowed to go Islamic militant. The 1979 treaty between Egypt and Israel was the first to recognize Israel, and Egypt was the first neighboring country to normalize relations with them and exchange ambassadors. True, it had cost the Americans a ton of money and military equipment and material to support the Egyptian military and maintain the peace, but not as much as the recent wars in Afghanistan and Iraq. Greta bet that the cousins were gnashing their teeth over their current foreign policy that supported democratic governments everywhere in spite of reality and local conditions.

She smiled when she remembered that she had twenty pounds riding on a bet that the duly elected government of

Afghanistan would collapse within two weeks of the departure of the last American troops. Merry, who had served there at various times had bet twenty minutes while Julia held that the current government people would beat the last troops out by at least two weeks. Well, at least she would see Lucien when she got to the airport to settle the problem of where to keep him.

"Ma'am?" said Charley. "Uh, we're ready if you are."

"Sorry," said Greta and shook her head and smiled, "lead on, sergeant."

Greta, Joey and Charley trotted down the drive to the bridge and up to the gate. Charley nodded, and the gate swung open and they all jogged out into the street that was strangely quiet in the early dawn light. Greta noticed with some amusement that Charley and Joey had changed into sweat pants and hooded sweatshirts. She wondered what was hidden inside their loose clothing then started running. She would hurt later but now it was starting to feel satisfying as her muscles loosened and her breathing stabilized. Maybe having an SAS sergeant major as a batman was going to work out, since she knew she didn't have the willpower to force herself to get up and run every morning but apparently he had enough willpower for two people, maybe three.

Greta was setting a fairly easy pace and Charley and Joey were staying with her, one was in the rear and one on her street side. They had been running for about twenty minutes when the Mediterranean Air Service building came in sight.

"Go," yelled Greta and took off as fast as she could run. Charley looked surprised and Joey dug in and sprinted with her. Charley was a bit slower but dug in and soon it was a three-way sprint down the center of the street with Greta leading, but losing ground steadily. As they dashed up to the entry door, Greta was half a step ahead and they all tried to go through the automatic door simultaneously. Greta ducked under Joey's arm as he slammed open the door and Charley turned sideways and squeezed through next to Joey almost losing his balance. They skidded to a halt in the lobby as several passengers waiting for the early morning flight to Aswan looked at them in amazement.

One of the desk clerks looked at them and then said, "The flight will not leave for half an hour yet so there is no need to hurry that much. Please don't run in the lobby."

Greta turned and walked down the hall to the business office and restrooms and Charley looked at the clerk.

"Lady had a bit of an emergency," said Charley. "Be back in a minute."

Then he and Joey followed Greta down the hall and stood in front of the door to the EUOPS office. When they were all there, Greta took off her veil and then swiped her access card and the door opened into the airlock door space. When the outer door closed, it activated the electronics in the inner door and Greta typed in her access code. The door opened into a small room with a full body scanner. Greta removed her pistol, shoulder holster and two clips of ammunition and put them in a plastic basket she placed on a scanner belt then she walked through the scanner. On the other side of the scanner she waited for Charley, two pistols and a fighting knife, and Joey, an Uzi machine pistol, two grenades and a knife. They all picked up the baskets with their weapons and walked through the door into the office to go to work.

The office was fully manned, and people were talking on phones, looking intently at real time satellite images of various areas and typing on computers. They glanced up as Greta walked toward her office and some of them smiled and waved and others nodded. She waved and walked into her office and sat down, then punched a button on her communications console.

"Yes ma'am," said a crisp female voice, "What can I do for you?"

"Is Lucien up yet?" said Greta, "I need to speak with him."

"Not yet ma'am," said the voice, "Would you like me to wake him?"

"No, nothing pressing," said Greta, "do I have messages?"

"Yes ma'am. I'll bring them in," said the voice, "two are in your personal code."

Greta looked at Charley and Joey standing against one wall and made a decision.

"Gentlemen," said Greta, "I believe I should finish my jump training along with Dove. Now, since you are bodyguards I am going to move a desk in here for Charley, so he can guard my body and put a desk in Dove's office so Joey can guard hers. You are also going to be personal assistants and we will work out exactly what that entails as we go along. Now, the selection of who guards who was based on Dove's pronouncement that she is going to get a red sports convertible and have Joey bleach his hair and wear sleeveless muscle shirts and mirror sunglasses when he drives her around. I would not like to disappoint her in this girlish fantasy and if you have no objections, Joey, I would like to present the red convertible sports car as an inducement to get her to finish parachute training."

"It would be my pleasure to assist Miss Abraham in any way that I can," said Joey, "actually driving a pretty girl around in a fast sports car doesn't trouble me at all."

"I didn't think it would," said Greta. "Now why don't you two arrange for desks and phones and computers and things then both of you go get something to eat. After that drive back and get the others and change while I see Lucien. Have Dove bring me some office clothes."

A secretary came in with a stack of papers and Greta took the download of the two coded messages in her private code and quickly typed the first one into her cell phone and pushed a button. The screen blacked and then cleared, and the message came up. It was from Julia. Julia was Lady Julia Robertson, Duchess of Montgeave and Viscountess Rhayader. She currently was the head of security and interrogation at a Welch EUOPS safe house, interrogation, and confinement compound. The compound was in an isolated valley in Wales where Greta had spent her pregnancy with Elise. When Elise had arrived, Greta had asked Julia and Willard Robertson to be two of Elise's godparents and they had accepted.

Julia was a nurse and also a retired MI6 assassin and operative from the cold war and considered to be one of the great ones. Greta, Dove and Julia were very close since they had all as the saying goes "picked up a gun" and become assassins. Although there was a degree of awe about Julia's past from the younger women, they could relate to each other and talk without constantly guarding their tongue. Julia had seen a lot of raw talent in Greta and had taken her under her wing during the Syrian gold theft operation and was instrumental in having Greta appointed to her current position as chief of the local EUOPS office. Probably the most important thing about Julia was she was a member of the Royal Security Oversight Committee, which is effectively the decision maker and sometimes the implementer for all aspects of English foreign policy. They decided what Whitehall did.

Julia's message was typically Julia:

Be there tomorrow. This whole thing stinks. Even Blossom agrees. Bringing some decent tea and the lanolin baby cream. Love Julia

Greta frowned. This would mean they needed more living space.

The second message was from Merry:

Almost everyone at conference would benefit from having one or more people killed. Analysis section said they would send me a few hundred of the most probable combinations but not to get too excited about any of them. They suggested that we allow the assassination next time and then analyze the results. Julia is on way with fire in her eye.

Greta cleared the messages and then looked over her desk for any other right now items. The door opened, and Dove walked in with a crying Elise.

"Here, feed our daughter," said Dove. "Charley just told me you authorized him to line up the training to finish my jump training. If it wasn't that I can't feed our daughter I would probably shoot you. What in the world is wrong with your head? You're going to have to go back for clothes because we were on the way already. After you feed the baby, you can go home and take a shower and get dressed and I can take her to see her father. What are you going to do about him?"

"Give me Elise," replied Greta. "You see this little hour glass on my desk? It is a nursing timer that doesn't go ding and wake up babies. I am going to finish the parachute training with you and see if it is something that we should be adding to the curriculum along with more make-up and disguise and remote assassination options. I don't know what to do about Lucien and the rest of them. He needs rehabilitation assistance and physical therapy at least and he isn't getting it here. The rebuilding at the jail is going to take time and we need to get Celeste and Nicole in school, too. I'll just wear my pilot uniform today and bring some clothes over later.

"Your timer just ran out of sand, change Elise over," said Dove. "You are getting fixated on the training school for female agents. What is a remote assassination option for heaven sakes?"

"Well for one thing, an armed drone," said Greta, "Mark just sent me a memo that he had swapped Merry out of four Whirligigs for us to evaluate and see if we can figure out somehow to kill people with them without wrecking them. He is putting the operators at Ben's place, but they are ours."

"Interesting," said Dove. "How are they armed?"

"Well they really aren't," said Greta, "They can carry twenty pounds of anything, caustic, poisonous, or radioactive, or a couple sixes of beer and a pizza. We got them to play with. Julia will be here today."

"If Elise is finished, I will go see Lucien and you can take a shower and get dressed," said Dove. "If you are going to run to work every morning, which is not a bad idea, you need to keep some stuff in a locker here."

"Yeah, well with Charley around, I probably will be running or getting nagged," replied Greta. "You got your sweats unpacked? I'm just an office person but you need to keep in shape to go in the field, you know."

"I am taking Elise and going and seeing Lucien before you finish that thought," said Dove. "You have already put a major strain on our relationship this morning with the parachutes."

Greta chuckled and walked down the hall to the pilot's lounge and transient quarters and swiped her staff card in the reader. She entered the ready room and looked at the service board. Units eight and three showed empty so she went and got a clean Mediterranean Air uniform from a locker marked Cpt. Steiner and grabbed her pilot's bag and hat. She walked to unit three in the transient pilot's overnight quarters and swiped her card and opened the door. The light came on when she opened the door and walked in. The bunk had been freshly made and the bathroom had fresh towels. She locked the privacy lock and then pulled off the sweat suit and her thigh holster and tossed it on the bed. Then she thought better of it and took the pistol and holster into the bathroom. She turned on the shower and stepped into the water and stood with her back to the spray as the hot flow of water softened the muscles in her neck. She held up her hair and let the water run unimpeded down her back and soak out the tension.

She did not need any more complications. She had an overflowing plate what with being a new nursing mother, getting her office organized, lining up somewhere to stay, taking care of Lucien, and figuring out what to do with his grandson, and oh yes before I forget, trying to prevent a potential nuclear war in the Middle East. The problem with motherhood was that she had not conceived Elise by being repeatedly raped by Mark. Far from it, she had been a full willing participant in all the sex and had occasionally flown back to the office for an overnighter when she was supposed to be in the field. Not only that she, well actually Mark, had the films to prove it. The fact that she was in a relationship with Dove and did love her and didn't want to hurt her or lose her did not alter the fact that if Charley walked in right now she knew exactly what would happen, maybe three or four times if he was up to it. That boy could sure kiss.

Greta poured shampoo on her hair and washed it vigorously and then climbed out of the shower and looked in the mirror. Not bad for a mama. She looked critically for stretch marks and didn't see anything and then turned sideways and admired her large breasts. She would still make out all right in the harem girl section of a North African slave market. However, harem slave is a relatively short messy career, and being the head of the Southern Operations Office of EUOPS might be, too, if she didn't get with the program. She would need to figure out what to do with Joey and Charley and Lucien and Sara today. Greta pulled fresh underwear from her pilot's bag and dressed in her uniform and a shoulder holster then coiled her hair up under her blue visor cap and put on a pair of mirrored sunglasses. She added pale pink lipstick and just a touch of rouge and looked at herself and nodded. She put the sweats and dirty underwear in a laundry bag and took it and her flight bag and unlocked the door and walked out.

Greta walked to her locker and opened it and threw the bag of dirty clothes in it. She would grab them tonight and take them home and wash them. She turned to the pilots' lounge and thought about a cup of coffee and whatever looked nourishing in the pastry bar and decided that it wouldn't kill her to have a donut if there was one available. She walked to the coffee bar and got a mug of coffee and looked at the various rolls and pastries. She shrugged and took a fresh croissant and a strawberry yogurt and put them on a tray and walked to the window side of the lounge and sat down at a table with a copy of the London times from yesterday open on it. She started reading about the latest guesses on when there would be an addition to the royal family and then turned to the newest scandal in the banking world. She supposed that she would have to take more interest in all things English now that she was a citizen.

Two crewmen in the maroon uniforms of Sahara Heavy Lift came in and looked around the room. They waved at two of the Mediterranean Air pilots sitting at a table on the other side of the room and then got coffee and sat down. The four pilots talked for a minute and then the two Mediterranean Air pilots got up when the scheduled flight to Luxor was called in the lounge. One of the Mediterranean Air pilots pointed at Greta and waved. Greta waved back and then started reading her paper again. There was a scrape as a chair was pulled back. Greta looked up. The two pilots from Sahara indicated the chairs. Greta smiled and indicated they were welcome.

"Hi," said one of the two men, "The guys just told us you are qualified in the Mi38 heavy. Been flying them long?"

"Not recently," said Greta, "They don't have any here, but they may get one or two if the business warrants it. You boys pretty well have the heavy lift business sewn up. I've got three or four hundred hours in the Mi38, though. I used to fly ferry flights from the Mil plant to here a couple years ago and I hauled freight for an oil company. Why?"

"We are in an embarrassing position right now," said the other pilot. "We have a client that has been having us fly various things to a camp out in the desert west of here and we have two choppers full of, umm boxes, that need to be delivered today. They pay well but they are a bit trigger-happy. Two days ago, one of their jumpy guards took a shot at one of our helicopters that was a bit early and it had to land with a hole in the fuel tank. They apologized and paid for the repairs and a bonus for the pilot and are picking up the costs for everything, but it's fixed now, and we need to get it out of there to keep up with scheduled flights. The problem is we only have two pilots available today because our one backup is off sick, and the other backup just got in a car wreck on the way to work. Everybody else is on a flight and we need someone to help us pick up the helicopter."

"They shoot at people?" said Greta. "I don't know. Who are they?"

"Like I said, we didn't ask because they pay really well," said the first pilot, "If I had to guess, I would say some kind of a training camp for a group of fundamental Muslims since they sure act that way. The thing is, there are a lot of them around out there and there are getting to be more all the time. Since they are the kind of people that are big in the government right now, we fly freight and keep our mouths shut."

"So, what do they pay?" said Greta. "And how long is the flight?"

"About an hour west of here in a big wadi with some old ruins and a bit of water," said the second pilot. "Not a bad place to land but a bit tricky when the sand is flying around, which it isn't."

"If you will fly in with us and take one of the choppers back, we will pay you five thousand dollars American," said the first pilot, "cash. Half now half when you land."

"Okay," said Greta, "but on the condition that I stay in the cockpit of the chopper I fly out in and I don't receive visitors since I don't think that Muslim fundamentalists are that big on women pilots. Whoever is flying out can supervise the unloading of my chopper and then take the other chopper and we can all leave together. I will need to be back by noon or somewhere about then for my own schedule. Is that doable?"

"No problem," said the first pilot. "Who are you?"

"Oh, just call me Julia," said Greta, "shall we go?"

Greta finished her coffee and stood up and grabbed her flight bag. She opened it and pulled out a thermos and filled it at the coffee bar and put it back in her bag and walked to the bathroom. The two Sahara pilots grabbed a few more donuts and some napkins and filled take away cups and sipped them as they waited.

Greta walked into the bathroom and pulled out her phone and hit Maurice's number. The phone rang and then Maurice came on the line.

"Get hold of the people that are running the Whirligigs and Taranis test drones," said Greta, "I just got recruited to go pick up a Sahara Heavy Lift Mi38 at what appears to be a big Muslim militia training camp in the desert west of here. I will go ahead and put a tracker in my flight bag. Follow along and get some film with the drones. The location of large militia training camps could be important to lots of people including us. I'll be back by noon."

"I'm on it," said Maurice. "We will also have a plane in the neighborhood for armed cover. Be careful."

Greta scrubbed off the make-up and tied a scarf around her neck to slip up over her lower face. She looked down at her breasts and shrugged. There wasn't much she could do about them right now. Then she walked out of the restroom and went to her locker and opened it. She stood behind the door and got another clip of ammunition for her pistol and a tracker. She thumbed on the tracker and dropped it into her bag next to a hand-held emergency transponder and grabbed a pair of headphones. Then she walked back to the Sahara pilots and they all went out the crew door and got in an electric cart and headed down the field to the Sahara terminal.

CHAPTER 9: SHOW AND TELL

Lucien was sitting in a recliner with Celeste standing on one side and Nicole sitting on the arm when Dove walked in. He was dressed in khaki drill pants and an open collar white shirt and his hair was freshly cut and combed. He looked alert and almost normal if you didn't know him. There was a bit of a wooden look and a slight downward twist to the left side of his face. A walker was sitting beside the recliner in easy reach and his shoes had been replaced with a pair of bedroom slippers. He had a tablet computer on a lap desk in his lap and was touching it with his right hand while his left hand lay across his lap.

"Very good, Signor Francisci," said Nicole. "Now if you want to save an Internet address and not a mail address. What would you do?"

Lucien looked up at Dove and smiled a slightly lopsided smile and gave the tablet to Nicole and pushed back the desk and held out his right arm. Dove walked over and kissed him and then sat Elise on his lap. He put his right arm around Elise and she looked up at him curiously. Did she know him? Elise brightened when she saw a familiar sock puppet and laughed and tried to grab the pig puppet on Nicole's hand. The puppet swooped down and tickled her stomach and she waved her arms and giggled. Then Nicole picked her up.

"I think I should move her before she gets you wet, Signor Francisci," said Nicole. "Here Celeste, take Signor Francisci's pad and we will go and see to our little girl."

"Well, that was a complete hijacking, Lucien," said Dove as she bent over and kissed him again. "How are you feeling?"

"Betr, Dob," said Lucien. "stl knt tk good. I got pad."

"I see that, and also two teachers," said Dove. "I should probably come take lessons, too. Do you have an account yet?"
"Fasebok," said Lucien, "klrgrnpa, gve pad."

Dove gave Lucien his pad and pushed the lap desk back over his lap and he put the pad down on it and started typing.

"This one finger typing takes some getting used to but then my two-finger typing was never that good anyway. Where is

Greta? We need to get somewhere today. Armand has arranged for us to go to a guesthouse at Saint Athanasius the Great school and hospital. It is located in the Zamalek District and is inside the cloister walls of the monastery. A sizeable donation to the building fund has allowed a few rules to be waived and Armand is supplementing Alonzo with a few of my people from the estate. Nicole and Celeste will be able to attend school there or continue their studies using internet. One of the sisters at their school in Corsica makes up lessons for girls that are sick or absent for acceptable reasons and sends them out every day. That way the girls can keep up with their studies. But I think that the chance to go to a foreign school for a while would be a good thing."

"Do you think that it is safe, Lucien?" said Dove. "I really am a bit worried about you being somewhere I can't keep an eye on you."

Lucien snorted and started typing again:
"I managed to get by for a number of years without you looking after me. I am grateful for you and Greta getting me away from the estate and my family and assorted wives and mistresses, but I don't think that it would look too good for us to be closely associated other than on a business basis. The monastery has managed to withstand mobs and even soldiers for over six hundred years and we will be taking a few extra precautions too. Where is Greta? We need to talk about my grandson and my daughter."

"She will be back for lunch," said Dove. "She is currently flying a load of contraband to what appears to be a training camp for one of the local terrorist organizations. We have a tail on her and we are going to see what is going on."

"Do one thng at time evr?" said Lucien, "rit aftr lunch thn."

"All right Lucien," said Dove. "Do you want me to do anything now?"

Celeste and Nicole came running back into the room with a shrieking Elise riding in Celeste's arms and pointing forward.

They stopped, and Celeste whirled in a circle while Elise waved her arms and giggled.

"Oh, look Signor Francisci," said Nicole. "See what our brilliant clever girl can do."

Celeste put Elise down and held her up, so she was sitting. Nicole took an inflated beach ball she had been carrying and sat down opposite Elise. Nicole rolled the ball slowly at Elise and Elise batted it with her hand so that it rolled back to Nicole. Nicole rolled the ball again and Elise batted it again and then looked at Dove and Lucien.

"Very good Elise," said Dove. "We will have to show your mother your new trick."

Lucien focused and then said very clearly, "Bravo."

Then he smiled and said it again and held out his right arm for Elise. Celeste picked Elise up and carefully transferred Elise to Lucien's arm and Lucien raised her to his face and kissed her cheek. Then he blew on her stomach and she laughed and squirmed. Celeste took her again and sat her on the floor and leaned her against a pillow. The girls got out the sock puppets and started telling the three little pigs in French.

"M fine now," said Lucien watching the girls and baby. "After lunch?"

"I guess I will leave Elise if Celeste and Nicole want to watch her," said Dove. "At least until lunch."

Celeste and Nicole nodded and continued with the puppet show they were putting on for the wide-eyed Elise.

Dove walked from the guest quarters and into the office area and went to the room where the tracking equipment was. Maurice was standing and looking at one screen where a red dot was slowly moving across the map of Egypt. Above the screen, a large screen television showed a picture of two helicopters flying across a landscape of grey broken hills, tumbled rock, and dry sand. Dove watched as the shot pulled back and the two helicopters shrank to dots against a grey background.

"Where are these pictures coming from?" said Dove, "This isn't from a Whirligig."

"No, Mark conned Merry into letting us have the use of a Taranis since everyone is interested in large groups of men at camps out in the western desert," said Maurice. "There is a theory that it could be a group of terrorists linked to Al-Qaeda or, get this, a secret Egyptian army training camp."

"Why would the Egyptian army have a secret training camp?" said Dove. "This is their country."

"No, that is where the problem for them is," said Maurice. "If they are planning on moving against the Morsi regime, they might feel they need something special. Unless you have prepared troops, a coup is hard to spontaneously field. As a matter of fact, I can't recall any really spontaneous coups."

"I sure wish Greta hadn't gone," said Dove. "She is driving herself too hard. Granted she was uniquely qualified since she is the only one of us that can fly helicopters, but we also could have just put a tracker on one of the Sahara ships now that we know about the camp. When she gets back we need to go see Lucien immediately, Maurice. What do you know about the Saint Athanasius the Great school and hospital?"

"Really old, really swank, really good, and really, really exclusive," said Maurice. "Why?"

"Lucien has got a guest house there and wants to move in today or tomorrow," said Dove. "I'm not sure if Greta wants him out of her sight although Armand arranged it."

"Why don't we talk to Armand and check this out when Greta gets back," said Maurice. "This sounds fishy and I am quite surprised since Armand more or less said Greta was supposed to keep an eye on Lucien. Anyway it is to late to do anything today."

"Sir," said one of the technicians, "look at this."

Dove and Maurice turned and looked at the screen of the television showing the direct link from the jet powered Taranis. The picture showed two helicopters that had been following a broad valley with a meandering dry riverbed turning into a narrow high walled canyon. The Taranis turned and followed the line of flight of the helicopters and caught them settling onto a flat area in the shadow of the eastern wall of the canyon. Another helicopter was already there, and the two landing helicopters kicked up dust from what was a small playa covered with tire tracks.

"We are recording, aren't we," said Dove, "We need IR too. I don't think we should make another pass right now. The Taranis is stealthy but there is nothing to mask the sound after the helicopters land and there is an awfully lot of quiet out there."

"Yes ma'am, we are recording UV, IR, three densities of visible light and a false color image. I suggest we go around in a big circle and climb to thirty thousand feet and reduce power until we see the helicopters taking off. Then we could try another pass. Or just go back tomorrow now that we know where it is."

"Yeah, Greta is going to want to see this," said Maurice, "look at all the tents and there are six or eight white trucks coming out from what appears to be an overhang. Since the canyon runs north south, the light is subdued except at noon and the tents are the same grey as the dirt. Tire tracks are harder to hide though but I don't think that anyone has a reason to look here for anything. I wonder what she is going to do?"

****

As the helicopter settled, Greta looked out at a large military camp. There were probably three or four hundred two-man tents pitched on the floor of the canyon and under the overhand on the east side there were a dozen or so large wall tents located next to a small pond. Against the back wall of the canyon there were the ruins of a large stone building and numerous smaller mud brick buildings. The whole complex was enclosed in a thick stone wall with an open gate. Above the gate an ornate cross was carved in the keystone. Several white Department of Antiquities trucks pulled out of a motor pool and drove toward the helicopters. The pilot finished the shutdown and unplugged his helmet. Greta pulled hers off and then looked out the window as one of the trucks pulled up to the helicopter and the freight door came open.

"Interesting," said Greta. "What is this? An archeological site?"

"If it is, they sure want to protect it, judging by the amount of ammo and machine guns we have been bringing in," said the pilot. "I'll go back and keep them from wrecking everything and you can stay here. When they finish unloading, I'll do the walk around and shut the door. I'll take the mechanic and the chopper he repaired and head out first and you can follow. If we need to talk, I'm Sahara one, you're Sahara two and the other chopper is Sahara three. Land at the terminal and we will pay you off and give you a ride back to Mediterranean Air."

Greta nodded, and the pilot walked back and yelled at the men unloading the helicopter to leave at least something without a dent. Greta closed the pilot's compartment door and locked it and then pulled out her phone and hit Maurice's number. It clicked a few times and then emitted a burst of static that cleared as Maurice came on the line.

"Greta, are you all right?" said Maurice. "We got your phone call. We have a Taranis loitering around and taking pictures and acting as a relay. What have we got here?"

"We've got a bunch of skin heads in white tee shirts and combat boots with Department of Antiquities trucks unloading crates of ammo and barrels of water," said Greta. "There is what appears to be an abandoned monastery built under an overhang and a pond of water and date palms. This could be the same bunch that jumped our car at the Garden City apartment since they are using Department of Antiquities trucks and are dressed the same way. We should be out of here in under an hour."

"Okay, we will stay with you on the way back," said Maurice. "You need to see Lucien when you get in and Julia and Willard are here already. They have borrowed an estate in the Zamalek District on Gezira Island from one of Julia's cousins. They would like you to come to dinner tonight and Ben just said that Southerland Oil bought the jail. He would like to talk to you about it today or tomorrow."

"Okay," said Greta. "I'll be back in an hour or so."

The lock clicked, and the cabin door opened, and the pilot slipped in. Greta slipped her phone back in her pocket and looked at the pilot.

"Yeah, no signal," said the pilot. "I guess satellite phones work about half the time but nothing for us poor slobs. Look, what time is your flight?

"It's the one twenty to Luxor," said Greta. "Is there a problem?"

"Kind of," said the pilot. "We have a very strong request to ferry one of the bigwigs back to Cairo. Apparently, he has a plane to catch and our problem this morning has put him in a bind. Could you just go ahead and go back on your own and haul him?"

"Yeah, no problem," said Greta. "When does he want to go?"

"Now," said the pilot. "I'll have him load up. You care if he sits right seat?"

"Not if he keeps his hands in his lap," said Greta. "You did the walk around?"

"Not yet," said the pilot. "They still have some stuff to unload. I'll walk and then give you a thumb up. The guy you are ferrying back has your cash."

"Okay, send him in," said Greta. "I'll start a preflight right now."

Greta plugged in her helmet and put it on and then started checking the controls and electronics. She pulled her scarf up to cover her chin and mouth in case the passenger was someone she knew and then pulled out her phone again and hit Maurice's number.

"Okay, I am going to leave my phone on for a while," said Greta. "I have a VIP passenger to haul back and will be leaving first, as soon as the ship is unloaded. I'll try to get him to talk a bit if possible. Apparently, he is someone important and maybe we can learn something. I'll put the phone in the back of my helmet and you should be able to get the conversation. Use a computer to sort the noise out."

Greta slid her phone up under the back of her helmet and pulled her collar up to anchor it in place. Then, she started setting radio frequencies and consulting her flight chart. The Mi38 was equipped with the latest moving map GPS but it had been turned off during the flight out and the pilot had used a sectional and compass headings. Greta flipped on the GPS and set it for the Cairo airport and then when it was apparent it was working got her location coordinates. Then she looked at her sectional and located where she was on it. The map showed a canyon adjacent to a dry river canyon with no name. There was a large dry lake a couple of miles to the south that should be a landmark that would help find the place if all else failed.

Someone touched her on the shoulder and she looked up at a man wearing a white cotton keffiyeh or ghutra, the traditional Iraq head cloth with one end pulled across his face. Greta indicated the helmet lying in the copilot's seat and the man looked at it and then picked it up and pulled off his headscarf and uncovered his face. Then he put on the helmet and Greta plugged it into the intercom.

"Can you hear me?" asked Greta. "The volume control is on the right side of the helmet. Twist forward for softer backward for louder, one, two, three, testing."

The man nodded and then sat down and started fastening the harness and adjusting it. Greta looked out the front of the helicopter and saw the pilot standing with both hand in front of him and both thumbs pointing up.

Greta waved and then said, "Okay, I am going to check the freight door and then I will get you to Cairo as soon as possible. They told me you had a flight to make. What time is it?"

"Later tonight, but I need to talk to some people as soon as possible and before I leave," answered the man. "I would appreciate a fast trip."

Greta nodded and then unplugged her helmet and walked back to the freight door.

"Maurice," she said as soon as she was out of the flight deck, "Hamid Masoud is sitting in the copilot's seat. Monitor my calls and get ready to tail him as soon as we land at the Sahara terminal."

Greta checked the door and then walked back to the flight deck and sat down and belted in, plugged in her communications, finished her check list, and started the first turbine, then the second, brought up the power and went straight up. Then she banked left and headed for Cairo. Twenty-eight thousand feet above the helicopter, a dusty blue colored drone recorded the takeoff, then it flew back and forth with big slow turns to keep pace with the lower, slower MI38 as it flew across the desert.

*****

"I may have a potential seller," said Armand. "There is a Chechen general that is active in the current fighting on the Chechen side who says that he knows someone who might have a nuclear device that is for sale. It is a warhead off of an old Soviet GR-1. It was a replacement that had just been rebuilt just before the last round of reductions and was shipped but never installed. The old warhead that was installed was shipped with the missile when it was decommissioned and the new one was appropriated for potential use or sale."

"What are the specifications and how powerful is it?" said the hooded figure sitting across the table from Armand.

"I don't know yet," said Armand. "I have been unable to contact the party that has the device since the general is playing coy and wants a finder's fee, so we do not have an asking price or any assurance the device will be active or usable. Also, I still haven't received permission to broker the deal from my associates."

"In other words, you have still not found us a device," said the hooded man. "We may need to explore other options."

"That is not what I said," said Armand. "We have several leads, but this one appears to be the most promising and easily accessed. We still only have a vague commitment on your part and this is one of the reasons I have not been able to convince the people that I must satisfy to invest much more money or time in this project. It is exceptionally risky but does have the potential to place us in a good position in the weapons market. Still, things must be handled discretely since things do happen to people that engage in the buying and selling of this type of weapons. Remember the Estonians?"

"Everyone pulls that bogey man out of the bag when we discuss our proposal," said the hooded man. "We do not fear the displeasure of the western vigilantes and their ideologically bankrupt philosophy of suppressing the other people of the world. As for the Jews, they cannot touch us, and we are not interested in their petty struggles."

"You may not be troubled, but the potential sellers may be," said Armand. "After all, the Estonians are the one who sold the missiles and they were destroyed, along with the buyers. But if you want us to continue negotiating with the current leads, I am afraid I am going to have to ask you for something tangible to present to my associates."

"What would you suggest?" said the hooded figure.

"Oh, a moderate amount to defray expenses and provide assurance that you can actually pay for a device," said Armand. "How about six million euros, in gold."

"I will present your suggestions to my superiors," said the hooded man. "How should I contact you?"

Armand reached in his briefcase and pulled out a pair of cell phones in plastic bubble wrap packages and handed it to the hooded man.

"I will call one of these phones with another one like it later today," directed Armand. "Don't answer the phone just recall the number in the missed call menu and phone me from the other phone. If I cannot answer, leave me a message to call back. I will call the phone you used to return the call with within twenty-four hours to arrange a meeting. Throw both phones away when we have arranged a meeting."

The hooded man accepted the phones and Armand stood up. They shook hands and Armand walked to the door followed by the man. Armand exited the room and the other man shut the door and then walked to the door of the connecting room and knocked. An Egyptian man in a casual outfit opened the door and the man walked into the room and took off his suit and packed in a suitcase. Then he put on a padded bra, a long wig and a scarf and veil and a cotton jilbab. The man in the casual outfit looked and nodded and then he went in the other room and pushed a stroller with a two-year-old in it out and to the door. The apparent couple with their baby went down stairs and got in a taxi and left.

****

It was mid-afternoon and Colonel Bryon McMillian was drinking a coffee in the dining room of the Intercontinental Hotel at a table that had a clear view of the lobby and entry. He picked up that morning's copy of Daily News, the only daily English newspaper published in Cairo and signaled the waiter. Although he was dressed in a blue business suit and a muted tie, he still wore his officer's shoes and it was apparent that either he had a particularly well-muscled left arm or was wearing a shoulder holster. The waiter hurried over and the colonel ordered another pot of coffee with cream and sugar on the side and two more cups. Then he opened the paper and read about the mess in Syria. Ten minutes later, Maurice joined him at the table and poured coffee and then gestured at the financial pages. He was carrying a folder and a brief case. The colonel handed him the financial section and filled another cup. Five minutes later, Armand joined them. Maurice and the colonel stood and shook hands with Armand and then sat down and folded the paper. The waiter came over again and asked if the gentlemen required anything else and Maurice ordered a basket of fresh croissants.

"Oh well, bring me and my friends a basket of Ka'ek Masri too. They are date rolls," explained the colonel. "And more hot coffee. We will be out on the terrace. We have a real estate problem to discuss."

"Oh," said Armand. "I thought it was only an ownership problem?"

"It appears we have a new player, or an old player that wasn't mentioned in the original deal," said Maurice. "We are somewhat puzzled, but we may have a partial answer about the things that transpired at the apartment a few days ago. We have several new things to consider this morning. I brought some pictures you need to see. What about your latest friend, Armand? Did you find anything out? Also does your Godfather know you are in town?"

"I was going to drop by later, but no, not now," said Armand. "How is he?"

"Much better," said Maurice, "but did you suggest he move to a bigger place?"

"No," said Armand, "I was letting his daughter and her group take care of that. It was his desire. Why?"

"We may need two more baskets of pastries and several pots of coffee," said Maurice. "First, your friend, Armand?"

"Let's go and get a table outside and have the waiter close the doors so we are alone in the garden room," said the colonel, "it is quiet during the day and almost impossible to observe. Still, I would guard my tongue these days."

"Yes," said Armand, "let's see what you have and let me make a couple calls and then we should probably go to visit my Godfather since he is the one we need permission from for anything."

"Excellent idea," said the colonel, "ah, here comes the food. I'll have the waiters take it to the garden room and give them a couple hundred pounds."

Armand and Maurice nodded and stood and followed the colonel who intercepted a group of waiters and followed them to a secluded gazebo at the end of the terrace. The inside of the gazebo was six sided and had couches on all the sides and a number of low round tables. The waiters spread the food on a round table with six chairs and then stood hopefully around. The colonel reached in his pocket and started handing out Egyptian fifty-pound notes until each waiter had received a tip. Then, they all bowed and disappeared.

"Knock when you check back," said the colonel to the waiters and shut the door, "the place has windows to keep out mosquitos and make it soundproof. It also has roll down black out curtains to keep it private. You could rent it for after dinner drinks for a ruinous price when I was in military college. The outside terrace on this end isn't screened and the mosquitos get something fierce at night, so everyone moves to the screened area on the other end. This was known as the lost and found department.

"Oh," said Maurice, "I'm fairly sure what got lost, but what was found?"

"Some of the young ladies found out if they actually liked it," said the colonel. "What photos did you bring?"

Maurice opened the folder of pictures at the desert camp. They showed an early morning picture taken from the east when the grey tents each cast a square shadow. Another picture showed the ruins under the overhang and the pool and command tents. The white Department of Antiquities trucks were visible backed into a parking area. A third picture had been taken straight down from above that showed the playa. The playa was covered with vehicle tracks and had four mesh screen helicopter landing pads in the center.

Another low angle picture showed that there was a strange heat signature further up the canyon where a large grey canvas the same color as the rock hung from pins. Several hot spots showed through the canvas and there were other shadowy reflections.

"There are six hundred two-man tents that we have photographed," said Maurice, "they have twenty-six Department of Antiquities trucks parked in the open and six or seven presumably armored tracked vehicles behind the camouflage curtain. From an analysis of the tread width and tire track spacing, we think the vehicles are a mixture of Russian BMP-3 tracked armored personnel carriers and either BRT-60 or BTR-70 wheeled attack vehicles. One of the things that we discovered after reviewing pictures of several trucks parked under the overhang is that the people at the oasis have SA-18 Igla ground to air missiles mounted on a mobile launch platform on the back of some of the trucks. The thing is, the Russians sold this type of antiaircraft missiles as well as the armored personnel carriers to the Egyptian army."

"And this means" said the colonel, "exactly what?"

"It means that these people have a better than even chance of being part of the Egyptian Army," said Maurice. "Would you like to comment?"

"I think I need to ask around," said the colonel. "But also, as you know, this type of equipment was also sold to Lebanon and Syria, among others. There were also about three thousand Igla missiles and a thousand launchers sold to Libya that have gone missing since Khadafy was thrown out and also dozens of Libyan armored vehicles can't be accounted for. You could be right, there are several opinions in the high command on what to do right now and they could be radical members of the Army or just terrorists. Can I have copies of the pictures to show my superiors?"

"Only the ones that do not show the ruins or the full layout of the camp," said Maurice, "partial views will be enough to provide proof. The chief said we don't want anyone phoning up and tipping them off and right now the camp could be lots of places. Also, we will be watching them now twenty-four seven."

"I will nose around and come over this evening," said the colonel, "now Armand, did you find out anything more about our purchaser?"

"Yes, I did" said Armand, "I have never met any of their representatives before and I told them that there was no chance of a deal if we were not going to meet since our side and the prospective seller were getting nervous about so much air time what with the American NSA and all. Their representative scoffed at the Americans and said they were, "degenerate capitalist pigs" and shouldn't be feared. Now, this is a naïve and unreasonable attitude, and something left over from a long time ago."

"Well, Americans are capitalist for sure, degenerate to a certain extent, although far too prudish to carry it off really well," said Maurice, "and the men are pigs if you listen to their women. But there are very few places in the world where this is knee jerk language anymore, and the American digital technology is very good, damn scary, and not to be ignored or discounted."

"So, what did you conclude Mister Gerard?" said the colonel. "Before you called me with your suspicions, of course."

"Well, their representative was wearing a ski mask and a blue suit of local manufacture," said Armand, "but his hands were bare. His manicure was abominable, his teeth were not even up to European standards and he was Asian."

"Yes, I see," said the colonel. "Strange how people don't cover their hands. Well, a man and an Asian woman and a child left the hotel when you signaled and so we followed them. They drove to the airport and the woman got out with a small suitcase and the man and child drove away. We followed the man and have an address. The woman went into the ladies room and an older Asian lady with long black hair, glasses, and wearing a blue suit came out a few minutes later and purchased a ticket to Shanghai using a debit card on a numbered account issued by the International Bank of Trade and Finance in Bern, Switzerland. One of our agents managed to get a seat on the plane and we will be hearing from him in this evening. We also sent six agents and a plane to Shanghai in case we want to bring the person back."

"This is rather curious," said Maurice, "an Asian negotiator representing a Middle Eastern terrorist organization?"

"I rather think that you may have that backwards," responded the colonel, "Shall we all go tend our other business and get together at eight or so for dinner?"

"Why don't you come to our place?" suggested Maurice, "You were there last night. I will order a good dinner from the Marrakesh Café and we can talk about what we find out today. Call if anything pressing comes up."

Maurice, Armand and the colonel stood up and signaled a waiter who was standing a discrete distance away. The waiter walked to the door of the gazebo and opened the door. The colonel nodded and signed the bill.

"Did anyone look interested, Yousif?" said the colonel holding up an American fifty-dollar bill.

"A man came in and tried to come out on the terrace," said the waiter, "I told him it was closed to be sprayed for mosquitos and he would have to sit inside. He offered me a bribe and I took it but told him if he didn't want to sit in a fog of bug killer, I would recommend the other terrace. He agreed, and I seated him and brought coffee. He said that a young lady would be joining him, and she did. They had a conversation and then left separately a few minutes ago. I took pictures."

Maurice pulled a hundred euro note from his wallet and held it up, "We would like to buy your memory card, please."
The young man took the card out of his camera and handed it Maurice who handed him the money. The colonel handed the waiter the banknote. Armand took two small envelopes of white powder out of his inside jacket pocket and held them on his palm.

"Who were they, Yousif," asked Armand, "I'm sure you know them."

"The gentleman is a member of the government and the young lady is a foreign television reporter," answered Yousif and reached for the envelopes.

"Names?" said Armand and closed his hand.

"He is the Assistant Minister of Defense and she is Margret Perry the journalist," replied Yousif. "They meet here once or twice a week and she gives him money."

"Very good," Yousif," said Armand. "Watch and see what they do. Someone will bring you a little recorder to put under their table and a little controller to turn it on and off. I will tell someone to come and give you your usual supply, free of charge, in exchange for the tapes. Tell them that Mr. Snow sent you."

Armand dropped the two bags of cocaine in the outstretched hand of the waiter and smiled. The waiter hurried away, and the colonel looked at Armand.

"You are aware that the penalty for selling drugs is very harsh in this country?" said the colonel. "You could be put away for years for what you did."

"Actually, I didn't sell anything," said Armand. "I gave away two envelopes of talcum powder for an embarrassing itch for all anyone can prove, colonel. Also, I was able to find out that your Assistant Minister of Defense is taking bribes from a respected television journalist, and incidentally a CIA operative, which you didn't know. We all work in the best way we can and it would appear cooperation should be based on trust, don't you think?"

The colonel sighed and said, "Yes, yes we should, and I do appreciate the knowledge. Now, I have to decide what it means and who to discuss it with. Until dinner tonight at eight, Au revoir."

Maurice and Armand watched as the colonel drove off in his car and a teen-age couple in jeans, tee shirts and helmets painted to match their Vespa pulled out of an alley and followed him. A taxicab with no passengers pulled away from the front of the hotel and joined the procession.

"Now that is interesting," said Armand. "The young couple is employed by us. Is the cab one of yours?"

"No," replied Maurice. "We have been relying on your surveillance people since they seem to be very dependable. Who do you think the cab belongs to?"

"I have no idea," said Armand, "Let's find out and then we can go talk to Lucien. Our car."

A Mercedes town car pulled up and a man got out and nodded to Armand and opened the back door. Armand nodded and then got in and slid across the seat. Maurice got in and the chauffer got in front and drove off. Armand dialed his cell phone and explained about the taxi and then nodded.

"Well that is taken care of," said Armand. "The couple are going to the stadium and attending a minor league soccer game and be observed by some of our people to see if there is anyone interested in them. Another young man, a messenger on a bicycle, is following the cab. Now what is this about Lucien moving to larger quarters?"

"That was something that came up first thing this morning when Dove dropped in to see Lucien," explained Maurice, "Lucien said that you had made arrangements for him to move to the Saint Athanasius the Great school and hospital today."

"No, I did not," said Armand. "Has there been any effort to remove him from the temporary quarters at the airport?"

"No, he is still there," said Maurice, "I think that I will call on ahead and put half a dozen armed men outside his quarters until we arrive. Excuse me."

Maurice dialed his phone and put it on speaker so Armand could hear. When Dove answered, he said that Armand had not arranged for Lucien to go anywhere and to put a bunch of guards outside Lucien's quarters right now. He also asked if there had been anyone trying to move Lucien.

"No," said Dove, "No one has come to try to move Lucien and we wouldn't haven't done anything before we checked anyhow. I did phone Armand's office, but they said he was on a flight and wouldn't be available until later this evening. I suggested that Lucien, Alonzo and his family might want to look at our place and see it, just to get out a bit, and we are there now. Lucien has a new portable computer that I got him, and Celeste is showing him how to do things on it. He is doing quite well typing with one hand. He has also started trying to squeeze a ball with his other hand. He has been working with the physical therapist you sent this morning. He took Lucien outside in a wheelchair he brought when Celeste and Nicole decided to go swimming a few minutes ago."

"This is Armand," said Armand. "Does the wheelchair have a safety belt?"

"Yes," said Dove, "It does why?"

"Shoot the physical therapist right now," said Armand. "I did not send him, and he is going to belt Lucien in the chair and hit him on the head and push him in the swimming pool. We will be there in ten minutes."

CHAPTER 10: QUESTIONS AND ANSWERS

Armand leaned forward and told the driver to step on it. The car shot ahead and started swerving through traffic. It shot up to the gate of the Heliopolis house and started honking the horn. The gate guard was nowhere to be seen and Maurice opened his door and dove out while pulling out his pistol. He rolled to one side and then sprinted to the gatehouse and looked into the yard. To the far side of the lawn by the swimming pool the guard was bending over a man and Dove, Celeste, and Nicole were standing looking at him. Lucien was sitting in a wheelchair facing the gate and saw Maurice. He waved and yelled something, and the guard came over to open the gate.

By this time, Armand had joined Maurice and they walked through the gate and over the bridge to the far side of the swimming pool. Dove was holding a phone in one hand and a pistol in the other she was talking on the phone and looking quite angry. Celeste was wet and shivering and Nicole was standing beside Lucien holding his hand and looking very protective while he patted her hand.

"These young ladies are very capable, Armand," said Lucien. "I would like to extend them my thanks in a more tangible way. Would you please set up an educational fund in their names? We will discuss deposits later."

"Certainly, Lucien," replied Armand. "What happened?"

"Well obviously someone has gotten to at least some senior people at the Corsican estate," answered Lucien. "I got a phone call from, well someone there, that said that you had arranged a house for me at a very exclusive hospital and school here in Cairo. One of Greta's local young ladies knew of the place and gave it a very good report, so I called our local representative and had him run a check. It is a very good location and has good facilities but is not somewhere I would feel comfortable. Also, there was no record of anyone arranging for a villa there for Alonzo's family and me. Besides, Dove and Greta have been taking care of me and my daughter and I was dubious that you would act without consulting me and so when Dove suggested we leave the airport and come here where the security is much better, I agreed. This is a very nice place, Armand, and I think I may want to stay here. Dove, Greta and my daughter live upstairs and there is a small, although very comfortable apartment downstairs. As you can see, the place is a fortress."

"What about the person by the pool?" asked Maurice, "Who is he?"

"Patience, Maurice," replied Lucien. "We will know everything in a while. But he came to the airport and presented a medical order from the hospital and said he was a physical therapist and nurse and was here to evaluate me. We hadn't told anyone at the airport to not tell people we were here so he probably just asked and they sent him on. I believe he actually is a nurse since he has been helpful in a number of ways, but when he arrived we were quite distrustful of the whole situation and I decided to let him in and see what he did or attempted to do. He examined me and helped me bend my arms and legs several times, which is painful, and then suggested I start squeezing a little rubber ball with my bad hand, which I can. Also, you can hear that my speech, while a bit slow is almost normal. If I slow down and think deliberately, I can speak almost normally."

"I am very thankful that you appear to be on the mend, Lucien," replied Armand. "Did you recognize who made the call about the transfer?"

"Yes, and they took sick at work this morning and left and can't be found anywhere," replied Lucien. "They either left by private boat or float plane or they could be hiding on the island since we always watch the airports and the ferry terminals. They might have taken the hydrofoil, but we have people at the terminal in France. I told security to find him but not to kill him."

"What about this man here?" asked Armand," I believe we should talk to him rather forcefully, and here Celeste, slip on my coat you're cold. When did you suspect him?"

"Ah well, their plan was rather well thought out, although it must have been spur of the moment, but I have seen this before," said Lucien. "You remember the German? Well, the nurse suggested that if the girls wanted to swim, he could take me out into the sun and so the girls put on their suits while the nurse transferred me to the chair and tightened up the seat belt. Celeste and I spoke Corsican for a second and she brought me a lap robe, a law enforcement grade Taser and a very sharp knife to cut the seat belt, which I did under the robe. We all went out and the nurse tried to push me in the pool, but Nicole jammed on one chair brake as hard as she could, and the chair spun around. I hit the nurse with the Taser and he fell in the pool. He was trying to climb out when I gave Celeste the Taser and she used it on his head. Apparently, they work better in water because he stopped breathing and sank. Celeste dove in and pulled him up and the gate guard pulled him out and gave him CPR and then handcuffed him when he started breathing."

"I called Sara and she is sending a plumbing van to pick him up and take him to Ben's new place," said Dove. "We can lock him up in one of the cells in the administration building basement and discuss things with him at our leisure. I do wish you had told me exactly what you were planning to do, Lucien. I was terrified when Armand called."

"I am truly sorry, my dear," answered Lucien. "But we needed a good gun to stay with Elise in case something else happened while the girls and I took care of this problem. They are getting very good, although they both have only been old enough to help their mother and father for a year or so."

Lucien sighed and then went on, "Armand, it is apparent that there is some disagreement among the senior leadership group regarding my continuation as the leader of the family. I highly resent this and will be resuming my duties as the head of the family immediately. I would like you to arrange a conference call tomorrow and I will talk to everyone. I am inclined to let the breach of discipline pass, since killing the wounded lion has a historic precedent, but I just cannot. Someone in our family tried to have me killed and they must be discovered and called to account. Set up a conference call and a time personally and notify Greta."

"Yes Lucien," said Armand, "Where would you like to take the call?"

"I will originate the call and will call everyone's number," said Lucien. "I will also be discussing living arrangements with Greta when she gets back. Now, tell me why you are here and not in Geneva talking to potential customers like you are scheduled to be?"

"The people who are interested in the device wanted an urgent meeting," explained Armand. "They indicated that they believed the situation in Egypt was deteriorating rapidly and we needed to act very quickly. I squeezed them for six million euros in gold as a good faith pledge to do business."

"Do we have anything to sell them," questioned Lucien, "and if so, what?"

"No, nothing," replied Armand. "We will have to see if they come up with the money and then figure out what to do. I'm not sure how much longer I can stall them. Maurice knows everything that happened at the meeting and since it appears you are right about opposition and are going to originate the call, I should really get on to Geneva. Everyone thinks I am on the way right now, which is probably why they made the attempt on your life now since everyone knew I was out of touch and no one could check with me on the proposed move. Perhaps a bit of engine trouble or passport problems would be a good excuse for my late arrival and pretended ignorance of anything happening here. I'll take the car and get a charter from Greta's company. Until tomorrow, Lucien, and I must say I'm relieved you are taking over again. I have my hands full with the people that want a bomb. I suppose I should look for one, but I guess I should discuss that with Greta and her people first. I do remember the Estonians."

Armand walked to the waiting car that had pulled through the gate when he and Maurice had run to the pool. The gate guard was just letting in a van that said Moussa and Sons Construction that was driven by a gigantic man with a shaven head. Armand waved a hand at the van and then got in the car and drove out while the van continued across the bridge and parked. The door opened and a large muscular man over six feet tall got out. He was huge, had a shaved head and had an expressionless face. He was brown from the sun and had flat pale blue eyes with no expression. As he walked he kneaded a tennis ball in his hands alternately crushing it flat and then letting it expand.

"Sara sent me," said the man. "She said you had someone that needed delivered somewhere."

"This is Amir Moussa. Amir, this is Lucien," said Dove. "Amir and his father are contractors, Moussa and Son. Their company did the rebuilding here at the house. They do quite a bit of work for Sara and now us. They are renovating the new facility at the old detention center for Ben."

"Sir," said Amir. "I am honored to meet you and wish you a speedy recovery, sir. Your illness has been the subject of some discussion and questions among the construction unions. Is this the package Sara wants transported?"

Amir prodded the handcuffed man who was still face down by the pool, and very quiet.

"Yes, could you take him to the administration building at the old detention center and put him in one of the holding cells in the basement," said Dove. "We will decide what to do with him later."

The man suddenly rolled over into the pool and sank. Celeste sighed and pulled off Armand's suit coat and dove in the pool again. She grabbed the man by his handcuffed hands and pulled him to the surface and Amir took hold of his arms and then pulled the man out and held him upside down by his legs. The man coughed, and a spout of water ran out of his mouth and nose and he started gasping and gaging. Amir held him suspended until he started breathing normally then walked over and put him in the back of the van and fastened him to loops in the floor with several industrial rubber bungee cords and shut the door. Then he walked back to the group by the pool.

"Will you be sending someone to tend him, Miss Dove," said Amir, "or should I arrange for a guard?"

"I'll get hold of someone to meet you, Amir," said Maurice. "If you could please take him there and take him down stairs without anyone noticing?"

"Not a problem, we have a lot of stuff stacked in the parking lot that shields the door," said Amir. "I am very pleased and gratified to meet you, Don Francisci."

Amir got in the van and drove to the gate. Dove looked at Lucien and at Maurice. Then she frowned.

"Celeste, you are going to freeze," said Dove. "Remind me to get the pool heater up and running so you girls and I can actually swim in the pool. You and Nicole can take Lucien to the house and get changed. We will clean up here and then come up."

Celeste got behind Lucien's wheelchair and pushed it up the path to the house and Dove and Maurice gathered up the Taser, lap throw, a pistol that had been taken out of the back of the nurses pants when he was pulled out of the pool the first time and Armand's suit coat. Then Dove walked around the pool looking for anything else. She picked up a couple of pieces of paper and a beer can that had apparently been thrown over the wall and put it and the paper in a trash container.

"I didn't tell Amir Lucien's last name," said Dove, "and I am not sure how much we should get involved in family business. Apparently, the Franciscis have interests in at least the local construction business, but then we have been using their people to do our local surveillance, so I don't know why I am surprised. Another thing is, that it does appear that Celeste and Nicole know what they are about, but then I was a field operative by the time I was sixteen and I know better than to underrate them. I wonder if they would like a little tutoring. I really would feel better if I know how much I can depend on them, if they are going to get involved in things like today."

"I would bring it up with Lucien in connection with their babysitting duties," said Maurice, "and let on it is about babysitting Elise and not him, which would probably disturb him. Well, we need to go and discuss the people trying to buy a bomb with Lucien. I wish Greta was available, but she is working with Julia on Hamid Masoud."

"Hamid Masoud?" said Dove. "What in the world is going on with him? We don't even know where he is or who he is working for."

"Greta actually gave him a lift back to town from the unidentified camp in the desert in her helicopter and we have had people on his tail ever since he landed," said Maurice. "I didn't mention this to Lucien or the Egyptian colonel since Hamid Masoud is not part of the problem we are working on with them and their organizations. Anyway, let's go and tell Lucien that the supposed Egyptians that want a bomb are Asians, well at least their chief negotiator is and he just flew to Shanghai. The Egyptians have a tail on him and a kidnap squad there if it is needed."

"Oh, give me a break," said Dove. "What a day this has been already. I think we need half a dozen men here immediately. When the nurse doesn't report in we may have more company. Thinking back, I missed lunch with everything that is goings on.

Let's go up to the house; maybe Clarissa has something we can eat while we talk. Then we need to touch base with Greta. Why is Julia here?"

"She said she and Willard were coming to bring some baby things and decent tea," said Maurice, "but she also said this whole thing stinks, which is an interesting comment. I bet she is going to come and see if we need a bit of hand holding on the bomb thing and probably Blossom asked her to come since Greta will listen to Julia and Willard."

"But not Blossom?" said Dove. "Well, I am not sorry to see them, which I haven't. I guess they borrowed a house somewhere and we are getting together tonight. I'll phone for backup and get some people here. Then we can eat and go and find Greta and Julia. I still haven't had any lunch and I am about ready to gnaw on one of the palm trees. Come on, there has to be something to eat at the house."

****

Julia and Greta were sitting in Greta's office talking when her phone rang.

She listened for a moment and then Greta turned off her phone and turned to Charley where he was sitting at his new desk in the corner and said, "Charley, would you organize half a dozen people to go over to the house and guard Lucien? Dove just called and said that a fake nurse showed up an hour or so ago and attempted to push Lucien's wheelchair in the pool and drown him. Apparently, Celeste or Nicole zapped him with a Taser and Maurice has sent him on to Ben's new office for further consideration."

"Right away, brigadier," said Charley, "and do you want me to go help?'

"No," said Julia. "We may need you to help us pick up Hamid Masoud when he is done flitting around town. So far, he met with someone in the Defense Ministry Building, spent time at the Department of Antiquities, had a long lunch, and has gone to the office of a dealer in antiques and curiosities. Right now, he is visiting the Chinese embassy. I really think that we should get him as soon as he gets to the airport."

172

"How do you think we should do it, Julia?" asked Greta. "I suppose we could send a cab to get him and then gas him. I don't think we should try a snatch in broad daylight at an airport with all those armed guards around. We could get him on the way out though."

"No, then everyone would know that someone put the snatch on him if he just disappears and he wouldn't be useful for them anymore," said Julia. "We need a believable story of why he is out of action, so he can surface in or four or five days without apparently being compromised so we can send him back and watch him. Umm, let me see, obviously he is going to have to be sick or in an accident, so we will need an ambulance and crew, we need someone to fill in for him at the hospital and a friendly doctor to take care of our stand in for him. I figure I will need three days to persuade Mr. Masoud to talk."

"What are you going to do, Julia?" asked Greta, "Or do I want to know."

"Actually, yes you do, dear," said Julia. "You have to know precisely what is going to happen to someone before you make a decision to do it. I have concluded that we need to have a lot more exposure to all parts of our activities for the field people. Greta, you and Dove and I worked in the problem-solving group, which everyone thinks is glamorous, but they concentrate on the flitting around the world shooting people and not the fact that you are on your own and fair game anywhere you carry out an assignment if they catch you. Francis worked in the honey girl division a bit before she joined the science group and she knows you need to be a very good actress when one of your subjects shows up sloppy drunk and amorous. Like most of the girls, Francis got burned out, but she got interested in dirty tricks and explosives, which is very dangerous, but she was very good at it. Confinement and interrogation is another whole division like the honey girls, where you need a strong stomach. As you now know we have numerous people that do things with and to computers and you are learning a lot about having enough toilet paper and people on the street and everything else about running an office but there is really no structure to bring field people like you up to command grade. It has been more or less hit and miss and we can't afford that any more. We need more solid preparation for our senior operatives.

Granted, there are not a lot of senior operatives, but quite frankly dear, you are still wet behind the ears. So yes, you need to know what I am going to do, and you are going to help so I know you know. Now, where is our target?"

"Still talking to people according to the message I just got," said Greta, putting her phone in her pocket.

"Well let me call Mrs. Caparoni and see if she and the girls are free for a little while," said Julia.

*****

Hamid Masoud got out of the cab at the Cairo airport and walked to the Singapore Airlines entry door. He was puzzled about the request to fly to Singapore to meet with an important man, which was all they had said, to undertake a very important mission that was different. This was not like the way they handled any of the various assassinations that he had done for these clients. Normally, they would just send his current open phone a text message stating where he could pick up an envelope. He would respond with a text message and a phone number for a new phone, after you subtracted the last four of the eight winning numbers of the Brazilian lottery for the day before. Then he would dispose of the current phone and have a messenger service pick up the envelope. When the job was completed, there would be a transfer to his Cayman Island bank account from his Chinese stock investment account. Since he was registered as a resident of Brunei, which has no income tax, and has only minimal interest in the financial dealings of its citizens or residents, he was about as insulated from his sources of income as was possible. The only inconvenience was when some of his friends asked how he kept beating the market by so much.

He wondered why they wanted to talk to him face to face and in Singapore. There had been some repercussions from the missed kill at the conference, but he had refunded the full fee and offered a cut rate if they wanted to have another attempt made. He was still worried about who had spotted him and how he had been located on the day he had finally set up the rifle for the shot after his days of studying the conference routine. He was also curious how he had been targeted in an apartment that was on a higher floor than anything for half a mile. He was more than half convinced that someone from the group that had hired him had fingered him. This was despite their huffy reassurances to the contrary. But relationships were strained now, and he had taken some precautions at the Singapore end of the flight so that the meeting would be as safe as possible for him, and as dangerous as possible for the important person if there were some treachery.

He pushed open the door and walked in carrying his bag and a briefcase with some blank pads and two or three paperback novels. He looked around at the terminal. There was a sweeper in loose white cotton pants and a long shirt using a push broom and dustpan to clean up the sand from a large tipped over ashtray that was to one side of the check in counter. A woman in a western suit and a veil and scarf with two young girls was standing on the other side of the check in counter from the mess. The girls were standing back from the workman and the older girl apparently was scolding an eight or nine-year-old girl that appeared to be her little sister about running and tipping over the ashtray. He walked to the counter between the woman, the children, and the janitor who moved in around him and shielded him from view as he presented his passport and reservation. He felt a jab in his back and spun around then looked down at the janitor who was kneeling behind him and was holding the push broom near the head while pushing the last of the sand into the dustpan. The shaft of the broom was waving around and he stepped back as the broomstick almost hit him in the face. Apparently the broom handle had hit him in the back. Hamid barked at the janitor to watch what he was doing since he didn't need clubbed to death. The man looked up with a puzzled frown and then got up and dumped the dustpan into a rolling waste cart and pushed it out of the entry door.

The woman and her children had stepped back from him and picked up some small carry-on bags while they waited for him to finish checking in. He smiled and winked at the smaller girl who looked like she was close to tears from the scolding. Then he turned and retrieved his passport and picked up his boarding pass. Suddenly, he had an intense pain in his head and his eyesight blurred. He grabbed for the edge of the check in counter and swayed as he fought for balance.

"Are you all right?" asked the woman with the children.

The smaller girl had retreated behind her mother and looked at him with big eyes while the older girl stepped back away from Hamid.

"My head," said Hamid. "I can't see, and my head is splitting."

An older white woman in a plain grey suit got up from where she was sitting in the waiting area and hurried over.

"What seems to be the trouble?" asked the woman. "I'm a nurse."

"My head is splitting, and I can't see," answered Hamid. "My vision is all blurry all of a sudden and my head is splitting."

"Here sit down. You," she said pointing at a man. "Help him to a chair."

The woman walked back to where she had been sitting and retrieved a black leather satchel and opened it. She pulled out a small flashlight and a stethoscope and then came to where Hamid was sitting. She pulled off his suit coat and shined the light in his eyes and then listened to his heart and neck veins and then took his pulse.

"Call an ambulance immediately," she said. "This man is having a stroke."

The woman with the two girls pulled out a cell phone and dialed it and started talking. The nurse reached in her bag and pulled out a syringe and gave Hamid a shot in the arm and then took out an IV set and expertly put it in his forearm and taped it down then held it up in the air. The pain in Hamid's head started retreating and he slowly leaned back and passed out. In under a minute an ambulance pulled up to the front of the gate and two men in white coats jumped out and rushed into the lobby pushing a gurney. The nurse met them and led them to Hamid explaining what she had done. The men nodded and then loaded Hamid on the gurney and put him in the ambulance. The nurse looked at her ticket and then shrugged. She picked up Hamid's suit coat and her bag and got in the ambulance and left with him. No one noticed that the woman and her two girls had disappeared along with their luggage and Hamid's briefcase and bag.

The ambulance hurried through the streets of Cairo and then instead of stopping at one of the nearby hospitals, it shut off it siren and proceeded to the street leading to the Sixth October Bridge and Gezira Island. It drove sedately through the Zamalek

District turning into the gated drive of a large villa on El-Khalig Street. The gate opened to admit the ambulance and then about ten minutes later it opened again, and the ambulance drove out and proceeded north. Suddenly, it turned on its siren and drove at high speed to Saint Athanasius Hospital and pulled into the emergency entrance of the hospital. The crew unloaded a man on a gurney and wheeled him into the hospital and started giving information to the emergency room staff.

At the villa, Julia checked Hamid Masoud. He was strapped on the gurney from the ambulance and was still unconscious. She checked the IV and then nodded and started pushing him down the hall to an elevator, motioning Greta to follow her. The elevator smoothly descended to the basement that was made from concrete, and despite the best efforts of the builders, it was cold and damp since it was below the water table from the Nile. Julia motioned Greta to turn on the lights and then pushed the gurney down a hall to a small windowless room that had been a coal storage room when the building was first built but had since been converted to a general storage room.

The room had been emptied and the various boxes, spare furniture, and plastic storage tubs had been moved into the wine cellar. The room was freshly painted black and the wooden door of the room had been replaced with a plain metal door also painted black and with a peephole lens installed in it. There was a heavy swinging bar on the outside of the door and it had two deadbolts mounted at the third points. There was a desk and two chairs with a floodlight in front of them facing the back wall where two chains dangled from the ceiling at a point that was invisible in the light of the floodlight. Julia wheeled Hamid into the room.

"Here," said Julia, handing Greta a hospital gown, "strip him and dress him in this. We'll put a piece of foam on a platform with a plywood top under him."

Greta started undressing Hamid and stopped and looked at Julia when she got to Hamid's shorts. Julia nodded, and Greta pulled off his socks and shorts and tee shirt and proceeded to get the gown on him. Julia came over and slipped two inflatable cuffs over Hamid's wrists and the lower part of his forearm and inflated them. Then she pushed the gurney over to the chains and snapped carabineers into reinforced holes in the cuffs. She walked out the door of the room and looked in to watch and pushed a button. Hamid was pulled upright by the chains and then off of the gurney. He hung in the air by his arms swaying. Willard brought in a platform with a sheet of foam.

"Okay, move the gurney out while I let him down," said Julia, "get that platform over there and put it under him. It is big enough to let him lie on when we don't want him hanging up. Now, I am going to lower him down and attach the plumbing to the IV and then we can get ready for the long haul."

Greta moved the platform under Hamid and Julia used the hidden winch to lower him down, so he lay on his back with his arms extending up. She checked the IV and then locked an extension tube into the IV. There was a bottle of glucose and a plastic manifold with remote control valves and several small bottles attached to it on the end of the extension tube. Julia fastened the manifold and bottle of glucose to the chain several feet above Hamid's wrist where it would be out of his sight and adjusted the glucose drip. Then she walked to the interior wall of the room behind Hamid and put an iPod on the floor where it would be out of sight to him and turned it on. She looked around the room and went to the door and motioned Greta to follower her.

Julia pushed the door shut and locked the deadbolts and then slammed the locking bar into place with a loud thump. She pushed a box with lights in it that covered the bottom of the door over to cover it and then she walked across the hall and into a lighted room while Greta followed. Maurice and Willard were sitting in front of a table with several television screens that showed the interior of the cell where Hamid lay unconscious on the platform.

"All right Greta, you are here to get your first lesson in interrogation 101," said Julia. "Maurice has had a bit of training but that was different and a lot more hands-on, so to speak. Both of you are going to be helping now, so get a cup of coffee because this goes twenty-four seven until he talks."

"Julia, I don't know if I can do this," objected Greta. "Pliers and electrodes and water tubs or things like that just aren't my thing. I will probably throw up at an inconvenient time and screw everything up. I will watch as long as I can, but I just don't know how long that will be."

"Um," said Julia, "you can kill people, but you can't hurt them? Dove said she once saw you jam a flick knife through a man's scrotum and threaten to castrate him. How about you, Maurice? Your file said you beat a man half to death and then held his head in a toilet until he answered some questions."

"Julia, I had to have the combination to a safe or the whole mission would fail," objected Greta. "I just didn't think. I acted because I had to."

"And you, Maurice? Why did you do what you did?" asked Julia. "Just for the hell of it?"

"I found out there was going to be a raid on my position and I had to know when or I was going to lose a lot of people," explained Maurice. "I guess I could have just moved everyone out, but I wanted to surprise some people with a few booby traps."

"So, in order to finish a mission, you both hurt someone but now without the adrenaline surge you get squeamish?" asked Julia. "Well without the knowledge that this man has, we can lose people or blow the mission or several missions. Now, I am going to take a few minutes and do a bit of teaching, so get the coffee and sit. First, if you hurt someone often enough and bad enough, they will say anything you want, they will confess to anything you want, and they will tell you anything they think will make you stop. This seldom yields good information. Brain washing techniques, where you just wear someone down by talking and drugs and sleep deprivation do work, but this takes a lot of time when the person involved is a fully formed adult. Whole populations can be manipulated and made to believe the silliest things if you get them when they are young, but you can convert a whole population to believers in a couple of generations using brain washing and propaganda. North Korea is a perfect example."

Maurice nodded and Julia poured coffee for everyone and put it on the table.

Then she took a sip and went on, "Of course, you have to have a good secret police and death camps that are not a closely guarded secret so that the stick is visible along with the carrot, which most starving North Koreans would probably kill for to get a whole carrot to eat. But anyhow, the information you get when you have reprogramed someone is a lot more reliable but usually so out of date that it is only marginally useful. Normal police interrogation techniques are not much good on really trained people since there are strategies that the police use and also easy counters to them since they can slap you around a bit but won't kill you. Of course the police in the southeastern United States are an exception. But we need information quickly and we do not want Mr. Masoud to show rough handling marks."

"What are you going to do, Julia," asked Maurice, "and how are you going to do it?"

"Ah, a glimmer of interest," replied Julia, "First, let's review a bit. We went to a lot of trouble to leave a trail for Mr. Masoud, so he could be tracked. A lot of people saw he was taken sick at the airport and left in an ambulance. He is not expected in Singapore for at least twelve hours and probably not at a meeting until tomorrow. When he doesn't show up then, someone will start looking. We probably have from twenty-four to thirty hours before anyone is really inquisitive. Now, why are we going to all of this trouble? Because we want to have it appear that he isn't blown, so that whoever is using him to assassinate nuclear scientists keeps using him and we can find out who they are and what they want and maybe take appropriate actions. And we also don't want a finger pointed at Mr. Masoud since he may be useful in the future."

"All right, so this is a good thing, but how do we get him to talk without pulling out his fingernails or something?" asked Greta, "and how do we do it in a couple days?"

"By screwing with his mind, dear," answered Julia. "Now, why don't you go and pump Elise some milk, there is a new pump over there, and I will start softening Mr. Masoud up. We are going to compress his consciousness so that he thinks he has been here for weeks. We will chemically modify his mental environment to compress about three days into an hour."

"So, you are going to drug him," said Greta. "One question, what's the silent iPod for? Are you recording with it and what is the box over the door?"

"We are already recording everything that goes on with a hard drive video system," said Willard. "We're making infrared, low light, and normal recordings. That is what the screens show."

"The iPod is part of the effort to convince him he was in the hospital," explained Julia. "It plays the sounds of an emergency room just below conscious hearing level. It is a subliminal clue for him to fasten on while he is passing out and coming awake and makes it easier to convince him of what we want him to think happened. The box over the door produces either light or darkness in the crack under the door where he can see it and lets us produce false days and nights for him. Also, the suspension cuffs are actually a close copy of cuffs used when people are in a coma and thrashing around. When he wakes up in the hospital, he will be tied to his bed with cuffs and that will explain the ache in his arms. Now we have twenty minutes until the first cycle. I am going to give him a laxative and a diuretic so that he messes himself and is thirsty when I wake him up."

Thirty-two "days" later, Hamid Masoud started talking to the pleasant voice that asked questions. Fourteen actual hours after he left the airport he was in a private clinic where a thin catheter was run up his nose and out through his sinus. A small lesion that formed a clot was chemically created in his brain and he was transferred to Saint Athanasius Hospital for testing. The ambulance went to the admitting entrance where he was sent to a room and then to x-ray. When he came back, his gurney passed another one with a figure under a sheet that was being wheeled out.

Hamid was wheeled into the newly vacated room, his restraint cuffs were tied to the bed, his newly cleaned clothes were put in the closet along with his briefcase and suitcase and his IV was connected to a mild sedative. A doctor redistributed the charts and x-rays between his file and the file of a stand in that had been in the hospital occupying a bed to prove that Hamid Masoud had been there. Then the doctor signed the DOA death certificate for a John Doe that had been admitted that morning had been sent to the crematorium. Hamid slept for ten hours before he was located and identified by a man who said he was a business associate. When the man left Hamid's room he talked to the doctor in charge of Hamid's treatment. Then the man went and sat in the waiting area and immediately called Shanghai for instructions.

CHAPTER 11: FAIRLY FULL DISCLOSURE

Greta and Maurice were sitting on the couch in Greta and Dove's apartment drinking coffee and relaxing after a hard night with Julia and Hamid while Dove changed Elise. Greta had just finished feeding Elise and Dove had taken her into what was now the girls' room to change her. Nicole and Celeste had moved upstairs and were sharing a bedroom with Elise since Lucien, Alonzo and Clarissa Caparoni, and Charley and Joey had moved in. Charley and Joey were sleeping on the upstairs sleeping porch that had been fitted with blackout screens and furnished. The third downstairs bedroom was now a guardroom for the half dozen armed people that were always around. Charley and Joey were in command, but the men and women of the security force were a mix of Lucien's young men, Ben's commandos, and Dove's direct-action force. There had been a bit of hostility to start with, but things had settled down when everyone got their assignments straight.

Things had also settled down in the house since Clarissa had taken over the kitchen and housecleaning. She was feeding a dozen people every meal but had refused any additional help besides Alonzo. When Nicole and Celeste moved upstairs, Greta had offered to move Elise into Dove's and her bedroom so that Nicole and Celeste wouldn't have to share and the girls had been insulted because she was trying to separate them from Elise who they considered their little sister. Greta had backed off and Sara had outfitted the biggest bedroom as a girl den before she left.

Sara had added two comfortable arm chairs with a small table and reading lamp between them, bunk beds, three bright colored gym lockers in the closet for hanging clothes, a double desk with a bookshelf partition between the two sides and office chairs. Under the window there was a large double dresser for folded clothing and a changing area on top for Elise. Elise's crib with a toy box under it were in the interior corner in the most protected spot in the room but she usually took her naps in the bottom bunk and also slept there with Nicole or Celeste when she was fretful, although the girls strenuously denied it.

"There, she's fresh again," said Dove coming into the sitting room and handing Elise to Greta. "Now, what did you find out from Hamid Masoud?"

"I really don't know everything, or maybe anything," said Greta. "When he started talking it was like someone had pulled a plug in the bottom of a barrel and I got lost. Willard and Julia and the information specialists are going over the DVDs they pulled off the hard drives now and they said that they would have an informal highlight report later this afternoon at their place. They are inviting Colonel Bryon McMillian and Lucien, if he is up to it. Copies of the tapes have been compressed and scrambled and are on the way to England for a thorough going over which will take three or four days. We are keeping the originals at Ben's new place at the old immigration center in the vault in the basement and Willard has a copy of everything on his portable computer."

"How useful is Ben's new office?" asked Dove. "What about the man who tried to drown Lucien? Any action there?"

"He is just locked up over at Ben's new building and worrying," answered Maurice. "Ben has already moved a bunch of his staff into the administration building since paint and furniture was all it needed. They have a new crash proof gate and a discrete plaque that announces the place is the Southerland Oil Cairo Operations Center. Moussa and Sons has ripped out everything in the detention building and have started construction of the hospital and living quarters and converting the cells in the basement. Sara left sketches and went back to her day job rebuilding the royal palace in the United Arab Emirates and won't be back for a while."

"Then maybe we can get on with the job now," said Dove. "What is the job, Greta?"

"I have absolutely no idea," answered Greta. "We have all kind of gotten sucked into this atoms for war program and no one has told us to do anything. I still have to figure out what to do about Lucien's grandson, which is kind of personal and kind of company business. Also, we need to talk about getting Lucien some physical therapy. What about the girl's schooling and... Where are the girls?"

"They're in school," said Dove. "You asked Asim to help with Elise and the girls. When the girls showed up she started helping them. She arranged for the girls to go to Saint Margaret's

Academy, a very well thought of Catholic girls' school that has a mixed racial student body. Most of the girls are local or from Asia and are predominantly Catholic or at least nominally Christian. Asim and I have also been working with them for an hour after school on self-defense and rifle marksmanship."

"Has anyone mentioned this to their parents?" asked Greta. "Nicole is what eight?"

"Nicole is nine, almost ten, and Celeste will be seventeen in a month or so," answered Dove. "I told Asim that we needed to know how much help the girls would be in a pinch and she found out she had a couple of willing learners. Besides, Saint Margret's Academy has field hockey, tennis, and jujutsu for competitive sports and the girls are allowed two. They are both doing judo and Asim is acting as their private coach. Celeste is doing tennis for her other sport and Nicole adores field hockey, although she may lose some teeth or get a black eye after practice if she keeps high sticking people."

"She is an imp, or maybe more accurately a tomboy," said Greta. "So, how much can we count on them in a pinch?"

"I think in the heat of the moment, Nicole would kill you without blinking, if it was to defend Elise or her family or Lucien," responded Dove. "Celeste is more cool and calculating, but probably more deadly and so smart it is scary. I wonder what we are doing to these children though?"

"When did you go in the field, Dove? It was when you were sixteen, wasn't it," asked Greta. "I was a late bloomer and didn't become a full operative until I was almost nineteen. The thing is, Dove, we are not training these little girls to go active. We are just training them to defend themselves. At least I hope that's all. In my opinion, every girl should know how to do that. Anyhow, you said they are in school. Since you and I both work, who is watching Elise during the day?"

"Well, a good defense would probably help a lot on first dates," commented Dove, "but on the other hand if it was too good there might not be a lot of second dates."

"Asim is filling in right now," answered Maurice "She takes over when the girls go to school and is assigned to the day time security detail here at the house. When the girls come home, they take over until you get here, if you get here, whenever you get here. Their mother watches Elise when the girls have dance lessons or sports competitions or something outside the house and Asim is off duty. The judo practice is on mats out in the garage and they shoot with paint ball rifles in the side yard. Normally, they take Elise with them in her carry seat when they are practicing. She seems to enjoy judo a lot."

"It's really great to know that someone else is taking care of my baby while I am out drugging some killer so that he spills his guts," snarled Greta. "I am about to sit and think about this whole situation quite a bit."

"Rough day at the office, boss?" asked Maurice. "I remember when my mom and dad both worked, and I went to school and then came home and did my homework while I waited for them."

"Just don't try to tell me you turned out all right," said Greta. "I know what you do for a living. Okay, I am grabbing a diaper bag, Elise, and my coat and heading for Julia's since she is giving us supper. Lucien is coming later, come on, Dove."

"I'll wait and bring Lucien to the meeting," said Maurice, "I'll catch a bite with Asim here at the house."

Greta looked out the window of the black Mercedes sedan with dark windows that Lucien had furnished for when Elise was going out. Greta didn't want to guess how much it weighed because of the armor and it always came with two or three other vehicles that changed every time and three or four young people that rode scooters or motorcycles. Greta guessed that there was enough firepower concentrated around the car to start a war or stop a battalion. Anyway, just the presence of the other cars and outriders probably tipped the streetwise off to the fact that someone that should not be trifled with was in the car. This wasn't far from the discovery that the passenger was a woman with a baby or a couple of women and a baby, like now. This would result in someone looking for the man who was providing the car. Eventually, someone would connect it to Lucien and then it would all be downhill from there.

Since Blossom had fingered her and she had rescued Lucien, EUOPS didn't have much of a secret organization left in Egypt, especially with the Egyptian security services in the loop too. Greta wondered if Dove had hit the nail on the head when she speculated that Blossom still wanted to stick it to Greta. The Egyptian EUOPS operation was seriously compromised and she was again the one standing with her head above the trench looking for snipers. Back when Mark was running the office in Damascus with the Southerland Oil cover, there might have been some suspicions, but no one had ever come calling. It was kind of like Ben and the Southerland Oil operation here. Everyone was on her case and Ben was floating along below the surface just keeping on keeping on.

Strange how she hadn't thought about that when the Southerland operation had been jerked out of her control and although it was supposed to report to her, she didn't seem to be getting a lot of reports or anything else, except Charley and Joey who were supposed to be coordinating with Ben's operation. She wondered about them and if they were making regular reports on her but not to her. Charley and Joey had been too damn good in the bluffing match at the hotel with Colonel McMillian. What did she really know about them? They were SAS, but then maybe Charley had implied something else when he said she had never asked if they had worked in intelligence.

"Dove, who was the first one to spot Hamid's set up at the conference?" asked Greta. "You said that one of the high-altitude drones saw something and someone called us?"

"Yes, one of the Taranis drones saw the shadow wasn't moving and alerted headquarters and they called us and we sent a Whirligig to take a look," answered Dove. "Why?"

"Taranis drones are operated by headquarters," answered Greta. "They belong to the English and we get them loaned to us for specific missions. They are supersonic high altitude stealth drones and are used for mapping, surveillance, and rocket attacks. Mostly they look straight down at a small area with a high detail camera or at a larger area with greatly reduced detail, like they can see a car at large scale but not a window shadow. Why would a supersonic high-altitude drone just accidently hold position and use high magnification to watch a shadow long enough to see it hadn't moved?"

"You know it is rather thin when you think about it but what are you getting at, Greta?" replied Dove, "I know it must have happened because we were there, you know, and watched the whole thing."

"Wrong, we watched the whole thing after the Whirligig saw him," pointed out Greta. "We have absolutely no confirmation that a Taranis saw a bloody thing. Besides there is no way a Taranis could have spotted an unmoving shadow because it would have had to stay in one place for several minutes. And I will go you one better, a Taranis can't hover and watch anything. They must keep flying or they fall down and go boom, literally. Also, we get involved in this while we are trying to get set up to do things. Then suddenly headquarters tells us to jump on the nuclear bomb problem, and then Blossom immediately rats us out to the Egyptians. I don't think that they counted on Lucien having a stroke and us rescuing him or him adopting Elise, but they had to go along with it since it happened."

"Who is they?" asked Dove.

"Blossom, of course," replied Greta. "She has blown us and eventually someone on the other side, whoever they are, is going to try something. Hell, they already have. The attack on Lucien at our place and the attempt to snatch someone out of the car at the apartment can't just be coincidences. Colonel McMillian says it wasn't his organization at the apartment and they have only a tangential interest in Lucien anyway, so it wasn't them. Blossom is using us to smoke out whoever is trying to buy a bomb and we are the lamb tied to the stake for the tiger. I may kill the bitch."

Greta grabbed her cell phone out of her diaper bag and hit the button for Maurice's phone. It rang three times before he answered, and she told him to stop at the central city mall and do a bit of shopping before he came on to the briefing. She also said to pick up a bunch of flowers for Julia.

"Why the flowers for Julia?" asked Dove. "I mean a hostess gift is nice, but we are more family than that."

"I might want something to go on her coffin if she knows anything about us being set up," answered Greta, "and I have a little task for you later too."

The escort cars scattered and parked down the block and across the street while the motorcycle outriders went on to circle the block when the Mercedes turned in at the driveway of the villa. There was an open Egyptian military scout car with a manned heavy machine gun parked just inside the gate. Two uniformed soldiers stood behind the car with automatic weapons and an officer in the uniform of the Republican Guard stepped into the center of the road and held up a hand. The driver looked back at Greta and she held up one finger for him to pause. Greta pulled out her cell phone and pushed the call button for Julia. The phone rang and then was picked up.

"What in hell is going on?" asked Greta. "Should we have general invitations to your briefings in my operations area printed and air dropped for the public? Now, short sentences and quickly Julia, or you are going to have a whole bunch of dead toy soldiers when Lucien's security gets back."

"Calm down, dear," replied Julia. "Merry and Blossom are both going to be calling in tonight and we have a special guest that I can't mention as well as a cousin from the states. Things are getting bigger and bigger and we are getting in deeper and deeper."

"And Blossom didn't think to call me up and mention it?" asked Greta. "I am getting seriously put out with that woman and we need to have a little mother daughter chat, momma, before your goddaughter's mother has a hell of a humdinger of a tantrum."

"Umm, it would appear you have been thinking again," answered Julia. "Come on up to the house, dear, and please don't kill anyone."

A green light on the dash of the scout car flashed and the officer stepped aside and saluted. The driver put the Mercedes in gear and drove to the front of the villa. There were four Republican Guards standing at attention outside the door. When the car stopped, one stepped up and opened the door and saluted.

"If the young ladies would please surrender all of your weapons to the corporal inside the door, the general would appreciate it," said the soldier and stepped back and saluted again.

Greta looked at the guards and turned to Dove and whispered, "Distract them while I get a camera out of the baby bag."

Then she stepped out and waited for Dove. Dove smiled and then swiveled on the seat to face the guards and pulled her skirt up to expose most of her legs and her thigh holster with the commando knife. She slowly pulled the knife out as it rucked her skirt up higher and higher then handed it to the soldier. Then she extended her hand to be helped out and smiled. While the soldier assisted Dove out of the car and everyone watched, Greta reached in the baby bag and pulled out a small blue plush teddy bear with a camera in it. She tucked it in Elise's blanket. Elise looked at the bear and then put its ear in her mouth and started sucking then looked disgusted and turned away from it.

Dove and Greta walked to the door while the soldiers watched Dove sway down the hall with appreciation. Greta and Dove stopped and gave their pistols to the corporal. He saluted and then another armed soldier along with a woman dressed in a western suit came down the hall and stood while the corporal made out two receipts and gave them to Greta and Dove.

"If you would follow me, please," said the woman, and grinned. "I don't believe a total strip search will be necessary."

"I don't think a strip search would even be possible, sweetie," said Greta. "Now, where are Julia and Willard before I become very inquisitive?"

The woman smiled thinly and then turned and walked down the hall and to a door on the left of the hall. She gestured to the door and then reached for Elise. Greta smoothly turned the reaching hand around into a hammerlock and reached in the baby bag and pulled out a silenced Uzi machine pistol with her other hand. Dove used her elbow to hit the male guard in the stomach and then helped him to bend over as she brought up her knee into his face. She grabbed the soldier's collar and threw him through the door to open it as Greta tripped the woman and shoved her inside. Greta switched hands with the machine pistol, handed Elise to Dove, then crouched and knelt and held the muzzle of the gun just above the top of the table that occupied the conference room.

"If anyone moves you are all dead," said Greta in a conversational voice, "and the silencer on this gun is so good they won't even hear it at the door. Now, what in hell is going on and I am in a mood where I just might just kill someone for practice."

Dove stepped in holding Elise and casually kicked a pistol out of the hand of the woman on the floor.

Dove picked it up and then addressed her, "Have you ever wondered what a steel reinforced six-inch Gigallio spike heel will do to your face? Do you want to find out?"

Then Dove closed the door and slid a chair under the knob to jam it and turned and smiled. A man in a blue civilian suit was sitting at the head of the table along with a man in a general's uniform. A familiar looking blond woman was sitting next to the man in the suit. Julia, Willard and Colonel Bryon McMillian sat on one side of the table and three locals sat on the other side of the table

"Your commander did not lie when she said you were one of the best she had," said the general. "Allow me to introduce myself. I am General Abdul El-Shazly, the gentleman on my right is the Assistant Egyptian Minister of Defense, I am the head of the Military Intelligence and Reconnaissance Department and the young woman is Margret Perry, the American television journalist. We are here at the request of several people, both here and in other nations, regarding a plot to purchase an atomic device and get the nation of Egypt blamed for God only knows what."

"Julia?" said Greta. "When did this develop and why wasn't I notified?"

"Blossom thought that you could be informed tonight in person, dear," said Julia. "We know this area is not compromised. That was quite an entrance, but totally uncalled for."

"Yeah well, bullshit, mama," said Dove harshly. "Guess what's behind the door three? Then, this woman tried to grab Elise. Well, excuse me for overreacting. Actually, I was about to garrote her with my scarf since she had made a couple shitty comments about strip searches, but Greta took over. Now, put her on her leash or I will actually show her what happens when you stomp on someone's face with a reinforced spike heel. Also, I am getting a little tired of Blossom's shit but that is another conversation for a little bit later tonight."

"It certainly is," said Greta. "Now, let me see how much I have straight so we won't have to waste a lot of time explaining things we already know. The minister is working for the CIA and Perry is his handler. The general is the head of the anti-Morsi faction of the army and the lady on the floor that is still trying to figure out a way to do something to get her seriously killed is part of Perry's group. I bet Colonel McMillian got preempted by the general, who is the head of Military Intelligence, on the bomb business when someone, probably Colonel McMillian, figured out that the people out in the desert at the old monastery are Morsi's people and they are the ones dickering for a bomb, thereby implicating the president and by extension the nation of Egypt. I kind of run out of steam here because the people that appear to have the money for a bomb appear to be Asians, not Egyptians."

The general nodded and said, "Yes that is all correct but there is more to it than that."

"I would suspect that there is," said Greta dryly. "Since the minister, the CIA and you all got invited to Julia's briefing, general. I guess Blossom and Merry are now in this up to their, let's just say necks, along with England, EUOPS and the Americans. There are a few other things too but they are internal, and I don't think that we need to wash our dirty linen in public before we save the world. Now, call your dog, Perry and I will put away my popgun since this looks legit, if very poorly handled. We need to let Maurice and Lucien in any time now and call Blossom and Merry. It appears that some rather big twos and twos got put together to make fours when headquarters was going over the tapes from Hamid's interrogation and you called Blossom and Merry, Julia. I have no idea who the gentlemen along the far wall are or why they are here. I assume you will explain."

There was a discrete tapping on the door and Margret Perry waved at the woman who Dove had allowed to stand while she covered her with the Walther PPK that had been in the lady's possession a few minutes ago. The woman marched up to stand behind Margret Perry and look mad.

"Who is it," said Julia.

"Maurice Toubon and Lucien Francisci," said a voice, "They are on the list."

Dove pulled the chair out from under the knob and opened the door. A man in the uniform of the Republican Guard looked in and then down at the unconscious soldier on the floor.

"He just tripped and fell, and hit his head on the table," said the general. "We were just calling for someone but since you are here take him to the infirmary. He might have a concussion."

Lucien drove an electric scooter into the room followed by Maurice. He stopped it at the side of the table nearest the door, and watched as the unconscious soldier was carried out and the door was shut, then he stood up. Everyone else stood and he waved them down. Dove handed Elise to Greta and helped Lucien into a chair facing the Assistant Defense Minister and the general and he squeezed her hand and smiled. He nodded to Julia and Willard and the Egyptians and then held out his hand for Elise. Greta put the teddy bear that she had been taking pictures with on the table and gave Elise to Lucien who smiled as Elise tried to poke a finger in his nose. Elise was reaching for the blue teddy bear and Lucien put out a hand to get it for her. Greta saw the sweat on his forehead as he forced his left hand to grasp the teddy bear and then Greta took Elise and picked up the teddy bear.

"Maurice, did you bring the things from the store?" said Greta, "If you did, I really need to change Elise. I will just take the diapers and pop into the study next door, unless you have a good air freshener in here, Julia."

Maurice handed Greta a plastic shopping bag that he had been carrying and she smiled and took it. Greta picked up the diaper bag and put the blue bear in it and walked through a door in the back of the room. Lucien asked for some water and Maurice inquired if there was coffee. Julia pulled a bell cord and a young lady in a maid's uniform came in and took orders and then walked out.

"I am quite surprised to see you here, Lucien," said General El-Shazly. "But then I guess the rumor of your recent demise are exaggerated."

"Yes, they definitely are," said Lucien, "I had a small stroke because my blood pressure had gotten clear out of hand, but as the doctors say, I have had my warning and am taking better care of myself. I came to Egypt with Greta when one of my associates brought up the problem with the atomic device and I learned she was involved. As with all of you, we too are in a delicate position, and we all do need to cooperate to survive, if not to look like saints. Just for the record, I do not intend to sell an atomic bomb to a bunch of terrorists."

In the next room, Greta changed Elise, uploaded the pictures of everyone in the meeting to her office to be identified by using her phone and dropped the bear with the camera between the wall and a couch where it would be found sometime later. Then she walked back into the room with Elise and sat down. She took a bottle out of the baby bag and started feeding Elise.

"Where were we, Julia," said Greta, "this is, or was, your meeting. Do we have Merry and Blossom on the line? What happened?"

"We have been on the line since before you threatened to shoot everyone," said Blossom. "I really do not approve of your style sometimes, young lady, although it is predictable."

Dove stood up and looked at the speakerphone sitting in the middle of the table and said in a cold voice, "And I really think you should…"

"Dove, we will discuss any communication problems we girls are having when we have finished with the gentlemen," said Julia, cutting Dove off. "Now, I will start off with some things I found out from Mr. Masoud. The group in the desert is part of a radical Islamic group that is loosely allied with Al-Qaida and, well almost every other radical Islamic group in the region. They are also getting support from the current administration. They are the ones that were trying to obtain a nuclear device last year to blow up something…Buckingham Palace, the UN, the American capitol, the Olympic games…something. They have several sympathetic adherents, not only in the Egyptian army, but also among the more dimwitted members of the Egyptian Muslim Brotherhood. For some reason the radical portion of the brotherhood think that by shooting off a nuclear device in a western country, they will somehow gain the upper hand against the western nations instead of guaranteeing the total destruction of Egypt and probably a significant portion of the Middle East."

The general glanced at the unidentified men sitting at the table and said, "Apparently, the current regime is allowing sanctuary for the radicals at a few camps in Department of Antiquities protected areas and providing assistance. They are listed as contract workers conducting preliminary digs and other archeological investigations for the Department of Antiquities and are being supplied by that department. Unless you dig up a solid golden something or a new tomb, no one really watches what the Department of Antiquities spends its money on or how much it spends. Also, since the revolution, tourism is at an all-time low so there is not much international interest in new unproven sites. Therefore, no one on the outside has noticed there is a moderate sized army hidden in the desert."

"Were you aware of them, general?" asked Greta.

"That is partially true, Miss Steiner," said the general, "we have been watching them, but they have mostly been doing calisthenics, target practice and attending lectures. I suppose I should clarify who we are. There is a large group of both senior and junior officers in the army that are not supporters of President Morsi. He has done nothing to relieve the economic problems of the nation and is apparently preoccupied with separating the nation into warring religious camps. He has not kept his promises to respect the constitution and has, in fact, forced a new Islamist leaning constitution on the country. He is instituting more and more laws favorable to Muslims and turns a blind eye to attacks on Christian institutions. The secular nature of the country is under attack and the whole country could become nothing but another theocracy like Iran. It may seem strange to say it, but I definitely prefer corrupt politicians to fanatic imams."

"That is what we believe, too," said one of the Egyptian men that had not been identified, "I should introduce us, but our names would be meaningless and there is a good chance we will all be dead in a few weeks anyway. We represent a group called Tamarod, which means rebellion in Arabic. The movement was founded by a friend of mine, Ahmed Adel, to register our dissatisfaction with the state of the economy, the lack of work, the reductions in electrical power and interruption of water service as well as the skyrocketing costs of food and gasoline. Currently, we have over fifteen million signatures on petitions to remove Mohamed Morsi as president since he is unfit to hold the office. With the discovery of the radicals seeking a weapon of mass destruction, it is apparent he also a danger to the survival of our nation."

"There is also a great deal of dissatisfaction with the current president in the civil departments," said the minister, "However, I am not working for the CIA, Miss Steiner. I am the Assistant Minister of Defense and the type and kind of defense funding that the United States provides the nation of Egypt is my responsibility. Miss Perry is a trusted messenger for the United States and we have been exploring options through more informal channels. It is clearly in the interest of the nation and the western powers that Egypt remains a willing ally, so we can all work toward maintaining stability in the region. This requires a unified government and unfortunately we do not have that now."

"As you can see, Greta, there is a great deal of discontent with the current regime," said Merry over the phone, "When we located the assassin, we were mostly curious about why he was there and Blossom and the EUOPS control committee decided to let you sniff around a bit since you seem to turn things up. When the atomic bomb purchase came up and Mr. Francisci contacted you, we didn't see how things fit, but we have been turning up more and more things that are too closely related to be coincidence but still don't fit together into a clear picture yet."

"As your famous fictitious English detective said, more or less, a coincidence is where we are not well enough informed to see all the connections," volunteered Lucien. "One of my associates has just realized how several things that happened are part of the current situation. Let me explain. Last year, a ranking member of the newly elected Egyptian government made an initial contact with my organization about obtaining a nuclear device. We asked how they would finance such a purchase before we considered any action and were informed that they would pay in gold. They said that the army was going to seize twenty tons of gold bullion from criminal revolutionaries hiding in the desert, but this apparently miscarried."

"What," exclaimed Greta, "so the Egyptian government was going to seize twenty tons of gold bullion from a bunch of terrorists somewhere in the desert? How interesting."

"Yes," said Lucien. "Isn't it? As some of you are aware there was an attack on the office of a charter airline we use. An aircraft we had arranged for that was carrying a group of people was hijacked with the intent of kidnapping the passengers but independent actions on the part of the passengers disrupted the planned abduction and it failed. But as part of the plot, the kidnappers killed some airline ground crew and office people that were under our protection since they were working for us. My organization learned who was responsible and we eliminated the local perpetrators after determining that they were part of a widespread radical group. My associate has just confirmed that the group that are currently camped in the desert, the government person and the army unit that was going to capture the gold are all members of the radical group that wanted to buy a bomb last year. I believe we are not square yet and they still require a bit more of my attention since they killed our airline people last year."

"Thank you for your information, Mr. Francisci," said Merry over the phone speaker, "You and your group are to be commended for your initial handling of the question of the atomic weapon and the latest information is very interesting and explains a number of things. Greta, EUOPS council is pleased with you locating the camp at the monastery and identifying and capturing Hamid Masoud. You and your group and have done excellent work starting with just a minor question of a failed assassination attempt. You and your team's efforts have been duly noted at the very highest level."

"We can discuss the failed assassination attempt and our involvement later, Merry," said Greta, "but what else did you have, Julia?"

"I think the most significant thing is that Hamid Masoud actually confirmed what Mr. Gerard suspected. The people buying the bomb are Asian," said Julia. "Hamid Masoud has been doing work for them during the last two or three years, but he isn't sure of their nationality or allegiance. They usually phone him with a target or request and he quotes a figure. When the job is over, he gets paid with a bank transfer to his account in Dubai from his Chinese stock investment account where he keeps a decent balance in stocks and bonds so large transfers are not unusual. He was on his way to Shanghai to meet with someone important for some reason when we intercepted him and debriefed him. Unfortunately, he was unable to make the meeting and so we don't know who he was meeting and or for what purpose."

"My associate who was discussing terms with the current person seeking an atomic device informed him that we had several leads but that a cash assurance, in gold would be needed to prove that they are serious," said Lucien. "We asked for six million euros in gold. Their representative said he would ask. It is not beyond the realm of possibility that they wanted to have Hamid Masoud bring the funds here. He does odd jobs like kidnapping and smuggling, as well as shooting people."

"The Asian person we followed flew to Shanghai after the negotiations meeting," said Colonel McMillian, "We have a six-man team there in case we want to remove him, or we can just keep watching, which I would recommend. He could be the person Hamid Masoud was meeting or it could be someone further up the chain of command."

"You mentioned that you had several leads on a device," said Margret Perry. "Is that true?"

"No," said Lucien. "We haven't really tried to find one yet because even looking around for a nuclear device attracts too much attention, usually unwanted attention."

"I'm glad that you realize that, Mr. Francisci," said Margret Perry. "People that have them are very protective. However, things have been arranged for you to have the use of a one-megaton B-83 thermonuclear bomb. It is one of the kind that are currently in use by the United States and this one is going to be listed by serial number as being lost in an aerial refueling accident just off the coast of Africa two years ago. The crews in the KC-135 and the B-52 that collided were killed and were never recovered due to uncertainty about their location and so no one can say if the B-52 was carrying anything except a few empty beer cans in the bomb storage area. Since there is no way to verify if there were bombs on board and since the planes were never recovered, then someone else could have salvaged one of the bombs and we can all claim we are innocent."

"That is very surprising," said Lucien. "Ah, I assume there is some reason that your country is making this overly generous offer?"

"There are actually several, but I am not cleared to know all of them," said Margret Perry. "What I have been told is that the Egyptians are going to be taking delivery of the device for a third party who is paying them with munitions for their services as a cut out. The third party is planning on removing the bomb as soon as it is delivered. The Egyptians are supposed to handle final payment to you and the third party is going to give them very good counterfeit securities and money to use to pay the Francisci organization."

"That is not going to work," said Lucien. "We would, of course, require a verified transfer of funds prior to releasing anything. We do not deal in cash or paper documents. If they don't have real credit at a bank that we will choose, they will never see anything."

"That's not even the half of it," said Margret Perry. "The Egyptians are planning on stealing the bomb as soon as it is delivered. That is one reason they have over six thousand off-the-books soldiers tucked away in camps around Egypt. Using them, they can field a force that is big enough to swamp any opposition at the delivery point."

"How do you know this, Miss Perry?" asked Julia. "Hamid Masoud had no information about any of this."

"We have been listening in on phone calls," answered Margret Perry. "The problem is that we haven't been able to get any names since we have to use voice recognition software because the parties keep using one time throw-away phones. This is one reason we record everything we can get our hands on. Voice recognition software can run through thousands of calls a second and find people that need to be listened to but it doesn't work to identify them when they only use a phone number once."

"So, the people trying to get a bomb are actually Egyptians," said the general. "When did you learn this, Mister Minister?"

"Just now," said the minister. "What does the United States want to happen to the bomb, Margret?"

"We definitely want it to go to the Asian purchasers," said Margret Perry, "and all of us here need to help make that happen."

CHAPTER 12: FAMILY SPAT

Greta, Julia, and Dove were sitting in a small withdrawing room off the dining room, having coffee and dessert and talking. Greta was nursing Elise but was eating a lime ice with one hand. She changed breasts and then turned the little egg timer that she carried in the diaper bag over and held up her coffee cup with one hand. Julia nodded and started to get up, but Dove pushed her down gently and brought a silver coffee server over and filled Greta's cup. Then she added cream and one spoon of sugar and stirred it before giving it to Greta.

"I know you don't like cream and sugar," said Dove, "but if it is all the same to you, I would like you to come to bed at a decent hour tonight. Julia, I cannot believe that Blossom just hung up without talking to us. She knew we wanted to talk to her."

"No, you didn't," said Julia. "You wanted to scream at her and have a fight, Dove. You and Greta feel that you have been used in this assignment and that she had no business exposing your operation to the Egyptians. Well, the thing is, that Blossom works for someone, too and they have other more important things in mind than letting you track down an assassin and a few local terrorists so the Egyptians were told to contact you."

"I don't care if they are saving Santa Clause," said Dove. "They have put us in a position where we might just as well post a sign on our front gate that says EUOPS Southern Headquarters-knock and start shooting. Well, one thing is, if their actions resulted in anyone hurting Lucien or Elise, there would or will be pay back, big payback, on whoever the Franciscis decided was to blame, including Blossom, her boss or her boss's boss. Now, I personally love Lucien. But having him as a house guest in a place everyone knows about is like having a ticking bomb in the front room. Quite flatly, all of the double domes that are in charge of the big picture and the greater good owe their continued happy existence to a nine-year-old girl and her sixteen-year-old big sister."

"I believe that the attempt was not connected directly to the operation we are involved with," said Julia. "There is currently a power struggle going on in the Francisci Family and Lucien's location is already known to the various people that would profit if he were to be eliminated. "

"Yeah, that is an interesting concept to explore," said Greta, "I sure hope that all the people who would be involved in payback if Lucien was killed believe it wasn't our fault. I'm done with my creamy coffee and Elise needs to be changed and put down for the night. Remember what Lucien said about a coincidence is where we don't know enough to see the connections? I agree and I for one don't think that any of this is just a coincidence."

"What do you mean, Greta?" said Julia.

Julia stood and gathered up the coffee cups and dessert bowls and put them on a tray. Then she walked toward Greta and held out her hands for Elise.

"You always surprise me when you start thinking," said Julia. "Sometimes it is paranoid little girl thinking but then you can also be quite insightful."

"Meaning, I don't think very much," said Greta surrendering Elise and the diaper bag to Julia, "Well, you are probably right. Sometimes I need to think a bit more before I react. However, I am not apologizing for tonight. Blossom was playing games again. She should have contacted me about the change in plans. Blossom does not do anything without a reason and my grand entrance was a result. I didn't know if the Army was here as a guest or not. Why didn't you call me?"

"I assumed Blossom had notified you and you knew," said Julia. "I agree that Blossom doesn't do anything without a reason which makes me very curious why she didn't let you know about the Americans and the general and the minister. Your normal reaction to anything that is unknown is get a gun, actually both your normal reactions is get a gun. She must have known that you would probably not actually kill anyone out of hand for no reason but that you would be ready to start shooting if needed and would not feel cowed or blindly cooperate. Which, I would say, is probably why you were not informed. Ummm, it appears that Blossom might have had some questions about the company we were keeping and was sending a message to someone. I don't think it would be the general; he is an actual patriot and is worried about his country. The minister is a bit more of an open question, but he has a pretty good thing going with the expense money he gets every month from the Americans and the kickbacks from the people that supply the medicines and other supplies and arms. I don't know about Margret Perry. She is vicious and jealous of her position as a newsperson, but she has been a CIA operative for years, and that is partially why she is a very well known newsperson. The cousins have quietly promoted her image and allowed her access to a lot of people and things. I doubt if she would rock the boat about the bomb situation though."

"Which leaves us with a bunch of random soldiers that normally change without warning, some Egyptian dissidents that are all expecting to die for some reason, and a lady that is who?" said Dove. "She reached for Elise and that is why Greta dumped her in the room and followed with a machine gun."

"She is Serena Watson. She is the producer and sometime cameraman for Margret Perry at American Press. She is also an operative for one of the numerous letter agencies," said Julia. "I'm not sure who, but supposedly she works with Perry and Perry provides cover for her. She provides protection for Perry. I have no idea why she would reach for Elise."

"That is exactly what was running through my mind when she made the grab," said Greta. "Women instinctively try to get the kids out of the bomb blast or barrage of bullets. I thought something like that was coming through the door when you didn't come and meet us. I just didn't realize it until I thought about it now. I didn't realize why I did what I did, now I realize I was expecting an ambush."

"The other reason women grab kids is to run off with them," said Dove. "I suggest we get hold of Miss Watson and apologize for manhandling her and ask her what in the hell is going on. She didn't have a reason to pull out a gun when she was down either, but then maybe she was just pissed. I wouldn't spend a lot of money on her as a bodyguard."

"It is a trifle late for that," said Julia. "She left with Margret and the general and minister, but I would like to discuss a few things with Lucien and Willard now. Maybe we can see if we can eliminate some of the uncertainty here, at least among us."

Greta nodded and carefully wrapped a sleeping Elise in a blanket and then looked around for somewhere to lay her down. She finally motioned to Dove to pull a seat cushion out of one of the leather sofas and put it on the floor in one of the front corners of the room in the shadow behind a wingback chair. She put a throw on the leather and laid Elise down on the cushion then pulled the drapes shut and dimmed the lights. Julia carried the tray of dirty crockery out and a few minutes later Lucien, Maurice and Willard came into the room. Lucien was riding his scooter, but he was smiling, and he had a glass of whiskey and water in the cup holder that was mounted on the handlebars.

"Should you be drinking and driving, Lucien," said Dove and smiled. "You look good. Are you feeling a lot better?"

"Yes, I can move my left arm and leg and my speech is almost back to normal if I speak slowly. As a very learned man once said, 'There would be much less trouble if you had to think of everything you are going to say and then write it down before you say it.' Anyway, I think that I should try to hire Amir Moussa full time," said Lucien. "He is a magnificent specimen and he has been working with me an hour or two each day for the past two days. He told me he lifted one hundred and eighty kilos in a local tournament recently without binding his wrists or arms. The other thing is, he has a university degree in kinetics and is licensed in sports medicine and physical therapy. His father is a friend of the family and I am very grateful to them for volunteering his services. Maurice said that you hadn't located anyone you felt that you could implicitly trust to help me yet."

"Well, that among other things that aren't done, Lucien," said Greta. "If you are happy with Amir, he seems to be helping and he is safe. Lucien, who would profit the most if you were to die? You also said that someone at the estate was behind the fraudulent move to Saint Athanasius the Great school and hospital. Who was it and did they catch them?"

"First, who would profit if I died? Hmmm, that is a question of deep philosophical implications, but I assume you mean directly profit from my death," said Lucien, "Well first Armand Gerard, Valentino Guérini, Carlo Conein, or John Carbone since one would probably take over as the head of the family. They have all seen what is done and needs to be done.

AND NONE SHALL REMAIN

Armand would have my backing because he is more practiced in the buying and selling business as well as being a sharp bargainer, but he wouldn't be the best for the financial operations, Valentino would be a better banker and is shrewd, John is not the best choice although he is competent but sometimes needs help with decisions, and Carlo is fine in his job but tends to settle all arguments with a gun. Present company excepted, ladies."

"You're stalling, Lucien," said Greta. "Who would be trying to kill you?"

"That is a problem for sure," said Lucien, "the person that notified me of the move to a hospital was found trying to get off the hydrofoil ferry in France dressed as a nun by some of my people and they attempted to question him, but he expired before any useful information could be extracted. This leaves me with a bit of a problem. I could have some other people at the estate questioned but I need to have some evidence of complicity before I act."

"Julia, does Ben still have the nurse that tried to drown Lucien?" said Dove. "I think that we should call right now and double the door guards or maybe even move him somewhere. How about the little cell downstairs at your place? I really don't think that someone you want to extract a bit of information from dies while being questioned just like that. Who caught the person from the hydrofoil?"

"I'm not sure exactly who, but some of the amateur questioners do get exuberant," said Lucien, "and accidents happen."

"Bull, Lucien. You said you wanted to talk to him and wanted him found, you did not say you wanted him dead," said Dove. "As a matter of fact, you said not to kill him. He should be alive and kicking right now and tuning his voice to sing. You are procrastinating, and you know it. Whose men caught him?"

"I am not sure, Dove," said Lucien, "as a matter of fact, I don't know who to ask right now since I am unsure whom I can trust. I would normally turn to Armand but that could be misplaced trust too. What would you suggest?"

"I think that we should run and fetch the nurse from Ben's place while he is still alive and let Julia talk to him at her place or somewhere else of her choosing," said Greta. "I believe Dove is right. He is in a lot of danger since he is a loose end that knows something, and they cannot afford to have him hanging around."

"I'm calling right now, and I want to send Elise's car to go fetch him," said Greta. "Maurice, could you head up the transfer? By the way, why wasn't Ben here tonight?"

"That is a question that bears some thought, Greta," said Maurice, "but they obviously didn't want him to meet all the people, or at least all the people to meet him. Call Ben and I will take all the guns and cars and motorcycles and what not and bring the nurse and Ben back."

"Why Ben?" said Lucien, "What does he know?"

"Good question," said Greta. "Very good question. First let's see if we can find out if he knows why he wasn't invited."

Ben sat in the back seat of the Mercedes with Maurice and fidgeted. The man that had tried to drown Lucien was riding in the trunk of the car with tape over his mouth, a plastic bag with air holes cut in the back of it over his head and snap ties on his wrists and ankles. The ride to the new Southerland Oil headquarters near the airport had been uneventful and the pick up at the building had been without incident. Ben wondered why Greta had rather forcefully requested his presence at the villa that Julia and Willard were using. He had been keeping his head down, as ordered, and staying in the background on this whole situation.

EUOPS headquarters had authorized the purchase of the old Egyptian immigration detention complex in the name of Southerland Oil and he had been busy establishing a presence in the oil exploration and exploitation operations in Africa and the local area. The disintegration of the Damascus office had left a hole in the oil well service business that the new operation in Cairo had moved into. The additional new work in Crete would keep the office hopping and the additional work from EUOPS would be hard to cover without more staff. He wondered if he had been nuts to accept Merry's proposition to retire and take over the Southerland and EUOPS operation that Mark Saint Martin had run. True, he was getting to the stage where it was more reasonable to sit at a desk instead of charging the machine guns and he was good at organizing things, but the thorny patch with Greta and the split in Mark's original organizations left him in an uncomfortable position. Now he didn't know what was up, but he had a feeling that he might be pressed for some answers.

Ben looked up at the rear-view mirror and noticed that a large covered white truck was moving up on them in the outside lane. A white van moved in front of it and the truck moved back behind them and attempted to pull to the curb lane and pass the cars directly behind them. A young man on a motorcycle slid in front of the truck and the truck kept moving up and then swerved and shouldered him aside. The motorcycle swerved off of the road and into the grounds of the new Occidental American hotel.

"Hey," said Ben. "Did you see that?"

"I sure did," said Maurice. "Quick, duck into the Occidental's parking structure, the truck won't fit. Go up."

The driver nodded and pulled the wheel of the car to the right and pulled in front of the truck that was gaining on the car in the curb lane. The car accelerated off the road and ran through the barrier of the parking garage sending the barrier arm flying into the building. The driver turned right and shot up the inclined ramp as the truck hit the ceiling of the entrance and jerked to a halt. Men with automatic weapons and balaclavas dressed in desert camouflage fatigues started jumping out of the back of the truck. An officer started waving men into the parking garage and then started shooting at the car as it turned to go up to the second floor.

"Where to?" said the driver. "It's a long jump from the top. This thing is eight stories tall."

"Good," said Maurice. "Head for the top. Are there any light poles or anything on top?"

"Yeah, they have light poles on the outside walls," said the driver. "Nothing in the middle, it's all parking."

"Head for the top floor. We're driving, and they are running so we should beat them by a minute or so," said Maurice. "Park the car crosswise so it blocks the ramp. I wish we had some grenades."

"In the trunk," said the driver. "There is a whole case and a half a dozen submachine guns and ammo under the trunk floor where the spare would be if we had a spare."

"Okay," said Maurice. "Ben, you grab the prisoner. Uh, what's your name?"

"Seth" said the driver. "I'm Elise's regular driver and this is her car. It is armored."

"That should slow them down," said Maurice. "All right Seth, block the up ramp and open the trunk. Ben, I'm calling for a blacked out twin Huey helicopter to come and pick us up. We will set the car to block the ramp. Seth, you grab some guns and ammo, Ben you get the prisoner and I will grab the grenades. We will run to the opposite end of the ramp where we have a clear field of fire at anyone coming up it. The helicopter should be here in less than ten minutes from lift off and we should be able to hold them that long, easily."

Maurice dialed his phone and barked some orders as Seth exited the ramp and then spun the wheel of the Mercedes and stopped it. He put it in gear and backed it across the entry and exit ramp so that the car almost filled both lanes. Seth popped the trunk. Then he opened the door and jumped out and took a position behind the hood of the car with his pistol out. Maurice and Ben got out and ran to the trunk. Ben lifted out the prisoner and threw him over his shoulder and ran toward the other end of the parking level. Maurice lifted the interior lining of the trunk and pulled out a submachine gun and pointed it down the ramp.

"Come on, Seth," said Maurice, "I have the ramp covered." A figure in a balaclava and camouflage uniform ran into the end of the ramp and Maurice fired a burst down the ramp. Then he pulled the pin on a grenade and threw it over the car so that it rolled slowly down the ramp and exploded. No one else showed up at the end of the ramp, although there was some shouting.

Maurice grabbed another machine gun and gave it to Seth and then slung an extra over his back for Ben and scooped loaded clips into his pants pocket. He took out two grenades and handed the rest of the box of grenades to Seth, then closed the trunk.

"Can you lock the car, Seth?" said Maurice. "We don't want them to get any more guns."

"Sure," said Seth.

Seth clicked the lock button on the key and then picked up the remainder of the case of grenades and ran for where Ben was crouched below the concrete safety wall above the entry ramp to the floor. Maurice got down behind the front of the car and waited. Half a dozen men ran out of the shadow of the lower floor at the lower end of the ramp, firing wildly. The bullets sprayed and glanced off of the heavily armored car, tracing it with dents and lines of pits in the paint and pockmarks on the glass. Maurice rolled a grenade down under the car and the men at the bottom saw it and jumped off the sides of the ramp. Then Maurice pulled the pin on a grenade and flipped it over the car so that it hit well beyond the ramp near the rolling grenade. They exploded one after the other and filled the whole floor with shrapnel. Then he shot several bursts of machine gun fire down the ramp at the floor so that the bullets ricocheted through the garage hitting cars and walls and pillars. About this time, a firefight started at the bottom of the building as the people from Lucien's escort cars and the scooter and motorcycle people arrived at the scene.

Maurice listened, and he could hear the beat of a helicopter closing from the airport. There were a number of cars parked on the roof of the building, but the far end of the floor only had two parked near the hotel entry bridge. It would be a bit tricky but not impossible to land. He looked down the ramp again and then noticed Seth running for the first car parked on the far end. Seth swung the machine gun at the driver's window and then pulled up the lock and got in the car. The car started and then backed up with its tires spinning and shot backwards toward the Mercedes. Seth backed the car out of the open part of the ramp and then jumped out and ran back to the other car parked on the far end and smashed the window with the gun and started it and backed it out of the way of the helicopter.

The firing in the lower part of the building was intensifying and Maurice could hear the helicopter very close now. Then sirens announced the first police cars arriving. He ran and grabbed the box of grenades. Ben had put the prisoner over his left shoulder and had a machine gun in his right hand. Seth was peering over the edge of the railing on the entry ramp when a burst of machine gun fire arced up and he pulled back.

"Get over here," yelled Maurice, "We have a clear field of fire on the upper part of the ramp and they can't even see us here. Now, when the helicopter gets here, Ben, throw the prisoner in and then you and Seth get in. I'm going to ride the skid out."

"Bullshit," said Ben, "That is my job. I am trained to hit things with a machine gun while hanging out of a Huey. I'll ride the skid and you get ready to drop some grenades down the ramp to discourage anyone running out in the ramp opening and shooting at the chopper. Where are we going?"

"Airport," said Maurice, "I'll phone Greta and tip her off and I think we should take our prisoner and go to, ummm, someplace. You better come. This attack pretty well tells us that someone in the family is behind it since it looks like they were after our prisoner and that is troublesome but also fills in some more blanks."

"I'll take your word for it until we have time for you to explain it in short sentences with little words," said Ben. "Get ready to move, here comes the chopper."

A black Huey with the slide door open slid over the railing of the parking garage above two light poles and settled lightly in the cleared parking area. Ben ran for the open door and threw in the prisoner and Seth ran for the Mercedes. The trunk of the Mercedes popped open as he sprinted behind it and then reached in the trunk and pulled out two more machine guns and a dozen clips of ammunition in a gym bag. He held them up and Maurice nodded then threw two grenades over the rail onto the ramp and then ran toward Seth. Seth crouched behind the car as the grenades exploded. Then he stood and emptied his machine gun down the ramp and threw it over the side of the garage. Maurice slid to a halt and grabbed the extra submachine guns and clips.

"I'll stay with the car and act scared, which won't take much acting," said Seth, "I'll back it out of the ramp before the police get here and stop where it will look reasonable to be hit with all the shooting and tell the cops I got caught in a fire fight between a dozen people who looked like they were stealing cars. I'll need someone important to be at the hotel as my fare. Have the limo service call me with a name I can give the cops. Now go."

"Prints?" questioned Maurice.

Seth held up his hands to show his driving gloves. Maurice nodded and took the extra ammunition and loaded the two extra sub machine guns and ran toward the helicopter alongside the railing of the ramp. Every so often he stopped and fired a burst over the edge of the railing with one of the guns and scattered the spent cartridges around. He reloaded and ran toward the outer edge and fired into the air at several points, scattering spent cartridges. An examination of the cartridges would show that several guns had been involved and it would look like there had been a lot of people shooting. Then he put the machine guns in the gym bag and ran to the helicopter and jumped in.

Ben had rigged the door gun and he swung it out and handed Maurice a helmet. Maurice put on the helmet and the blacked out Huey lifted straight up out of the light of the parking garage. It swung north away from the airport and climbed.

"What?" asked Maurice.

"Julia wants us to fly over to the river and head upstream under the radar," said Ben, "We will land at a small military post north of here and she has arranged for the Egyptians to pick the prisoner and you up. The Huey will get a medic and a suspected heart attack and take off as a medical evacuation flight and I will fly right seat. I'm supposed to meet you at the airport later. What is going on?"

"That is what we are going to discuss," said Maurice, "Ben, you have been doing not much of anything. Is there a reason?"

"Yeah, the home office said to make like a gopher and tend to Southerland business," said Ben. "Blossom said Greta and your guys are very visible and would be taking this one and I am supposed to fade back and be ready with all the troops since it looks like things are going to blow up in the near future and we may need to either shoot our way out or take over when you have to run."

"Well, she didn't explain that to us," said Maurice. "But that really isn't surprising. You know about the bomb?"

"You mean that someone is trying to buy one?" said Ben. "Yeah, I know that. Have you figured out who yet?"

"No, but the Americans just gave us a medium sized H-bomb to sell to the people who are trying to buy it," said Maurice, "and they said we all have to cooperate to get it to them."

"No shit?" said Ben and shook his head in disbelief.

Maurice reached inside his suit coat and Ben reached into his hip pocket and they both pulled out flasks. They smiled and traded flasks and drank and then traded back. Then they sat down in the side seats of the helicopter and watched the reflection of the moon on the surface of the Nile as the river streamed by at over a hundred miles an hour and twenty feet below them.

****

Lucien was sitting on his electric scooter holding Elise and using both his arms. Elise had tried to stick her finger up his nose and giggled when he pulled back his head and then she wiggled down in her blanket and went to sleep. Greta was sitting at her desk drinking a cup of coffee with cream and sugar and Dove was sprawled on the settee folding and refolding a piece of paper.

They were waiting for a breaking TV news report on the local Cairo station they had been told was coming. The normal program was interrupted and Margret Perry came on. She was holding a microphone and standing in front of the Occidental American Hotel with an Egyptian police officer where a cascade of flashing blue and red police vehicle lights and portable spotlights illuminated the parking garage. There was a white Department of Antiquities truck crashed in the entrance of the garage totally blocking it and a swat team vehicle parked on the lawn. A man in a flack jacket and helmet was yelling through a megaphone at the structure and several policemen were crouched behind the various cars and vans holding pistols and shotguns.

"Less than an hour ago, armed gangs waged a gun battle in the parking garage of the luxurious Occidental American hotel where I was attending a press conference announced by members of a group called Tamarod that opposes President Morsi. My hired car and the driver were caught in the crossfire when dozens of men shot it out on the roof. My driver said one group appeared to be stealing high value cars and suddenly another group showed up and everyone started shooting. After a prolonged gun battle, with an unknown number of casualties on each side, a helicopter landed on the roof and members of one group escaped. My driver said they were carrying their dead or wounded and loaded them into the helicopter as they left."

There was a burst of automatic weapon fire from the parking garage and everyone, including Margret Perry, ducked for cover. Her cameraman swung the camera to where several policemen were beating a hasty retreat down the entry ramp of the garage. They took cover behind police cars that were barricading the entrance behind the crashed Department of Antiquities truck.

Margret brushed back a lock of her singnature long blond hair and addressed the camera, "As you just heard, the battle with the police continues. There are still an unknown number of people defying the police and barricaded in the garage. A police negotiating team has been called in to try and get them to surrender. I have Capitan Zakaruia Salem from the Ministry of the Interior with me. Capitan, do you have any idea who was involved in this gun battle?"

"At the present time, we have not identified any specific group or groups, but it looks like two criminal or terrorist factions with different plans may have become involved in a confrontation," said the Capitan. "I doubt if this was a planned incident. We will know more when the remaining holdouts surrender, and we can question them."

"What are the police going to do now?" said Margret, "Has the negotiation team made any headway?"

"They are talking to a member of the group who contracted us on a cell phone a few minutes ago," said the Capitan, "Since they initiated the contact, it appears that they are willing to talk. I will keep you informed. I have no further comments at this time."

"Thank you, Capitan," said Margret Perry, and turned to the camera, "a witness who works at the hotel said that a covered truck with the emblem of the Department of Antiquities crashed into the vehicle entrance of the garage and blocked it and unloaded armed men dressed in uniforms with their faces hidden by scarves shortly before the gun battle started. You can see the truck rammed into the entrance of the garage behind me. Speculation here is running high that the people from the truck were planning on attacking the press conference that was going to be held in the hotel ballroom by a group called Tamarod, or rebellion in the Arabic language. Tamarod claims to have collected over fifteen million signatures demanding the resignation of President Morsi who has been in office less than a year. They have been agitating for action and it is speculated that they were going to announce an ultimatum or call for a return to the streets like the one that toppled Hosni Mubarak. We will be updating you live as the drama unfolds. From the Hotel Occidental Cairo, Egypt, live, this is Margret Perry reporting for American Press. Stay tuned for updates and further developments."

"It was fortunate that Miss Perry was at the hotel for the press conference and could help us," said Lucien, "She sounded very convincing about the suspected attack being on the Tamarod people."

"Even though we think the attack was actually on the man in the car who tried to kill you, it actually is easy to believe that the attack could be aimed at the Tamarod people, Lucien," said Greta, "It actually makes sense to the public."

"I wonder why they had people in a truck to attack the car?" asked Dove, "It would be more reasonable to just have a motorcycle drop a briefcase bomb with a magnet on top of the car and then swerve off and detonate it if it was an attempt on the passengers. Even the best armored car can't resist twenty pounds of shaped charge C-4."

"You're right," agreed Greta. "Attacking a moving car with a truckload of soldiers is crazy. But why did they jump out and start shooting at the car in the garage?"

"I just wonder how long the truck followed the car or if they were actually just going the same way," said Dove, "It could be that they thought that we were there to break up their attack and they were taking offensive action first. It's not normal for a car to have a bunch of escort and outriders. Also the car didn't act normal when it swerved for the parking garage especially after everyone in it attacked them by throwing grenades and shooting. Then the other Francisci cover people showed up shooting in a classic front and rear attack. No wonder they thought we were out to get them."

"I wonder if we are wrong to be so sure the attack was directed at the car?" said Lucien, "Greta, I think that my daughter needs a change, again."

"Let me take her, Lucien," said Greta, "I think she may not be the only thing here that smells, though."

CHAPTER 13: TALK TO ME

Julia was sitting in a room that looked out over the Mediterranean on a private Greek island. The leaded glass French doors that led to the room's marble balcony were currently standing open to catch the sea breeze. The dozing sunlit sea lapped gently on a narrow rocky beach at the end of a cove, three hundred feet below the balcony. The room was a cross between a library and an office with built in shelves full of books and closed cabinets for files. The style of the room was masculine useful with paintings of sailboats and horses on the walls. A room size antique Turkish geometric carpet covered the floor and a large antique mahogany Georgian library desk where Julia was sitting was situated in front of the open French doors. There were two computer screens and a wireless keyboard and scroll ball on the desk and also an official British dispatch box in its distinctive crimson leather covering. Two leather easy chairs were located in front of the desk and faced a leather couch with an antique table holding a tray of decanters and glasses between them.

Julia looked up as the man who had tried to kill Lucien was escorted into the room by two very large blank-faced guards. He was bathed, shaved, and his hair was trimmed and combed. He was wearing loose white hospital scrubs and his hands were shackled to a wide leather belt around his waist. He looked curiously around and bowed to Julia as the guards withdrew.

"Madam," said the prisoner. "I can assure you that I can tell you nothing of importance since I know nothing of importance. You should just as well kill me now and save your time and a lot of unpleasantness on my part."

"Oh, I doubt that you don't know anything," replied Julia. "Would you care for some tea?"

The man nodded, and Julia unlocked his right hand and poured him a cup of tea. Then she added two sugars and lemon and handed it to him.

"I won't ask if I got it right," said Julia. "I know I did. You should already know you are going to tell me everything you know, important or not. You see, the thing is, everyone knows something that is interesting or important and they may not even realize it. You are a trained nurse and reported to be a very good one until you started sampling the pharmaceuticals. Now, I do know from my own experience that the shifts in the emergency room are brutal. Especially if you want any kind of an outside life and that if a bit of something is available that will keep you functioning at one hundred percent, it is better for you and the poor sods that get dragged in missing pieces or shot full of holes, right? The thing is, that way lies a bit more and a bit more and the next thing you know you kill someone by being high and making a mistake and you get caught and lose everything."

"You know about me?" asked the prisoner. "How did you find out?"

"We know about everyone. Now, as a trained medical professional, you know what I can do to you with various things. And you are right, sometimes it gets very unpleasant and messy, but I have a deal for you," said Julia. "We are interested in your recent employer and some of the people you have been rubbing shoulders with for the past few years, not you. What I would like to do is to talk to you and have you answer questions and then we will be sending you to England for further discussions with others. We will not turn you over to the Francisci Family but will eventually set you up in practice as a physical therapist in the midlands or Scotland or give you a government job. I will find out if you are lying about anything so just answer truthfully or if you don't know, say so. If you speculate or give me gossip, that is fine, just let me know it is speculation. We are not interested in punishing you for anything you did but you are ours now for the rest of your life and you can decide how long that will be. Now its your choice."

"Isn't this one of those offers you can't refuse?" asked the prisoner. "I really have no choice."

"Your feet are not restrained and the window to the terrace is open," pointed out Julia. "If you made a beak for it, I doubt if I can stop you. The fact that when you leap off the terrace, it is three hundred feet down to the beach is a problem, but there is always a choice. Now, if you choose to cooperate I will have your hands released. We will call for some more tea and a few sandwiches and cakes and we can chat for a while. Oh, and just so you know it, there is now a tracking device installed in your back adjacent to your spine. It contains a quarter ounce of explosives that can be detonated with a rather long and involved sequence of digital numbers to prevent accidents, but then time is nothing to a computer on a relative scale and we only need to push a button."

"You won't give me to the Franciscis and I will get a government job or a practice when I have told you everything I can remember?" asked the prisoner. "You swear to this?"

"Subject to you staying clean. If it will make you feel better, I can give it to you in writing," said Julia dryly, "but as you know things can change at the drop of a hat."

"I'll chance it," said the prisoner. "They tried to kill me last night, as you know. Thank you for rescuing me. Is there anything stronger than tea available?"

"Not while we're working," said Julia. "Now, who hired you to kill Lucien Francisci?"

"I don't know for sure," answered the prisoner. "But I know who contacted me. He is a member of the Francisci Family that works in collections and enforcement in Cairo."

****

Greta was sitting in her office at the airport sipping a second cup of after breakfast coffee with cream and sugar, which she was getting used to, watching the television. Charley was leaning against one wall and Maurice and Dove were sitting on the sofa. The English language channel had been broadcasting periodic updates on the standoff and final surrender of the group at the parking garage three hours ago. Margret Perry was standing in front of the hotel broadcasting another special update.

"Three hours ago, the last opposition at the parking garage here at Cairo's upscale Occidental Hotel ended when special units of the security service accepted the surrender of the remaining terrorists and loaded them in armored vans. The government has not released any further information about the identity of the group involved in the attack or where they are being held. There is also no information on how the group obtained a Department of Antiquities truck that was used in the assault. There has been no official comment or information released on the group that appeared to be preventing the terrorists from entering the hotel through the top floor sky bridge."

The television showed a hall jammed with tables and chairs and wheeled serving carts with a few sofas and garbage cans shoved in at the rear.

Then the picture showed Margret again, "When the gunfight started, quick thinking hotel employees stacked the bridge full of furniture from the top floor restaurant making it impassible and called the police. Witnesses in the restaurant at the time stated that there were an at least twenty or thirty men involved in the fighting on the top floor of the garage. We have been unable to confirm rumors that the defenders were either members of a special government antiterrorist team or Tamarod supporters that were already in place on the roof guarding the Tamarod press conference. According to eye-witnesses in the restaurant the defender on the roof of the parking garage were evacuated by a black helicopter as soon as regular police and security forces arrived. In response to last night's failed assault on their news conference at the Occidental Hotel, Tamarod, the anti-Morsi political protest group, has released a statement calling for mass protests against the government next weekend. We are currently seeking an interview with a representative of Tamarod to obtain more information. This is Margret Perry for American Press, reporting from the Hotel Occidental American in downtown Cairo. Stay tuned to this station for updates on this story and other important news."

"I don't know how she looks the same degree of disheveled all the time," said Greta as she punched the mute button for the TV. "Her hair must be professionally mussed, and I have no idea where she got a flack jacket that has cleavage."

"You're just jealous," said Dove. "Although I think right now you could fill out that flack jacket better than she does. Maurice, we need to talk to Mark and see what he knows about what the hell is going on and who wants us to see that a hydrogen bomb gets bought and sent to some group of Asians. We also need to get together with Armand and Lucien and see what is going on with the negotiations for the bomb and with the Egyptians about the people that attacked the hotel. Also, where are Julia and Willard and Ben and the guy that was going to kill Lucien?"

"When we got picked up in the helicopter last night we flew into a small military base that has a helicopter pad. Julia and Willard were waiting with a car. They took the prisoner and then a man on a gurney was loaded into the helicopter," said Maurice. "Julia told me there had been a change in plans and that they were leaving but would contact us sometime today. They handed me a white jacket and I got in back and Ben went up front as the copilot and the helicopter flew to the airport. We landed, and Ben stayed with the helicopter and left. I got in the ambulance that was waiting and it drove to the hospital waiting area and parked. The guy got off the gurney and I shed my jacket and we walked to a car in the doctor's lot and left. He dropped me off at home without having to ask directions."

"I don't like the fact that they have your address although Julia and Willard probably told him. I have never been so out of the loop on something that was supposed to be my mission since, well since last time I had a mission," said Greta. "I am seriously considering resigning and going to work as a freelance pilot or moving in with Lucien on Crete. What do you think we should do Dove?"

"I think you should stomp your foot and threaten to have me shoot a bunch of people if we don't get some straight answers right now," replied Dove. "I, for one, am getting tired of us being the point man on this since he is normally the first one speared. However, I think that if we take Elise and move to Crete to be kept women without clearing up the little question of who is gunning for Lucien, we will have to spend the rest of our lives looking over our shoulders. Where is Lucien this morning?"

"He has a two-hour session of PT with Amir," said Greta. "Nicole is swimming with him and Celeste is watching Elise and doing homework at the house. I need to go back to London for Elise's pediatrician appointment in a couple weeks, so I would kind of like to clear all this up by then."

There was a knock on the door and Greta glanced at the screen above the door. Colonel Bryon McMillian was standing outside. He was dressed in a blue London cut pinstripe suit with highly polished smooth-toed black shoes and a white oxford shirt and school tie. He was carrying a black leather briefcase and had on mirrored sunglasses. He looked like a moderately successful lawyer, a minor criminal or a military officer in a blue suit. Greta pushed the buzzer and the colonel pushed open the door and came in. He put down the briefcase and pulled off his sunglasses and looked around. Dove indicated the coffee pot and he nodded and walked to the end of the room and got a cup. Then he turned and nodded.

"First, the general would like to congratulate you on breaking up the raid last night," said the colonel. "Then second, he would like to know how you found out about it."

"Maurice," said Greta. "You're on."

"We didn't find out," answered Maurice. "We thought that they were after us since we were transporting the nurse that had tried to kill Lucien and this white Department of Antiquities truck muscled one of our outriders on a motorcycle off the road. We swung the car into the parking garage since we knew we could keep them off us until we could get one of the standby helicopters there. The subsequent firefight was mostly sound and noise. Did any of them get wounded or better yet killed?"

"No, I don't think so, although I don't know where they are," said Colonel McMillian. "They surrendered to a special security unit that works for the president and then just disappeared. It seems that no one knows anything. We did get our hands on the driver of the truck. He got knocked out when the truck hit the entry and was unconscious when the police arrived and they transported him to a hospital in the first ambulance. We are holding him in a secure location here and he has confirmed that the Tamarod was the target. This is one reason they have set a date for the protests."

"Well I will be damned," said Dove with amazement. "The nurse wasn't the target? Are you sure?"

"Yes," said the colonel, "They were after the Tamarod press conference and not the nurse, you just blundered into the middle of something. I doubt if the general will believe you though. How did Margret Perry get there?"

"She rode with her crew to go to the news conference, but she was already there and took on the limo to give it an alibi," said Maurice. "She also started the rumor that there was a special security force already guarding the sky bridge to protect the news conference."

"Where is the nurse you were transporting and what has happened to him?" asked Colonel McMillian. "What have you found out from him?"

"He appears to be part of a power struggle in the Francisci Family," said Greta. "He is out of the country now. I guess you can say he has defected. Julia is working with him for a few days then she will be sending him on for further debriefing. He is now what we call a library asset. We will fix him up with a new identity, get him a job in Derbyshire or somewhere keeping bees or writing life style books, and keep him around to ask occasional questions or identify people."

"What did you learn from the nurse?" asked Colonel McMillian. "Did he know anything about the rebels or the bomb?"

"Lets see what did you learn from the van driver," said Greta. "Did he know anything about the rebels or the bomb? Come on colonel, you know how it works you tell me and I tell you. Right now I don't think that you are telling us everything that you know about the terrorist group or who is backing them and how they just managed to disappear into thin air. Somebody on your side of the fence is giving these boys a lift. You don't just find a bunch of Department of Antiquities trucks parked in a vacant lot with the keys in them and you don't get a bunch of terrorist troops listed as summer help without someone being in your corner."

"True, but the driver was just that, a driver," said Colonel McMillian. "He is a Saudi and part of Al Qaida in Yemen. The group in the desert is not primarily Egyptian, although there are a number of Egyptians involved in it. He is however quite vocal about his theological leanings and the jihad against the west. More important, he told us that the leadership at the camp has promised an action to destroy the will of the west in the next few weeks."

"Why the attack on the press conference?" said Dove. "What did he say about that?"

"They were going to slaughter the reporters. They were supposed to kill all the western journalists as a lesson to the world press," said the colonel. "I checked and there were only three western journalists there. They were Margret, a BBC stringer, and a commentator and local crew from American public television. It's fairly evident that Margret, who is the top CIA agent in the country, was the target."

"Why would anyone try to wipe out Margret," asked Dove. "No Margret, no bomb."

"I don't think they know that," said Greta. "They think that they are dealing with Lucien's people. At least I think they think they are."

"First, I want to know what you learned from the nurse and not just that it is all family business," said the colonel. "Unless you haven't noticed, the Francis have been chosen by lots of high level people to deliver an atomic bomb to a group of terrorists. Doesn't this make you just a little bit nervous? Remember the Estonians? That could happen here, you know."

Greta stopped talking and looked at the colonel. He was holding his coffee cup in two hands at chin level and gazing at her over the top with a slight smile.

She looked at him and then said, "El Lawrence of Egypt? You are an Egyptian officer and what else, a MI6 agent, military intelligence or diplomatic corps? I should have guessed it. The Estonians are not a topic of conversation except for the people who know about the Estonians and the Egyptians don't. You think that someone is trying to set the Franciscis up to take the fall on the bomb if something happens? That wouldn't surprise me at all knowing the parties involved, but then I'm not sure I know all the parties involved. Okay, everyone sit down and grab some more coffee. I want to do a review here."

"What did you learn from the nurse?" repeated the colonel. "I want everything he knows, it could be improtant."

"Not much yet," replied Greta. "Julia called in from points unknown this morning and said that the nurse said that someone fairly high up in Francisci Enforcement and Collections in Cairo contacted him for the job. He has been doing a few injections and standing on breathing tubes for various people the last few years. I don't think he has been pushing people in wheelchairs down hills, but you never know. Apparently, he learned about the Francisci enforcement man when one of his patients told him who he was nervous about and showed his new private nurse some ID pictures before he went to sleep the last time."

"Why would Francisci enforcement people contact an independent hit man?" asked Dove. "That is awfully chancy for them to get directly involved."

"What if you didn't want anyone in the organization to know?" said Greta. "If you are planning on snuffing your boss you really don't want anyone that could move up into his job to know. You would have a fairly low level individual like one of the local collection and enforcement people you knew would keep mum and who worked for you do the arranging. "

"That probably explains why we fished Giorgio Solari out of the river this morning," said the colonel. "However, I would like to point out that Solari was so far down the food chain that he had to be taking orders. I think that the direct contact was made by him because he was ordered to do it and the reason he went swimming is because Lucien didn't. I doubt if they are too happy that the nurse is now somewhere and they have to assume we, or someone, have him and are squeezing him."

"Whom is they? Or is it whom are they?" said Dove. "This is one of those stupid tricky English things like the basketball team is tall, or the basketball team are tall. Anyway, the whom I got that right at least, are you talking about?"

"Whoever is trying to take over the Francisci Family," said the colonel and laughed, "The deal with the bomb is too important to have a family squabble derail the transfer. There is a lot of muscle behind this. Where is Lucien actually at now?"

"Two hours of therapy with Amir at Amir's club," said Dove. "Celeste is babysitting this morning and Nicole went to the club with Amir and Lucien to swim since the pool is heated. They should be back to the house for lunch in a minute. Why?"

"I really think that we need to talk to him and get his opinion on the situation. He is the obvious expert" said the colonel. "Besides, I know that Clarissa is making meat and cheese pies for lunch since I stopped by on the way over"

"We should probably leave now then," said Maurice. "That way we can get some before Amir gets there and eats them all."

Colonel McMillian, Greta, Dove, Maurice and Lucien were sitting at a table under the shade of a cloth pavilion on the terrace having lemonade after lunch. Elise was in her carry chair under a beach umbrella at the target range where Nicole and Celeste were practicing with paint ball rifles under the supervision of Asim. Lunch had been as good as anticipated and serious discussions had been delayed until the food had settled. Now Lucien set down his glass and looked at the others.

"I truly think that I may just retire when this is over and move back to Corsica," said Lucien. "I have made Amir an offer to work full time for me as a trainer and bodyguard and he said he would consider it. I think that if I offered him the job of construction and maintenance director for the estate and my other properties on the island with a side job as trainer for me he would probably come. After considering the news you brought colonel, I believe that I should have a talk with Carlo Conein since Giorgio Solari worked directly for Carlo as a fixer. I doubt if he was taking orders from anyone else when he contacted the nurse."

"Do you think that Carlo is behind the attempt on your life?" asked Greta, "Do you think he could take over the family?"

"It is likely that Carlo saw my stroke as a chance to take over my leadership of the family, but I don't think that he counted on my recovery," answered Lucien, "As for Giorgio ending up in the river, Carlo is a very direct person, not unlike you and Dove, Greta. He always settles things by the most direct action available. I don't think Carlo's actions in this situation will directly impact anything but internal family business. I will make enquiries about Giorgio and Carlo on my own. However, there is another item that is of interest to all of us. This morning, Armand informed me the Asian person dickering for the bomb is sending six million euros, more or less in gold. I am not exactly sure how you get six million dollars more or less, although taking market fluctuations into account, it actually is reasonable."

"When is the gold going to get here?" asked the colonel. "How is it going to be delivered?"

"It isn't coming here," said Lucien. "It is being delivered to Marseille in a container with some other things in about three or four days. We will move it to Corsica, which is what would be normal and would be expected by everyone. The thing is I think we should start arranging to get the merchandise for them."

"Lucien, I know it is heresy to ever question the actions of your companions in an enterprise but the colonel had a real point," said Maurice. "He said that there were a lot of real big players in this and that they had chosen you to deliver a fair sized hydrogen bomb to a bunch of Asians of unknown persuasion or if there is a slip-up in a group of radical Middle Eastern terrorists."

"Then he brought up the Estonians," said Dove. "Lucien, I don't want to see you get hurt."

"I have been considering this," replied Lucien. "Now, why would someone want one atomic bomb? As Greta pointed out, either to shoot it off to make a point, like we think the people in the desert are planning on doing, or if they are a nation, to place it on display as proof that they are members of the nuclear club. There are several nations, including a few locals, that would like to join the club, including Iraq and Syria, but showing off an atomic bomb in this region usually attracts the attention of Israel with dire consequences. The thing is, that the people that are trying to gain possession of a bomb appear to be a group of Asians. The price of a bomb is huge. It is in the nation state range, so I believe that we should look for a nation in Asia that wants to give the impression of having a nuclear arsenal but doesn't, as our customer."

"That makes sense," said Greta. "We have been leaning that way too. Who would you nominate Lucien?"

"Well, I don't have all of the contacts that most of you do in that area and I am just guessing but first I would think about who it wouldn't be," answered Lucien, "India has bombs, as does Pakistan, North Korea, and China so in my opinion they are not worth considering. I don't think that anyone like Afghanistan or Iraq could raise the money and besides, they would be painting a target on themselves because of the Al-Qaida association. I doubt if Japan would be in the market for one, since if things get out of hand with China, they can probably borrow some from other people and the same for Taiwan. South Korea is a possibility and so is Vietnam. However, we now have logistical and payment problems as well as considerations of security to make sure any device reaches the right people, we only have a few weeks to deal with all this and I don't want to upset anyone. I believe we all should get together and talk, and by that, I mean the group that was at the meeting at Julia's house."

"This is an awfully involved operation to have evolved from seeing a sniper getting ready to shoot someone," observed Dove. "By the way, who was he going to shoot?"

"I don't think that Julia ever said," said Greta, "and somehow I think that it may be relevant. I still think that this is all one piece somehow. And I agree with Lucien, it's time for everyone to get together. I am calling Mark and Julia and having them get hold of Blossom and Merry. When does the down payment get here, Lucien?"

"In about a week," said Lucien. "The boat is coming up the Red Sea now, according to Armand's contact. I will call him and verify that, but I would suspect a meeting in a day or two to discuss how to handle the transfer and collections would be advisable since we will need some time to make arrangements."

"I will contact General El-Shazly and Miss Perry," said the colonel. "Now I must go. I'll call again later."

The colonel stood and walked to the gate where the guard picked up a phone and called. A minute or two later, a car with darkened windows pulled up to the gate and the guard checked it and then let it into the parking area. The driver got out and saluted the colonel and opened the rear door and then colonel got in the car and left.

"Why do you think that the target that Hamid Masoud was after is relevant?" asked Maurice, "Any real reason?"

"Yeah," answered Greta, "Dove and I figured out that a high speed, high altitude drone is not going to notice a shadow on a window, so this means that someone either knew that he was there, or he was spotted some other way. So, we got lied to at the very beginning. This means that they, Blossom and Merry and others that will come to light as we keep digging, wanted us to break up the kill. The colonel said that the Egyptians had figured out that Hamid Masoud's employer was having him kill people who are experts in enriching uranium. Now, everyone assumed that this is to keep any of the current nations, like Iran, that are trying to enrich uranium to make a bomb from doing it. This is a logical assumption, but it has also occurred to me that the reason that Hamid has been getting steady work is not to keep someone from making a bomb for strategic reasons like Israel verses Iran but to keep anyone else from making a bomb and widening the playing field any farther. Have you ever played croquet, Maurice?"

"As a child, we played it in mid-summer at garden parties," said Maurice. "Why do you ask?"

"Because there is a move called Roquet where you bang into your opponent's balls to knock them away from scoring or even get them clear out of the game. It is one way that you win," answered Greta. "If you are trying to build a nuclear bomb, and be the first one of the people trying to do it lately, one way you can do this is by knocking off everyone else's key people. If you keep sabotaging your neighbors so that they are always playing catch up, you win the race and get to have a vote in the look we got one club."

"Now that is an interesting insight, Greta," responded Maurice. "Who would you think is doing that?"

"Someone who is trying to win by buying a bomb instead of making one." said Greta, "Or is trying to pass off carry out for homemade. We do have a lot of things to discuss with everyone."

Asim, Nicole, and Celeste walked back across the yard from the practice range toward the table. Nicole was carrying two paint ball guns and the baby seat and Celeste was carrying Elise. Elise had been transferred to a front carrier sling and was looking around curiously. When she saw Greta, she waved her arms and started crying. Celeste walked to Greta and took Elise out of the carrier and handed her to Greta. Elise started trying to nurse and Greta sighed and pulled open her blouse and shrugged off the strap of her bra. Elise stopped crying and started sucking.

"I guess this ends the discussion," said Greta. "Maybe it isn't a good idea for a section chief to have kids, at least babies. I'm going in and get some strained pears for her. Do you want to come, Celeste? I think you have more spoon practice than I do, and I might need some help."

Lucien held out his hand to Nicole and she handed him one of the paint ball guns. He looked at it and then handed it back and Nicole showed him how to load the paint balls and then charged it and handed it to Lucien. He pointed it at the wall and pulled the trigger. A single paint ball sped across the lawn and hit the wall making a red splatter mark.

"It's an air gun?" asked Lucien. "What about the spot?"

"These are what are called soft mark paint balls," answered Nicole. "They wash right off. They also make hard mark balls for tournaments and engagements. That's where a bunch of people get together and fight. Everyone gets a color and when you get marked everyone can see who got you. The hard mark paint is pretty permanent and has to wear off. I guess some of the boys that are really into paintball games smear themselves with cold cream to make it easier to clean up."

"How many times will they shoot, Nicole?" asked Lucien. "By the way I have noticed that you are a very good shot. We will have to get you a small shotgun and we can go and shoot at the trap range when we get back to the estate. I find it very entertaining."

"That would really be fun, Signor Francisci," said Nicole, "Here, now shoot."

Nicole flipped the auto feed lever on the paintball gun and handed it to Lucien. He pointed the gun at the wall and pulled the trigger and splatters started appearing as dozens of balls hit the wall. Lucien looked at the gun with more respect.

"Nicole, can I borrow this until tomorrow?" asked Lucien. "I would like show it to Armand when he comes."

"Certainly, Signor," said Nicole, "Do you have time to help me with my French tonight? The sister is giving a test on pronouns tomorrow and I'm not sure if I know all the rules."

"Certainly, Nicole," said Lucien, "and thank you for calling this paint ball gun to my attention. I'll tell you what, I will give you ten euros for every point over eighty you get on your French test and that should make studying easier, all right?"

"Yes sir," said Nicole, and smiled. "I think I will go and start now."

Nicole ran into the house and Lucien turned the paint ball gun over in his hand and looked at it. He took one of the packages of paint balls that had been left with the gun and looked at the package and the manufacturer. Then he started examining the gun.
"This looks quite realistic," said Lucien. "How many shots, balls, does one hold and how many times can you fire it before you need to reload the air supply?"

"Actually, these are custom made to look like an actual assault rifle, Lucien," answered Asim. "I was going to move the girls up to an actual twenty-two caliber rifle in a few weeks. Skeet shooting would probably be a good hobby for them, especially if you were to participate since they would like to impress you. These guns aren't typical though. The guns that the tournament and serious players have use a hopper to feed them and have large air tanks. I would say that one of them could fire seven hundred to a thousand times without replenishing the air supply and you just keep dumping paint balls in the hopper until the air runs out. They are just toys, but they are a good way to teach some basic gun handling."

"Still, they are interesting," said Lucien, "I think I will go on in now and take a little nap before anyone sets up another meeting or discovers a crisis."

CHAPTER 14: CONTINGENCY PLANNING

Merry, Mark, and Julia were sitting on one side of the table in the library at Julia's borrowed villa on Gezira Island. Dove, Greta, and Lucien were sitting on the other side and Margret Perry and Blossom were sitting at the head of the table. Blossom was sitting with her hands in her lap and Margret was tapping a pencil on the table and looking sharply at everyone.

"Well, now that everyone is finally here I would like to finalize the directions for the operation," said Margret Perry. "We have been informed that the six million in gold will be reaching Marseille by the end of the week. I would like to know why the gold went to Marseille instead of coming here, Mr. Francisci? Was this one of your cute little tricks?"

"Actually, Miss Perry, the negotiators agreed to use an already developed channel for supplying material from Singapore to our organization," answered Lucien. "They felt that it was a tested channel and there was no reason to change things. As for cute tricks, I really don't know any. When I was younger, I could wiggle my ears, but it has been years. I would, however, like to know where the bomb is and how and where it will be delivered to us."

"Where the bomb is currently located is not something you need to know and how it will be delivered here is our business," answered Margret. "After consideration, we have decided to handle the delivery of the bomb to this location ourselves."

"So, there is really no further reason for my organization to be involved," said Lucien. "Thank you, Miss Perry. Where would you like the six million in gold sent?"

"Keep the gold and anything else you can squeeze out of them. We still want you to deliver the bomb to the buyers," said Margret. "They think they are dealing with you and we wouldn't want to do anything to make them nervous. I cannot stress that this is vitally important. We need that bomb to go to the buyers."

"And who exactly is that?" asked Dove, "The terrorists out in the desert or the Asians who have the money or someone else.

Where are our Egyptian buddies, by the way? Aren't they invited to this little tea party and chat?"

"As a matter of fact, they are not for various reasons and you know damn well that the bomb goes to the Asians somehow. I cannot stress how important it is for that bomb to get to where we want it to go," said Margret, "I will not stand for any more crap from any of you, do you understand me?"

Dove started to stand up and Lucien put his hand on her leg and pushed down while Greta kicked her ankle. Dove sat very stiffly in her chair and then relaxed and leaned back.

"And I was just wondering, Margret, where is your side kick?" asked Dove, "You know, your trusted producer Serena Watson? I heard a nasty rumor that she was last seen on a plane that was leaving town for parts unknown right after the screw up at the hotel where we kept you from getting snuffed. Any comments?"

"Serena Watson is no concern of yours or your whole organization, for that matter," responded Margret, "she is our problem, if there is a problem of course, which I deny."

"Oh, of course, and if you have a traitor that has flown the coup, it is our ass to bail out your little project since we are the visible part?" said Dove with a sneer, "I don't think so, baby."

"I want her out of this now, right now, and her boss and your whole local office, Blossom," demanded Margret, "and while you're at it, I think we can handle any further coordination in the delivery and forwarding of the bomb without EUOPS assistance. We will be working directly with the Francisci. Consider this an American show from now on and thank you, oh so much, for your help. Now, if there are no more useful comments, I will be leaving. You all know to keep your mouth shut, or there will be repercussions."

Margret Perry abruptly stood up and walked out of the room. Blossom looked at Dove and sipped her tea and then pulled a face and held up her cup. Julia sighed and then walked to the sideboard and poured another cup of tea and brought it to Blossom who sipped it and looked at Dove.

"Why did you do that, Dove?" asked Blossom, "We were just barely hanging on to the corner of this whole thing. Merry, do you think that you can still talk to any of the Americans and keep us informed?"

"Probably," replied Merry, "Margret is not popular in her organization, but she is very highly placed politically. Dove, I have a great deal of respect for you and your opinions but what in the world did you antagonize her for? Did you want to get thrown out of the operation?"

"Of course she did, Merry," answered Blossom, "I recognized what you were doing, Dove but I was hoping we could stay engaged a bit longer. Well, I guess it is time to make a clean breast of what has been going on, as far as we know and then you can tell us what is going on that we don't know."

"That would be appreciated, Blossom," said Julia, "and I think the girls do need a bit more of an explanation on what has been happening. Also, I did talk to Hamid Masoud for quite some time and found out a number of things that have not been discussed yet."

"Well, Julia said that you girls figured out that a high altitude supersonic drone would be a very poor way to spot a shadow that wasn't moving," said Blossom, "but everyone was thinking on the fly and sometimes that is not very good at providing answers that survive a logical analysis later. I myself did not think that you would fall for it, but the Americans seem to have a very low estimation of our female field operatives, an opinion I seek to further at every opportunity. We were informed by the Americans that Mr. Masoud would be there getting ready to shoot the head of the Iranian technical negotiation team only a few hours before he was going to do it. Your team was the only one active, if not actually physically present, in the area at the time, Greta, and so, against my better judgment, I gave in to pressure from the Americans and had you scare him off. They said that I should have you file a report about the effectiveness of the little drones, tell you thanks, and have you go and measure your apartment for drapes."

"Blossom, I am going to have to learn to count to one hundred every time I see an American operative," said Greta, "They still owe Francis a dead body and Margret leaps to mind."

"You are getting calmer, Greta," said Blossom, "The Americans, of course, underestimated your curiosity and immediate interest in the assassin. Which lead to your attempts to investigate before you could be stopped, if that was vaguely possible. Then, with the attempted kidnapping at the Garden City apartment, the situation became even more confused and you got even more interested. When you contacted Lucien and found out about Elise's adoption and the fact that the Egyptians had contacted Armand about the bomb, I just shrugged since you were in full involvement mode already and I let you run with it."

"But what is it, Blossom?" asked Greta, "We can talk about Dove getting us thrown off the operation in a minute. I would also like a straight answer about why you blew our cover with the Egyptians."

"As far as I know, this particular situation is a plot that the Americans and English and some Asian countries and a few locals have been hatching to get an atomic bomb into the hands of a particular country in Asia. But I am not sure who, since I am only top-level security cleared," said Blossom bitterly, "Merry, do you know what is going on?"

"Not fully, Blossom. I only run a national security agency," said Merry. "This is one of those things that the various unnamed inter-agency, multi-government cooperative strategic and policy committees dreamed up and ran up the political ladder to the various tops and back down and then handed it to the CIA inner circle and Her Majesty's very dirty tricks group at Portsmouth for implementation. I hear the Israelis are actively involved, too. It is not an individual operation so much as a philosophy lesson on atomic weapons. I hear that these particular thinkers and doers were in charge of the recent sabotage of the Iranian centrifuge program and the air attack on the Iraqi reactor in eighty-one, as well as the Estonian explosion."

"Well," then since they appear to be dedicated to limiting the development of atomic weapons worldwide, and since they did the Estonian operation, it appears that they are currently trying to get someone else to accept a Trojan horse or maybe a Trojan death sentence," said Julia. "There are a few things that need consideration here, though. In the first place, when the bomb exploded for the Estonians, it was in a deep protective bunker and it didn't truly go off. It was extremely dirty and not very powerful as atomic explosions go."

"True, everyone in the base and a few people outside were killed and some radiation escaped, but it was only a partial atomic reaction," said Merry. "The missile may have tried to fly indoors, or the warhead may have tried to explode prematurely, and the devastation was major but not catastrophic. No one wants something like that to happen on the surface. In the first place, it would be too noticeable, and people would start asking questions about global nuclear security. This put some constraints on this operation. They don't want a big bang and they don't want it on the surface. So we know the policy group is against the development of more nuclear nations, but they intervened at the talks to stop Hamid Masoud to save a top Iranian nuclear scientist, very curious isn't it?"

"Before we drift totally off the subject, I would still like a straight answer about why you blew us with Egyptian security, Blossom," said Greta. "I'm waiting."

"You are also quite tiresome, young lady," said Blossom. "In the first place, we had to be engaged in this or the Americans would have complained to the top-drawer people and this is one of those sticky little political things. Actually, you were an obvious choice and I did not, as you so colorfully put it, blow you, which is vulgar. You were already in contact with Lucien and he had been contacted to get a bomb and also you were scaring off assassins and doing other high-profile things here in the country, so you were the logical choice to work with the locals. Besides, they knew who you were from the rather colorful films they had."

"That is a low blow, Blossom," said Greta.

"I don't know one way or the other. I haven't seen the films," said Blossom with a sniff, "Also, Greta, I must confess that I wanted Ben to establish a potential long term stay in place organization under the radar. In the first place, Southerland is a known quantity, Ben is comfortable in the local environment and he has a background and experience that are reasonable for the Southerland cover. Besides, you were already on the local radar or they wouldn't have put surveillance cameras at your apartment and you were also connected with Mark who was suspected of being someone's agent."

"Besides, we were ordered to cooperate with the Egyptians from on high. It is vital that Egypt stay firmly in our camp," said Julia. "And Colonel McMillian isn't exactly a stranger."

"Yeah, well, we already figured out he is a plant," said Dove, "One of yours Merry? Now, what can you tell us about the attempt at the apartment by the guys who tried for our car."

"I think I may be able to shed some light on that, Dove," said Lucien, "I have asked around and also I have been able to do quite a bit of thinking since I have been freed from so many administrative duties. The attack on your car was made after I had adopted Elise and at about the time I had the stroke. I think that someone in the family has been very naughty. I think that they arranged for the terrorists to attack the car to eliminate Elise before I could officially acknowledge her. I think that the car was targeted since it had been identified, including the license plates, from when you had it in France. You and Dove had also been seen driving it to your old apartment here and it was not anticipated anyone else would be driving."

"This would mean that quite a few people are sharing information," said Blossom, with a frown. "Someone in your organization is sharing information with the terrorists, Mr. Francisci, and apparently, the Egyptian security services are also sharing with the terrorists."

"Why do you say that, Madam?" said Lucien. "It is probable that someone in the family sent the terrorists to harm Elise and Greta, but why do you say that the Egyptian security service is working with the terrorists?"

"I doubt if anyone in your organization knew Greta's address in Egypt," responded Blossom, "Besides, we know that the Egyptian government, at some level, is providing cover and supplies for them. I doubt if there is any reason the Egyptians wouldn't be providing information too. The attack on Margret also supports the conclusion since she had not announced to the world that she would be at the press conference. We were unaware that she was there, but someone must have known and that is probably the Egyptians."

"Is Colonel McMillian a plant, Merry and for who?" said Greta. "Do you think he is the leak?"

"No, he is not a leak. Colonel McMillian is an Egyptian patriot that is tasked with maintaining contact and providing cooperation and coordination with MI6 and other western military security agencies," said Merry. "He is a legitimate Egyptian and English dual citizen and has been engaged with us in several very high profile joint operations that no one will ever hear of. The colonel is just a working rank. He really is a general and in charge of national security for the northern area of the country. The reason that he is personally involved in this is that he is very worried about what is going on now. He wants to make sure that any atomic weapon that comes through Egypt does so with no tracks that can lead back to the soon to be changed government."

"An interesting choice of words, general," said Lucien. "I assume you know something?"

"I don't know anything for sure, but I have my suspicion that if the population takes to the street like the Tamarod wants, which is likely, the military will step in to restore order," said Merry, "and they will do that by kicking out the Morsi government, including whoever is supporting the people in the desert. They don't want any connection to the bomb even breathed about, except that they cooperated in the western plans to move it on. The military has run this country for a long, long time and probably will for the foreseeable future."

"So, you think the Tamarod is not bluffing?" asked Blossom, "That gives us a very short window to get this done. We will only have a few days after the money gets to Marseille to effect the transfer."

"What do you mean by us?" asked Dove; "I thought I just got us thrown off the operation."

"Oh, don't be silly, young lady," responded Blossom, "You and Greta are only officially dismissed for Margret's comfort, as is EUOPS. I believe you two wanted it that way? Why?"

"Blossom, I haven't been this jerked around since I used to get towed on skis by my Uncle's horses in Russia," said Greta "Dove, why did you shoot off your mouth and Blossom, why did you let her and then do what you did?"

"Well, I got the hint when Lucien broke my leg and you hammered my shin to a pulp that you really didn't approve what I was doing, but the fact is you were both wrong," said Dove.

"Blossom, I believe that you and I both figured out that what the Americans really want is a fall guy to cover their rearmost body portion when this blows up, literally. The Asian government is going to want blood for real and they will come out shooting since they are being shipped a fake or defective bomb. You set us up to be the very visible presence here, Blossom, and to take the fall if anyone screwed up. True?"

"Almost true, Dove," said Blossom and sighed, "I am going to have you and Greta come home and work in the central office for a while and learn something besides gunfight diplomacy. I admit that I have thrown you in the water to sink or swim recently, but you have managed not to drown, which is handy, although there has been a great deal of splashing about. As Merry has explained, Egypt is going to explode in a week or two and Ben is hunkering down as a legitimate business. When this happens, you girls are leaving and going somewhere safe and he is staying. He has no association with the bomb that anyone can prove and yes, you are the ones that everyone can point at. The thing is, now that you are officially off, we don't dare let things miscarry or it will be your fault because you refused to cooperate. Do you see the position you put yourself and EUOPS in?"

"Yeah, screwed either way," said Dove. "All right, I admit that I don't like Margret Perry and I was mad at you because you don't explain what you wanted us to do, but you sure didn't help us any."

"On the contrary, Dove," said Blossom, "by letting you run with the assignment, and run off at the mouth just now, we have finally clarified the rules. If it works, then we are squeaky clean, but not involved since we were dismissed, if it fails, it is kind of our fault but since we had been dismissed we are still not directly to blame. Sometimes, two easily defined extremes are the best position. Especially when you are not involved either way and now EUOPS is not involved at the local or international level. You heard Margret. It is now an all-American show, thank God. We will need to tell Colonel McMillian immediately, so he can get clear too. Now, Lucien what do you intend to do to help us all along?"

"To begin with, the six million in gold is being delivered at Al Ghardaqah on the Red Sea about now and will not complete its voyage. It will be loaded on a cargo plane and proceed to Switzerland where it will be evaluated, and a value determined by tomorrow. The other thing is, I become nervous when someone says I should sell their home and keep the money, Lady Covington," said Lucien. "It is apparent that the Americans do not expect there to be any meaningful reimbursement for the bomb or they would be here with their hand out. I know that Margret said the Asians are planning on giving the terrorists a large amount of counterfeit securities and bonds to pay us with, but the terrorists plan on capturing the bomb with their troops when it is delivered and probably plan on keeping the money too. This will not happen since, as I pointed out, we will not accept a trunk full of money on delivery and someone will need to have made a verifiable payment to a financial institution of our choice before we give them the code to arm the bomb or remove the tamper proof explosive charge. The buyers are going to need real money or negotiable credit and they know it. If there is ever a transfer of counterfeit securities, it will only be to assure the Egyptians."

"What tamper proof explosive charge?" said Blossom, "I didn't know anything about that."

"The one we are going to inform them is included in the package containing the bomb, Lady Covington" replied Lucien, "Who knows, we might even slip one in if we can locate the bomb before we are supposed to turn it over. I am sure you are aware the bomb will be booby-trapped in some way and will explode at a time and place that the Americans have selected. I am not at all happy with the Americans expecting the family to be the identifiable agent in obtaining and selling what will appear to be a defective nuclear weapon to a nation, Lady Covington. I believe the buyers should demand that their experts see it and get to examine it before concluding any deal."

"Oh, call me Blossom. In what way would it be dangerous, Lucien, if I may call you Lucien," said Blossom, "I can think of several things that would be dangerous, but what do you mean exactly?"

"I would be honored to call you Blossom. In a way it is like the difference between our organizations, Blossom," said Lucien, "As the leader of a criminal organization, I can have you killed or have your house burned, or your children kidnapped.

What I can't do, is call in a drone and shoot a missile at your whole family or get a court order and seize your property and I cannot have police and tax agents hound your every move. Governments are very dangerous because they are uncontrolled by anyone and are bullies. I believe I need to make sure that someone else is directly to blame for the sale of the bomb and not the family in general and definitely not Armand or me. I believe that you were hinting that you would like to have Dove and Elise and her mother stay at my estate for a while when we leave Egypt?"

"Yes, if that would be possible," said Blossom, "I think we would like to pull back to the northern Mediterranean for a while and let the Middle East settle down since I don't know how far the unrest in Egypt will spread. Since Greta and Dove have an air service that was previously located on Corsica it would be logical to relocate there when Egypt becomes chaotic."

"I will need to solve the current problems of the family before I return but I would be most honored to extend an invitation to the young ladies to stay as long as they like," replied Lucien, "There is already talk about Greta's plane visiting quite often over the last year and the fact I adopted Elise, so it would not be an unexpected relocation."

"Do you think we can finish getting this mess we are in the middle of now settled first?" asked Greta, "Although lying on a chair at the pool in the sun in my swimsuit while someone brings me cool drinks and headache pills has a certain appeal right now."

"Julia, you said that you had obtained more information from Hamid Masoud?" said Maurice. "Is any of it relevant to our current problem?"

"I'm not sure, to tell you the truth," replied Julia. "But Hamid said he had been hired to shoot the leader of the Iranian technical delegation who is also the head of the Iranian centrifuge and enrichment program. If Greta is right and the people that he keeps working for are trying to prevent anyone else from getting their own bomb first then this, and the information that Colonel McMillian gave us on Mr. Masoud's activities, would suggest that the people he is working for are having trouble producing highly enriched uranium, which is the key ingredient of an efficient atomic bomb. The rest is just engineering."

"What would that mean?" said Lucien. "They wouldn't be able to make a bomb?"

"Well, not exactly," said Merry. "They could make a bomb, but it wouldn't work quite right. The impurities would cause a damped reaction and it would fizzle. The thing is, how many impurities does it take to make a bomb not a bomb? There is always some residual non-fissile materials in any bomb but it still is a bit of cut and try with while you are learning to make them and everyone leaning toward having more purity than less."

"Except when they can't do it," said Greta. "So if you couldn't quite pull off a bomb and you have been telling everyone you had one and the first one you try is a total bust, you really have egg on your face. In some Asian cultures screwing up is not an option. If you had already had one fizzle and your second try was a bust too but you were already bragging up another test happening real soon you would be desperate to get something that you knew would work really spectacularly. When you got something, you could make up a story to go with whatever you got. Explain it as a small bomb for missiles, a big bomb for rockets, a medium bomb for rickshaws or whatever, the press releases would be adjusted to fit the bomb you got hold of."

"I see what you mean, Greta," said Blossom, "Now, how about that? It would also mean that it would be tested underground, which would be very nice as far as we are concerned, it would fulfill a bunch of announcements that they have made but not carried out, and it would boost a very young leader's credibility. It would be tough on a small nation's economy though."

"The costs would be tremendous," said Lucien. "I don't know how much it costs to develop a competent nuclear technology and actually build a bomb these days, but we were planning on asking half a billion dollars, American, for the bomb we were selling, as a reasonable middle of the road figure for a functional weapon. Hmmm, I need to talk to Armand and some of the gentlemen that are involved in weaponry. I hear that these things eventually go dated."

"Yes, they do, but the one we are getting is about four or five years old and although it was supposedly lost at sea, the details of its presumed recovery and where it has been are very vague," said Merry. "We will need to patch that up before we proceed any further, I think. I'll handle this and put a bug in the ear of some of my American friends. In addition, I believe we are all considering the same country as the potential purchaser?"

"Well, they fit the pattern as though it was made for them," said Blossom. "Isn't it strange how the facts actually reflect reality sometimes."

"Excuse me, but I just mostly kill people for a living and am just learning all the niceties of slipping them a booby-trapped weapon of mass destruction," commented Dove, "Whom are we discussing, please and why do you think it is them?"

"I'm sorry, Dove," replied Blossom, "A little history then. This country announced with a great deal of fanfare that they were going to test a multi kiloton atomic device in October of 2006. When they pushed the button, the results were rather underwhelming. Their great socialist weapon produced less than a half a kiloton of explosive force and some rather interesting radiation signatures. However, the presence of radiation did show that there had been at least a partial nuclear reaction. Medium sized fusion bombs are relatively easy to make, the American trinity test in 1945 turned out to be a twenty-kiloton device although they were expecting less. To make a device that is very large, or very small, demands a lot more technological know-how than this country had then or probably has now. Everyone decided that what they had produced was a defective device or in the highly technical terminology of atomic scientists, a fizzle. The next time they gave it a whirl, in 2009, there was another great deal of talk and a loud noise, but no one ever detected any radioactivity from the test. This would be a first in containment. The Russians overrated the explosion and the other scientists that do that kind of thing said this atomic test could have been a big pile of fertilizer, ammonium nitrate, and the claims were the other kind of organic fertilizer that we have come to expect from these people. Dove, I think you and Greta should work at the home office and get some training and background and go to university after this assignment. I really have been expecting far too much from you girls without advanced training."

"Well who is this country for heaven sake, Blossom," said Dove. "It sounds like they are a likely candidate."

"North Korea, dear," said Julia, "and I agree with Blossom. Both you girls should get a university degree to help your potential for advancement. You just might learn something useful along the way too."

CHAPTER 15: SURPRISE, SURPRISE

Greta was dozing, and Elise was tucked in and sleeping between Dove and Greta, a bad habit that had gradually developed. Elise still occasionally needed her middle of the night feeding, even though she was almost six months old now and had been sleeping through the night more and more, but when she demanded attention, Greta had been lazy about taking her back to the girls' room. A small sliver of light shone on the wall of the bedroom as the door opened a crack and Greta rolled over and saw Celeste peeking in the door.

"She's here, Celeste," said Greta, "She was hungry, and I got her. I thought you were in your bunk."

"No, I was downstairs studying," answered Celeste, "We have examinations next week and I was worried. When I finally couldn't think anymore, I came up and Elise was gone so I thought I should check. I'll take her back now."

Greta looked at the clock. It was almost three thirty and Celeste needed to be up by seven to be at school by nine.

"Celeste, what's troubling you?" asked Greta, "Just a minute."

Greta got up and picked up a soundly sleeping Elise and walked to the door, grabbing a robe off a chair on the way by. She slipped through the door and closed it softly and motioned Celeste into the girls' room and put Elise in the bottom bunk with Nicole who immediately made room for the baby without waking. After arranging the covers over the two small sleeping girls, Greta motioned Celeste to follow her into the sitting room and indicated one of the chairs.

Greta sat on the couch and looked at Celeste. Really actually looked for the first time in months. Celeste had become a fixture in Greta's life. It seemed she had always been around doing duty as a nursemaid and helper and babysitter when Greta needed her. Celeste had become the younger sister you dumped the kids on when something came up you had to tend to. She was always there and never complained, and it never occurred to you that she had a life and plans and needed to do things too.

241

What Greta saw was a young, just blossoming woman, dark, pretty, and petite with a dancer's litheness and figure and huge dark worried eyes. There were dark circles under Celeste's eyes and she unconsciously clenched and unclenched her hands.

"Celeste, things have been hectic, and we have all been taking advantage of you and dumping all the odd jobs and extra chores on you," said Greta, "I'm sorry. Now, what's wrong, Celeste? Have you been sleeping any recently?"

"I'm scared," answered Celeste, "I'm scared all the time. I'm scared for Elise and Nicole and me and everyone else. At home everyone respected us and we had men with guns around all the time and we knew they were there to protect Don Francisci because he is an important man, but we never had anyone try to kill him. We have guards here too, but the man tried to drown Signor Francisci and the guards didn't stop him. Nicole and I had to stop him, and I didn't know if I could do it and I was terrified. And no one likes me, and I don't have any friends at school and they all speak Farsi or Saudi and laugh behind my back and call me the gangster. I don't know what you are doing and how I am supposed to act or what I am supposed to do here. I'm scared I am going to screw up and you will all be mad at me. I can't concentrate, and I am behind in my school work and the sister said men came to school last week and asked about me and Nicole and our records for some reason and I can't sleep, and my stomach hurts something awful and I've got a period."

Celeste broke into tears and tried to stifle the crying by biting her lips. Greta stood up and walked to the chair and knelt and took Celeste's hands in hers.

"Okay, first, you are not going to school today," said Greta, "You are staying home and getting some sleep and TLC and then we need to have a long talk about what is reasonable to expect from you, besides your school. I think we may need to send you and Nicole back to Corsica, not because you have failed in any way, but because it may be too dangerous here very suddenly. I think I will send Elise with you just to keep her safe, if that is all right with you and your mother. I need to talk to Lucien about this, but first I want you to get some sleep. I will go and get you some warm milk and some aspirin. Go and put on your pajamas and then you can sleep on the sleeping porch since Charley and Joey have moved out. That way you can sleep in. I'll sit with you until you go to sleep."

Celeste nodded and walked into the girls' room and Greta went downstairs. Clarissa Caparoni was standing at the bottom of the stairs with her lips compressed and a worried look on her face. She had a bottle of aspirin in one hand.

"I assume you heard everything, Clarissa," said Greta. "We still need some warm milk though. I think Celeste probably needs her mother right now more than she needs me. Did you know about men checking at the school for Nicole and Celeste?"

"No, I didn't," said Clarissa. "I am suddenly very nervous about that. What do you think?"

"I think that the girls should stay home for a while and we should think seriously about getting you and your family the hell out of here, pronto," said Greta. "We are all sitting on a box of dynamite and watching the fuse smoke. I don't think that any of this should be your problem. I also think that Lucien should go too. Right now, and not then. He doesn't need to be here, and this place is going to go up in flames."

"I agree with you," said Lucien getting up from a chair where he had been sitting in the dark, "I just talked to Armand, the gold has arrived at the bank and has been certified and accepted. It is in an escrow safety deposit box in Switzerland with three keys, one for us, one for the purchaser, and one for the bank. Greta, I have been thinking and I believe it is about time I suffered a dreadful relapse and Armand suffers an accident that will lay him up for several months minimum. We can talk about it tomorrow after Armand arrives, but first I think you need to get some warm milk and I will get an extra blanket since it is cool, and Clarissa can bring the aspirin. Then we all need to go up and tuck a young lady in and assure her that none of this is her fault and that we love her very much and we are all going home, and then we should sit with her until she goes to sleep."

"I think I will stay with her tonight," said Clarissa, "I think she may need me."

Greta hadn't managed to get back to sleep by six o'clock when Clarissa stuck her head in the door and quietly held out a cup of fresh coffee. She beckoned to Greta and Greta slid out of bed and walked to the door, Clarissa slid in and handed her the coffee and then went to the closet and looked at what was hanging there. Clarissa pulled a long white floor length satin dressing gown with puff sleeves and ostrich feather collar trim out of the closet. It was an impulse purchase that Greta had made in Monaco because it made her think of Princess Grace, who had died before she was born. Greta had never worn it, but she took it and slipped it on. Then Clarissa picked up a hairbrush and pushed Greta down on the bench at the dressing table and started brushing her hair.

"Now, go and wash the sleep out of your eyes," said Clarissa, "Armand arrived a few minutes ago and Mr. Francisci would like to see you now. Evidently, there is something important that won't wait. I will find you some slippers and a ribbon for your hair while you do a cold-water wash."

"I can go right now, Clarissa," said Greta, "I don't need anything."

"It is never good to let them forget we are women and the mothers," said Clarissa, "Otherwise it endangers us all. Go, wash your face and then put on these gold sandals and I will put a pink mother's ribbon in your hair. They should not expect us to appear like a genie out of a bottle. I will make a light breakfast and bring it in. Do not forget you are the most important woman in that room."

"Hardly that," said Greta, "Blossom and Julia and a lot of other people out-rank me."

Clarissa stood back with her hands on her hips and shook her head.

Then she said, "That is just your job. You are the most important woman in the family. You are the acknowledged mother of the daughter and heir of Don Francisci and are more powerful than a queen, probably richer too."

Greta looked startled and then thoughtful and nodded. Greta went to the bathroom and washed her face with cold water so it glowed and then grabbed an eyebrow pencil and some mascara and did her eyes. Then she stepped back and nodded. She was getting a lot better at this. She put on light pink lipstick and brushed her teeth and came out and slipped on the gold sandals while Clarissa put a half inch wide pink ribbon in her hair like a coronet. Clarissa inspected her and then took a bottle of *Forbidden*

Passion perfume from Dove's side of the dressing table and touched the applicator to Greta's throat.

"I don't normally wear that. It is downright slutty," objected Greta, "especially in the morning."

"Then it's a good choice I'd say," said Clarissa, "they are in the downstairs living room."

"I should get a gun," said Greta, "just in case."

"I would say off-hand, you are already fully armed already, but here," said Clarissa and handed a small automatic to Greta, "don't put it anywhere it will make an unsightly bulge."

Greta looked in the mirror and shook her hair so it fluffed out then settled around her shoulders and smiled. Then she nodded and handed the gun back to Clarissa and walked out the door and down the stairs

"Damn," said Dove from the bed. "That is really impressive, Clarissa. How is Celeste?"

"Sleeping," said Clarissa. "She has been having cramps. My little girl is truly a woman now. I had expected it when she started taking care of Elise. Girls want babies, not lovers or husbands, but babies and they grow up when they get one regardless of the source. Are you getting up?"

"Only if you sneak me up some coffee," said Dove. "I'm taking a good hot shower and then putting on some jeans and a top since I have the strangest feeling we will not be going to the office officially today. I'll check on the girls while you go and make breakfast."

When Greta was about half way down the stairs, Lucien saw her and pulled himself to his feet. Armand and Maurice glanced at her and then stood. Maurice grabbed an easy chair and turned it to face her and Armand and Lucien bowed.

"I am sorry we disturbed your rest, Greta," said Lucien. "Armand has important news and we need to determine a plan for us now. Seeing you though, I must admit that I wish I was a great deal younger than I am now, but you do remind me of how it was then."

"Would you like coffee or tea or juice?" volunteered Armand. "I can fetch you something, anything."

"No, I'm fine gentlemen," answered Greta and leaned back in the chair then curled her feet up under her. "Clarissa is making

245

something for us and I've had coffee. She said something was important?"

"Yes," replied Armand. "The Asians delivered the six million in gold and we cut off the shipment before it left the Red Sea and had it examined. Since we don't care about registered bars we melted it down and did a composite assay. The results are that there is a bit over six million euros in gold now in our hands in new registered bars. There was only one counterfeit bar and we informed them of that. I mentioned it when I told them they had complied with our request. They offered to send another bar, but I told them that it was unnecessary. They then asked when they could examine the bomb and where was it without prompting. I told them that we had not yet received it and that it would be a day or two before we would take possession and that they would have to make the payment by credit transfer before we would deliver the device and the firing keys. They were somewhat puzzled about that and said that they were paying the Egyptians to make payments and handle logistics. I said that was fine but we would need payment in full for our client and certification from the financial institution that the payment was valid and in the hands of our client before the bomb and firing codes were turned over."

"What did they say?" asked Maurice. "I don't believe that we had discussed any of this with them."

"They were somewhat put out," responded Armand. "But I told them that we were just the facilitators and that the owner had some requirements too. They said that they would like copies of the manuals for the device and pictures of the outside of the device with me holding a current newspaper in every frame so that they could verify it was a valid working device before they put up a dime and that we would need to outline delivery and payment procedure that everyone is comfortable with in detail."

"Oh my," said Lucien. "How wonderful. They give us a license to steal without even knowing. But first, we need to get someone else to take the fall for selling a bad bomb to the Koreans."

"How did you determine it is the Koreans," asked Armand, "and which set, North or South?"

"We were just kind of guessing," answered Greta, "but you know, that is a reasonable question. There are a lot of good reasons for the South Koreans to have a bomb when you think about it. It would kick a lot of sand in the face of the North Koreans if the south could test a bomb that was big and scary. Especially since the North Korean tests have been less than spectacular. Still, there is a lot that says it's the north. They have had one or maybe two at least partial failures and people are starting to laugh at them, and not behind their back anymore."

"I don't really think it matters," said Armand. "The people who own the bomb and a whole lot of other people want us to get it to whoever it is."

"And EUOPS has been told to get off the team," said Dove smugly.

Dove was standing on the stairs with Celeste. They were both dressed in flannel pajamas and terry robes and slippers. Celeste's hair was in pigtails and Dove had two ponytails, one over each ear. Both had scrubbed faces but had on light eye make-up and lipstick.

"Hi Armand, Maurice," said Dove brightly, "Greta and I have been told by Margret that our services are no longer needed and that the whole thing is an American show now. We need to call Colonel McMillian right now and tell him too. Celeste is staying home today since she is a bit under the weather and has been worrying herself sick. She needs a bit more information about what is going on since she doesn't know what to do. I thought that she and I could have breakfast and work on her essay for tomorrow and then if she feels up to it I could explain a few things to her later. Then the girls and I might go to the zoo. Nicole has still not seen a camel."

"I am sorry you are not feeling well, Celeste," said Lucien. "I find a day of rest and relaxation every so often is something I need to stay sane. And remember what they teach you for one day or even one week in school is not as important as staying sane. Besides, you will either not need what they taught today or learn it somewhere else if you do. Do you need an excuse? Should I call the school?"

"Thank you, Signor Francisci," said Celeste. "Mother said Nicole should stay home too and that she would contact the school. Mother also said we might be returning to the estate in Corsica in the near future. Was she right?"

"Actually, I think we will all be going to the town house," said Lucien. "It is just a few blocks from your school and in the city where most of your friends live. You can go to the shops or visit them. We will probably have to get you a scooter though."

"Oh, I would like that, Signor," said Celeste, "When will we be going?"

"In a few days," replied Lucien. "Now, go and have something to eat and have your mother bring us some more coffee please."

"You are going to the town house, Lucien?" asked Armand. "Why are you doing that?"

"As an old man who is handing over the leadership of the family after suffering another stroke in the fairly immediate future, I feel that the new leader should have the estate," said Lucien. "Don't you? Now, let me explain what is going to happen, and Greta, since you are officially out of the operation, may I request your help, totally unofficially, of course."

"Maybe you should explain a bit more, Lucien," answered Greta, "but I will help you as much as I can."

"First, we need another meeting with the negotiators for the purchaser. I suggest we tell the Americans that the buyers demand pictures and the manuals and that the bomb needs to be moved to somewhere we can take the necessary photos since they need pictures showing Armand and the latest newspaper with the bomb. Then we take the pictures and get the various instruction books and things that the prospective buyers want and then give them the books and pictures," explained Lucien. "Then I think that the buyers should demand a hands-on examination in a place we choose and an explanation of how the bomb was acquired and who had it. Finally, I think that we should figure out how to follow it around so we know where the bomb is so it won't get lost."

"I think that the things you suggest will tend to reassure the purchasers, and we do still need to work out a payment method that is acceptable to all parties," said Armand. "But how will this help us, Lucien?"

Then he told them how.

Armand was sitting in the outdoor terrace of the Intercontinental Hotel at a corner table behind some potted palms in the screened area. He had already looked under the table and chairs for recording devices and had ordered some melon and hard rolls and coffee when Margret Perry arrived. He stood as she approached the table and sat down without a greeting. He nodded and then told her what the negotiators wanted.

"That is totally impossible," said Margret Perry. "There is no way that bomb leaving where it is now."

"Then why is it an impossibility?" responded Armand. "They just want manuals for the bomb that are paper, an inexpensive commodity, and pictures of the inside and outside of the bomb to show there is no damage or problems. Then they will want a hands-on examination to make sure the bomb is as advertised. Also, they want to know who had it and where it has been and how they got it."

"Well, it ain't going to happen," declared Margret Perry, "Tell them you will cut the price but no information."

"I hardly think that will be an incentive since they will obviously just think there is a problem with the bomb and someone wants to unload damaged goods on them," said Armand. "I would be very dubious about buying something as potentially dangerous as a damaged atomic bomb. I will tell them and they will probably refuse and we can return their gold and all go home.".

"We can't do that, for God sake," yelled Margret Perry. "This is too important. Convince them that they don't need pictures and stuff and no access to the bomb."

Armand looked at Margret Perry and folded his hands so that the two index fingers pointed up from his folded hands. He put the fingers in front of his mouth and his thumbs on his chin and pulled his lower lip down with the sides of his fingers. He half closed his eyes, pursed his lips and shook his head no.

Margret Perry stood up and looked at him furiously. She had been in on the planning of the whole thing as part of the nuclear policy group and it had been a simple and easily workable plan. If it blew up now, it would seriously damage her career. How in the world had it gotten so complicated? All she had to do was to convince some crooks that worked for money to slip a gimmicked bomb to the people who were desperate for it. Now everyone was making all kinds of demands. The damn EUOPS people had challenged her authority and she had kicked them out without informing the rest of the nuclear policy group. This had stripped one layer of protection from the operation, but she had gotten a belly full of the silly old biddies and the two teenage wet workers that thought they knew everything and now the crooks were getting cold feet.

She had slipped up when she had told EUOPS and MI6 that the Egyptians were going to pay for the bomb with half a billion dollars' worth of fake bonds and securities. The crooks had already gotten six million in gold and that was also a screw up on her part. The gold was supposed to come here where it could be scooped up by the Ministry of Defense and confiscated as soon as the deal closed but at least it was gold the Asians had furnished.

When the problem about the transfer of payment had come up she had convinced the nuclear policy group to authorize real, off the book, agency slush funds for the half a billion so it would be possible to make an actual above-board transfer of credit. The money had come from the CIA and was in the Bank of Hong Kong. The agency would authorize a payoff to the crooks, so the bomb and codes and manuals would be transferred to the Egyptians from the crooks. The Egyptians hadn't been informed about the demand for a verified credit transfer and still thought that the payoff would be with paper cash and phony securities while the Asians thought that the Egyptians were using the promise of securities to back a loan from the bank, which was fine. But when the bomb actually changed hands and the money moved out of the Bank of Hong Kong the agency would know where it went and could confiscate it immediately. Since the United States had put up the money when the cash was recovered it would go to the treasury and then quietly back to the CIA slush fund. But first, she had to get the train back on the track.

Okay, so the buyers wanted some paperwork and some pictures. This was actually not a big deal. The bomb was already in Egypt although no one but her knew it and it could be moved after the photo shoot. She needed to take two deep breaths and think. One of the current problems that had her worried was that no one had seen Serena Watson since the night of the gunfight at the Occidental hotel. She hadn't left town and she hadn't been back to the hotel, she hadn't phoned and most telling was that she hadn't used her credit cards. Margret hoped she was either safe or dead somewhere. Serena could cause some real problems if someone had picked her up, since she knew about most of the operation.

In the movies the heroes bit their cheeks to bloody ribbons and died with a smile on their lips after hanging by their wrists and being beaten to a pulp, also usually missing fingernails, eyes, and other more intimate parts of their anatomy, all without spilling the beans. Realists knew heroes didn't exist. Everyone could be broken eventually and Serena wouldn't even put up a useless fight before telling anyone everything she knew about the plan. Now Margret needed to change things enough to avoid detection and move fast. Thank God, the man she was looking at was the only one who had handled negotiations with the Egyptians. It might be an American show now but there still needed to be a fall guy when the bomb went boom.

"All right, you can come right now and we can buy a camera and a newspaper on the way," said Margret, "The bomb is in Egypt. I'll take the pictures. You can give them the pictures and we can email them copies of the manuals. Tell them the official manuals were lost in the plane crash."

"Fax the printed manuals to me and I will make copies and take the pictures and enough manual pages to prove they are genuine with me to the meeting," said Armand. "Use a fax because you can't hack into a fax machine like you can email. If something goes adrift I won't mention that the manual pages and pictures are in my briefcase and if there is a problem later they won't have a full manual until they pay. How many pages are there?"

"I haven't got the foggiest idea," replied Margret, "I'll get them scanned and transmitted starting as soon as I can. You should easily have them tomorrow before the meeting, I guess. Now, let's go see the bomb."

An hour later Armand downloaded the chip from the camera and sent the pictures to Lucien from his hotel room after being dropped off by Margret. Then he waited as the manuals downloaded to a fax. At midnight they were still printing and he put another ream of paper in the printer and went to bed. The next morning, he ordered breakfast, added two more reams of paper and fresh ink to his fax and finally put the pictures and some pages from the printed manuals in a suitcase and drove to the Heliopolis house in a car with darkened windows. When he walked into the first floor living space, Greta was sitting in an easy chair looking at bomb pictures and having after breakfast coffee.

"So, this is what a hydrogen bomb looks like," commented Greta looking at the pictures with the newspaper held against it, "Not very impressive. I thought it would be a lot bigger."

"You have probably only seen the pictures of the first ones from the history books," relied Armand. "Unlike American cars, they do not get bigger and bigger every year, except for destructive power, and even that has been stopped since blowing up everything in an area the size of Ireland is not really reasonable if you want something left to invade. Recently, atomic weapons have gotten smaller, both in power and size. This is really a fairly new one and as you can see, it will go in the back of a delivery van, crate and all. Which is how they moved it after I took the pictures."

"They moved the bomb after you saw it?" said Greta, "How do we know where it is then?"

"I put on one of the little paste-on micro trackers that looks like an inventory label," said Maurice and pointed at a picture. "This one, right here, under the big data plate by the two other little stickers. It pings only when you send it a command, so it's really good for tracking things in trucks or planes since you can verify stuff is there with a single ping and then ignore it until you want to check again. Currently, the bomb is on the other side of the airport in a charter jet."

"Whose charter jet?" asked Armand.

"Ben's," said Maurice, and laughed, "a Southerland Oil heavy freight 737-700C. Ben converted the plane to the cargo configuration and leased it to the Egyptian government and gave them the keys. He doesn't have any people there either. The plane is in a Sahara Heavy Lift hanger."

"Interesting," said Greta. "Sahara Heavy Lift is the one who has been flying supplies to the terrorists in the desert and now we end up with the bomb in one of Ben's planes that is in one of their hangers. We should look into this."

"Yes, we should," said Lucien. "I have been admiring the pictures you took, Armand. Celeste has copied them to my pad and showed me how to greatly increase the size so the smallest detail is visible. Truly amazing the things that are possible now. You have a meeting tomorrow with the negotiator for the purchaser?"

"Yes, I do," said Armand. "I have been requested to carry a little recorder since our Ms. Perry doesn't trust me."

"Well, she probably shouldn't," said Dove. "Why are we making two copies of the how-to manual for the bomb, Lucien?"

"You never know when you might need one, Dove," said Lucien. "Suppose we were to lose the set we now have or end up with another, what is it called, Armand?

"Well, the manual claims it is an A/N B-83 bomb, thermonuclear multi fuse high altitude one-megaton yield general purpose device. The errata and upgrade appendix refer to it as a B-83 Mark four series three neutron boosted general purpose device," said Maurice. "The instructions are over eight thousand pages long and the appendix is another seven thousand. Both of them are full of little things with a skull and crossbones mark about how you will kill yourself and most of the surrounding villages or city if you unplug the blue safety lock initiator wire on the reset module before you unplug the battery for the barometric fuse sensor. I can see why we have never had a nuclear war. No one has ever learned how to shoot one of these things off."

"Interesting," observed Lucien. "Well, take them the pictures and the operating manual, Armand. Also the first few page of the upgrade manual. Tell them they get the rest of the manuals, firing codes, and trigger and activation module when we get the money."

"Are you really going to charge them half a billion dollars for the bomb, Lucien?" asked Dove. "I really can't even believe there is that much money in the world."

"Actually, Dove, we bring in that much money every three or four weeks from our various activities," said Lucien. "It's not all profit, of course. Salary and overhead expenses like retirement and travel and medical, liability, and fire insurance eat up quite a bit. Still, we do manage to clear a few billion every year. But then I guess you are right, it isn't money, it is bookkeeping."

"Greta, I take back everything I ever said about going and living with Lucien and being a kept woman," said Dove. "Can we leave tomorrow, please?"

Lucien laughed and then reached over and patted Dove on the cheek.

"You can come and live with me any time you want to, dear," said Lucien. "With no duties or requirements anymore, sadly enough. However, I think that we should make arrangements for Elise and Alonzo's family to go back to Corsica in the immediate future. When will Merry and Colonel McMillian be here?"

"Any minute, Lucien," replied Maurice. "How do you plan to transfer the money? I assume that everyone in the world, literally, will be looking for the transaction."

"Yes, I'm sure they will, and the Americans know that the funds are, in fact, legitimate since they are providing them," said Lucien. "Although they don't know we know that too, and they undoubtedly will know where they are credited as soon as it happens. The thing is, I thought about how Hamid Masoud was getting paid and I have an idea. Ah, Colonel McMillian and Merry are here."

A bright red SUV pulled through the front gate and then proceeded to the new gate blocking the bridge over the swimming pool moat. The guard at the bridge looked into the car and then opened the gate and the SUV moved into the rear parking area by the garage. It stopped and Merry and Colonel McMillian got out. They were wearing golf clothes and Colonel McMillian stopped and hit an imaginary ball as they walked to the kitchen entrance. Maurice got up and walked to the door to buzz them in and then laughed as they looked down at their feet and then took off the cleated shoes before they entered the living area and walked on the hand tied antique silk carpet.

"It looks like you two were up early," observed Lucien. "I used to play but I don't know what I would need for a handicap now."

"Don't listen to the old fraud," said Armand. "He plays bets by the hole at his estate and loses on the front nine then trims suckers on the back nine by tripling the bet. Anyway, how was the game this morning?"

"Rather like cat and mouse," replied Merry. "The Assistant Minister of Defense was not too subtle in trying to find out where the bomb was and when it would be delivered. He is acting very nervous and was quite surprised when I informed him that the Americans had politely told us to go away. Bryon, Colonel McMillian, had already briefed General Abdul El-Shazly the head of the Military Intelligence and Reconnaissance Command on the situation and had pointed out the fact that if you were only an observer nothing could be your fault, regardless of what happened and the general had agreed. But the minister invoked national pride, sovereign rights, international agreements and the fact that everyone had agreed that Egypt would take the lead and so the CIA was out of line. He said he was going to complain to Margret Perry and informed everyone that everything that the CIA did was his business and that he and Egypt could not be dismissed out of hand. We agreed that it was all between the United States and Egypt now and totally his responsibility. I don't think he liked that."

"We also confirmed that Margret's sidekick has disappeared," said Bryon McMillian. "She hasn't been seen since she got a call just before the Tamarod press conference and the shootout at the hotel. She told the film crew she was going to go back to her hotel and they should film the news conference without her."

"Right before the shooting started?" asked Maurice. "Do you think there is a connection, like someone tipped her off?"

"An intriguing thought, at least," replied Bryon McMillian. "I immediately made some inquiries at my office and she was last seen by a hotel surveillance system camera entering a white nine passenger government van in front of the hotel. It is a typical type used by everyone and one of the doormen remembers a white government van parked in the waiting area for a few minutes. It was a plain door van from the motor pool. We couldn't see the back of the van in the picture from the camera so we didn't get a vehicle number or the plate number. There were over forty vans checked out of the motor pool that night and yes some of them were checked out to the Department of Antiquities, but we have no way to determine where any of them were without some way to identify them and tracking all forty is impossible."

"So," said Lucien, "if any of my people who were in the area saw the van and got the number, we could see who had it out? It could be important to know who spirited Miss Serena Watson away and why."

"She could be dead," said Greta. "But that could just be wistful thinking on my part. I sure would like to know where she is and what she really does for a living. What did General El-Shazly and the minister have to say about her disappearing?"

"The general was slightly troubled, and the minister just shrugged and huffed about the bomb and how he needed to know everything," said Bryon McMillian. "I also asked about the people that were captured at the gunfight at the parking garage. Neither one of them admitted that they knew where they were or who was holding them, or even if anyone was."

"What do you think is going to happen on the thirtieth with the Tamarod call for a general strike and demonstration," said Lucien. "That is less than a week."

"I think that there will be a massive popular demonstrations," replied Bryon McMillian. "Some of them may turn violent. The Morsi government has made a lot of people very angry and has not improved the economic position of the country. There is also a great feeling of betrayal by the Christian minority and the young people that supported him."

"What is the military going to do?" asked Lucien. "Will they act to suppress the demonstrations?"

"I doubt it," answered Bryon McMillian. "The active military is not enamored of the Morsi government any more than the people are. He does have the support of the Muslim Brotherhood militias so it could get bloody. I think the next move is up to our president. Now tell me about the bomb."

"It is in the country and I took pictures of it last night," said Armand. "The people negotiating the purchase wanted copies of the manuals and some pictures. They are going to demand a hands-on examination of the bomb and they want a detailed explanation of where it has been."

"I set up some back story and the CIA said thank you very much," said Merry. "You know, eventually Muammar Gaddafi is going to be used up for all of the lies we tell and no one will believe us anymore. Thank God that hasn't happened yet. To make a long story short, we have told one of our Libyan pensioners who was a general in the Gaddafi regime to verify that Gaddafi bought the bomb from a Polisario general from Western Sahara, who is now missing. The story goes that the B-52 went down in shallow water and in sight of a fishing boat. The boat took coordinates of the location of the plane and a group of divers recovered the bomb a couple days later. When the Polisario general realized what they had, they didn't want anything to do with it and sold it to Gaddafi for five million euros and breathed a sigh of relief. Gaddafi was still wondering what to do with it when the people revolted and it was sold again to a rebel in Chechnya for one million euros in gold by one of the Libyan officers in charge of guarding it as part of his exit strategy. The Chechen rebels have supposedly been keeping it in storage in Libya and trying to market it since if they used it, the Russians would make Chechens a thing of the past."

"That is almost believable," said Maurice. "How do you back it up?"

"Well, there is the testimony of our Libyan general, a number of rumors we started about an unidentified Western Sahara fishing crew that got rich and left the country and another story that the Chechen rebels are about to get some major funding and were looking for some arms," answered Merry. "Armand's people are negotiating with the Chechens right now for a multi million dollar order and the CIA is going to make a sizable donation to them when the bomb sells so they can close the deal."

You're kidding," said Dove. "The CIA is funding a terrorist organization in Russia?"

"Well yes they are, there and in several other places," replied Merry, "besides the CIA likes Chechen rebels. But actually, the CIA is putting up the money and Armand's people are giving the Chechens a good price on everything since the agency approved the backstory and want to make it creditable and the Franciscis want it to be accepted too. I think the story will hold up fairly well."

"Now, just a few details to work out about how to deliver the bomb," said Armand, "and make sure we get the money, of course."

CHAPTER 16: SETUPS

A stiff wind blew off of the glaciers on the top of the Alps as the cold, pre-dawn air tumbled down the steep slopes and valleys and rushed toward the lake thousands of feet below. Armand had changed out of his tuxedo in the back of the disabled delivery van sitting in the turnoff with its front-end protruding into the travel lane and put on the ripped duplicate tuxedo stained with his blood that came out of a pint he had donated that morning. His highly polished handmade shoes had been exchanged for an older pair that looked the same and just as polished that he had been meaning to send in for re-soling but had donated to the present operation. He was sitting in the back of the van on a large box of paper plates and shivering. He took another drink from the bottle of excellent burgundy that he had ordered at the restaurant where he had hosted the dinner for the other members of the family council members.

At the dinner he had explained that Lucien appeared to have suffered another stroke and was thinking about retiring from active leadership of the Family. He had also told them that Lucien would be returning to the town house in Calvi in the near future and was withdrawing from the present business with the sale of the bomb. Armand said he would be handling the final payment and delivery details but that he felt nervous about having no backup if something happened to him or if Lucien had a major stroke. The council members, Mr. Valentino Guérini, Mr. Carlo Conein, Mr. John Carbone, had listened gravely and then John Carbone broke the silence.

"Armand, I don't know crap about arms or arms deals," admitted John Carbone, "I would volunteer but really almost anyone else is more qualified to take over if something happens to you. How likely do you think that it is that Lucien could have another stroke and why are you worried about yourself?"

"He has had two as far as we can tell," answered Armand, "the first one which was fairly major and a smaller one recently. It may even be something else, but we don't know and he is being cantankerous, as the Americans say, and refuses to go to the doctor. As for my health I am fine as far as I know but I need a back-up since I don't want to blow a half a billion-dollar deal."

"True," agreed Valentino, "that is a lot of money. I would like to suggest Carlo as the backup for you. He is the one that has the muscle and a general presence wherever in the world we do business. I don't have a lot to contribute to this operation, since I just run casinos, gambling and loans, which are at fixed locations. But the thing is, if Lucien has had two strokes, it is short odds he will have another one fairly soon. We may have to take on the management of the whole family sooner than we want to. I just as well may say that if he goes, you get my vote, Armand."

"Mine, too," said John, "You have the most business experience for general activities."

"I would go with the majority," agreed Carlo, "but I would offer to be your backup until we can bring some more people up. I would also suggest we examine the field for new blood for all of our positions. I have been worried about what could happen with an accident or plane crash or something. We need more people in second tier training to be in the decision making process."

"I totally agree with Carlo," said Armand, "I will talk to you tomorrow about what is going on with the bomb and the delivery, Carlo. I have my notes on the sale that I will leave with you tonight. It looks like you are it, Carlo."

The next day, Armand met with Carlo in the morning and explained that the purchaser's scientific team had examined the bomb during a flight in a chartered aircraft and had pronounced it acceptable, although there appeared to be some minor corrosion on the exterior casing. The delivery was set for mid-morning this Saturday. The bomb would be transferred from the hanger where it was still in the guarded airplane to another point of the purchasers choosing using a white van to be provided by the sellers. The counterfeit bonds and securities would be given to the Egyptians at that time. But only after a verified notification was received from the bank that the actual CIA funds had been transferred to the family accounts would the purchasers' representative be given a black briefcase containing the fuse, the arming codes and the manual of modifications.

"So the Egyptians are being scammed since they think they are getting the money and are planning on hijacking the cash and the bomb? It seems straight forward enough," said Carlo, "Where are the actual funds going to be transferred to?"

"An account in the Bank of Macau," said Armand, "Apparently, Lucien has an in with the management. Then they are going to use the funds as collateral to back a construction loan for a fictitious casino in Macau for Valentino and in a couple years they are going to declare the project a failure and the loan uncollectable and seize the account. It's costing us three percent."

"Three percent is better than anyone's taxes," said Carlo and laughed. "Do I need to know anything else?"

"No, not now," answered Armand, "If there is any future problem, contact Margret Perry, the news person. She is also CIA and in charge of this whole thing, since she assumed total control of the whole operation and kicked the other spies and spooks off."

There was a rap on the van door and Armand snapped back to the present. A large, very competent man in a white lab coat had just rapped on the van's rear window. Armand took another drink of the Burgundy

"Are you ready, sir?" a large man that Armand had never seen before asked.

"Yes, but I need to put this half bottle of wine in the car first," said Armand, "everyone saw me buy it."

The man nodded and Armand walked to the car. The crew had sprayed the inside and trunk with two gallons of petroleum and the smell of raw gas caused Armand to gag slightly. A dead man in a blue suit and mirrored sunglasses was sitting in the driver's seat. He had died of blunt force trauma but had been saved in a freezer until now. He had been thawed out over the last two days and now he was sitting behind the wheel of a Francisci Family owned Mercedes Benz S class. Armand gave the half bottle of wine to one of the technicians that was doing final arrangements and turned back to where the large man was pulling on a pair of special gloves. The gloves were padded on the inside but had metal inserts under the leather of the outer shell.

"What are the gloves for?" said Armand as he stood shivering in the dying wind.

"So I won't break any bones sir," said the man, "ready?"

"As much as I'll ever be," said Armand, "It's nice to know you won't break any bones."

"Yes sir," said the man, "it takes your hands a long time to heal."

Then he slapped Armand in the face and broke his nose. Armand gasped and the man punched him in the stomach and then in the ribs. Armand felt two ribs go and then when he was punched in the jaw he passed out. The man kicked him in the thigh to make a large bruise and then looked at his face and nodded. He ripped open Armand's shirt and scratched him with a jagged rock he had gathered on the roadside and then carefully put the rock down where he had picked it up. He ripped the leg of Armand's tuxedo and used a currycomb to make a large bloody scratch on top of a newly forming bruise. Then, he broke Armand's arm. He picked Armand up and nodded at the technicians. One of them brought the last of the blood from the donated pint and sprayed it on the pavement where the man holding Armand indicated.

A technician pushed the dead man over on the passenger's side and got in the car. He backed it up and then got up to twenty miles an hour and sideswiped the front of the delivery van and stopped. He backed up and got the car up to forty miles and hour and drove within an inch of the van and stood on the brakes locking the wheels and sliding the car past the van until it stopped. Then he got out again. He pulled the dead man over behind the wheel, and fastened the seatbelt so he would stay in the car during the fall and tumble, and turned the wheel to the right. Then he tied the wheel in the full stop right position with a piece of cotton string soaked in gasoline.

The technician opened the back door of the car and put the wine bottle in it to wedge it open then he stripped off the gasoline soiled white lab coveralls and gloves and put them in a garbage bag. He added the bag to a garbage bin in the back of a small truck with seats along both sides of the covered rear box then he got in the truck and sat down. A phone rang and the man in charge answered, then he nodded to three men in coveralls, gloves and shoe covers.

They pushed the car to the edge of the road and then one of them lit the driver's seat with a propane torch. The interior started burning as they pushed the car over the side of the road and down a rocky slope to the cliff. The burning car bumped and bounced down the slope and then fell and came to rest on a scree slope among some large boulders several hundred feet below.

The man carrying Armand walked to the front of the van and put him down on the shoulder of the road on the blood spot and where he would be seen. Then the man hit him so his nose started bleeding again and dug into Armand's arm with the currycomb so it was bleeding too. Then, the members of the special activities group got in the truck. They showed the man in charge their equipment and materials and he checked it off as they put it in the garbage bin along with their gloves, shoe covers, coveralls, and hairnets. The truck started and turned onto the road and the last man obliterated its tracks with a willow broom and got in. Then the truck proceeded up the road a quarter mile to a junction and then turned toward Italy.

The truck would be micro cleaned and returned to the family moving company in Lugarno and the men would be dropped off one or two at a time to pick up cars or board trains and buses so they could make their way out of the country and back to their duty stations.

Twenty minutes later, the overnight ski bus from Zurich came around the corner and swerved to miss the van. The driver saw the smoke and flames from the burning car and the man lying beside the road. He pulled off the road and ran back with a blanket to cover Armand while a young man on the bus called for help and the other passengers watched the gas tank of the car explode.

****

It was early in the morning at the Heliopolis house in Cairo. Lucien had just been informed that Armand was in the hospital in Lugarno with broken ribs, a broken arm, numerous contusions and a suspected concussion after a traffic accident.

The car Armand was riding in had gone off the road when it swerved after hitting a stalled vehicle and the driver had been killed but Armand had managed to jump from the moving car. Armand had a few broken bones and numerous scrapes but would survive. Lucien had not told anyone yet and he probably wouldn't tell anyone that Armand had been hurt until later. Everyone was saying goodbye to Alonzo and his family before they went to the airport to fly to Corsica. Alonzo's family was going back to Calvi in Corsica to get the town house ready for Lucien who was scheduled to join them in the next few days.

"Are you sure you don't mind, Celeste?" asked Greta, "I won't be long. Just a couple days at most."

"No, we don't mind," said Celeste holding out Elise so Greta could kiss her, "Do we, sweetheart? Now, give mommy a big kiss and then we will go home to Corsica and I will finish my tests and then we have the whole rest of the summer to go to the beach and play in the garden and eat sorbet and have fun."

"Celeste, do you have the extra lotion from Julia and the shampoo and...Oh, I am just chattering," said Dove sniffling as she kissed Elise. "I know you will take good care of her. If you need anything, call."

"I will," said Celeste reassuringly. "I need to go and join my family now. I will take care of Elise, and I do mean what I say about playing in the garden at the house in town. The gardens are beautiful and completely safe. Come quickly because she fusses if she doesn't see you two every day."

Dove looked at Celeste and smiled and winked. Celeste looked down and blushed and then came over and kissed Dove on the cheek.

"Thank you so much for your help, Dove," said Celeste, "I finally have a big sister too. Now I really do need to go."

Greta watched as Celeste pushed the stroller to the parking area and then put Elise in her car seat while the driver loaded the stroller. Celeste turned and waved, then got in the car.

In the past week, Dove had helped Celeste improve her wardrobe to reflect her new status as a young lady and more than just a schoolgirl in a uniform. Celeste was wearing a light flowered summer frock, hose and sandals. She had on a gold crucifix and a ruby ring and carried a white glove leather custom-made Georgiou Marchesi shoulder bag with a reach in pocket for a twenty-two-magnum automatic pistol with a high capacity magazine and one of the cute little pink military grade Tasers. Her hair had been cut and styled professionally by a very good beautician and her nails had been manicured and polished. She was still learning make-up, but Dove had helped her for the trip home and her large liquid eyes shone.

Elise's newly repaired armored car pulled out of the parking area and onto the street on the way to the Mediterranean Air Service terminal where a private jet would fly them to Corsica.

"There goes one of the future heart-breakers of the world," remarked Lucien. "I am going to have to post a guard on her."

"Don't you dare," said Asim. "I agree she is going to be unbelievable but she is entitled to a bit of fun. Seriously though you should have her watched to make sure no one kills her before we get her fully trained."

"Trained for what?" asked Maurice. "You haven't recruited her have you? She is only sixteen, for heaven's sake."

"No, we haven't recruited her," said Dove, "but I was already a wet worker at sixteen and look how I turned out. I have a respectable government job, a family, a pension, medical benefits and two weeks off every year for a seaside holiday. All of that, and I am still young enough to still get carded if I want to drink at the local pub."

"You are a baby faced leader of professional killers for a totally black undercover international spy agency," pointed out Maurice, "but on the other hand, the benefits are top notch, especially if you live long enough to get the pension. Now, wave and don't cry, Greta. Elise will be fine for a few days, she is used to being taken care of by Celeste."

"I know that, God damn it!" said Greta and ran into the house crying and Dove followed her.

"There are a huge number of things you could have said that would have been a lot better, Maurice," Asim commented. "She doesn't want her baby taken care of by someone else, and she sent Elise with Celeste because we all have a really good chance of getting in serious trouble or getting killed now. Otherwise, she would never have sent Elise away."

"Yes, we need to go inside and talk," said Lucien. "I have some news."

Lucien leaned on his cane as he walked into the house and Asim gave him a hand opening the door and guiding him through. Maurice brought up the rear and shut the door. As soon as they were in the house, Lucien put his cane over his shoulder and walked up the stairs to the second floor. He sat down in a chair and motioned for Asim to bring him a glass of whiskey with ice.

"Thank you, Asim," said Lucien. "I am missing Alonzo and his family already since they all spoil me. I really don't need the cane except for show but I am still winded when I climb the stairs."

"I wish you had gone with them, Lucien," said Dove, "but at least Elise and Alonzo's family are well out of it."

"I will go on home tomorrow or the next day. We need to talk about the bomb delivery," said Lucien. "Armand was fairly seriously injured in a traffic accident last night and is out of commission for several months. Carlo has now taken command of the whole process and is in charge of the delivery of the bomb and collecting the funds. I expect to see him contact Margret Perry and the buyers very soon."

"My God, is Armand all right?" said Greta. "What happened?"

"He was driving back to France from Switzerland to catch a plane after a meeting. The preliminary reports from the police say that his car hit a stalled van on a mountain road. The van was protruding into the road on a blind curve," said Lucien. "His driver tried to stop but lost control and went over the edge of the road and then the car fell several hundred feet and burned. Armand was either thrown free or got out and fell and slid on the road but didn't go over. He has broken ribs, a broken arm, a possible concussion and numerous scrapes and bruises but he will survive. He is however out of commission for several months."

"So, Carlo is taking over for the family?" said Maurice. "How interesting. Isn't he the one that hired a thug to drown you?"

"That is only a supposition," said Lucien. "Never the less it is a good one. But I trust him to do exactly what he normally does. He is competent but always wants just a bit more. Ah well. Come with me, Maurice, I need to show you something and then my ride will be here."

Maurice nodded and stood up while Lucien finished his whiskey and then walked to the kitchen of the house. There were two large cases sitting on the pantry table.

"Since Clarissa is gone I don't think the kitchen will get much use aside from coffee so I had them put them here," said Lucien, "I had them open a case so I could show you."

Lucien reached in the case and pulled out a paintball gun. He handed it to Maurice who looked at it and then held it to his shoulder. The gun had a forward grip and a rear grip with the air tank between them and a loading port on the right. Lucien handed Maurice a plastic bottle full of paint balls. The bottom of the bottle had a cap. Maurice unscrewed the cap and screwed the bottle into the loading port of the gun. The bottle partially blocked the view to the right of the gun but didn't unbalance it due to a slight offset in the alignment of the air tank. The whole gun weighed about two kilos, Maurice estimated.

"Interesting, Lucien," said Maurice. "But what do we want with a bunch of children's toys?"

"Not quite toys, Maurice," responded Lucien. "I was thinking about them after I saw the ones that Nicole and Celeste were training with. A paint ball gun is a weapon that delivers a large amount of balls of liquid at a high rate of speed for a fair range. The air pressure is limited by the toughness of the shell of the paint balls. I got to thinking that you didn't have to fill the balls with paint. You could use numerous other things, like anesthetics, or caustic soda or permanent marking compounds that don't wash off, or chemicals like nerve gas. Just because children play with them does not limit the offensive or defensive use. We have four of these here and six thousand rounds of ammunition."

"Loaded with what, Lucien," said Maurice. "Not nerve gas, I hope."

"No," said Lucien. "Actually there are two kinds here, one is a liquid form of powerful tear gas, and the other is an ultraviolet sensitive marker dye mixed with a synthetic cannabis compound of very high effectiveness. We have been developing it for use in the new electronic smoking devices. We are also working on ammunition with a quick acting anesthetic and tranquilizer."

"Synthetic marijuana, Lucien?" said Maurice. "Isn't that illegal?"

"Actually no," said Lucien. "But there is a really high dose in the paint balls and you don't come down for several hours. Both kinds of ammunition are very effective for crowd control without killing anyone, but I hope will be effective enough when the time comes to use them here, Maurice."

An ambulance with lights and sirens turned in at the gate and the gate guard opened the gate after glancing in the cab. The ambulance rushed across the bridge and into the side parking area and two men jumped out of the back with a gurney while two more jumped out of the cab.

"Ah, my ride is here," said Lucien. "I will be going on now. I'll talk to Mark, Merry and Blossom tomorrow before I go home to Crete. You go ahead and show Colonel McMillian the air guns and explain about the ammunition. Au revoir, I will see you all in a few days. Be careful."

Maurice nodded and buzzed open the kitchen door and the four men with the gurney rushed in. Lucien lay down on the gurney and two of the men put a blanket over him then they taped the tube of a bottle of saline on the back of his hand and one man held it up. One of the day guards dressed in ambulance attendant whites walked into the room and the four men pushed Lucien out of the kitchen door while Colonel Bryon McMillan stood aside. As soon as the men were out the door, one ran ahead to the ambulance and started the motor and lights and siren while two men guided the gurney and the third man held the bottle of saline in the air and talked on a radio. They loaded the gurney and Lucien in the back and then backed up and turned with a screeching of tires and accelerated toward the gate. The guard had started opening the gate as soon as the ambulance had turned around and it was barely opened wide enough to allow the ambulance to pass through when it did. The ambulance pulled into traffic and accelerated away.

"Well, that was dramatic," said Colonel Bryon McMillian, taking off his white ambulance attendant coat. "What did Lucien want me to see?"

"These," said Maurice. "It's a new thing and has some ammunition that would probably fetch twenty American dollars each on the street. You want coffee? Greta, Dove and Asim need to see these, too. Everything ready?"

"Yes," said Bryon McMillian, "Margret Perry called the minister and she was madder than hell. Apparently, the new head of the family wants more money as a personal bribe and told the Asians that a million dollars in small bills would be appreciated for him stepping in for Armand at the last moment. What happened?"

"It is a long story," said Maurice, "and we are out of coffee. Let's get the ladies and go somewhere quiet for a while. We do need to leave anyway, since it would be expected that someone would follow the ambulance."

CHAPTER 17: B-DAY

Every balloon, blimp, zeppelin, glider or airplane has a name, well actually a number. It's number is painted on the wing or tail or the body near the tail if it is a heavier than air aircraft, or on the envelope if it is a balloon. That number is its Civil Aircraft Registration Number. When there got to be enough aircraft to need to be sorted, the international community got together in 1913 at the International Radiotelegraphic Conference in London and assigned numbers to aircraft based on radio call signs. As the number of aircraft increased, the registration numbers became more numerous and finally the International Civil Aviation Organization formalized a system so that almost every civil aircraft has its own international registration recognition number.

If you know the scheme you can identify where an aircraft is registered and a lot more. Take N-X-221, for example, the N indicates that the aircraft is registered in the United States, the X that the aircraft is an experimental, and by looking at the registry it will be discovered that the number 221 was given to Charles Lindbergh's aircraft, The Spirit of Saint Louis. However, strangely enough, no one goes around checking on whether the numbers displayed on the aircraft are in fact the correct ones that should be painted on a particular plane.

In the early evening of Thursday, the day before the nation-wide protests, a transport jet in Southerland Oil colors entered the outer limits of controlled space at the Cairo International airport. It requested landing instructions and then turned onto its final approach.

As it passed the runway's outer marker, the copilot keyed the radio and yelled, "Something just blew up in the hanger complex. It looks like there is a big fire in the charter area behind some of the commercial hangers. We are committed, but I think you should shut things down until you get things sorted."

"Ground control," said a voice, "please identify and say again."

"Southerland 737 N8387," said the Copilot, "There is a fuel truck on fire in the Sahara Heavy Lift area right next to the runway and it looks like it is spilling burning fuel onto the ramp. We are down now and past the fire. We would like to proceed to the ramp parking area at the far end of the field as far from the fire as possible."

"Southerland N8387, proceed to ramp parking area E-3 and stay with your aircraft for further instructions," said a voice, "we have the fire brigade on the way. Thanks."

The 737, that had the registration number N1033A, not N8387, painted on the side, turned off of the active runway and taxied to a large ramp where it turned and moved to the far side of the parking area and right next to the taxiway where it would be the first plane to leave and idled its engines as a swarm of fire engines roared toward the spreading fuel fire.

There was another explosion as a propane tank next to one of the Sahara Heavy Lift office buildings exploded, throwing chunks of tank and plumbing through the air like shrapnel. An Erickson S-64 Air Crane was hit by flying debris and started spilling fuel. Something hot hit the spill and the helicopter caught fire. To the rear of the burning helicopter, one of the pilots managed to get a Mil Mi38 into the air and skim out over the taxiway to altitude and climb to a holding pattern. There were figures running everywhere as ground crew ran to move aircraft that could be saved, or pilots tried to start them.

A pickup truck pulled up to one hanger and a pilot in coveralls and a helmet jumped out and ran to a padlocked hanger with two guards. The guards were standing outside the hanger watching as the fire reached a fuel cart that blew up spreading five hundred gallons of high test gasoline in a wide circle that included the tank farm.

"Open the God damn hanger now," yelled the pilot, "then get the hell away, move it."

"We're not supposed to let anyone in the hanger," objected one of the guards, "There is something important in it."

"Yeah well, I know what it is, and we do not want it to get hot or catch fire or explode do we, right?" yelled the pilot, "Now open the damn door or he'll shoot you."

The driver of the pickup leveled a submachine gun across the bed of the truck at the two guards and they raised their hands. The pilot shot the lock off of the door using a heavy handgun and then ran and hit the door switch. The doors started sliding open as the first fire trucks pulled up at the blaze and started spraying foam. The fire staggered back for a minute and then the truck filling hose on the jet fuel tank burned through and the gravity feed tank started spilling fifteen thousand gallons of jet fuel out through a two-inch diameter pipe. The guards in front of the hanger looked in horror at the swirl of fire that flamed up into the air a hundred feet as the pilot kicked out the chalks on the only jet in the hanger and turned and ran up the steps. The door hatch shut and a minute later one engine started spooling up as the fire spread to the next fuel tank in the complex and the firemen retreated.

"Get in the back of the damn truck, you two idiots," the driver yelled at the guards as he put down the submachine gun and started the truck. "Do you want to stand there and get burned up?"

The two guards got in the back of the truck and it started moving down the taxiway as both engines on the jet in the hanger came up. As soon as the engines had power, the jet pulled out of the hanger and turned down the taxiway and started gathering speed. The pickup dodged into the grass between the taxiway and the landing strip and stalled, as the jet roared passed it. The plane rolled to the end of the taxiway and slowed and finally paused at the end of the airfield before crossing to parking ramp area E-3 along with half a dozen other planes that were being moved out of the danger area. The pickup driver swore and tried to start the stalled pickup. It finally started and then the driver drove slowly down the taxiway and waited until he could cross the runway to the parking area without hindering planes. When he got there, he started driving slowly between the rows of accumulating airplanes until he stopped where a figure was waving a flashlight.

"Okay, the plane is here right out front," said the pilot, "now you two guys stay right by it. No one gets in and no one moves it until someone gets here from headquarters, right? I'm heading back to see if there is anything else I can do."

The two guards nodded and then moved to the airplane. The pilot got in the truck and drove it back along the other side of the field from the fire until it reached the Mediterranean Air Service flight center. It pulled into a parking area with a group of parked trucks and the driver and passenger got out and walked to the crew door and went in.

In the back of the ramp parking area, two mechanics on ladders at the rear of a plane in the back row were finishing smoothing down the second of two dry stick decals the same color as the plane's paint that said N 8387 and that covered the painted-on registration number N1033A. They finished and then folded the ladders and put them on their service truck. Then they stood under the wing and watched as the firemen used flame shields and fire suits to try and reach the blazing fuel tank's shut off valve.

****

Margret Perry snapped awake. She was sprawled in the back seat of an American Press Network van with her feet on a briefcase full of mixed twenty, fifty, and hundred-dollar bills that totaled one million dollars. She had pulled the money from the contingency fund cash drawer in the safety deposit box in the bank downtown last night. She was almost ready to shoot Carlo, the bastard, and do the delivery herself but sanity had kicked in. Whoever delivered this little baby would be blamed for the resulting fiasco when it exploded. When that explosion was going to take place would be dictated by the actions of the new owners. But that wouldn't be her problem. All she needed was to get Carlo to load the damn thing in a van and get it out of her hair. She assumed that the new owners would take delivery somewhere on the airport and fly the bomb out after the bank confirmed the fund transfer and when they got the firing codes, manual, and fuses. This was where it would get tricky since the Egyptians would get the fake securities and would make a try to hijack the bomb.

The agency's person in the bank would notify her group where the funds were going to be transferred to as soon as they knew. Once the funds were moved, the agency could step in and claim them at any time, since they would have all the information about the account that would be receiving the funds, including any numbers for numbered accounts. But the funds would only be seized after the notification of deposit was made to the crooks and the bomb, codes, manual, and fuse was safely on its way to its new home.

When she got the call about the fire last night, she had called her support team and headed for the airport. Her journalist credentials and two hundred euros had gotten her through the car gate and into the private and charter area and she had driven to the area where they were relocating and parking the planes. Her crew had set up cameras and she had started broadcasting and recording as soon as she could. One of her crews had headed out to do interviews and look for the plane with the bomb. When they found it, they interviewed the guards, who had been near the original fire and were good material, and then an expert had checked to see if the bomb was okay. A quick inspection using the camera lights had shown that the packing crate was still there and a scan with a Geiger counter confirmed that the crate was leaking a bit of radiation, so the bomb was assumed to still be there. She had confirmed the seals that the buyers had put on the crate during their inspection were still in place and unbroken and then went out to report on the fire after while the guards watched the plane. When the fire was out she crawled into the van and went to sleep.

Margret sat up and twisted her head to crack her neck and then got out and looked at the first light of dawn. The sky was a purple black with a few hold out stars still visible in the west. In a few minutes, the first sliver of the round golden disk of Ra would throw the immensely long shadows of the three great pyramids across the ancient necropolis and just touch the apartment buildings and offices across the Nile on El Faoum Desert Road before they were rejected by modern Egypt and spent the morning crawling chastened back to the great lumps of stone that cast them.

Margret looked around, the guards and plane were still there along with a bunch of other planes that still needed to be sorted. The original hanger at Sahara Heavy Lift hadn't done well in the fire and had finally buckled in the heat from the burning tank farm. One wall had kind of sagged and the doors and door tracks were crooked and jammed but the plane and the bomb were safe thanks to one of the Sahara Heavy Lift company pilots. She still needed a hanger for the transfer where the bomb could be loaded in a van privately and out of sight. Then when she gave the bribe and the triggers to Carlo she was done with the whole thing, except for having the soon to be identified bank the family was using confiscate the money. Someone banged on the side of the van and she looked out. Carlo was standing by a large black car. It looked suspiciously like the armored limousine that she had taken over at the shoot-out at the hotel.

"Ah, Miss Perry," said Carlo. "The guards said I would find you here. If you have my fee and other things, we will take the airplane and leave. We have rented a hanger near here where we can work without a problem."

Margret looked at Carlo and thought about the million dollars she was giving him along with the briefcase with the remainder of the printed addendum to the manuals she had received that morning, the two arming keys that were only together on a combat training or picket flight and the USB drive with the code for activating the bomb. She smiled and handed him the two briefcases and he walked to the car. The chauffer took them and put them in the trunk and locked it. Then he opened the door and Carlo got in. There was already a person sitting in the rear seat of the car. He was wearing an Egyptian robe and a blue Taureg veil and his hands confirmed he was Asian. Margret looked the other way and suppressed a slight smile.

A Southerland Oil tug and van pulled up and two young men wearing khaki outfits with ball caps and earphones hanging around their necks got out of the van and walked to the plane containing the bomb where it was parked on the very edge of the parking area right in front where it could directly access the taxi way. They checked the tail number, N1033A, and then hooked up the tug and removed the chalks.

The tug towed the plane to the Southerland Oil flight complex followed by the armored limo and van. The tug pulled the plane into a hanger where a large white panel van was already parked and the limo and van stopped outside. The tug unhooked and came out and the hanger doors rolled shut. The man in the robe put a padlock on the door and nodded and the two guards stood in front of the hanger. Now, all that needed to happen was for the money to be transferred by noon and the bomb to be unloaded into the transport truck. She had no idea how the fake funds would get to the terrorists or even if that part of the charade would happen. One thing though, she'd make sure good old Carlo got his, sooner or later and a million bucks wouldn't stop that.

Other crews and aircraft tugs started showing up at the parking lot as the airport finally opened for business and the rest of the parked planes were sorted, towed away to be fueled, checked, and then put back in service. She idly watched as another Southerland plane, N 8387 from the back of the parking area pulled past her and moved down the taxiway. It was towed to an open ramp at the Mediterranean Air Service operations area and stopped. A closed aircraft service truck pulled up and the side freight door on the plane was opened. Several men got in and some seats were loaded into the plane to be installed in the freight bay to add passenger capability. The freight door was closed truck pulled away and a tug and luggage cart came and stowed luggage and some bins in the luggage compartment.

One of her camera crew walked up and handed her some vile coffee in a paper cup and she drank it greedily.

"Are we all done here, Margret?" asked the man, "We should probably go and do a story from right across the field from the fire and then see if we can catch a fireman for an interview. I have some fire and explosion footage that hasn't been shown yet and we could do a recap segment for the evening news and then get the hell out of Dodge."

"Yeah, come on, let's go and get done," agreed Margret, "we got some down time coming. I need to book some flights out of here later today after the riots start."

"What happened to Serena?" said the man, "I hear she got jerked out for something else."

"Yeah, that's right," said Margret, "I guess we will find out someday. Come on, let's go to the terminal and find someone to give us an official statement about the fire and get something reasonable to eat and go to the bathroom. Then we can go out and report on the riots and head out later this afternoon before everything explodes."

****

Serena Watson stood in the French doors to the balcony and looked out at the Nile sliding slowly past the island in the warming morning sun. She had been hiding at the Assistant Minister of Defense's small, insert laugh here, cottage in Garden City since she had been told to get out of the news conference because the terrorists were going to attack it. She wondered if she

275

had enough ammunition to ensure her survival now that things were coming to a head or if she should be making plans.

But half a billion American dollars' worth of fake securities and cash was five hundred million any direction you sliced it, and even if the securities were counterfeit, they were darn good counterfeits produced by a government program. There wouldn't be any problem in unloading them for thirty cents on the dollar and a third of a billion dollars was well over a hundred million, even allowing for some slippage and once they were in circulation it would be impossible to get them all. The problem was the securities and the bomb were both part of a too involved web of deception that was becoming more and more convoluted and unworkable.

When the Assistant Minister of Defense had come to the hotel and contacted her, she had acted shocked and then she had considered and finally she had taken him up on his offer to switch sides. Margret quite flatly had the personality of a horse rasp, one of the big coarse ones that farriers used to trim down the hooves of horses in a few quick strokes. The minister had gotten fed up with Margret and had contacted Serena with an offer of ten million dollars and a damn good alibi if she would help him and the current government, read the terrorists, locate the bomb and determine where the trade of money for bomb would happen.

The official plan, as dreamed up by Margret and the other deep thinkers at the International Working Group on Nuclear Limitation, was for the Egyptian terrorist group in the desert to buy an atomic bomb from the Francisci Family and then give it to the Asian purchasers. The Asians would then smuggle the bomb out of Egypt on their own. The Asians were furnishing the terrorists with half a billion dollars fake cash from various countries and phony commercial and government bearer bonds, gold certificates, and commercial paper to use to pay the Franciscis for the bomb. The terrorists would then be supplied with military equipment and supplies for acting as a cut out for the sale.

The Franciscis were supposed to take the crates of funny money and go home. Then, when they finally found out the money was off, the terrorists group would be dissolved and gone, and no one would know who the Asian buyer was. The fact that the terrorists were already a terrorist group meant that they didn't give a whoop about double-crossing the family or suffering the weight of world opinion and displeasure. They were already on the eliminate as soon as possible list and the fact that terrorist groups had no country and disband and reformed more often than teenage rock bands made them almost immune to retribution. So, the unnamed Asians got the bomb, the terrorists got the weapons and the Franciscis got stiffed, end of deal.

The only problem was that things had started unraveling with the original buy a bomb operation when the CIA had discovered a couple hours before it was going to happen, that an assassin was going to take out the head of the Iranian nuclear centrifuge and enrichment program who was with the Iranian technical delegation at a conference. They had panicked because he was also the chief CIA spy in the Iranian nuclear program. The only group that had been available to break up the attempt was a new unit of EUOPS that was testing little drones and doing surveillance practice. Unfortunately it turned out they were lead by a particularly nosy and pushy person that had become curious and started asking questions.

Suddenly, EUOPS and MI6 were right in the middle of things. The fact that the head of the EUOPS was a very close friend of Lucien Francisci the head of the Francisci Family who had already told her about the request for a bomb had totally screwed things up. Suddenly, there were more players than it was possible to control and Margret had watched her potential promotion to Director run toward the cliff with all the other lemmings.

One problem, thought Serena, was that no one ever did what they were supposed to or played by the rules in these things. The terrorists were planning on stealing the bomb and the half a billion in fake money and bonds and had gathered enough of their troops out in the desert, where they were pretending to be summer help for the Egyptian Department of Antiquities, to do the job. It was fairly obvious to Serena and probably everyone else that someone very high up in the Egyptian government was involved in protecting them. The only thing was no one knew just how involved the Egyptian government was. But this didn't matter now because before the terrorists could steal the bomb, they needed to know where it was and who had it. This lack of information had resulted in the offer of ten million American dollars to Serena by the Assistant Minister of Defense who was obviously part of the group involved in protecting the terrorists.

Actually if it worked the terrorist plan left the Franciscis stiffed, the Asians with no money and no bomb and the terrorists with both. But Serena knew the CIA and the Franciscis had worked out a side deal without the purchaser or the terrorists' knowledge on the purchase of the bomb for real money and delivery by some transfer method unknown to anyone but the Franciscis and the CIA.

Serena and Margret actually had been working together and they both knew this. Margret still had the bomb's triggers and arming codes and she also had a source in the bank of Hong Kong where the CIA money was being held in a numbered account. When the money moved, her source would tip Margret off to the destination so the gears for the Americans to seize the funds could start turning. This would allow the United States to recover the money after the crooks thought they had it and had moved the bomb to the Asians, as originally planned. Under this scenario, the terrorists got the counterfeit securities, the Asians got the bomb, and the Franciscis got stiffed. But the plan depended on some tricky timing. Before the Franciscis' accounts were frozen, but after they had been notified that the money was there, they needed to release the bomb, manuals, and triggering device to the Asians with the real bomb.

Meanwhile, the terrorists, read current Egyptian government radicals and the Assistant Minister of Defense, were still clinging to the 'steal a bomb and the securities too' plan since they didn't have a clue of what else was going on. Currently, it looked like the way things played out, the Asians got the bomb like the International Working Group on Nuclear Limitation wanted, the Franciscis got a transfer of real money that would hopefully be taken away from them and the terrorists got no arms but did get a bunch of really good peculiar securities and cash, a whole half billion dollars' worth, and that cash was what Serena was interested in.

Serena finished her cup of morning coffee and looked at the clock. It was nine thirty in the morning and she still needed to pack. Well, today was the day. She still had time to get a shower and pack before noon. She had used her phone to book tickets on a KLM flight to Paris, a British Air flight to London, another British Air flight to London two hours later and an Air France flight to Milan in between. Starting at about noon, when the transfer of the bomb was scheduled, she had a flight out of the airport every thirty minutes or so to somewhere until two o'clock. She went to her closet and got a pair of safari pants, a white shirt and a bush jacket out and laid them on the bed. Then she got in her underwear drawer and pulled out some plain cotton briefs, cotton socks and a sports bra. She looked at a high sensitivity miniature wire recorder she took out of a bag that contained a tangle of chargers and cables and headphones. She looked at it and pursed her lips and then made a decision and put it with her clothes.

Serena showered and dressed. She slipped the recorder in a small pocket in her bra under her left arm where she could control it with her arm and pinned the microphone, which looked like an American Press lapel pin, on the front of her shirt and connected it. She finished dressing with a pair of trainers and put a khaki ball cap that said ICCA on the front in black letters in her shoulder bag. She slipped her computer in her shoulder bag and added a miniature still or video camera and two memory chips for it and a small automatic pistol. Then she packed her two bags and set them by the door.

Serena shook the thermos pot from that mornings breakfast and drained the last of the coffee into her cup and drank it cold. Margret had recently kicked everyone else off the team and was desperately trying to recover her plan, but Serena didn't think she could do it. But she had changed the time of the delivery for the manuals, trigger, and codes to dawn although the transfer of funds and the bomb would still take place at noon. Serena looked at her watch and decided to leave immediately. She wondered how things would go. Oh well life was chancy at best.

She shook her head then she called the Assistant Minister of Defense on his private line and told him, "I'm leaving for the airport now."

****

Margret Perry and her crew had taken over a balcony waiting area at the El Al passenger terminal. Some of them were dozing and some of them were idly reading newspapers or magazines or watching their phones. Margret was sprawled in an easy chair dozing and holding her phone in her lap with one hand. As soon as she was notified that the money for the bomb had been transferred to the Francisci account and had been taken out of the plane, she would wait half an hour and make a couple calls, then see about getting a plane home. Her back was getting stiff from the chair and probably the night spent in the van didn't help and besides she needed a rest stop too. She stood up and stretched and then looked down into the lobby and café area below on the main floor. A woman in a safari gear outfit was pushing a luggage cart over to a table in one of the window alcoves that had a view of the runway. Margret looked down and then waved as Serena turned around.

Serena looked up and then touched her ear and made an okay signal with her right hand and then touched her eye and spread her hands and shrugged. Margret thought for a second and then walked back to her crew.

"Serena is down there," said Margret, "She just signaled me that she has sound but needs pictures. John, take a camera with a turret lens and walk around the balcony to the side where you can get a good side view of her and her table but stay out of sight. She is in the third alcove waiting for someone. I want a camera set up here to get what she says and one across the hall to get pictures and lip movement on whoever she is meeting but I don't want them to see the cameras."

"Right," said John, "What is she doing?"

"I don't know," said Margret. "I thought she might be dead for a while until she called me. We can ask her later but I bet there is a damn good story in it."

Margret walked back to the railing and looked down. Serena was looking at the airplanes moving around with a small pair of field glasses. She barely glanced at the railing where Margret flashed an okay sign and smiled. Serena reached in her bag and pulled out a small camera and put it on the table and sat her bag down beside it to shield it from view. She pushed a speed dial on her phone and Margret's phone vibrated. Margret plugged a small cord into her phone and then plugged it into the side of the camera focused on Margret.

"Okay cameras are rolling," said Margret, "sound check?"

"Loud and clear, Margret," said Serena, "now, mute your phone. I don't want anyone to know mine is on."

Serena put her cell phone on the table by the camera. Then she glanced at the clock. It was a bit past eleven. No reason to panic yet. She wondered what Margret was doing hanging around the terminal since the balloon was supposed to go up on the general protest today too and Margret should be getting background interviews. Margret being here now was a bit of luck since she had given Carlo Cohen the manuals, bomb triggers and codes this morning at dawn and there was no reason for her to be involved now except for authorizing seizing the money. There was actually no reason for her and the crew to be at the terminal. Anyway she had not counted on Margret being here but Serena was glad for the extra cameras.

Serena glanced at the television in the bar and saw Margret standing in front of a massive fire. Something exploded in the background and the picture widened to show blazing fuel tanks and scurrying airplanes. The sound was turned down so you couldn't hear but a ribbon showing English and Egyptian ran along the bottom. The ribbon was describing the massive fire at the Sahara Heavy Lift hanger and service complex last night.

Serena sat up straight and looked at the burning buildings and helicopters. She saw the Erickson S-64 Air Crane burst into flames and then saw the hanger in front of it open and a Southerland jet freighter taxi out and hurry down the runway away from the fire. She breathed a sigh of relief and then turned and saw the Assistant Minister of Defense and two bodyguards approaching. Now, where had the airplane ended up? She was in serious trouble if she couldn't locate it.

"Ah, Miss Watson," said the minister, "I see you have already packed. The staff at the cottage is already going through and removed all traces of you right down to changing rugs to limit DNA fragments from your skin and wiping everything for fingerprints. I guarantee you that no one will ever be able to connect you with that house. Now, it is approaching noon and you said the transfer was supposed to take place then?"

"Yes it is," said Serena and took a pair of small powerful binoculars out of her purse and looked around the field hoping to see the plane.

"Good, now what is going to happen?" said the minister. "Has the transfer started yet?"

"The bomb is in an airplane and is going to be loaded into a van," said Serena, "I don't know where the van will be going but I don't think you want to have a gun battle here at the airport where there are so many troops and security guards. It will probably be very easy to hijack the van on the street, or at its destination. The bomb will be loaded in the van and will probably leave first and the trigger mechanism will be provided as soon as the transfer of funds is completed, probably half an hour later."

"And where is this airplane," said the minister, "They may choose to fly it away instead."

"I'm not sure," said Serena, "it is a Southerland freight plane number N1033A. It was supposed to be in that hanger there that got melted in the fire, but I saw on the news that it got out. They have had to relocate it naturally but I would assume it is in either the Southerland or Sahara Heavy Lift areas. I trust that you could locate it rather quickly."

"Actually, Miss Watson, I already know where it is since I am in charge of delivering a large amount of money to the hanger," said the minister. "Where are the triggers and the manuals and so on?"

"I rather thought you would be informed since it was necessary to deliver the money and I had already gathered that you had a connection to the people in the desert and the Department of Antiquities trucks," said Serena. "The triggers are in the possession of the Franciscis at a remote location and once the money has been delivered, they will be turned over."

"And where is this remote location?" said the minister. "No one, alas, knows about that and that is why you were tenured a very generous offer."

"And don't forget, a perfect alibi," said Serena. "Well let's have lunch and then we can check and see that my account has been reimbursed and then I'll tell you where the triggers are at."

Serena glanced down the field with her field glasses and saw another Southerland plane, N 8387 sitting on the ramp at

Mediterranean Air. A passenger ramp had been pushed up to the front door and a number of people were boarding the plane. Most were in local garb and there were several veiled women. One of the veiled women carried a baby and another was helping a man in Saudi robes and a headscarf that was pulled across his lower face climb the ladder. Half a dozen young Asian men in conservative suits boarded the plane and then an older European man in a blue suit with sun glasses and carrying a briefcase walked to the stairs with a short person wearing an Egyptian robe and a blue Taureg head dress and veil. The two men stopped at the bottom and talked for a minute and then they glanced at their phones and shook hands. The man in the suit handed the person in the blue veil his briefcase and then the veiled man opened it and looked inside. He nodded, climbed the steps and boarded the plane. The man in the suit walked back into the building and the ramp on the plane was pulled back. The plane taxied to the end of the runway and got in line for departure.

"Ah, Miss Watson, it is almost noon," said the Minister. "Where are the bomb triggers, codes, and manuals?"

"They will be following the bomb in a car," said Serena, "as soon as the money is delivered and verified, the triggers will be given to the purchaser's representative who is will be riding in the car. The bomb and triggers are going to be smuggled out of the country in a shipping container. Now, shall we check my bank account? And what is my alibi?"

"Yes, go ahead and call your bank and check," said the minister. "Then we can talk about your alibi. I need to make a call."

Serena pulled out her computer and the khaki ball cap and set up the computer. She connected to the airport Internet and punched in her code for her bank account. It showed a balance of slightly over two thousand dollars. She glanced up at the minister who was walking over to the window talking on his phone. Across the field a white van and a black limousine pulled out of a hanger and stopped on the ramp. A white Department of Antiquities truck pulled up alongside the car and the two drivers rolled down the windows and talked for a minute. The Department of Antiquities truck pulled into the hanger and the door shut. The van and the car drove toward the private owner's gate and parked.

"There seems to be a bit of a problem with the deposit I was expecting," said Serena "What's going on?"

"You didn't really think that we would give you ten million dollars, did you?" said the minister. "And the truck that just went in the hanger is full of cartons of paper with a top layer of boxes full of fair counterfeit securities and a few hundred thousand in real American money. Now, you are under arrest for something."

Serena reached in her purse and one of the guards pointed a pistol at her chest and smiled as he clicked off the safety.

"Hold it right there," said a voice from Serena's purse, "Please turn to your left if you would like your good profile on the news, mister soon to be ex-minister. The whole thing is on tape and film and General El-Shazly says it will figure prominently in your trial as well as on my story on the news tonight. If you want to include murder of an international agent in the charges he said he is sure you can avoid a death sentence. The new president can just have you sent to the Central Prison of Port Said in the hard labor battalion for the rest of your life, you know about six months or so, your choice. The exits are all sealed and there are about sixty soldiers closing in on you, so make up your mind."

The minister looked wildly around and then put up his hands as General Abdul El-Shazly flanked by four hand picked Republican Guard members carrying submachine guns walked across the lobby.

"What do you think you are doing," said the minister, "I am arresting this woman on charges of treason and aiding and abetting a terrorist organization. Besides, I am a minister of the government and have immunity from civil charges, general."

"Well, I wouldn't put much stock in either the minister thing or even the government much longer," said the general. "The streets are already full of protesters and there is a firefight going on a couple of blocks away. I'll be sending some troops there to calm things down in a minute. Alexandria, Port Said and Aswan are warming up for the main event on the anniversary of Morsi's election tomorrow. The military will officially be declaring martial law then. But right now I am arresting you for treason and aiding and abetting a terrorist organization, counterfeiting, receiving stolen securities and false arrest of a member of an international law enforcement agency, and there is not a civil charge in the whole lot. This has been a rather involved sting operation and we caught you red handed. We are already inventorying the fake securities at your home. You don't need to put on the hat Miss Watson we'll take it from here and contact your office. Have your people stand down."

Serena nodded and made a sweeping motion with her hands. Half a dozen men in blue and black suits carrying briefcases put their ICCA pocket clip badges back in their inside coat pockets and their Uzi submachine guns back in their briefcases and went to the restroom, or to buy more coffee, or book an earlier flight to Switzerland. The Republican Guards troops handcuffed the minister and his two bodyguards. Then they took them out through a crew only exit to the field and loaded them in a military troop truck.

"Serena," said the voice from her purse. "Get yourself up here. The whole country is starting to explode, and we need to get on the street for some footage before we run. General El-Shazly has offered us an escort of armed Republican Guards and an armored Humvee in exchange for a copy of the complete tapes of you and the minister's little chat. We will need to cut something short with the general making the minister's arrest for the evening news, but right now we need to get to the gun battles and then the riots in the square downtown. The riot police are not making much headway on the crowd there and the army is staying home until tomorrow. We also need to either get out of here or find someplace safe."

"Be right there, Margret," said Serena. "I got the whole thing, picture and sound, on my camera too if you have the recording in your camera I'll change chips and give the original to the general to copy and then I'll head up."

Serena picked up the camera and popped out the chip. She handed it to the general with a smile. He picked up her ball cap and looked at it.

"ICCA?" said the general, "International Currency Control Agency, the Swiss and Germans and Euro securities and money bank guards? You were actually interested in the counterfeit securities, not the bomb?"

"Yes," said Serena, "There are several rogue nations that like to use funny money for their expenses and we like to make it as hard as we can on them. I'll phone home and the office will get hold of your people about the queer securities, general, and thanks a bunch. I suppose I should kiss you. I think they were going to shoot me as part of the arrest procedure."

"That would have been a criminal waste of both exceptional talent and great beauty. What will you do now?" said the general. "Are you staying in the city?"

"Yeah, until the news runs dry or it gets too dangerous. Then we'll leave," said Serena. "I'll give you a full briefing when I can and see if you can have access to my final ICCA report. But my cover is Margret's producer and director so I need to go to work there. I guess we will go out and roam the streets and let Margret talk to people and then finally see if we can find someplace safe to spend the night."

The general picked up a napkin and took a ballpoint pen out of his pocket. He wrote a phone number and an address on it.

"Here," said the general. "My place. It has a big tall wall and is full of soldiers and has lots of guest rooms. Also, I am not married so there is no one to be upset with extra dinner guests and you are always welcome. Bring the thank you kiss over after work and have a drink and dinner. You can bring your friends, too."

"I'll seriously think about it, general," said Serena and smiled. "Now I better get to work."

Margret met Serena at the top of the stairs and they walked out of the entrance onto the departure roadway. The crew was loading cameras and luggage into the back of an army truck and handing around combat gear. Margret got her own special signature outfit and then handed Serena a flack jacket and helmet. They dressed and stood by the armored Humvee. Three army trucks full of Republican Guards pulled up and led the convoy as it pulled away from the curb heading toward the sound of gunfire.

"What was that all about with the general?" said Margret. "What's the paper?"

"It's an invitation to prove how grateful I am for having my life saved," said Serena, "and an offer for someplace we can stay with only a slight chance of getting shot."

"Oh," said Margret. "Well keep it. You never know when it might be handy. Looks like the second exodus has started already."

Scheduled and charter aircraft were taking off as frequently as the tower would permit and turning in any direction that left Egypt. As Serena looked out the window of the Humvee, a Southerland Air Boeing 737 screamed overhead and climbed out to the north. As she watched a small colored tape or label tore off of the tail of the airplane and fluttered toward the ground and the tail number changed from N 8387 to N1033A. The plane climbed out and headed east toward the Orient.

"I wonder what that is all about?" she asked, "Airplanes normally don't wear pasties or change numbers in mid flight."

Margret's phone rang and she answered it and listened and finally threw her phone across the car.

"Oh shit, shit, damn, hell, shit," said Margret.

"What is it," said Serena. "I take it something bad happened?"

"The money was transferred all right," replied Margret, "But not into another bank account. It all went right into a Chinese investment fund at the bank of Hong Kong where it was. The Chinese Army operates the fund and the money was immediately invested in stocks and Chinese government bonds. The fund shares were immediately used to back a loan from the fund to itself so there is no money involved anymore and we can't seize the loan because it is just a credit for future construction costs of a proposed Francisci Hong Kong casino. The loan will be used by the fund to reimburse construction costs as they occur. There is absolutely no way that we can touch a bloody dime of it. I have just managed to lose the agency half a billion dollars."

CHAPTER 18: CLOSING CEREMONIES

Things were a mess at the Heliopolis house. There was a Department of Antiquities truck with its front end wedged firmly in the wall of the swimming pool and the rear end just barely on the opposite bank. The truck had rammed open the gate and then tried to cross the bridge. Maurice had triggered the charge that cut the bolts that held the two arches together and the truck had gone in the swimming pool and started sinking immediately. The driver had gotten out the window and the back door had been flung up and had fortunately stayed that way while a dozen men in combat gear and fatigue uniforms had jumped and crawled out the back. A couple of the men had managed to keep their rifles while they exited the back of the truck and had taken cover behind the rear of the truck. They were shooting at the house and the concrete planters where Colonel McMillian had posted his men.

Every so often, one of the men behind the planters would stick his submachine gun over the top of one of the planters and fire a burst that would take chips out of the compound wall on one side or the other of the flattened gate. So far, none of the terrorists had gotten past the idea that there was a twenty-foot wide seven-foot deep moat between them and the car with the triggers for the bomb.

"If they don't figure something out really quickly, we are in trouble," said Colonel Brian McMillian. "I just got a text from General El-Shazly that he has the Minister under arrest and is heading to the hanger where the boxes of fake money are so he can arrest whoever doesn't have sense enough to run. The thing is, he is sending troops here to stamp out the firefight. We have to get the triggers and manuals to the terrorists in the next few minutes."

"They do have the fake bomb?" asked Maurice. "I hope it fools them."

"Maurice, I couldn't tell the difference," answered the colonel. "Everything right down to the duplicate seals the Asians put on at the inspection were perfect. It looks like the bomb, it has the same weight as the bomb, the packing case is an identical forgery, including the scuffs and handling marks. It even leaks radiation like a bomb. Where in the world did you get it made so quickly?"

"To tell you the truth, Lucien had it knocked off at the prop department of a major movie studio in Rome a couple of days ago," said Maurice. "The people there are very fast, very good and very expensive. They do the occasional forged painting and most of the antique furniture, silverware, and curios that are sold in the gallery stores at Francisci casinos. The prop people even requested a copy of the paper that was used to show the date for the inspection pictures to measure it. The scale on the bomb and the packing case and everything is good to the hundredth of a centimeter. How did the terrorists get the bomb, but can't figure what to do now?"

"The bomb was fairly easy," replied Colonel MacMillan. "They boxed the van out at a stoplight and then started unloading troops to carjack the van and kidnap the driver and guard. As soon as the driver saw what was going to happen, he and the guard had their seat belts off and when the van stopped they hit the doors and ran. The driver has won the hundred-meter dash in the Regimental Games for the last two years, but he said the guard darn near passed him. Anyway, they made it into a street demonstration crowd and started yelling about army troops. The terrorist troops got mobbed by the crowd since they thought it was the army, but the terrorists managed to get the van and bomb out although they were losing men to the rioters really fast."

"Why doesn't someone here figure out they should get a ladder and climb the damn wall or something?" asked Maurice. "Another couple trucks have stopped outside and there must be almost a hundred people out there getting ready to shoot at us and I hear sirens. We are also attracting a bunch of citizens that probably want to loot the place. We may have to start shooting people and then they won't get the triggers and manuals, which will screw up everything."

"I've got an idea," said the colonel. "I'm calling General El-Shazly."

The general's phone rang. He was looking at the boxes of real American cash and counterfeit securities that had been on top of the load of copy paper in the truck and wondering how much of the money to turn in. He had already sent his aid into the

Mediterranean Air office to grab a couple boxes of copy paper, including the boxes.

"Yes," he answered absently, "General El-Shazly."

"General, this is Colonel McMillian," said the colonel, "We currently have a few hundred people shooting at us from the square and no one trying to get in and retrieve the briefcase which we have conveniently left in the limousine. Did the minister have a phone?"

"Yes," replied the general. "It's in my car in an evidence bag. Why?"

"I think that you may be getting a lot of phone calls on it," said the colonel. "Now I can hear sirens about five minutes away and we are tight for time. Could you check the phone and if they have called call back and tell them to form a human pyramid and put some people over the wall, or get a ladder, or drive a truck up where people can get on top and jump over the wall and get the damn briefcase with the trigger and manuals. We have a whole bunch of civilians mixed in with the terrorists and we really don't want to shoot them, or even the terrorists, as far as that goes. We need them to get the briefcase and run before your men get here."

"Hang on, colonel," said the general. "I'm on it."

General El-Shazly ran to his car and opened the trunk. There was a cell phone in the trunk in a plastic bag. It was ringing. He pulled it out of the bag and answered it.

"What is it?" barked the general.

"Sir, the truck with the interception troops went through this gate in a wall and then fell in a pool of water before we got the briefcase. What should we do now?" asked a scared voice, "The car is on the other side of a moat inside a wall and we can't get at it."

"Go around the outside of the wall and make a pyramid and climb the wall," ordered the general. "Get the briefcase and throw it over the wall to someone and then get out. Call me back when you have it."

A departing jet screamed by and anything that the phone said was lost.

"Do it now," yelled the general, and then held the phone out toward the runway where another jet had started accelerating to take off. He turned off the phone and ran back into the hanger and sighed and then told his aid and two guards to load all the boxes of money and securities into the back of an armored Humvee and go to the security service headquarters. He ordered the rest of his men to stay with the plane and guard it. Then he got in his car and phoned Colonel McMillian.

"You were right colonel," said the General. "I told them to come over the wall and then throw the briefcase over and then get out. What's happening?"

"Well your troops have arrived and are attempting to control the crowd with batons and shields. The terrorists have stopped shooting, so they won't attract attention and we are holding our fire too. I think we have some people coming over the wall on the far side of the compound. Yes, we do. One of them is sprinting toward the car and has the back door open. Okay, he has the briefcase and is running back toward the wall. Just a second."

There was a burst of machine gun fire and then several pistol shots.

"Okay, we missed him, and he tossed the briefcase over the wall and has surrendered," said Colonel McMillian. "Since we are all in plain clothes I think we will just tie him up and leave him. It looks like someone is organizing a rush on the front gate. I think we will pull out in a second."

The Minister's cell phone rang, and the general answered.

"We have it but there are a bunch of soldiers at the end of the square," said the voice on the phone. "What should we do now?"

"Can you mix with the crowd and walk to the other end of the square?" asked the general. "Take three men to go with you and the briefcase. Throw away your guns and mix with the crowd and walk to the other end of the square. Have anyone you see drop their guns and tell everyone they can find to drop their guns and then all of you take the bus to the airport or get a cab to the meeting point. But you bring the briefcase and leave right now. Can you do that?"

"Yes sir," said the voice, "but what about our other men that we can't contact?"

"Can you help them by staying?" asked the general. "How many of you are there and how many soldiers are there? Do you think if you all stayed and fought and we lost the briefcase it would turn the tide of battle? Now, talk to as many as you can and have them spread the word but go get on the bus and let the ones you can't get hold of gloriously cover your withdrawal and then leave if they can. Do it now!"

The general turned off the phone and closed his eyes and leaned back in the seat of his car. He sat for a minute or two and then opened his eyes and shook his head. If this was what the opposition was working with, his troops were all safe.

"All right, head for the square and let's see if we can avert a blood bath or at least a small shaving cut," ordered the general ordered his driver.

Colonel McMillian looked over the planter. There were about thirty soldiers with riot shields at one end of the square trying to contain the crowd. An officer with a bullhorn was yelling for the crowd to go home. Most of the crowd was turning to meet them and scream insults and tearing bricks out of the square to throw but there were maybe fifty or so men in fatigues gathering two or three ranks back in the crowd and they were facing the gate. The other thing was that unlike the crowd they had a variety of rifles, submachine guns, and rocket propelled grenades.

"I think that we have a problem, Maurice," said Colonel McMillian, "The soldiers are not getting control the crowd and the heavily armed random participants are gathering to rush the gate. I am afraid we may need to start shooting to save our lives and this is going to get a lot of the civilians."

"Here take this," said Maurice.

Maurice handed Colonel McMillian a paint ball gun with a full canister of balls. The canister and the balls were pale yellow. Maurice handed another one of the guns to one of the EUOPS security guards and motioned to one of the colonel's men. The soldier ran for the planter where Maurice and the colonel were and dropped behind it.

"All right, these are a new riot control device we have been developing but haven't used," explained Maurice. "The paintballs contain a permanent florescent dye that glows green under florescent light, so we can find people involved in riots and a powerful, hallucinogenic agent. If the soldiers can shoot off a few tear gas grenades into the crowd to provide a bit of confusion and smoke we will probably get charged. Then the first thing I want to do is open up with the paintball guns when they get to the gate and then if we must, the light machine guns when they get across the swimming pool. But let's see how the paintball guns do first okay? We have plenty of ammo but only four paint ball guns. I am going to move up to the planter closest to the gate."

"I'll come too," said Colonel McMillian, "you two men go out on the flank and pick off anyone that gets in and runs right or left. Maurice, give me another magazine and I'll call for some tear gas."

Serena was standing at the rear of the armored Humvee and watching the crowd that was confronting the group of badly outnumbered soldiers trying to prevent the crowd from getting out of hand. She could sense the mood of the crowd as it moved from indignant to really angry. They were collecting bricks and stones and pretty soon the mood would turn to vicious. When the first bricks flew, the first tear gas would be fired and then the rubber bullets and finally the real stuff.

Margret was standing at the front of the Humvee behind the corner of the cab with the cameraman. They could still get a good panoramic view of the crowd and soldiers over the hood but they were protected from any flying objects or bullets. She was doing a live uplinked breaking news segment for immediate broadcast in Europe and was recording it for the US and Canadian evening news. Serena moved back and took a pair of small field glasses out of her purse and looked at the crowd. Then she motioned to one of the other cameramen.

"You see the group in fatigues and ball caps back by the gate?" asked Serena. "They aren't your everyday rioters and they all have weapons. In a minute, they are going to charge the gate on that compound where the truck is in the water. Put a long lens on them and follow the action. We can get some narration later and develop something from it when we find out what's going on."

Someone walked up behind her and touched her on the shoulder. She turned and looked at General El-Shazly who had just arrived from the airport.

"General," asked Serena. "What's going on here? The Asians got the bomb and the trigger and codes and paperwork and flew out, right? So you see the bunch with the fatigues and ball caps that are getting ready to rush the gate? Why are they getting ready to do that?"

"I'm not really sure," said the general. "These are the people from out in the desert and they think they have a bomb."

"You say they have a bomb?" said Serena.

"No, they think they do," said the general "A long story, but I think that the group getting ready to rush the gate are a little behind on the action and didn't get the word to leave. They should be sneaking off with the rest of the men."

The general's phone rang, and he absently pulled it out of his pocket and looked at the caller ID.

"Yes?" said the general. "As a matter of fact, I am standing on an overpass watching the whole thing, colonel. All right, we can do that. Give me a minute. We will fire in one minute. Ready, hack."

The general stepped out from the shelter of the Humvee and stood next to the overpass railing. He took off his hat and put it carefully on the hood of the Humvee then pulled out his pistol and pointed it in the direction of the crowd.

Then he yelled at the cameraman, "Here, on me."

The cameraman turned and obediently focused on the general who smiled at the camera and said, "There is a group of terrorists in the square that are seeking to overwhelm a building where they believe a large amount of cash and securities are being stored temporarily. The building is being rented by a foreign corporation that has asked for assistance from Egyptian security forces in protecting their staff. The terrorists have incited a crowd of antigovernment protestors to gather here by spreading wild rumors so that they can use the innocent civilians as a human shield. We are about to use a new nonlethal crowd control device on the terrorists but if it becomes necessary we will have to use live ammunition. I am now going to give the signal to launch smoke projectiles into the terrorists to confuse them."

He stepped back from the railing and went to his car and got out two boxes of teargas canisters and a couple launchers while the camera followed him. He motioned to Margret and held out a launcher. She joined him in the picture and the camera followed them to the center of the overpass.

"Here, Miss Perry, put the bottom of the launcher on the pavement and then hold it at about forty-five degrees," said the general, "point them in the general direction of the armed terrorists getting ready to charge the building and then fire as fast as you can reload."

Margret nodded then motioned to another cameraman who pointed his camera at the square. Margret shot the first round. It was a bit early but the general shrugged and fired too. Because of the extra height of the overpass they had been launched from the two canisters arched up high over the crowd and started spewing white trails of CS gas as they flew through the air while the camera recorded their flight. They fell short of the terrorists and the general decreased the angle and fired again. This canister fell in the center of the group of terrorists and they started coughing and charged the gate of the house. Margret fired again, and another round fell in the center of the rioters and the first bricks flew.

"Oh shit, we have a situation," said Serena. "Now what? No, keep filming everyone."

"Use up the gas," said the general. "It may dissuade them. If not, we get in the trucks and run."

Maurice and Colonel McMillian were crouched behind the first planter box when the tear gas landed in the center of the terrorists and blew back across the crowd. The terrorists started firing and ran at the gate. Maurice stuck the paint ball gun over the top of the planter and pulled the trigger while hosing it back and forth. The paintballs were falling short but finally the terrorists ran into the hail of paintballs right at the edge of the water. Suddenly the firing stopped. The assault faltered and then some of the men sat down. Others fell down and a couple fell in the water but started laughing and started peeling off their clothes and swimming.

After Celeste had become so chilled when she dived into the pool while saving Lucien, Greta had ordered a combination solar and gas heater for the pool so you could actually swim in it. Heating the pool was frightfully expensive and the other equipment also cost a bundle to operate but it kept the pool pleasantly warm and free from germs. The swimmers were definitely enjoying the pool.

More of the terrorists in the initial assault group who were sitting or lying down started striping and diving into the pool. Several them were not wearing the normal issue underwear and bright colors of silk or absolutely nothing outnumbered the white cotton briefs. A few of the initial assault group hadn't been hit and they were screaming at their comrades and pointing across the pool. The swimmers made rude gestures or ignored them. Colonel McMillan peeked over his end of the planter and then brought up his paint ball gun and sprayed the remaining assault team. Then, he ducked behind the planter as a halfhearted burst of fire came in his general direction.

Finally, both the colonel and Maurice stood up and walked toward the pool. The troops that had attacked were swimming across the pool and then pulling themselves out onto the lawn side to lie in the sun on the patio. A cold drink and falafel cart had pulled in next to the wrecked gate behind the deserted guardhouse and people were buying drinks and food. Twenty or so civilians who had been hit by the paintballs, including some women and girls, had stripped to their underwear and were swimming or sitting on the grass next to the edge of the pool eating, while other members of the crowd tried to remove very happy friends or family who had been hit and wanted to swim too.

"My God, what is in these things?" asked Colonel McMillian, "I must say they are effective."

"Actually, the paint balls have a heavy dosages of a synthetic teterahydrocannabinol, or THC, you know marijuana oil that Lucien's people have been developing for the new electronic smoking devices. The high lasts for a couple hours," said Maurice. "They also contain a green dye that is invisible in normal light but you can see it for weeks under ultraviolet light."

Colonel McMillian's phone rang and he answered it.

"Yes sir," said the colonel. "It appears that way. I'll ask Maurice about the problem. Maurice, the general says the people at the other end of the square are throwing bricks and pushing on the soldiers. Could we break it up?"

"I think so," said Maurice. "Let's go get on top of the pool house. It has a parapet for protection and most of the square should be in range. Grab another magazine or two and take your guy. I'll stay here and hold the fort, so to speak. Then call the general and tell him we are going to need someone to come and load up a lot of really happy people pretty soon, before they all crash."

The general was standing by the railing of the overpass watching the crowd, including many of his soldiers wandering aimlessly around the square or walking down to join the swimming party. A few food carts and an ice cream truck with a blaring music system had showed up and people inside the wall that had been swimming had moved down to the patio and were dancing.

"Okay, that is it," said General El-Shazly. "Now, we are all going back to my place and we are going to watch while you cut some acceptable news releases that do not show a bunch of naked rioters cavorting around in a swimming pool or doing a conga line while dancing up to an ice cream truck to buy cones. You are now all my guests until tomorrow."

"Your guests or your prisoners, general?" asked Margret. "As a duly authorized and accredited member of the press corps in your country I demand an answer."

"Margret," said the general. "Just shut up. We are going go to my palace and do an official release on the activities here today for your evening report and then you can have a good dinner, a bath, a couple of drinks and a good night sleep in a comfortable bed where you will not be killed or molested. Otherwise, I can throw you in jail for a couple weeks and confiscate all your cameras, tape, disks and hard drives and give them back to you, empty and broken, along with a sincere apology after everyone including the Wet Springs Wyoming Monthly Tattler has scooped you on the story. I don't care if you are CIA. We don't officially know that, and things are going to be in a relatively dangerous state of flux for the next week or two until the military steps in and kicks Morsi out. You may not quote me on that yet. But you might want to stay at my place until things calm down because no one is going to come riot there. I have two regiments of troops with heavy weapons in the front yard and I cut a deal with the Tamarod."

"So, you are offering us official government protection and assistance," said Serena. "As soon as you are the government?"

"I guess you could say that, Miss Watson," said the General, "You just can't quote me quite yet but we will be available for interviews on the situation and I will provide armed escorts."

"I had already decided to stop by for a nightcap," said Serena, "I guess I'll just bring my luggage now. And you just as well call me Serena, general."

****

Colonel Ben Mac Glencoe stood in the early morning light and looked around the deserted Cairo headquarters of Mediterranean Air Service. There were a lot of desks and chairs and phones but no people in the office. The pilot's lounge had some stale donuts from yesterday and empty coffee pots and someone had cleaned out all the lockers and bathroom supplies, although there was one roll of toilet paper in each bathroom. The sign on the front door said that service had been suspended during the current unrest. Out back on the tarmac and in the hangers were four Shorts, a couple Falcon fifties and twenties and two Q 400 aircraft in Mediterranean Air colors. There were also four helicopters of various kinds with and without guns and missile hard points.

Ben looked at Maurice and said, "Okay, so what happens now?"

"Well, Blossom said I am in charge here and we need to clean up and reorganize. Most of the staff has been reassigned and Blossom is ordering Dove and Greta back to the home office in London for as she said, additional training and exposure to education, reason and patience after their furlough in Corsica," explained Maurice. "This includes some university training in various things like international relations, banking, economics, and diplomacy. She said they especially need training in diplomacy, manners, and following directions. EUOPS is trying to redefine the career path from field agent to supervisors. Both Blossom and Julia, for example, had already completed degrees before they entered the service, whichever one they entered, and this was normal in the forties, fifties and sixties when everyone in the spying business recruited from good colleges and universities. The thing is at the present time so many of our recruits come from situations where they have not been able to obtain formal training or establish personal relationships with the core people in the intelligence community and we need to accommodate that."

"I guess I just kind of expected that everyone would still know everyone else and their family and so on like it used to be," said Ben, "but that was before electronic surveillance, computer analysis, satellites, drones with cameras and rockets and everyone in the world getting in on the game. I must admit I had never met Dove or Greta before last year but then they were so young and after all they did come recommended by Merry and he is practically mister Anglo-American intelligence. I was in the army so long that I got used to having lots of raw material to choose from and didn't think about what is going on in the civilian end."

"Actually, not much with everyone getting on in years and Europe all one big happy family," said Maurice. "Of course, the Middle East and Far East are problems and that is why we are here. Anymore, a spy must be a linguist, a technician, and a diplomat so that they can work with everyone in the various intelligence and enforcement agencies. It used to be the other way around, everyone knew that the military charge de affairs at the embassy was a spy and half the secretaries were honey traps or foreign agents."

"So, no Southern Operations Area Headquarters to run operations in the Middle East and Africa?" said Ben, "Who am I supposed to be supporting then?"

"Just no local office in the area right now," said Maurice. "You have a good cover with Southerland Oil and do a lot of real things for them so you are just supposed to be keeping on doing things for them. The home office will be sending specialists to do anything sneaky that needs to be done and will get hold of you for support on an as needed basis. Asim and I are going to get half a dozen street agents that travel and go out and walk around and the Francisci Family is going to be sharing information with us, but we will just be data gathering and reporting to Mark on Cyprus for the time being. Anyway, Asim and I are supposed to clean up the loose ends here and then come and set up shop at your place at the jail and maintain a presence. The Heliopolis house and the Garden City apartment have been leased to Sara and she is repairing the damage and then renting them. Asim and I are getting married this fall and living in Asim's old apartment, if no one burns it down. The air service is going to be run out of the Corsica office by some professionals with some mechanics and ground staff here when things clear up locally."

"I cleaned up the coffee bar and pots when you were poking around in the office and made coffee," said Ben. "Want some?"

"Yeah," said Maurice, "how old are the donuts?"

Maurice and Ben sat on the leather couch in the waiting lounge across from the ninety-inch television and drank their coffee and ate three-day old donuts. Ben idly picked up the control and turned the set on. It blossomed into life and Margret Perry, dressed in her black helmet with dangling straps and one lock of loose hair and her flack jacket with cleavage popped up on the screen. She was standing in the desert in front of a brown cloud that was hanging on the horizon a few miles behind her. It looked like the leading edge of a sandstorm but there was no wind blowing and the cloud didn't move a lot.

"… less than an hour ago," said Margret, "Scientists who recorded the blast on seismographs at the university estimated it to be the equivalent of over ten tons of high explosives. The force of the blast was enough to rattle windows in Al Jizah and was heard in Cairo. There are unconfirmed reports that military helicopters surveying the area of the blast have detected radiation in the cloud of smoke and dust. We have been stopped about five miles from the suspected site of the explosion by members of the Republican Guard that are currently investigating to determine what happened. It has been suggested that an aircraft carrying a nuclear device may have crashed and there was a partial detonation. I will be speaking with General Abdul El-Shazly, the commander of the Republican Guard troops here who is arriving momentarily. This is Margret Perry, American Press, with breaking news about the massive explosion east of Cairo, Egypt. Now back to the studio for a discussion of the event with the experts."

The television cut to a local studio and several morning personality people who had been on the morning show that was supposed to feature an interview with a new chef and a fading female singer and were now trying to talk about the massive explosion until something came in from the reporters who were racing to the site and running down people to get them to come in and speculate.

In the desert, Margret grabbed a bottle of water from a cooler sitting on the ground between an armored Humvee, that now had a white magnetic door sign that said American Press, and a bright red Range Rover that was General El-Shazly's personal car. The General was standing behind Serena Watson who was dressed in a pair of red sandals, red short shorts and a red bra top with an open white shirt tied in a knot over her stomach. The General had one arm around Serena and had his hand on her stomach below the bra top. He was pointing over her shoulder with the other arm and Serena was looking through a pair of field glasses at the cloud on the horizon.

"Right there just below the top of the cloud," said the General, "It's hard to see because it is a flat pale blue. It shows up against the brown dust every so often though. You might see better without the glasses till you know what to look for."

"What is it?" said Serena, "I still don't see anything."

"That's the idea," said the General, "it's an English Taranis drone. They are made out of carbon fiber and only the jet engine shows up on radar, and not very well since it's shielded. We might be getting some pictures from the helicopters though and radiometric data. So, what actually happened, Margret?"

"I called in last night and they told me Lucien set them up to steal a booby trapped fake bomb," answered Margret, "It wasn't an atomic bomb. It was just a shell loaded with high explosives and radioactive medical junk waste to provide radiation. All the wall panels in the closed truck it was in had been pulled out and the inside crammed with four inches of explosives and half inch steel balls before the panels were put back in. The padding in the bomb box was explosives not padding and so was the eight-inch built up truck floor. Lucien is sending a message that it is not a good idea to try and cheat the Francisci Family or steal from it."

"So you think it is just payback from the Franciscis?" asked the General.

"Well partially," said Margret, "Terrorists don't have a country that you can bomb or anything like that but then neither do the Franciscis, and they are a lot better at payback. There were still some debts to settle regarding a small charter airline and some staff that got killed. Since there were a couple hundred or maybe a thousand people in the valley it was just too good an opportunity for the Franciscis to do some payback and to send a message. I doubt if you find anyone alive in the whole valley and if there are they will probably die from radiation poisoning. There was enough high level radioactive medical waste in the pseudo bomb to poison a big area and everyone in it and the explosion was confined to a narrow canyon. Okay, stop the tummy rub General and come look military. We need to do an interview about what happened and why it is the current outgoing president's fault."

Ben had clicked off the television after watching Margret's interview with General El-Shazly and finding out that the Morsi government had totally dropped the ball and allowed terrorists to endanger the whole country with weapons of mass destruction.

"That's it then?" said Maurice, "more weapons of mass destruction in the hands of terrorists?"

"It worked in Iraq for the Americans," said Ben, "I guess we need to put some of my guys here to guard the planes until the Egyptians get done mobbing the palace. Then we can see about staffing up and providing an airline again."

CHAPTER 19: THE BLESSING

It was the middle of Saturday afternoon and the sun was shining down through the pine and cypress trees in the garden of the Corsican town house where everyone was staying while Armand and Lucien recovered. The garden was cool and the sunlight dappled the thick lawn with blotches of moving silver and gold. Water gurgled in a stream that flowed down from a grotto at the rear of the garden in a stone channel through a rock garden and into the central koi pond where a pump returned the water to the grotto. The landscaped and tree covered mound containing the grotto also served as a guard and observation position and the surrounding twenty-foot-tall brick privacy wall made the lower garden invisible from the outside.

Armand was sitting in a patio chair with his arm in a cast. His bruises and scrapes were mostly healed and although he still had tape on his ribs they didn't ache all of the time. He was watching Dove, Greta, Nicole and Celeste sitting on the corners of a blanket on the grass in the garden with Elise in the middle. Elise would crawl toward one or another of them and then stop and laugh and head for another person. It was her personal game of keep away and she enjoyed it very much.

Everyone had just come from Celeste's graduation ceremony at the school and Greta, Dove and Celeste were wearing light make-up and summer frocks in pastel floral patterns from the House of Valentini. They were barefoot and looked like a group of teenage schoolgirls playing dress up. Nicole was wearing a short white dress and tights from a collection by Richard d'Abery and had her hair down in a loose bob with a ribbon. Lucien claimed he like to play with dolls when he was a child and used to dress them up. He said that since he now had a full set he was going to spend some money and play dressing them up and the girls had to indulge him because it was his second childhood. He had been flying to Paris for physical therapy weekly and would normally bring back a few designer clothes for all the girls, including Elise.

Lucien sat at one side of the garden drinking a glass of white wine and watching the girls play with Elise. He was sitting in a recliner next to a bright red electric scooter that he rode around town and whenever he was outside the house. He was actually in better shape than he had been in years and sometimes he would secretly go to Wales and Scotland just to wander around at the various EUOPS country stations and hike and fish. Here on Corsica, he maintained a slightly different appearance.

Whenever he went to town, he was accompanied by half a dozen guards on bicycles or motorbikes and followed by a handicapped hoist van. He never spoke to anyone in town but had a tablet attached to the handlebars of the scooter that he used to painfully type messages with one hand. Lucien kept a paper cup of small obsolete gold twenty-franc coins in the scooters cup holder. Occasionally, he would give one away to someone when he sensed or observed a need or when it looked like someone just deserved a good dinner and a weekend away.

The town folk were more courteous and thoughtful to him now since they knew about the strokes and the women curtsied and men took off their hats when speaking to him. They remembered how easygoing things had been before Carlo had taken over the running of the family after Armand was injured and almost died in a motoring accident that had scrambled his thinking, due to a massive concussion.

Lucien's phone rang and he looked at the text message from Merry.

"Girls," said Lucien, "Help Armand into the house, we need to watch the news channel."

Celeste scooped up Elise and blew on her stomach to make her shriek and then handed her to Greta. Nicole and Celeste folded up the blanket and then followed Dove who had an arm around Armand and was helping him into the house. When they got inside, Lucien jumped off the scooter and Armand nodded thanks to Dove and went to the bar to fetch a whiskey. Greta clicked on the television and then sat down on the couch with Elise on her lap. Celeste settled beside her and Elise took one of Celeste's hands and stared at the television. She wondered if it would make music and have strange blue and red singing animals on it this time.

"The blast was estimated at four kilotons by Russian scientists in Moscow and slightly more than two by the Americans," said a talking head, "There has been radiation detected by stations in Japan that indicates a full thermonuclear reaction. The actual location of the blast is in question. While the official announcement indicated that the test took place at the northern testing grounds, the epicenter of the blast indicates it was further south at the nuclear development center and breeder reactor site. The regime is claiming that it was a test of a small weapon intended for use on their new rockets but there is speculation that it was an accident at the development center. There is no word if satellite images of the reactor complex show damage to one or more of the facilities there."

Armand walked back to the bar and poured another whiskey for Lucien. He walked over and handed the drink to Lucien and then picked up his glass and raised it in a toast.

"How did it happen, Lucien?" asked Armand. "You never even saw the bomb. Was it something the Americans did?"

"Remember the page in the addendum that said that you should unplug the blue safety lock initiator wire on the reset module before you unplug the battery for the barometric fuse sensor or the bomb would explode?" asked Lucien, "The warning was all by itself on the last page of the first section. I just took it out of the copy they got. A regrettable omission, but not actually our fault."

"I wonder if they will see it that way?" answered Armand, "We should know very soon."

"Oh, they will probably register their displeasure in the normal fashion. Then it will be business as usual for all of us," said Lucien "As I said, it was not our fault since we made it abundantly clear that we did not guarantee the manuals and documentation since we didn't have anything to compare it with. Since there is no record in any of their copies of a single missing page or in any copy that isn't controlled by the Americans, how could they prove anything or even know what to suspect, and the bomb worked as guaranteed. They will be mad and I do assume they will register their displeasure in the normal fashion on Carlo for selling defective goods. Are you ready for my remarkable recovery? I am going to my villa in Spain for a while and letting you run things. Carlo was right about one thing. We do need to look for new talent to train for leadership roles and you are now in training."

CHAPTER 20: AND THE BENEDICTION

Hamid Masoud looked out of the window of the condominium. He had opened the terrace door at sunset and watched the sun sink into the sea. He smiled and thought back to a cartoon film he had seen when he was a boy where the sun had sunk into the sea and there had immediately been steam and boiling water as the sun went out and the stars flamed into existence from sputtering flying pieces of the extinguishing sun.

The night wind through the open door was slightly chilly and he slipped on his suit coat and sat on the chair at the dining table where he had set up his rifle with its control carriage and infrared laser aided sight. The sight was connected to a laptop computer with the newest targeting software from China. A USB cable ran from the computer to the rifle carriage that controlled the position of the rifle and that compensated for wind, temperature, air pressure, and gravitational variation due to the height of the rifle above ground. Everything was measured to an accuracy of half a wavelength of the invisible infrared laser light the new measuring devices used, and the rifles aiming point was continuously updated by the motorized carriage based on the laser measurements. The screen of the computer showed a white dot about the size of a pea for the uncertainty in the point of impact, a zone of probability that made the shot of over five thousand feet with a drop of over nine hundred feet, not only possible, but also precise.

He glanced at the luminous dial of his watch and wished he could have a cigarette but he had to minimize his presence in the room. It was after seven in the evening and the meeting would be breaking up soon. The people involved in the meeting had usually only held meetings every few weeks to report and discuss problems with their various operations but apparently there were either more problems currently or some major disagreements within the organization because the new head had been holding meetings every few days, and with a total disregard for security had not changed the meeting location. Someone had spotted him and called Hamid's principals. They had called Hamid and made arrangements since they were still smarting from what they considered a raw deal for defective merchandise. The bright overhead lights of the area under the portico of the casino and in the entryway had been provided to allow illumination for cameras to record celebrity arrivals and departures and would allow ample light and time to identify his target.

The Chinese cursed their enemies with the statement "May you live in interesting times." Well, all of us were living in interesting times now and Hamid's life was a bit more interesting than some. Funny how conditions shaped your life, he thought. His older brother had joined the family business and it was prospering despite his father's death. His two sisters were happily married with children. And he was prosperous, if not yet settled, but that was about to change. He was feeling much better now, but there was still a bit of droop to his eyelid and some arm weakness he was working to overcome. The weakness and some weird memory lapses and blanks were all that hinted that he had ever had a stroke.

The computer gave a pleasant chime and Hamid looked at the screen. The split screen showed a live view of a man in a dark suit standing under the portico at the casino and a photograph of the same man. Hamid nodded and touched the screen. The silenced fifty-caliber rifle barked softly, and the man fell. Hamid smoothly closed the computer and removed the memory card with the sighting program data and put it in its case. He unplugged the USB cable and curled it quickly around his hand and thrust it into a backpack with the computer and the memory card.

Then he released the two clips holding the stockless single shot rifle to the mounting carriage and put it in a foam carrier block. He slid the carriages padded u shaped holding clamps off of the edge of the heavy table, hit the release buttons and folded the carriage into a compact bundle of rods and tubes. He put it in the bottom of a metal toolbox and then put the foam block containing the short stockless rifle on top. He closed the lid of the box and swung the backpack over his shoulder.

Then he closed and locked the terrace door and turned and looked around one last time. He saw the computer charger still plugged into the wall and something stirred in his memory. Damn, he was getting old and careless. He had never left a charger before, had he?

He retrieved the charger and cable and added them to the backpack with the computer. Then he picked up the toolbox and backpack and walked to the private elevator. Hamid rode it to the basement and stowed the toolbox and computer case in the trunk of a car that he would park in the airport parking structure when he left and would be picked up later tonight. He pulled his carry-on bag out of the trunk and put it in the passenger's seat. Tomorrow, the decorating crew would come and remove everything and get ready to paint and change the carpets and furniture in the Sheik's penthouse and he would be visiting his sisters in Ankara and looking for a place in the neighborhood to buy. He should probably pick up a few gifts for his nieces and nephews at the airport.

****

"Greta, Dove, come quick and look at this," yelled Armand as he muted the television.

Armand was sitting in the Lucien's town house in Calvi watching the late television news. Lucien had gone to his place in Spain and Greta and Dove were on their way back to England for, as Blossom said, some smartening up and training. Armand finally had all the casts, and tape off and the various stiches had healed to faint red lines. Lucien had told him to take over running the family again but there had been resistance from Carlo, which had been anticipated.

Carlo had been, not a disaster, but not a steady influence in the reorganization and changes that had been necessary after both Lucien and Armand had apparently been put out of action. The arms and materials sales division that had been Armand's key activity had deteriorated as Carlo had allowed infighting among some of Armand's lieutenants who had sought to take over. Instead of stepping in and organizing an orderly transition, Carlo had ignored the problem and there had been several people killed and Armand was not sure about the current group leader. Determining secession with pistols was not what an efficient organization did and as soon as Armand took over there would definitely be a talent search and tables of organization developed that named names and positions. There would also be some training programs implemented.

The problem was taking over without causing major dislocations and hard feelings. Carlo had been holding a series of meetings trying to have John Clarborn and Valentino Guérini support him instead of Armand. Carlo had pointed out that the effects of the concussion could cause lingering problems with Armand's abilities, but this bit of speculation had not yielded any concrete results and both John and Valentino had said that Armand had been the original choice, and he was backed by Lucien, so when Armand came back they would see how he was. Carlo had tried to rally the young second tier managers in a rebellion but his lack of action in the arms leadership fight hadn't really generated a lot of trust among them, so Carlo had been holding meetings every few days at the Dubai casino to gather support, mostly by cutting deals with anyone who could be bought. Armand thought that the almost public meetings were chancy at best and not something that a prudent man would do but Carlo thrived on attention.

Dove walked into the room and sat down and Greta came in carrying Elise.

"What is it, Armand?" asked Greta, "I was just putting Elise down."

Armand hit the mute button and Margret Perry, without her flack jacket but with the slightly mussed hair and two blouse buttons undone was standing in front of the Jinni casino. It was dark outside so the reporting was probably live.

"I am standing in front of the glamorous Jinni Casino in Dubai, United Arab Emirates," said Margret, "Less than two hours ago someone shot and killed Mr. Carlo Conein, an international businessman and banker, as he exited the casino. Mr. Conein has been quietly holding a series of meetings here in Dubai concerning the reorganization of the banks, businesses, and holdings of Mr. Lucien Francisci, the billionaire financier and banker, who has retired after a series of strokes. Mr. Conein has been acting as the interim CEO in the absence of Mr. Armand Gerard, Mr. Francisci's designated successor. Mr. Gerard was severely injured in a traffic accident in Switzerland where his car left the road and his driver was killed. There are also rumors that there is a power struggle going on between Mr. Gerard and Mr. Conein. The police are investigating the death of Mr. Conein but have not released a statement. However, eyewitnesses say that he was shot as he exited the casino although no one reported hearing any gunfire. We will be providing updates on what appears to be the murder of this prominent international businessman as more information becomes available. This is Margret Perry, American Press, at the spot where the news happens, signing off this live report. Stay tuned for updates as more information becomes available."

Greta was soothing Elise who was definitely ready for bed and Dove had gone to the bar for a glass of white wine. Armand got a glass of brandy and they all looked at one another.

"Well it looks like Lucien was right," said Armand, "It makes the casts and stiches almost worthwhile. I believe I should go and rally the troops tomorrow. No, I had better go tonight. You can have the house since I won't be back for a while. When you leave, have the staff shut things down."

"All right, Armand," said Dove, "You think it was the Koreans and not the terrorists or Egyptians?"

"Probably," said Armand, "The Egyptians are fairly well tied up with getting reorganized internally and besides they didn't really lose or gain anything. The terrorists just don't do things that don't get them publicity and besides they got a lot of people blown all over the landscape recently when they messed with us, so I hope they learned something. The Koreans are big on face, so they needed to pass the blame on to someone else, so I nominate them."

"Well, at least it will clear up things for you to take over," said Dove, "If Lucien doesn't call up every twenty minutes with suggestions."

Armand laughed and said, "That is a possibility. But at least, it is over, and we can say it was a benediction."

"Isn't that a prayer?" said Dove, "You're going to pray for Carlo?"

"No," said Armand, "I went to a very strict boy's school that gave me a classical education. They thought you should speak Latin and Greek and read the great books. Benediction comes from the Latin word *benedicite* that originally meant an expression of surprise. Although, I guess we shouldn't have been surprised."

"There could be another possibility. I don't think Margret was surprised at all," said Greta, "I wonder why she just happened to be in Dubai anyway?"

More? Read the opening of the latest Greta Steiner Novel:

In Darker Dungeons and Despair
A Greta Steiner EUOPS Novel

Robert L. Fenton

"Let the sighing of the prisoner come before thee; according to the greatness of thy power preserve thou those that are appointed to die;" Psalms 79:11

Coming for Christmas!

CHAPTER 1: TRIBAL RITES

"Check," yelled the jumpmaster.

Greta Steiner looked at Dove Abraham and then at the lights on the bulkhead of the KC-130. The lights were still yellow and burning steadily. Six nervous people in high altitude pressure suits stood huddled in a group at the rear of the plane, waiting. The jumpmaster nodded at the training group leader and he nodded back. The group leader inspected the suits, rigging and helmets of the trainees then looked at the quantity gauge on the oxygen supply bottle attached to the full pressure helmet. Everyone in the rear bay of the plane was dressed in the pink insulated coarse nylon waffle weave pressure suits needed to maintain life six miles up in the hostile atmosphere.

It seems that our mother earth was quite willing to punish her children when they strayed into areas that they shouldn't be in, thought Greta, and anyone was a damn fool to annoy Mama. The group leader walked up and checked Greta and then winked.

"We hardly ever kill anyone in qualifying, brigadier," said Sergeant Major Charles Russell Whittingham, SAS, Retired, "Just remember, do not hold hands with the lieutenant colonel when you jump out or you could both break your arms. The plane will not be slowing down, and it is traveling over three hundred miles an hour. Don't fight it, but as soon as you stabilize, open your parachute and head for the green assembly area light you'll see behind us. The closer you can glide toward it, the shorter the swim. Are you okay? I ask everyone because you can step out now and come again if you don't think you are up to it tonight."

"No, I'm all right, but thanks for asking," said Brigadier Greta Steiner, Special Air Service, Twenty Second Regiment, Reserve, as well as a Senior Supervisor for Operations, EUOPS, currently unassigned.

The lieutenant colonel, that the sergeant major had referred to, was Dove Abraham, Field Operations Supervisor, EUOPS, also unassigned, and Greta's live-in and second mother of Elise Steiner, Greta's daughter.

Dove was the reason that Greta was about to jump out of a perfectly good functioning airplane and into the ocean six miles below. The HIHO jump had nothing to do with singing dwarves. HIHO, pronounced Hi Ho, stood for high insertion high opening and Greta and the others were about to jump out of an airplane going over three hundred miles an hour six miles up in the air and parachute into the ocean five miles minimum from the on land rally point. This was happening because Dove and Greta needed to complete their training for the SAS parachute wings that they had already half qualified for in Egypt last year. The reason they wanted to qualify escaped Greta now, but it had seemed like a good idea at the time.

For the last three months, Greta and Dove had been on leave in Corsica as a reward, after kind of foiling a group of terrorists, if killing them is foiling, assisting in delivering a more or less dud nuclear bomb to a country on everyone's naughty list, so they could blow up most of their country's nuclear capability and scientists in a big accident, and saving Lucien Francisci, the head of the Francisci crime family, after he had a stroke. In return, Lucien had adopted Elise Steiner, Greta's daughter, and made her his heir, thereby qualifying Elise as potentially the richest person in the world under the age of two, and EUOPS had given them three months off for recovery time, but no raise in pay or bonus.

Greta looked at Dove and smiled and Dove took her hand and squeezed it through the insulated zip on glove of the pressure suit. She nodded as the sergeant major plugged his communications cord into the intercom circuit to make the final announcements.

"All right, it appears we are all ready and willing, or at least ready, so just to make it exciting I forgot to mention that you will all get your own personal AR-15 to take with you and bring to the assembly area. If you do not make it, we will assume you drowned, if you lose your rifle but make it to the assembly area, you fail and owe the government four hundred quid. If you make it and bring your rifle, there is beer and a barbecue at the assembly area. Oh, and there will be no communications net on the way down or on the swim-in since we don't want to hear anyone screaming about faulty parachutes or sharks or something. It unnerves the other trainees. Are there any questions? No? Start your oxygen from your internal thirty-minute supply and unplug communications and air from the plane, now."

The sergeant major handed Greta an AR-15 and she slung it over her shoulder and fastened the sling with the Velcro tabs attached to the suit. She checked her GPS and made sure the coordinates of the assembly area were entered and the luminous arrow was pointing toward a place she had never been and couldn't see. She rotated in a circle then nodded as the arrow pointed in the same direction despite her movement.

"Ready," snapped the jumpmaster.

He depressurized the cargo area, turned off the lights, and lowered the rear ramp. Suddenly, the plane was full of thin swirling subzero air and fog. A few surfaces steamed as the residual moisture boiled off and although it was hard to hear, there was a thin scream like a banshee sitting on the roof of the manor house next door. Greta shivered even though she couldn't feel the cold. Then she looked up and out the back of the plane and froze. Rubies, emeralds, citrines, and diamonds were heaped on black velvet. Nothing flickered, and nothing gave the scale of the tipped over chest of precious stones spilled on the abandoned black velvet gown of the night. Jewels burned from the infinite soft black fabric of the gown that had been torn off in a passion of total possession and flung aside. A treasure of beauty and giddy abandonment where everything would be hidden in plain sight by the sun although it would still languorously stretch out its arms to call you wantonly back when night reawakened.

"Beautiful, so beautiful," whispered Greta softly, "cold and deep and dark and dangerous and beautiful enough to stop your heart."

"Stop talking about yourself," said the sergeant major over the command channel, "Be careful, brigadier, you can lose yourself in the stars and never open your chute. Just take a couple deep breaths, look down, and get ready. I will be jumping with the trainees and will look in on you."

Greta turned and smiled at him in the darkness, although he couldn't see, and then heard a buzzer. The yellow light was blinking faster and faster and the trainees lined up two by two. Dove found her again and stood beside her just as the yellow light went out.

A green light came on and the jumpmaster yelled, "Go, go, go."

The first two trainees ran down the ramp holding their arms across their chests and jumped out and assumed a sitting position. Then they were whirled away and Greta and Dove ran and jumped. Greta spun and tumbled forever, end over end and around and around and finally stretched her arms and legs out as she stabilized. The guide lights on two parachutes were visible below her and to her right and she also saw the green signal light of the assembly area off in that direction. She pulled the ripcord and her airfoil parachute opened with a jerk, and then she was flying. She glanced at her GPS and the arrow pointed to the green light. She breathed a sigh of relief. While it was easy to tell the land from the water from five or six miles up and she could see which direction to swim now, it would be another kettle of fish while actually in the water. She maneuvered her parachute to swing toward the light as a body hurtled past her and another parachute blossomed just to her right.

She looked around and then up. There was another parachute above her that blotted out a wing shaped piece of the sky. One of the two had to be Dove and the other was probably the sergeant major. She checked to see that her AR-15 was still firmly attached to her suit and looked at her wrist altimeter. She had another five or six minutes of airtime and the green light was still a long way off. All right, she would stretch her glide as far as she could and then cut away after she landed. The jump suit was buoyant and would keep you afloat indefinitely, but you only had thirty minutes of oxygen with the helmet if you got tangled under your chute.

She watched the water coming up and trimmed her parachute to squeeze as much distance out of it as she could. The green light wasn't visible anymore but the GPS arrow pointed straight in front of her. She felt like she was falling into a well and everything got totally black just before she hit the water. She landed with a splash and then went under as she released the parachute. She relaxed and let the buoyancy of the suit carry her up. Greta put one hand above her to feel for the chute and her hand broke the surface. Apparently, the parachute had gone away like it was supposed to. Well, what to do now? Greta turned over and floated on her back and confirmed the direction of the assembly area with the GPS. Okay, now the swim. Five miles wasn't much after the last six weeks of brutal, the service had called it rigorous, training at the refresher course.

After a few months off in Corsica, Greta and Dove had been told to go to the base in Crete for a refresher course in tradecraft and physical conditioning before they were reactivated. They had been given married officer's quarters at the SAS compound at the Akitori airbase and Nicole and Celeste Caparoni had come from Corsica to stay with them to see the sights, play on the beach and take care of Elise for a couple of weeks. The two Caparoni girls had minded Elise while Greta was running the EUOPS operation in Egypt that had resulted in the dead terrorists and probably a bunch of dead nuclear scientists halfway around the world. The girls were the children of the housekeeper and the bodyguard of Lucien Francisci and had come to believe that Elise was their special responsibility, with some justification.

When Dove and Greta had started the refresher training course, Greta had shipped them home to take a little time off themselves before they went back to school and let Francis Saint Martin, who lived on Crete and was married to Mark Saint Martin, Elise's biological father and Greta's former lover and boss, come and take care of Elise. Francis was pregnant and said she needed some hands-on baby time and any help would be appreciated. Greta had agreed, and Francis had showed up with a big box of inappropriate toys, a bunch of baby clothes, and some books on childcare.

Francis and Greta looked so much alike that Francis had been Greta's body double, although she had primarily worked in the dirty tricks section of EUOPS making exploding Bibles and inflatable airplanes. Francis was now retired because she had taken a bullet through the head that had been intended for Greta. The Americans had shot Francis, thinking she was Greta, to stop Greta from stealing a couple tons of gold, including some very interesting bars that proved that the American gold supply had been compromised and looted by one of their presidents. The Americans hadn't admitted anything about shooting Francis but had coughed up a settlement that would cover all of Francis and Mark's kid's college costs, including buying the college and paying the staff.

Well, thought Greta, Elise was safe with Francis on Crete and she was floating around in the ocean, wool gathering. Someone knocked on her helmet and she rolled over and saw Dove. Dove pulled the clips on the helmet and it came off and sank.

"Get out of the all over," commanded Dove, "We need to get moving or we are going to miss the barbecue and beer. Give me the popgun. You notice that there is no ammo and they are definitely training pieces since they are all rusty?"

Dove had stuffed her rifle inside her pink suit and zipped it closed and was now using it as a float. The suit floated high in the water and Dove was leaning on it with both elbows.

"Okay the rifles need to come back but the suits are not necessarily a return item?" asked Greta, "I gather that they have a tracker in them and someone in a helicopter gathers them up later. What about the helmet?"

"They can take it out of my pay if they want to," responded Dove, "I am not trying to swim in a candy striper pink coverall with limited air. But I did keep the zip on boots and gloves and stuff them in the suit I am using as a float, along with the rifle."

"What exactly are you wearing for the swim, if I may ask, Dove? I don't recall what you had on when we got the suits."

"I am dressed appropriately for a beach barbecue, although God only knows what my hair will look like. Now stop chattering or we will look like prunes when we get there. I figure we can make it in a couple hours even fighting the currents if we get with the program. Stuff your gun in my suit and we will go."

"I think I will stuff their rifle in my suit and keep my gun in the thigh holster where it currently is. Keeping the boots is a good idea too, Dove. Anyway, let's take two suits just in case, and head out. Shut off your GPS and we will use mine. It's good to have backups."

Greta handed the rifle to Dove and struggled out of her jump suit and then stuffed the rifle, boots, and gloves inside. She zipped the suit up and started swimming towing the suit on a length of the decent rope that's used to get out of trees that she took from the suit's leg pocket. They had been swimming easily for five or ten minutes when an inflatable kayak came up and a dim light shown on them.

"Hello," said Charley, "You two all right? Please put away your unauthorized pistols you have pointed at me. I assume they are stainless steel and totally submersible?"

"Hi Charley," said Greta, "Everybody all right?"

"Yeah, we had one person land under his chute but he just pulled it all to him and dumped it on the other side until he got out," replied Charley, "Well, I need to go herd the other ducks. I'll see you on the beach."

Greta and Dove slogged on but it was over two hours before they finally got to the beach and they had drifted down the shore from the assembly area because of the currents. They pulled the suits up on the beach and put on the zip on boots then they picked up the rifles and walked up the beach to the high-water line and sat down in the shelter of a large log.

"Something isn't right," said Dove softly as she leaned against Greta, "That is the quietest beach party I have ever not heard. We are only a few hundred yards away and nada, I know someone must have beat us in but no music and sounds of raucous laughter to guide the troops?"

"You got a point," said Greta, "let me take a look and then get back to you."

"Bull, we are going to go together and I am going to lead," said Dove, "If we need to shoot, come in shooting. If it looks too tight we go back in the water and lay low for a couple hours until someone comes to pick up the suits. Remember, Elise needs a mother. You got your boots on?"

"I thought I was in charge," said Greta, "what's with you running things?"

"I ran an assassination and kidnap squad for the Mossad, sweetheart," said Dove, "That means I have lots of field experience in make it up as you go along situations. You worked alone on set up situations where everything was thought out to the last detail, so let me do this. Besides, I remember, I was in charge of field operations the last time we were active."

"Okay, but be careful," said Greta, "yes, I have boots on. What are you wearing?"

"Boots from the suit with a pair of beach sandals inside, a tie died bikini, a crucifix and a nine millimeter Glock 42 with a stack of three eighty hollow points and one extra magazine. How about you?"

"Black shorty wet suit, Glock 17 and an extra magazine, some rubber beach sandals and an oversized beach towel. Here, tie on the towel and protect your legs"

Dove pulled the towel Greta handed her out of its plastic bag and tied it around her waist like a skirt then checked her gun and walked carefully toward the glow of the assembly area light. Greta moved to one side of Dove and then when they entered the trees moved swiftly to pass her. She moved to the side of the clearing where the light was and looked in. There was no one in sight. Several coolers sat on the ground next to a large bottled gas barbecue. There were half a dozen picnic tables and twenty or so chairs clustered around a fire pit that was circled with rocks and that held an unlit beach fire. There was not a sound. No crickets or birds or even the rustle of the trees. In the center of the clearing, was the green assembly light immobile and alone. It was on a tall aluminum mast mounted on a small trailer covered with batteries. There was also a high intensity light mounted on the mast below the glowing green light. Greta faded back from the edge of the clearing and cooed like a dove. She crouched down behind a large tree and cooed again. Dove moved from behind a clump of bushes and crouched beside her. Dove put her mouth next to Greta's ear and whispered.

"You went ahead of me," whispered Dove, "You could have been shot or killed or something. Don't do that again. What did you see?"

"There is a set up for a barbecue but no one is there that I could see. There are chairs and grills and tables and coolers but no people."

"They must have been moved," whispered Dove, "I don't believe that they got the drop on the people one at a time so it must have been a trap. I'm going to sneak in and look around."

"I'll cover you," Greta whispered back, "run back if there is any problem and I'll keep up covering fire. Hit the ocean and swim out and then back to the suits and we'll wait off shore."

Dove nodded and then crouched down and slipped into the clearing moving quickly and silently toward a table sitting on the edge of the clearing. As she crouched behind it, the high intensity light snapped on and Dove dived for cover and rolled. As she tumbled behind the first bushes she centered her Glock on the light and shot it out.

Coming This Winter, 2019

Made in the USA
Coppell, TX
30 October 2021